Praise for the *Embrace* series

"If you're into *The Vampire Diaries*, you'll love this book."

—Seventeen.com Book Club, on *Entice*

"Fast-paced action, a strong warrior heroine, a forbidden romance, amazing history—it's all here! Fans of strong-warrior-chick books like *Vampire Academy* will embrace the sequel to *Embrace* for the adrenaline-rush/heart-pumping romance combo it so deliciously provides."

—*Justine Magazine*

"A terrific story…a worthy follow-up to *Twilight*."

—*The Los Angeles Times*

"Entertaining and addictive. With buckets of thrills, *Entice* is a roller-coaster ride. With love triangles, angels, and bad guys, this is the perfect summer read."

—*RT Book Reviews*

"Hot, spicy, wild, dark, and crazy, *Entice* is a must read."

—Examiner.com, Lori Calabrese

"Strong, compelling and wonderfully flawed, Violet is the kind of heroine who will keep readers enthralled and rooting for her until the final page is turned."

—*Kirkus*, on *Entice*

"Addictive...add to your must-read list."

—*Entertainment Weekly*'s Shelf Life

"Jessica Shirvington sets up a delicious romantic triangle."

—*USA Today*

"One of the best YA novels we've seen in a while. Get ready for a confident, kick-butt, well-defined heroine who will let nothing get in her way. And the heroes! Oh my."

—*RT Book Reviews* on *Embrace*

"*Embrace* is a dark and heart-racing tale, filled with action and secrets that will keep you on the edge of your seat, and reading deep into the night...It's a combination of the badass-action of *Vampire Academy*, the complex love triangles of *Twilight*, and the angel mythology of *Fallen*, taken one step further."

—*Book Couture*

"Fans of romantic fantasy with a paranormal twist will find Violet and her adventures captivating."

—*VOYA*

"[An] absorbing debut...Fans of otherworldly stories will likely enjoy this edgy, suspenseful romance and anticipate its follow-up."

—*Booklist,* on *Embrace*

"Violet remains an engaging, contemporary protagonist whose absorbing narrative interweaves intricate mythology, action suspense, and romantic complexities."

—*Booklist,* on *Entice*

EMBLAZE

jessica shirvington

sourcebooks fire

The author and publisher would also like to acknowledge the following works from which the author has quoted: *The City of God* by Saint Augustine, *Douay-Rheims Bible*, *English Standard Version*, *The King James Bible*.

Published by Sourcebooks Fire, an imprint of Sourcebooks, Inc.
P.O. Box 4410, Naperville, Illinois 60567-4410
(630) 961-3900
Fax: (630) 961-2168
teenfire.sourcebooks.com

Originally published in Australia and New Zealand in 2011 by Hachette Australia.

Library of Congress Cataloging-in-Publication data is on file with the publisher.

Printed and bound in the United States of America.
BG 10 9 8 7 6 5 4 3 2 1

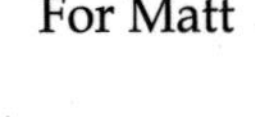

For Matt

"God did not spare angels when they sinned, but cast them into Hell and committed them to chains of gloomy darkness to be kept until judgment."

GREEK TARTARUS, PETER 2:4

prologue

"When I bring clouds over the earth and the bow is seen in the clouds, I will remember my covenant..."

Genesis 9:14–9:15

Evelyn

She didn't have to see him to know he was there. It had been a very long time since Evelyn had needed to rely solely on her eyes.

She released a final, ear-piercing scream, its song a double-edged sword that heralded both life and death. It was done—her ultimate joy now within her reach, just as her ultimate sacrifice extended its hand to her.

"It's a girl," the midwife said, placing the baby in her arms.

Evelyn stared down at the tiny child and wondered how she would find the strength to let her go.

"She's perfect, Eve. She looks just like you. My two beautiful angels," James said.

He was still crying. He'd been a blubbering mess since the first contraction, but his words brought the first silent tear from Evelyn's eye. He swept it aside lovingly.

"I knew you'd cry," he teased as his eyes drifted between his wife and their daughter. He tentatively brushed the top of the baby's forehead, barely using the back of his little finger.

Evelyn's heart clenched. Leaving him was not something she'd planned for. She'd always assumed it would be her that would outlive him. All the time she had spent deliberating over when to tell him everything—how to explain he would grow old while she would merely age a few years. Time wasted now.

She looked down at their daughter, her eyes opening slightly. It would be her choice now if he should ever know.

Evelyn pulled James's hand to her mouth and kissed it, letting her lips linger on his skin, inhaling his vanilla scent and committing it to memory. She wished they had more time, but she sensed the magnets of power around her. She couldn't ignore it much longer.

"James, could you give me a minute to tidy up?" It was her last lie and she still hated that she had to. Lying to her husband had never sat well with her.

He kissed her quickly. It was too quick.

"I'll be back soon, 'Mom,'" he said with a wink before leaving. It was heart-wrenching to know that she would hear it just once.

Alone with her daughter, Evelyn kissed the top of her perfect head. She already had a full head of hair, dark brown like Evelyn's, and she smelled...intoxicating. It was a fragrance she could get lost in for all eternity. She wished she could hold her like this forever, inhaling her and playing with her tiny, tiny fingers.

But she knew...they weren't really alone.

"Do I have you to thank for the dreams?" she asked the empty room.

He materialized, a corporeal form confirming the presence she had already felt. It was as if he had always been there.

She sensed him with her whole body. She had always been able to feel them. She could smell them too. Always flowers, but he smelled of lilies only.

And she knew—lilies held all the power.

He introduced himself, unnecessarily. She knew exactly who he was and why he was there. He'd been haunting her dreams for weeks now.

He stood by the window that looked out over a small park. There had been a time when he was able to frequent the world regularly, but that time had long since passed. He wanted to at least see the grass and sky from this point of view during his short visit.

They both knew how this was done. New life and new death equaled a gateway.

"Do you realize what you're asking?" she said.

"I do."

"What will she become?"

"The Keshet." He spoke with a reverence that made Evelyn nervous.

"The Rainbow?" she repeated, recognizing the Hebrew word.

He nodded. "The bow that holds our arrow. The link between the realms."

"The bow," Evelyn whispered to herself. "Why her? Why me?" It didn't seem fair—she had already given so much.

He could feel her pain but stuck to information; that was what she needed from him.

"Through you, she is already more than human. She is one of a kind. There may never be another like her."

Evelyn shook her head in disbelief, even though she knew he spoke only the truth. "You already know I'll agree, or you wouldn't be here," she said, resigned, then inhaled a broken breath. She had to stay strong. "Is there anything you don't know?"

"I do not know what she will choose."

Evelyn circled the child's face with her finger—so soft, so innocent. "She will choose with her heart."

"Then let us hope that she finds love," he said.

Her head lifted, now more determined. "I have terms."

He already knew what they were, had discussed them with her in her dreams.

"They have been accepted as long as you are willing to pay the price. Do you have it?"

She nodded and reached under her blanket, revealing one of her silver wristbands. She slipped it on her arm carefully while cradling the baby, and raised her brow; she hadn't expected it to be that easy.

"You really need her."

He tilted his head once in mute confirmation that carried remorse. It was hard for him, to admit their failings, admit that they had to turn to humans to make these sacrifices because they could not contain their own forces.

"Swear you will make sure she wears the amulet." Evelyn pushed herself up a little with one hand to sit. As she did, she felt the strength draining from her. She ignored it as best she could and focused on her daughter again.

"You have already defeated her. It is not certain she will return," he said.

"Swear!" She wasn't going to let this drop; she had seen too much, fought too hard.

"I swear," he conceded, impressed by her intuition as much as with her sacrifice.

She shook her head, silent until finally she let a tear escape, and whispered, "Just another lamb to the slaughter."

He pulled himself away from the view and walked toward her. "Not just any lamb. You forget—you are part angel too."

"When?" she asked, though she could already feel it.

"Now."

"I'm one hundred eighty-seven years old. Has it all been worth it?"

They both looked at the baby.

"You'll have to tell me," he said, surprised by the effect the proximity of the child was having on him.

Evelyn knew she had only minutes left. She took hold of the nurses' call button.

"Give me a moment to be with my family. Stand away, where I cannot sense you. I want to finish this as a human."

"You still believe in humanity after all you have seen?"

The heart rate monitor started beeping frantically. Evelyn kissed the top of the baby's head, inhaling her scent again and again as she pressed the alarm.

"Only a human can have this, however briefly. I would not give you my life and hand you her fate if I did not believe."

"I will travel with you, to a point, if you like," he offered.

She couldn't deny her fear. "Company would be nice."

The doors flew open as the midwife raced in, followed by the doctor with James close behind.

The midwife couldn't hide her horror when she saw the state of the sheets, now red. She started pulling the bedding off as the doctor began trying to fix the problem Evelyn knew he never could.

James's face had turned ghost white. Evelyn held out the neatly wrapped bundle of life to him. His arms shook as he took the baby. He knew this was bad. He could see it in her eyes.

Evelyn watched him, savoring her last moments with him.

"Tell me what's happening!" James pleaded, trying desperately to avoid his wife's all-too-accepting, fire-blue eyes.

The doctor didn't answer, yelling for more people instead. It would be too late.

"James," she said, but he couldn't look. She tried again, softly. "James, I've thought of a name."

"What?" he asked, through quivering lips.

"She is the heart of the Keshet, James. She is Violet." It was all she could muster. The most she could offer as explanation for what lay ahead. She'd told him tales of the Rainbow before. She hoped he'd tell Violet one day.

"Violet." He nodded and wiped his tear-streaked face.

"It's okay," she reassured.

James looked at the doctor and watched, disconnected, as he responded with the slightest shake of his head. His heart fell to a depth it had never known.

"I love you both."

"We love you, Evelyn," James whispered.

He was there for her the moment it was over, and he stayed with her through the journey. Later, he returned to the child Evelyn had named Violet and he left with her, the part of himself he could only ever give once.

Now all he could do…was wait.

chapter one

> *"As memory may be a paradise from which we cannot be driven, it may also be a hell from which we cannot escape."*
>
> John Lancaster Spalding

Smooth black lines bled from me—soul to hand to paper—begging for release. Charcoal wasn't my usual medium, but lately it seemed appropriate. With my back to the window, the sun cast a bright glow around my shadow on the remaining white. Beyond that, the charcoal began to carve out stronger, sharper lines as I dived deeper and lost myself in my work. That's what art did to me—it almost made time stand still.

Almost.

I was different, despite my efforts not to show it. I couldn't fool myself. The best I could do was stick to the rules. It was the only way. School, training, and research—when I was of any use. That's how I held on to the control that had never been so important or so fragile.

Lines had been drawn. Phoenix had gotten what we wanted—the

Grigori Scripture—and yet he'd be willing to do anything to get his hand on what we *had* gotten. And if I should die in the process of him getting it back? Well, he'd see it as a well-deserved victory.

That didn't mean I was going to make it easy for him. If the Grigori Scripture remained in the hands of exiles, an unfathomable number of innocent lives would be at stake. So, that left us with his suggestion—the trade. It wasn't ideal. If Phoenix got the Exile Scripture, he was going to do something so devastating we could not even begin to comprehend the price.

Or how many would have to pay it.

How does one really calculate the cost of resurrecting the mother of all darkness from Hell?

I tasted the apple, sweet and young, and smelled the flowers, so heavy with pollen the air thickened. I flinched at their nearness, but I was slow to react, still lost in my haunting thoughts. My charcoal slashes grew rigid and intense. I channeled the sound I heard of wings crashing, along with the flashes of morning and evening. They ripped through my vision, into the paper on my easel.

I finally snapped out of it at Miss Kinkaid's distinctive throat clearing. She was hovering over my artwork. I didn't need to guess why.

"Ah-hem, Violet—"

But now that I was aware of my surroundings again, my entire body rang with alarm bells.

Damn it, not again.

Griffin was going to be pissed.

"Miss Kinkaid, you need to move away from the window," I said, cutting her off before she could start her critique.

I stood and took a few deep breaths to steady my angelic senses. It was bad enough for normal Grigori, who had one, occasionally two, senses. I was the first to experience all five, and it was more than overload.

"I, *well*...I beg your pardon?" She slapped her hand over her chest as if I had just insulted her very existence.

I rolled my eyes.

Same reaction every time.

"Yes. Now. And the rest of you!" I called out to my art class. Luckily, we were a relatively small group of fifteen. "Backs against the far wall!" I ordered, grabbing my cell phone and typing in 0103 before hitting send and dropping it.

Out in open, three exiles en route.

Yeah, we'd even come up with an abbreviation for my...spells. Sometimes I just couldn't stop my defenses from dropping—especially when I was working on art. I just forgot about everything else. And when I didn't have my shields up, I drew exiles like a magnet.

My classmates looked at me like I was a freak, and even though I didn't have time to care, it still grated on me.

Maybe because they're right.

"I'm really sorry, everyone, but move it!" I said, starting to drag people from one side of the room to the other, the display of my inhuman strength leaving my fellow students' eyes popping out of their heads and mouths hanging agape. The outright screaming would start later, when they realized that this wasn't some practical joke. For now, everyone was affecting a certain amount of cool, just in case there was a hidden camera. As it was, I could already see Tristan Newland holding up his cell phone.

Exiles were almost here. I cursed myself. If I'd just kept my shields up for another half hour, I would have been outside school grounds and this whole thing would be easier.

The thing about exiled angels is there aren't many rules they have to—or bother to—follow, and while it's difficult for them to locate Grigori, angel-human hybrids like me, in our homes due to some kind of protective barriers all homes naturally emit, every other place, including school, was fair game.

I pulled off my sweater. "The windows are going! Close your eyes!" I commanded my classmates, who were now starting to react. Only half of them took me seriously, burying their faces in their knees. Maybe they thought I was taking them hostage. It probably didn't look good when I pulled out my very lethal-looking dagger from its sheath, a glamour acting as a camouflage to ensure no one even knew it was there. Once revealed, though, all eyes could look nowhere else.

"Oh dear God," Miss Kinkaid whimpered.

But there wasn't time to help them anymore because right then, three exiles came crashing through the windows with the force of a freight train, showering almost all the glass and surrounding woodwork straight into the room and over everyone.

Exhibitionists!

I saw a few people hit by stray shards of glass, but nothing major. Yet.

Three against one was bad. Three against one who also had fifteen defenseless humans to protect was worse. A white-haired exile zeroed in on me immediately and started lunging in my direction. I had less than a second to react, knowing I couldn't leave the other two free to get expressive with their own version of art—maim and torture—with my classmates.

As the exile prepared to land, I dropped my dagger and rolled, narrowly missing his fist and giving myself just enough time to grab the next exile, a strawberry-blond one this time, and hurl him like a bowling ball into the third one before Whitey was back on top of me. I paid for the move, my head pounding into the nearest desk, splitting the desktop in two.

Whitey threw me to the ground and straddled me before proceeding to pummel fist after fist into my face, all within seconds. I managed to wriggle enough to get a knee to his gut and scrambled back, jumping to my feet.

Two more figures came flying through the now glassless windows, landing gracefully behind the three exiles. They didn't hesitate, just pulled their daggers and jumped into the fray. I breathed out a sigh of relief before landing a fist in the face of the exile moving in on me. My strike packed enough force to throw him into the wall, giving me a chance to grab my dagger and draw upon the power that welled in the base of my stomach. I called it up.

My signature amethyst mist cloaked the room and I smiled as it encircled me. The exiles all stopped moving, stilled by my power and unable to break the hold.

I could feel a trickle of warm blood slipping down the side of my face. That earlier head-pounding had caused some damage.

"Hey, guys," I said to Beth and Archer, biting my lip.

My classmates started to scream or cry. I didn't blame them.

The two Grigori simultaneously raised their eyebrows.

"This is the third time in five days, Violet."

I walked over to Whitey, slumped against the wall. He could hear me and could talk if needed. He watched me coming, knew what I could do to him. The very same thing that had led them to me let him know just how powerful I was. Yeah, apparently...I radiate the stuff.

He was young. Not just in looks but in experience. I was willing to bet he hadn't been here much longer than a year, which was more than I could say for the other two. Millennia of existence as angels really didn't prepare them for taking human forms. This one looked awkward in his body, like it was the wrong fit. No surprises, he was male. They all chose to be male, at least *almost* all. From their point of view, males were superior and females the lesser gender, with no power and the added disadvantage of monthly bleeding.

Idiots.

This one didn't look more than my age, his bright white hair standing tall. He'd used one of those granny hair dyes and it was turning purple. I almost laughed, imagining him becoming human and then spending the next few weeks experimenting with hair colors.

Miss Kinkaid rose to her feet, shaking like a newborn foal against the wall, leaning against it for support.

"V-V-Violet, put…put that w-weapon away. We need to call the…police," she said, losing almost every other word in a hiccupping sob.

I sighed. This wasn't good. And even though we had it covered, I wondered if we might be causing some kind of psychological damage to these people later in life. Griffin, the head Grigori in the city, assures me not, but still…

At least the art studios are in a separate building; otherwise, the entire school would have charged in on us by now. As it was, I could hear people moving in our direction already.

"I wish it were that simple," I mumbled, not taking my eyes from the exile who would have killed me while smiling, before finishing off everyone in the room out of a misplaced sense of righteousness and, more practically, to cover the evidence. Exiles were thorough if nothing else.

"Do you want me to make you human?" I asked, glancing at the other two exiles. During an outright attack like this, we weren't required to make the offer and I knew what their response would be anyway, but I still felt the need to verbalize it.

Yeah. Sentimental.

The exile didn't respond; he just continued to look at me like he was envisaging ripping my head off. I tightened my grip on my dagger.

Archer cleared his throat. Unfortunately, I knew why.

I held back a sigh of frustration. "Do any of you have a message for me?" I asked, sticking to our latest protocol.

The exile didn't pause to consider his words, while the other two simply growled.

"I exceed you in every way! I'm more powerful than you can imagine, and when I kill you, others will bow at my feet!" he exclaimed, unable to contain the anger in his human form, an emotion that his previous, incorporeal self could not process. He was already well down Delusional Way.

Not exactly the message I was looking for, but good enough. In time with Miss Kinkaid's shriek, I ran my dagger through his chest, being sure to make it a fast killing will. It didn't need to go through the heart; lots of other places would ensure an exile's end. The only essentials are that a Grigori blade inflict the injury and we make it count. Otherwise, exiled angels are damn near impossible to get rid of.

Archer didn't hesitate, taking out one of the exiles and then spinning on the spot to face the other, his blade slashing straight across his neckline.

I looked away. Archer is old school and very good.

Two of my classmates, Jeff Willis and Meredith Faro, chose that moment to break out of shock and into hysterics. Jeff's pitch was the highest. At least no one was trying to bolt this time.

It wouldn't last long. Beth had already moved in on the other students. Every Grigori has a particular strength and we are all a bit different. Beth's strength is memory. Like all of our gifts, though, it isn't endless. She had about a ten-minute window of opportunity and only about a half hour "wipe" capacity *and* she needed to have touched her target in each case.

She started with Miss Kinkaid, who was now silent, despite her mouth being wide open and paused in a potential tense scream. Beth brushed her hand comfortingly.

"It's okay. Everything is okay now."

Beth moved by her, then on to the next, touching everyone in some way, even those who cowered from her, before moving to give them each a good stare.

"Help is on the way," she said soothingly. "Would you all look at me for a moment?" she continued, pushing a little sweetness into her voice, which had everyone slightly entranced. Beth is old school too.

Archer jumped back out the window and disappeared while I walked around, making sure all evidence of the exiles' presence had gone. Their bodies were the easiest part; as soon as they were "returned," whatever magic had given them a physical form quickly disappeared along with their remains, but every now and then, other remains were left behind. Weapons usually, but more recently, we had started to check for other things that might hide a message, even though I knew Phoenix wouldn't bother with such plotting. He liked to deliver messages in person.

"You have all been in art class, like any other day. Vandals have been causing havoc in the area and just like they did on Friday last week"—Beth shot me a loaded glance—"a gang of guys rode by on their bikes, hurling rocks through the windows. It was just lucky Miss Kinkaid was so quick to act that you all managed to huddle into the corner in time. A few of you were hit by flying glass, but you're all okay and know you are safe now. Unfortunately, none of you managed to get a look at any of the perpetrators. Does everyone agree?"

My teacher and peers all began to nod.

Beth waited until she was satisfied. "Okay. Now sit silently until we are gone. Do not pay any attention to us, and you will not remember us once we have left, all except for Violet, who is your classmate and was huddled in the corner with the rest of you."

They all nodded again.

Archer made me jump when he came bounding back through the window with a number of brick-sized rocks hammocked in his Road Runner T-shirt. He scattered them around the room to explain the shattered glass, dropping a couple on top of the desk I had broken with my forehead.

"It's just lucky your school doesn't have video cameras; otherwise, this would be a lot more difficult," he noted.

Rapid footsteps sounded down the hall. Beth and Archer both tensed.

"It's okay. Just Spence," I said. I could sense Grigori. Not as easily as I could exiles, but I ran with Spence every day—I knew his gait well enough to be sure this was him.

Spence almost slid into the room, then looked at my classmates, saw they were held in a momentary daze, and took about one second to put all the pieces together. He snorted. "I've missed it, haven't I? Jeez, Eden, you could've at least called me!"

Yeah. I felt bad. He'd been close and Spence loved a fight.

"Sorry. I barely had time to call in Beth and Archer."

We all knew they were first call in these instances. Beth's ability to make problems…go away was essential.

"Shields?" Spence asked, just as I started to feel the purr of another arrival.

"Yeah," I admitted, hating that I still wasn't strong enough.

There was another thump as two more feet were propelled through the window. I raised my eyes to the roof.

Did everyone have to be here?

Lincoln took in the scene in much the same way as Spence. His eyes landed on me immediately after. "You're hurt," he all but growled.

I sighed. "No. I'm fine. Stupid but fine," I said, trying not to focus on him, not that it made any difference. His very presence sent every part of me, human and angel, into overdrive.

He looked like he wanted to come closer, but after a considering look at my head, he must have deduced the wound wasn't that bad and instead turned to Beth. "How long do we have?"

"About thirty seconds until this group comes around," she said, taking Tristan's phone from his hand, no doubt deleting his recent footage.

"And about a minute until the school rains down on this building," Spence said.

I grabbed a few tissues from Miss Kinkaid's desk and started mopping the blood from my face. It really wasn't bad.

"Violet, are you okay from here?" Lincoln asked.

I sheathed my dagger and tied my hair back into its original ponytail. "Yep, you guys go."

Spence went back out the door the way he'd come. Archer and Beth leapt out the window. Lincoln moved to follow but paused briefly.

"Is that yours?" he asked, gesturing to my charcoal drawing, now on the ground.

"Yeah."

His brow furrowed. "It's beautiful...and awful too. What is it?"

"It's me."

chapter two

"The defects and faults of the mind are like wounds in the body. After all imaginable care has been taken to heal them up, still there will be a scar left behind."

Francois de la Rochefoucauld

I didn't know if I'd ever truly be able to function again after our trip to Jordan. Or if I wanted to. Losing Rudyard...and Nyla—the way their souls had so beautifully intertwined and then been so savagely torn apart. The scream, the last noise that fell from Nyla's lips, sounded in my ears constantly. Haunting me. And even though I pretended I was fine, it took everything I had to force myself not to scream along with her.

The hardest moments were when the thoughts I'd failed to hold at bay snuck into my mind. The selfish ones that made me wish Lincoln and I hadn't waited, that we had allowed our souls to come together completely before Rudyard's death, before knowing that to do so would be damning each other to a tormented fate like Nyla's.

I shivered, wrapping my arms around my waist and quickly pushing those feelings that made me hate myself from my mind.

Steph was already waiting for me at my locker. She was talking to Marcus, her ex-boyfriend. Somehow, they were still friends. Only Steph could manage that situation so well.

Maybe I should get some pointers.

When I arrived, he was already saying good-bye, planting a kiss on her cheek and giving me a charity peck too before dashing off to catch up with his friends.

I smiled when I looked down at the folder resting in her arms. She had an English paper on top, and a big A+ was circled in red. With all her extracurricular work lately, you'd expect things might have slid in other areas, but Steph stayed on top of everything with her particular brand of Steph-finesse.

She moved in close to me, lowering her voice.

"I heard about your art class. Are you okay?" she asked, looking over her shoulder nervously as if she expected secret agents to drop from the ceiling at any moment.

I held back the sigh. "Yeah. It was my fault."

"Was there, you know…did Phoenix send a message?"

"No," I said a little more forcefully than I'd intended. It seemed like the only thing people asked me these days.

She nodded, looking worried but also sensing my need to move on to a different topic. "Sal sent me a text today," she said, expertly transitioning. "They've asked for permission to return, but it's not going well." She frowned. "Spence's decision to stay here without consulting the Academy didn't exactly smooth the way. He thinks it'll take another couple of weeks before they decide what to do."

It had been six weeks since Salvatore and Zoe had returned to New York. In some ways, it seemed like only yesterday that we were all standing in Dapper's apartment unraveling the Exile Scripture after I had "returned" the Exile Jude—or rather, *Judas*.

I smiled, trying to muster some compassion for Steph. I *was* happy for her and Sal, the Italian Grigori she'd fallen for. I just had trouble convincing myself of that sometimes.

"Are they getting much pressure for details about what happened in Jordan?" I asked, feeling guilty. Griffin had put a gag order on everyone who had been present in those caves when Phoenix made his big revelation about me being the first Grigori to be created by the highest-ranking angel, the Sole. It is a fine line Griffin is treading, withholding the information until he is absolutely certain of it. Which is also why he's made it very clear to me he doesn't want to know anything I might know on the subject—like, for example, the time my angel maker visited my dreams and confirmed, well, everything.

"I think the Assembly has given up on getting anything from them. Sal said there are plenty of rumors going around anyway."

I shrugged. We'd expected that. As well as fellow Grigori, the cave had been full of completely unhinged exiled angels. We were sure they would be spouting the news along with their intense desires to be the one to kill me.

"They'll work it out," I reassured, pushing the other thoughts aside in an expert mental maneuver of compartmentalization. "Sal will find a way."

She gave a frustrated sigh. "Yeah, he said Zoe was working on something. It's just...you know."

"Yeah." I swallowed, trying to hold it together.

Oh, I know.

A bag thudded heavily at my feet, and I turned around in time to see Spence slide down the lockers and slump onto the ground.

"This school thing was a bad idea," he groaned. "Eden, you gotta do something, pull rank or something."

"No can do, buddy," I said, not really feeling sorry for him at all. Spence had been strongly urged by Griffin to finish his education if he intended to stay in this city. "And anyway, I hear you had a great time in PE," I added, raising my eyebrows at the last. His second week at school and already Spence had been pushing the boundaries of humanly possible sports.

He looked at me sheepishly. "You saw that, huh?"

"No, but everyone has been talking about it since lunch. Apparently, you're God's gift to the basketball court."

"Couldn't you at least *try* to blend in?" Steph asked, snappish with him, I suspected, for other reasons.

Spence took pause, but then just slumped lower, letting his hands flop to the ground. "I needed a release."

Steph rolled her eyes at him and then said to me flatly, "He flunked the pop quiz in chemistry."

"And history," Spence added. "And then I didn't even get to fight." He shot me a glare.

He looked so glum, I couldn't help but start to feel for him, but right at that moment, Lydia Skilton waltzed by with three of her plastic wannabes in tow. As she walked, her pink ballerina tutu—no joke—seemed to ride up of its own accord as she licked her lips in movie slow motion and curled a few cutesy fingers in Spence's direction.

"Bye, Spence. See you tomorrow."

Spence sat up a little and quickly changed from slumped idiot to laidback hottie as he threw a hand in the air to accompany his lazy smile.

"Bye, Lydia." He watched her ass till the doors at the end of the hall closed behind her.

"I'm sorry, but before I go to the bathroom and throw up, I just have to know—did you actually just *wink* at Lydia Skilton?" Steph asked, as if she had just witnessed a truly horrific moment. I was quite sure my expression mirrored hers.

Spence slumped back down to the ground to his previous life's-beaten-me position and shrugged. "Girl's hot." Then, speaking before Steph delivered a biting remark, he looked at me with an eager glint in his eye. "We out of here?"

I swallowed, relieved too, as I grabbed my training bag. "Yeah."

I shimmied out of my art smock, wiping my still-black hands on it in the process, and pulled on a pair of black leggings under my uniform before taking off my school dress. I always kept a black tank top on underneath to make quick changes easy.

"Training?" Steph asked.

I shrugged. It was no surprise. And anyway, training was the best part of my day.

"Lincoln?" she added quickly, looking past me, down the hall. She must have wanted to ask it for a while. She hadn't raised the subject in weeks.

"No," I said, trying to shut it down.

It didn't mean I never saw Lincoln, but through some kind of unspoken accord—aka avoidance—we had thought it would be better this way. Until things got easier. I wasn't sure if it was working for him.

"Oh," she said, giving me a pitying look, which I hated.

I pulled on a long, black sweater and strapped my belt and sheathed dagger around my waist. Steph watched intently, knowing what I was doing but unable to see the dagger with her only-human eyes. It still amazed—and irritated—her, the tricks the supernatural could play on her mind. Finally, I stuffed my bag into my locker in exchange for a baseball cap, which I slipped on with a sense of relief.

"It's all good," I said, throwing in a dash of fake cheer. "You want me to walk you to the library?" We'd taken copies of the Exile Scripture in the days after first discovering it and Steph had been working almost every day at the library, trying to decipher it. So far, not much. But she seemed to have more theories than Griffin, or the Academy for that matter.

"Actually, I'm going to Hades. The book selection in the library is running short and Dapper has some others he said I can look at, but you know what he's like." She rolled her eyes. "He won't let me take them away with me."

"Are you sure you're okay going there?" I still worried about Steph being a part of this world, and Hades was fast becoming the hub of Grigori activity in this city. She knew things so many normal people would never know, and she was defenseless against the power that surrounded her.

Plus, Onyx—a once very formidable enemy who, although now completely human, was by no means rehabilitated—was still living there. It seemed that had now become some kind of permanent arrangement.

"Yep. I think Samuel and Kaitlin are going to be there too," she said. Two other Grigori being there didn't ease my concerns. If anything, having Grigori escorting Steph only reinforced how essential she had become.

"Okay, well, we can catch the bus there together. We're training in the park today," I said, picking up my pace, eager to get moving.

"Finally!" Spence complained.

"Lovely," Steph said when she spotted the rain spitting against the windows. "Better you than me, I guess," she added, readying her Burberry-check umbrella. She gave me a devilish grin. "Then again, at least you get to hit Spence for the next hour or so."

She really *was* holding it against him that Salvatore couldn't get back here but…she had a point. She smiled and gave me a totally-Steph nudge.

A moment later: "I heard that," Spence said, a few paces ahead.

I smiled back at Steph, and within moments, we'd linked arms and were laughing. She always had a way of making things better. She wasn't just my best friend; she was my family.

chapter three

"We are each our own devil, and we make this world our hell."

Oscar Wilde

The rain had eased off by the time we reached the park, but there was still a persistent drizzle misting the cool air. As far as I was concerned, all-weather training was essential—Lincoln had taught me that early on. We didn't get to pick what weather we fought in, so the same should be applicable to training.

Apart from Griffin, the park—as usual—was people free.

"Hi," I said to him, tossing my bag next to his under the large tree we used as a base. "You been here long?"

"Hey, Griff," Spence said with a big smile and a not-so-happy glance in my direction.

Yeah, I hadn't mentioned we'd have company today. My bad.

Griffin looked up from his stretch. "Not long. Warm up and let's get to it."

Which was exactly what I wanted to hear. Spence's eagerness, however, was fading. He didn't share my all-weather views.

"I think you need to consider confining your art time to home. We can't risk involving innocents. Beth may not always be handy," Griffin said as I pulled off my sweater and started to warm up.

"Probably," I said, not offering to elaborate.

"Phoenix obviously has exiles near the school, waiting to try and sense you. It's a wonder they don't just storm the place, but for whatever reason, he seems to have restricted them to attacking you only when they are sure of your location. We can't ignore that advantage."

He was right, of course. I bent down to my toes so I didn't have to look at him. "It won't happen again."

I didn't know why Phoenix kept sending exiles to fight me this way. Other than consuming people's time and annoying me, it did nothing for him and almost always resulted in him losing his forces. I mean, protective barriers or not, Phoenix *knew* where I lived. He could have sent exiles after me easily, but none had ever entered my home. I knew part of it was his twisted sense of fighter ethics, but it was more than that. Tactically, none of us could work it out.

"Any contact I should know about?" Griffin asked, getting business out of the way.

"Nope." I kept stretching, hoping they'd both leave it. Griffin knew I wouldn't hold back if I had an update.

He seemed to pick up on the vibe and turned his attention to Spence. "How was school?"

"The place is already a faint memory, one I intend to keep in my past," Spence said flippantly.

Griffin smiled. "You'll adjust."

Spence scowled. He knew full well that if he wanted to stay in this town, he'd be finishing off his schooling. Finding somewhere to focus his retaliation, he came closer to me as I stretched out my calves. "Man, you've gotten cocky, Eden."

"Sorry?" I responded, but I knew where he was going.

"You really think you needed to bring the Griffster along?" he scoffed. "As if I won't be able to hand you your ass!"

I just kept stretching.

It wasn't that Spence wasn't a great fighter, but I was getting better all the time. Stronger and faster. Not as strong as Lincoln, but his training me had really paid off. Since I'd started doing my sessions without him, I'd been adding extra ones no one else knew about—taking long runs early in the morning and working out late every night, having converted half of my art studio into a gym. I was fitter than ever.

I knew all of Spence's moves, and he relied on the easy wins. When they failed, he had a flair for the dramatic, but to be honest, I think he was a bit scared to try out the wing-and-prayer stuff with me. Tactical fighting had me beating him regularly these days, and I needed to keep challenging myself.

"Okay. Leg-only combat. No hands," Griffin said, then added, "and no heads."

I smiled at Spence, jumping up and down on the spot to stay warm. "You told him I head-butted you."

He looked guilty. "That shit hurt, Eden."

"Let's go," Griffin said, clapping his hands together and taking up umpire position under the cover of the tree.

I wiped the rain from my eyes and quickly made sure we didn't have an audience. Spence came straight in, gung ho, like always. I dodged his first three kicks and worked to move him around, to keep his focus on staying in time with my movements. His leg struck out again and I dodged, but he kept swinging, hitting my ribs hard with his second pass. I stumbled back.

"You all right?" Griffin asked calmly.

"Yep," I said without hesitation.

I swallowed down the pain and told myself it was fine. I needed to be able to take hits too.

We faced up again. Spence was feeling good about getting the first blow in, but I had a renewed determination. I ran him around the same way as before, but this time it was my strike that counted. My leg went up and out, kicking him with the sole of my foot right between his shoulder blades. Before he'd even reacted, my other foot had followed, taking a swing out wide and smashing into his stomach.

He went down.

Griffin cleared his throat. "You all right?" he asked, not quite as calm this time.

Spence was on his knees, sucking in a few deep breaths, winded.

"Fantastic," he said, standing up to face me for round two. "Barely tickled."

We went six more rounds, each playing out fairly similarly,

Spence getting increasingly irritated that I had his measure. When I put my hand out to pull him up, he swatted it away.

"I'm not beat yet, Eden. I could go all night." He waggled his eyebrows.

"No doubt, Spence," Griffin said from the sideline. He pulled off his sweater, revealing a white, long-sleeved T-shirt.

Shock, horror, a deviation from his standard button-down!

Griffin is a conundrum. He looks like someone in his mid-twenties, acts like someone in his late forties, and is really in his eighties. But no matter how old he gets, he's always a little stuck in his time. That isn't to say he can't kick ass, though, which was clearly in the cards.

"How about we swap places for a bit?" he suggested.

Spence got up and tried his best not to hobble to the sideline. "At least you can heal me," he grumbled as he passed me. "Even if it does hurt worse than the damn kicks."

Healing other Grigori, bar Lincoln, tends to be quite painful and makes me a bit of an anomaly.

One more thing.

But I wasn't worried about that at the moment. I had my eye on the prize and I gave my full attention to my new opponent. I didn't often get a chance to spar with Griffin.

He kept a distance from me. Stalking me. "You're getting stronger."

I just nodded and pushed aside my fear that it wasn't true, reminding myself he meant physically.

"And braver," he said, which I took as a warning. Griffin is deceptively fierce and fights with his head. I couldn't outmaneuver him so easily.

"One round," Griffin said, still moving, backing up toward the tree.

"Why?" I teased, as if he couldn't handle it.

"Because you don't get practice rounds with exiles. Either beat me now, or don't bother."

Nerves tingled in my gut. But this was a challenge I wasn't about to shy away from. "Fine," I said, ignoring my dry mouth. I was up to it. I was sure I was fitter than Griffin; he didn't put nearly the hours I did into training. "I've got somewhere to be anyway. Any rules?"

"First with their back on the ground is out."

No way I'm going down on my back again today.

"Works for me," I said. But I didn't like the smile playing on his lips.

I moved in. I knew what he was doing, backing up the way he was, luring me in, but I couldn't show fear. I kept my footing, watching his feet and hands. He was almost beneath the tree as I closed in. Then, fast as lightning, his hand went out—a fist right across my face that felt like a metal bar. I stumbled but was quick to right myself. He'd have to do better than that to get me down.

He took another step back and that was his mistake. He'd cleared room for a kick and I was in the perfect position. I didn't hesitate. My leg went out and I put force behind it too. But instead of swerving, he moved into me, grabbed my leg, and used my own momentum to throw me. Straight up. Into the tree.

The wind was knocked out of me as my back and shoulder slammed into the thick, overhanging branches and then I fell down fast, my right arm snapping a large branch and several smaller ones as I ricocheted off them on my way down. But one crack wasn't from the tree. I hit the ground, hard. On my back.

"Whoa!" I heard Spence cry out. He was half freaking out, half laughing.

I opened my eyes and brushed away the dirt and bark from my face.

Griffin was standing above me. "Stronger and braver, yes, but years of experience count for something. I just spent the last hour sizing you up, picking your routine. You change it up, but everyone is predictable in the end. If you see the chance for a kick, you take it."

He put his hand out and I moved my right arm to grab it, but winced in pain as I did, working hard to hold back a cry. My head went back to the ground again.

"Broken?" Griffin asked casually.

I turned my face to the side, angry with myself. "I think so." That was the other crack I'd heard. *Damn it.*

"Perfect," Griffin said, as if it were all part of the plan. "This will help."

I glared at him. If he thought I was going to ask Lincoln to heal me tonight, he had another think coming.

"Whatever it is, it'll have to wait. I have dinner tonight with Dad," I snarled, pushing myself up with my good arm. Spence was behind me and helped me to stand. My head was spinning out of control.

"Easy, girl," he said, as if he was talking to a racehorse. I pulled my good arm out of his hold to stand on my own. Then desperately wished I hadn't.

While my stomach churned and I fought the urge to throw up, I took a few calming breaths and tried to center myself and control the pain.

That was when I felt it.

The invisible tendril that linked us sizzled. I could feel his heart beating, steadily at first, and then, as if recognizing me, it picked up.

He knows I've been hurt. What the…?

Then the connection snapped. I didn't know if it was him or me. Him, I think, because I hadn't thought to try. I could taste something in the back of my throat.

Honey. Since when could he sense me like that?

Griffin's phone started to ring. He walked away to answer, but I could hear him anyway. Grigori have better than normal senses too. We can't hear through walls, but we can hear, see, and smell better than average.

"It's fine…You knew?…Impressive…No…Training…No… We're exploring…I'll call you after." He sounded like he was trying to diffuse something and couldn't get off the phone fast enough.

"Lincoln?" I asked, trying not to look like I cared but knowing he was probably on his way by now.

Griffin raised his eyebrows. "You felt the connection too?"

I shrugged. I'd always been able to feel it, since just before I'd embraced and Lincoln had been hurt. It wasn't something I'd felt the need to advertise. I hardly needed to add anything else to the "special" list.

He watched me for a moment. Griffin saw all too easily through my bullshit, but he wasn't going to do anything about it now. He was good like that.

"He's worried."

I knew he was right—I even felt the little bit of truth he bled into the words for my benefit—but I just didn't want to have to think about it. Mostly, I didn't want to feel that intense desire to be near to him, to fill the emptiness in me that was always there when he wasn't. It's not like I couldn't hear the concern in Griffin's voice too. No one wanted Lincoln and me to be together. We weren't the only ones to see what had happened to Nyla and Rudyard.

Spence handed me a bottle of water.

"Violet, I want you to try and heal yourself. I've been looking for an opportunity, but you've been doing well in training so one hasn't come up till now." Griffin slipped his sweater back on, perfectly timed to cover his smile. Even Griffin was guilty of competitiveness.

No wonder he sounded defensive with Lincoln.

"Lincoln's not coming?" I asked, giving him a look that said I saw the smile and there would be a rematch.

"Not unless we need him," he said with a shrug, which also responded to my look. We were holding two conversations at once.

That part of me that had started to anticipate Lincoln sank.

"Okay," I said, trying to ignore my disappointment.

"Let me tell you what we are going to try," Griffin said before proceeding to talk through how he wanted me to heal myself.

At first, I thought he was mad. I'd only just mastered the ability to heal Lincoln. Sure, there had been some discussions that I might be able to do more, prompted by my sometimes being able to send the flow of power back into myself and heal injuries that would have otherwise been too great for Lincoln to do alone. And I'd managed to heal other Grigori—well, only Spence so far. We hadn't tried anyone else yet. But still…

Griffin suggested ways of tapping into my power, but they felt wrong. Lincoln was my partner—*he* was supposed to heal me. But things were…the way they were. He was trying to stay away from me, like I was supposed to be doing from him.

Standing in the dim light, rain still spitting, under a tree I'd just had a head-on collision with, I did as Griffin instructed and drew my power within, trying to coerce it to heal my arm.

To my delight…and horror, I received an answer.

chapter four

> *"No price is too high to pay for the privilege of owning yourself."*
>
> Friedrich Nietzsche

The full-length mirror inside my wardrobe shot back an image I barely recognized. I was wearing a little, black, A-line dress, and I'd opted for tights. I didn't usually like them but they were good for hiding the evidence. Over my arms, I draped a silver shawl I'd borrowed from Steph ages ago to cloak the bruising. Luckily for me, most of the damage had already healed on my face, and a layer of foundation covered up what remained.

It could have been worse. I'd actually managed to tap into my power earlier and manipulate the healing I usually sent to others. It hadn't done a complete job, but enough to fix the break in my arm and the cut on my head. It had also relieved some of the pain and bruising, even if my arm still hurt like I was plunging it into a vat of acid every time I used it. It would take a few more days to fully recover. Griffin had suggested I try again, but for now, I wasn't up to it.

I assessed my ensemble again. At least Dad would be happy. Fathers seemed to feel a sense of accomplishment when daughters dressed conservatively, hence my putting on the black knee-high boots Zoe had given me before she left. Along with a smudge of eyeliner, they changed the overall look just enough.

Petty, yes, but right now Dad invoked that reaction in me. I hadn't told him about what I was or *who* had made me like this. Most of the time, I felt terrible for him. And guilty. He'd had a wife who had deceived him the whole time they'd been together and then died, leaving him completely broken. Now, he had a daughter who really wasn't any better.

But he wasn't blameless either.

I came home regularly with bruising or blood on my clothes. I was always out—not that he wasn't as well, but a father is supposed to pick up on these things. Not to mention I'd flown to Jordan recently without him so much as noticing. The only thing he'd questioned was the thousand dollars I'd withdrawn from his account to pay off Onyx for much-needed information—about my likely demise. Half a dozen fabricated household bills later, Dad had accepted there was no drama and gone back to his work.

So sue me. I wasn't about to turn up to our quarterly, sometimes half-yearly, "family" dinner wearing an outfit that would make him relax into his seat and feel certain everything was as it should be.

I closed the wardrobe door and slipped on the silver bracelets I wore to hide my angelic markings and made a mental note to buy some new ones. I was sick of wearing the same jewelry every day.

Dad had arranged to meet me at The Orchard, our favorite Thai restaurant. When I was younger, he used to take me there three or four times a week, whenever we were nanny-less. It was as close as we came to a home-cooked meal. He knew the staff and liked it there. They called him "John" instead of "James," and I think, in some ways, he liked that the most.

Issues? Us?

I'd decided to walk to the restaurant. It was near our apartment building and I was early anyway, plus I knew Dad would be running late.

Not far into the walk, my angelic senses kicked in. I smelled the flowers first, which only ever happened with him, that distinctive bouquet dominated by scents of musk and jasmine, a particularly moreish combination. The taste of crisp, ripe apple came next, and I saw the flashes of power that echoed morning and evening. Even though he wanted me to know he was there, my senses were less perceptive of him compared to other exiles, the flashes more gentle but still, unnervingly, swaying in favor of evening.

I stopped outside a department store window and stared at a mannequin wearing a beautiful, strapless, black dress with an intricately laced bodice from which fabric flowed to the floor in a sublime drop, a long slit in one side. The model was emotionless even though it showcased one of the most stunning dresses I'd ever seen. I locked my own reactions down and tried to replicate her numbness while I waited.

I didn't need to turn to know when he was right behind me. He was so close, I could feel his breath on my back, feel the flickering emotion he was sending me, the kind that wrung my insides in terrible delight. I focused on being like the mannequin.

"Stop it," I said through gritted teeth.

He moved to stand beside me. The pushing eased and I could breathe again.

"That would look ravishing on you. Would you like me to buy it for you? I could even throw in the ravishing if you like," he said, teasing and not at the same time.

I looked down the street. A moment before, it had been filled with city-goers, hurrying from buildings, heading out for the night or trying to get home. Now, it was quiet. Apart from a few hesitant passersby, it looked like the area had been evacuated. Even the traffic had lightened considerably and seemed to creep past, as though the engine sounds were somehow muted. I knew it was Phoenix; I just didn't know if it was an illusion he was creating in my head, trying to give us some sick kind of privacy, or if he had poured something terrible into the minds of those surrounding us, something so awful that they had fled.

I could see our reflections in the window. He was taller than me, though he often slouched. He always dressed smartly these days. Today, he was in black pants and a charcoal shirt. He looked both handsome and dangerous, and I couldn't help staring at his hair in the glass—the way light danced across the black roots that were illuminated by ripples of deep purple and strands of dazzling silver. Even in the image bouncing off the window, it was mesmerizing.

He was watching me too. I knew what he was thinking, standing there surveying me the way I had him, and I hated that we looked so good together. I could feel that he hated it too.

Hates me.

There were other emotions there as well. He wasn't good enough to hide them completely—or didn't want to. And every time he bled those intoxicating feelings of lust and seduction into me, I sensed they were laced with an honesty he would deny even to himself.

But none of that mattered. Not anymore.

He recoiled, taking a small step back, into the shadows of the reflection. I wondered if it was a reaction to me and my emotions or to his.

"We need to agree on buildings," he said, his voice smooth and sure.

I nodded. It was the last of the pretrade arrangements. We'd left it that way on purpose. Too much could go wrong otherwise. At least I'd finally have some news to pass on to everyone.

He pushed a little at me again, emotions caressing me from inside out. It was divine.

I put up lazy walls and bit down hard. "I said stop it or I'll leave."

"But I could make this exchange much more pleasurable."

He tried harder this time and, like smoke seeping under a doorway, lust rose, my body craving more.

Phoenix laughed lightly. "You have such an appetite. I don't know why you deny it," he said, coercing me with his words.

"Because it's not me. I don't want your emotions running through me. It's like some kind of poison."

He didn't stop but didn't push any harder. Instead, he leaned in close, too close for comfort, and spoke with a low voice into my ear. "I would've given you everything."

I held my defenses where they were—caught in the moment, half up, half down, unsure for a second which way to go. But then I came to my senses, and my walls shot up. I stepped back and turned to him, showing I wasn't afraid.

"No. You would've taken everything I am until I was nothing but your puppet. You might not have planned to, but you wouldn't have been able to help yourself. And anyway..." I stopped. There was no way to discuss that, to talk about how I couldn't love anyone truly, anyone other than Lincoln.

Phoenix shrugged, but his expression remained intense.

"Guess we'll never know." He looked right into my eyes, making sure he had my full attention. "But then, neither will he."

Like I was back in Jordan again, I felt the tragedy of Rudy's death, of Phoenix calling out to his exiles to leave a moment later. I'd wondered since why he hadn't just grabbed the Scripture earlier and taken off. He was losing exiles and we were too evenly matched—it wasn't a smart fight. If he was any other exile, I would have understood. In general, they don't care and would be insane enough to take on any odds, but not Phoenix. He is an anomaly.

He was still watching me, and it was then that I realized why he'd waited so long to leave.

"You wanted Rudyard to die," I accused, barely able to push the words from my mouth. It was too horrific, and even after everything he'd done, I really didn't want this to be true.

His eyes flickered, then narrowed. At first I thought my accusation surprised him, but then he just let out a calculatedly bored yawn.

"An acceptable casualty of war." He put his hands in his pockets, showing he wasn't concerned.

He'd planned it all. Made sure Lincoln and I would never be...

My good arm went out so fast I hadn't even realized I'd decided to do anything. My closed fist swept across his face, hard. He hadn't expected it, and it hit him in the jaw, jerking his head to the side.

He stood tall again, as if it hadn't happened. He didn't even put a hand to his face to rub the spot I knew would be hurting. In fact, he left his hands in his pockets.

Bastard.

I kept my own hands fisted, anticipating his retaliation. But instead, he just growled, "Buildings."

"Maddox," I said quickly, still in a bit of shock.

"Fine. We'll be on the Brighton. Tomorrow night. Eleven p.m. No tricks."

"No tricks," I agreed, suspecting I wasn't the only one lying. "And you can stop sending your lackeys after me too," I added. "We've returned them all, Phoenix. Surely you're getting sick of losing fighters."

He smiled without any kindness. "Just making sure you have no more hesitations."

I glared at him. "No such luck," I sneered. My apprehension at drawing my dagger had ended the night I'd returned Jude. But I felt sure he knew that.

"*And* I thought you'd appreciate the extra training."

A shiver ran down my spine. The way he said it and waited for my reaction—I was suddenly convinced he'd been watching me, following me on my additional sessions.

He turned to walk away but stopped and looked back.

"Violet..."

"What?" I snapped.

"Thank you," he said, now touching his face. And then he was gone with a more forceful than usual gust of wind that pushed me back a step before I caught my footing.

"Shit," I mumbled nervously, taking a few calming breaths and trying to shake the quiver from my hands.

chapter five

"People only see what they are prepared to see."

Ralph Waldo Emerson

Dad was picking at a plate of spring rolls when I made my late entrance.

"You get lost?" he asked, but his smile paused mid-upcurl and he dropped his roll into the dipping sauce. "What happened?" he asked, looking worried as he stood up and carefully reached out to touch my arm.

In my haste, I'd let the shawl drop and bunch into the crease of my elbow. Dad was surveying a pretty big bruise on my bad arm.

I had to take a few steadying breaths, still working hard to pull myself together after seeing Phoenix. "Oh. I…bashed into a tree," I eventually said.

Technically…true.

"Accident," I added.

Technically…false.

"It looks painful. Must've been one angry tree," he said, something in his tone unsettling me.

Suspicion?

"It'll teach me for not looking where I'm going, I suppose," I said, looking at my arm as if only now noticing how bad it was while trying to ease it out of Dad's hold, pretending it didn't hurt like hell. Once free, I readjusted my shawl and took my seat. "Have you ordered anything else?"

He nodded, taking his seat too, still looking at me strangely. "The usual."

"Great," I said, pepping up convincingly. "I'm starving."

A plate of spring rolls, a chicken pad thai, a green curry, and two glasses of Coke later, I was looking for a way out. Fast.

It was like Dad had undergone some kind of personality transplant. Not only was he conversational, but he'd also never so closely scrutinized me or asked me so many questions in…my entire life. I was right; he was definitely suspicious.

I'd dodged the questions about my after-school activities, brushing off my busy schedule on preparing for the Fenton art course due to start after graduation and studying at the library with Steph. But when Dad started asking about Lincoln, not just if we were still friends, but what Lincoln's plans for the future were, if we were still training—since I was looking very fit—I knew I needed to get out of there.

"Dad, I, umm…I'm feeling a bit exhausted, actually. Do you mind if we just grab an ice cream on the walk home?" Okay, so blow me down or something, because *my* father, the man who usually jumps at the opportunity to remove himself from any personal moment, put down his napkin, and said, "To tell the truth, honey, I'd really like it if we could chat for another few minutes."

I sat there, dumbfounded. I considered asking him if he was feeling okay, if he had been struck down by some terminal illness and only had days to live. When I went to open my mouth…nothing.

"It's just that, well"—he cleared his throat, oblivious to my stunned state—"I know I'm not around a lot. And recently it's come to my attention that maybe I'm not…*there* enough in other ways too." He sighed.

My mind was reeling.

Come to his attention? Who the hell managed to get his attention long enough to bring anything to it?

"I'm not good at this, Vi. I know you probably think I'm a terrible father, and I…I wouldn't blame you if you did. But I feel like I've been caught between worlds since…your mother. I never really took up the reins, and you were always such a good girl. I guess I just let you carry the load."

Good God, did my father just use the word "feel"?

The front door to the restaurant swung open and a happy family left, calling out their thanks to the waiters as the boy swung between his parents' hands.

If I run, I could make it out that door before it closes.

"I know something is going on in your life, Vi."

Does he? Is it possible that all this time, Dad has actually known?

Or figured it out?

My hands went to my bracelets, rotating them around my wrists.

"And I can see that it has changed you."

He knows.

He sat up straighter. I braced myself.

"When we're young, lots of things happen that we think are the be-all and end-all, but really, they're not. I can see you're losing focus on school and I realize it's wrapping up now, but you still have work left to do, and I haven't heard you talk about university options or seen any applications lying about. Violet, if there is something going on that I need to know about, it's time to tell me," Dad said, sounding sterner than I'd ever heard him.

He doesn't know.

I took a moment, recovering from the roller-coaster conversation, followed by a speedy shutdown.

"I'm fine. Everything is fine."

Dad watched me as I sat there with a smile frozen on my face. He seemed a little disappointed. I suppose he had just said quite a bit and I hadn't offered much in return, but he'd obviously prepared for the conversation and I…Hell, I'd had no idea he was going to say anything beyond his usual, "How was your day?"

"Okay. I'll take your word for it." He stood up. "Let's grab that ice cream on the way home."

And right there was the first parental guilt-trip my father had ever successfully pulled on me.

I pulled my shawl close, feeling lonely and my arm still aching.

I should have taken some aspirin before I'd left home. We weaved our way between the tables of the busy restaurant, the owner stopping us at the front to ask Dad—"John"—how everything was. When I stopped walking, I felt a twinge in my chest and then a sharp throb at the base of my ribs. I jerked straight and concentrated on breathing deeply. I knew instantly. It wasn't my pain I was feeling.

It's not a bad one, I told myself. *Ribs, I think.*

I smiled when, from behind the desk, the restaurant owner gave me a cheesy grin—the same one he used to give me when I was nine.

Lincoln.

It was fading. But it had also been stronger than any of the others I'd felt. The feelings were getting more acute each time, and though they passed quickly, I hated the aftermath even more. Everything in my being wanted to run to him. Every breath felt like an impossible delay as instinct and something more took over, trying to control me. I took hold of one of the chairs and cemented my feet to the floor while I waited for Dad to finish being John so I could walk with him to the ice cream shop before heading home.

When we reached the front doors to our building, I spotted Spence resting against the wall.

"Dad, I'll meet you up there. I just want to say hi to a friend of mine," I said, motioning in Spence's direction.

Dad nodded to Spence—who he thought was just a school friend—briefly, but his smile was edged with something, sadness maybe.

"Don't be long," he said, walking inside.

There had been a lot of times I'd tried to talk to him and had gotten nowhere, so I knew exactly how he felt and it made me want to go after him. But I had to speak to Spence first.

I joined him against the wall after dropping my barely touched ice cream in the trash.

"I would've eaten that," Spence said. I ignored him.

"How bad?"

"You know, he'll find out I've been reporting to you on this stuff," he grumbled.

Spence wasn't a snitch. But even if he did live at Lincoln's now, Spence was my friend first and that gave me dibs.

"Spence," I warned.

"One rib, maybe two. He's fine. They'll probably heal on their own in a day or two."

"Where was he?" I asked, but part of me already knew. Phoenix had been sending exiles every few nights, but I'd suspected he was actually sending them more often than that—I just wasn't seeing them. Plus, there was a reason why I'd felt his injuries so acutely tonight.

"Ah…come on, Eden, don't push it," Spence said, wriggling against the wall.

I just stared at him.

"I don't know," he blurted out. "Around, in the city."

"He was patrolling near the restaurant, wasn't he? I felt it more—I know he was nearby."

Spence didn't answer, which I took as a yes.

"How many were there?" I asked, now regretting hitting Phoenix even more. No doubt he would have seen this as fair recompense.

"Three."

My eyes widened. "Who was with him?"

Spence didn't answer.

"Jesus! He was on his own?" I exclaimed, increasingly stressed that he might be in worse shape than Spence was letting on. Just today I'd had a glimpse into how impossible a confrontation with three exiles against one Grigori was. This was my fault. Phoenix had probably known Lincoln was nearby.

"Yeah. The man's a legend. Returned two of 'em too," Spence said, bobbing his head up and down.

Clearly Lincoln had found himself a fan.

"So," I said, trying to gather my thoughts, "where is he now?"

Spence shrugged. "Resting, I expect. I only know 'cause he called me after he couldn't get through to Griffin and asked me to let him know one of them got away. You want me to check the area before I go?"

"No," I said, then realized why he'd been so quick to come to me. "That's why you're here! Lincoln sent you to patrol, in case that other one came back. Oh my God!" I was seething. Did Lincoln have such little faith in me to protect myself? I definitely didn't need Spence guarding my front door.

He slid off the wall. "Hey, you *know* I know you can kick butt. I have the bruises to prove it. I don't reckon there'll be any more action tonight anyway, but you know—the guy can be persuasive."

I didn't really care what Spence did. I didn't believe that Lincoln would stay home and rest. There was still plenty of witching left in the night and, broken ribs or not, Lincoln was just about determined enough to come back out looking for the one that got away.

Fine by me. I'd be waiting.

Dad was sitting up at the breakfast bar when I walked in. He was sipping coffee and there was another full cup beside his.

Oh, come on!

He turned as I came into the kitchen, and I opted for standing on the opposite side of the bar rather than sitting beside him. He slid the coffee over to me. I swept a tired hand across my face. It had been a long day.

And it's not over yet.

"Thanks," I said, taking a grateful sip. Dad and I couldn't cook to save ourselves but we both made wicked coffee.

"How's your friend?" Dad asked.

"Fine."

He nodded, and an awkward silence settled. Normally at this point, Dad would get up to do some work or go to bed. He shifted in his seat.

"I…Vi…Actually, I'm going out tomorrow night. Ah, you know, an after-work drink thing."

I smiled, breathing out a little relief and breathing in the shift in power. "Caroline?" I asked slyly. I hoped it was Caroline. She'd been Dad's personal assistant for as long as I could remember and had always had a thing for him. I'd never thought Dad had noticed, but maybe I was wrong.

"Do you think it's a bad idea?" he asked, suddenly sounding a lot younger than he was.

I honestly didn't think Dad had been on a date in seventeen years. And I wasn't exactly the best qualified to be giving out relationship advice right now, but I bit back the *All relationships end in heartbreak or mass murder* comment on the tip of my tongue and settled for, "It's a great idea, Dad." And then I thought of a way to help myself out with another problem. "*And* I'm staying at Steph's tomorrow night, so you'll have the place all to yourself."

Dad stood up like a rocket. "Violet," he coughed. "It's just an after-work drink." He took his cup to the sink and emptied it before reaching over to give me his signature kiss on the forehead. "I'm going to bed."

"Sweet dreams," I teased, as he walked into his room at double speed, and I had to stifle a laugh.

That worked out well.

Not only had I slipped in that I wasn't coming home tomorrow night, but he'd also closed himself in his room, and I knew following *that* conversation, he would not resurface tonight.

I took my coffee and went to my art studio. I considered doing some painting, but when I walked in there, I was reminded I had jammed all my art stuff up against the wall—exercise mats now took up the majority of the space. I couldn't get to anything without rearranging everything. There was no point doing a workout. I'd get one shortly anyway, so, instead, I found myself sitting on the windowsill where my angel maker always hovered.

I looked out, down over the city street as cars flew by, headlights blazing on one side of the road, red brake lights flashing on the other. I looked toward the park at the end of the road and then I pushed out my senses.

The park it was.

chapter six

"My love lies bleeding."

Thomas Campbell

I changed into leggings and a gray turtleneck and slipped on a beanie. I was pretty sure Dad was asleep, but if I left through the building's front door, the security guy might say something to him in the morning, so I headed for the balcony off the living room instead.

Twelve stories is a big drop. Fortunately for me, on this side of the building, every floor has a balcony at the same spot. Quietly, I slid the door open, just enough so I could shimmy out. It had a squeaky spot, but I'd closed it enough times to know just when to lift it a little to avoid the telltale noise. Getting down was going to be tricky; getting back up, just plain hard.

I hoisted myself over the railing, sitting on it and letting my feet dangle down.

Come on, Vi, you've got this.

If Zoe could catapult herself up here from a tree and Spence could scale the walls, then surely I could bounce down. I held out my bad arm and fisted my hand a few times, deciding it would hold up. I slid down so my feet balanced on the small ledge, turned so I was facing the wall, and let myself fall.

With a slap, I caught the railing of the balcony below as my feet scrambled until they found a grip. My heart was in my throat, but I'd done it.

Only ten more!

Each time, the adrenaline rose as I let go and dropped another story. But by the time I reached the fifth floor, I had it in the bag. When I landed on the pavement, I almost took out some poor guy going for a night jog. He swerved and looked at me like I was some kind of lunatic but kept going.

I brushed myself off without making much improvement—the outside of the building really needed a clean, and cobwebs are hard to shift. At least I was in gray.

Once I was reasonably presentable, I felt for my dagger and headed toward the park. Despite my slipups in art class, I had become increasingly good at keeping my guards up. Unless I wanted them to, exiles couldn't sense me as easily as they had once been able to.

It didn't take long for me to connect with my angelic senses. An exile was near and not bothering with stealth. By the energy he was releasing that was now pulsing through my body, I suspected he was hunting.

I kept my guard up while I moved closer, wanting to size up my opponent before letting him sense me. I weaved between the trees rather than taking the path, using the shadows for cover. The anticipation of conflict ignited the combatant in me and I found myself almost hungry for the confrontation.

It didn't take long to find him, and when I did, I was surprised. I'd assumed it would be one of Phoenix's crew, but now I wasn't so sure. Phoenix kept his followers on a tight leash. If he'd sent this exile after me, he wouldn't be dragging a petrified woman to the back of the park instead.

I stopped behind a tree, testing my arm again, straightening it out to be sure it wouldn't be a problem when I needed it. It screamed with pain, worsened by its recent workout, but it was functioning. I closed my eyes and used a tiny bit of power to see what everyone else was seeing. Sometimes it was the other way around. Sometimes the exile was so strong that I'd be seeing what he was putting out into human imaginations and I'd have to use my power to break it down, show me the truth, but in the case of the weaker ones, which this one was, it worked the other way. A light misting of my power filtered out into the night sky; the purple glitter was absorbed in the darkness quickly and allowed me to see the glamour being used.

As far as any normal human was concerned, the exile was just some well-dressed guy walking through the park with a woman, as if they were out on a midnight stroll. I closed my eyes again and reopened them to the reality. He had her by the hair, dragging her as she clawed at the ground and screamed for help.

She'll be dead in minutes.

I felt for my dagger again, apprehensively. The only way to get the exile away from her was to give him something better to play with. It hadn't exactly been my plan heading out tonight. But it was now.

I took a step out from the cover of the trees and felt him instantly. I froze, biting down on my lip as I realized my mistake. I'd let myself get distracted by the exile and hadn't felt him approach. Now, his nearness washed through me, making me rigid yet like jelly at the same time.

I guess the original plan is going to work out after all.

"You shouldn't be here," Lincoln said, his voice low and gravelly. I couldn't stop it from vibrating through my whole body, teasing me beyond belief.

I didn't turn. I needed to keep my eyes on the exile who still hadn't sensed us. And it was easier not to look at him.

"Look who's talking," I replied quietly. "Do you even sleep anymore?"

The exile pushed the woman into a tree and she crumpled to the ground.

"Just staying fit," he said.

"So I hear."

He sighed and then said something bad under his breath, followed by Spence's name.

"Don't blame Spence," I said.

"I don't," he said. I wasn't really sure what he meant by that. Maybe he blamed me. Taking in the scene ahead of us, he added,

"She's covered in shadow. He's been preying on her for a long time." And now he was angry.

Lincoln was a shadow-finder. He could see the marks left on humans after exiles had penetrated their minds. The residue. It made him one of the best people for tracking exiles. Find the shadowed humans and you could bet on finding exiles soon after. But there was a price—he carried the burden that came with knowing their victims' pain.

The exile moved above the woman; he was going to hit her. Suddenly, the image of Claudia popped into my mind, remembering how defenseless my old classmate had been when an exile had attacked and murdered her.

It's now or never.

I dropped my shields quickly and completely.

"Violet!" Lincoln growled, unhappy with my decision.

I didn't care. I wasn't about to let that woman get hurt, and neither was he. I'd just beat him to it.

The exile's attention sprang up like a dog that had smelled a bone. He turned, his interest in his victim now fully extinguished. He started for me and his victim crawled away, fast.

Smart woman.

The exile, tall like so many of them, stepped into the glow of light from the street. He was strikingly handsome, also like many of them. Dressed in a well-fitted suit and with perfectly fixed hair, he looked like a metrosexual. It was easy to see how he'd lured that poor woman into his hold.

He stalled on his approach, feeling my power.

"What? You need an invitation?" I asked, sounding as angry as I felt. It was a shame that having this kind of power didn't mean they ran away and hid from me. No, instead, it meant he leapt into the air with freakish speed and height and headed straight for me with what could only be described as malice-fueled determination.

I stepped out of his way just in time and had my fist in his face before he'd even landed both feet on the ground. Of course, that barely slowed him. He spun, going for the obvious target—my neck. I let him take it—I was better off if he was one hand down—and quickly delivered a knee to his groin. In that split second, when his head dropped and his grip on my throat loosened, I followed through with a flat palm up and into his nose. It was neat and efficient, and I had him.

"Choose," I demanded, holding my dagger that had slid into my hand smoothly.

He stumbled back and laughed. "I know who you are."

"Good, then you'll know to choose quickly," I said, getting ready.

They never *choose* humanity. None of them believe they will truly be beaten, narcissists that they are. And even if they do, they could never live without the power that comes with their exile status.

He spat at the ground. Blood. I saw that as a compliment. It took a lot to get blood from an exile. I'd probably smashed his nose right back into his throat.

"You're Phoenix's whore," he said, laughing again.

I shrank back in shock. Part of me wanted to run and hide; the other wanted to make sure his nose was headed for his stomach. Lincoln put a hand on my shoulder.

"Violet?"

"It's only a matter of time. We have numbers beyond what you could dream of. Grigori are all but extinct!"

I just nodded and watched through glassy eyes as Lincoln, who'd been respectfully letting me take point, moved forward swiftly—showing no sign of his injury—put one hard kick into the exile's head, and followed through, planting his dagger into his chest. Like that, he was gone, disappeared.

"Not before you," Lincoln said, putting his blade away.

But words linger.

"Was he one of Phoenix's?" I asked, still looking at the spot where the exile had stood. If Phoenix had sent him to attack me, he shouldn't have been sidetracked with that woman.

Lincoln nodded. "Phoenix doesn't have as much control as he would have you think. A lot will never follow, despite what they promise him and no matter what the cause." He walked toward me and suddenly I was on the defensive.

"You can't protect me twenty-four/seven!" I said, using my anger to cover everything else.

He didn't respond for some time. Finally, he took another step closer to me. Closer than was safe.

"Violet," he began calmly. "Are you okay?"

"Am I okay?" I repeated, shaking my head at him. I took the

last step to close the distance, and he flinched as if he wanted to back away.

Just perfect.

I put a hand below his chest. I let my power run from me to him. It almost galloped out of me, it was so pleased to find him. His body's resistance dropped a notch, moving into my hand, and his chest heaved. His hand went out instinctively to my arm, returning the favor. I felt the warm honey of his power trickle through me and worked to stop myself from crying out in relief.

Stupid powers, betraying me.

"You shouldn't be hunting on your own," I said, my voice thick with want, my hand still resting below his chest. I could feel him breathing, his firm muscles moving up and down, each breath increasingly deep and at the end of each intake, the slightest tremor. I couldn't stop my eyes from traveling over that perfect chest, its contours showing through his black cotton sweater just enough.

"Like you just were," he said, sounding like he was feeling exactly the same way as me. His hand was still on my arm, sending a lick of fire through my body.

I dropped my hand, scared of what I'd do if I left it there a moment longer.

"I knew you were out here somewhere," I said, defending myself. "I'm not about to let you go out every night all Lone Ranger, just to protect me."

Lincoln let his hand drop too and took a small step back before grumbling Spence's name again. I felt his power pick up, the honey and cream that was unique to him and, in that, the intoxicating smell of early-morning sun on a hot day. I didn't know what had his power working so hard, but before I could ask, he had his own question for me.

"What did Phoenix want?" he asked softly.

I should have known he'd seen, following me, playing protector in the shadows.

"He took the Brighton building; we have the Maddox."

He nodded, looking past me. "Anything else?"

I shrugged, uncomfortable.

He stiffened. "He still gets to you, doesn't he?"

I'd never fully explained to Lincoln just how much Phoenix's power affected me, but I suspected he had a good idea.

"I can handle it. We don't have any other choice, right?"

It had been the condition of negotiations. We had the Exile Scripture, Phoenix had the Grigori Scripture, and the only way he had agreed to the trade was if he dealt with me. *Only* me. It was a spiteful thing to do, but we all knew that until he had the Exile Scripture, he wouldn't kill me.

He'll wait until after.

Which was why tomorrow night would be so dangerous. Lincoln was watching me.

"Looking to see if I'm falling apart?" I asked, bitter as well as testing.

"No, I just know there's something you're not telling me. And I'm wondering what he did to make you hit him."

I hated that he knew me that well, could read me like no one else. I guess it made sense now why he above all others had that ability—I wished that was the only side effect of being soul mates. I considered telling him what I'd discovered—that Phoenix had ensured Rudyard was killed so we would witness what happened to Nyla—but it would only hurt him.

"It's nothing," I said.

"If you say so," he said, still keeping a close eye on me. "I know you'd tell me if you thought I needed to know. And...what that exile said, about Phoenix and you..." He sighed with frustration and I wondered if it was at me, but then he surprised us both by stretching his arm out and letting his fingers glide over my forehead, tracing the rim of my beanie.

"It's not true."

I nodded, my heart pounding at his touch, but his hand fell away as his power flared again, sending out more silken honey.

"Would you like me to walk you home?" he asked, not pushing.

I felt like I was about to burst into tears. It was hard enough to hear someone call you a whore, but to call you the whore of someone who was killing people you cared about—and in front of the one person you most dreaded could think of you like that...

"I'd prefer to go alone. It's just up the road," I said, fighting to hold on to control until I could get away from him.

He nodded. "I should go and check that woman got away okay anyway."

I started to leave when I remembered something. "Linc, you felt me today, didn't you?"

He stopped midturn. "When you hurt yourself? Yes."

"No, I don't mean that. I mean you felt me respond to you, like we weren't just aware of each other, more like we were communicating."

He thought about it for a moment. "Yes..." he said uncomfortably.

As far as I had known, he hadn't been able to do that before. Any of it.

"Since when?" I checked.

Another delay before he answered. More honey stirring. Why was he pulling on so much power?

"Today."

chapter seven

"Through pride we are ever deceiving ourselves. But deep down below the surface of the average conscience a still, small voice says to us, 'Something is out of tune.'"

Carl Jung

Exchange night.

It had been in the making for six weeks, since that first text from Phoenix after he'd discovered Jude had betrayed him and handed us the Exile Scripture.

It took nearly four weeks to simply agree on the method of exchange. A simple face-to-face had been quickly ruled out in week one—too easy for Phoenix to use his power over me and reinstate the wounds he had once healed. He could bleed me out as soon as he got hold of the Scripture, or, if I got in first, he knew I could harness my abilities, disabling him completely. And this was only one of the problems we faced in a potential minefield. Almost every scenario had a similar bad ending based on the mutual distrust each side had for the other.

The drive-by drop would never work with Phoenix's speed advantages, and his suggestion of using normal humans was quickly tossed. The fly-by drop—Spence's idea, need I go further? Even the idea of the public place and intricate treasure hunt—as suggested by Steph—had flaws.

Of course, we didn't *really* care. We had our own plans in place, but we couldn't appear as though we didn't think this exchange was important. We'd even gone as far as to stage a few heated conversations at Hades and outside Lincoln's warehouse, arguing over my safety, given the role I would have to play. We knew Phoenix had exiles watching. I could sense them lurking.

In the end, we had agreed upon the exchange particulars, a combination of some of our earlier suggestions and Phoenix's all mixed into one. Two tall buildings, far enough apart that our powers wouldn't cover the distance, and a solitary high-tension cable connecting the two. The idea was fairly simple; with one person traveling from each side, neither force would be as quick to cut the line. In addition to Phoenix and I, we were each permitted to have two people on the roof and one on the ground, just in case. We had Beth stationed below, though if it came to it, a fall from that height would be fatal, so her services would be more about containing the scene than recovery.

I'm not usually scared of heights, but standing on the rooftop, looking over…Well, it was a *lot* higher up than my apartment building.

I shivered and wrapped my arms around my waist. I'd given my coat to Spence as a precaution hours ago and regretted not thinking ahead as another blast of high-altitude air sent cold right through to my bones. I tugged my beanie over my ears and crouched back down, out of sight.

It won't be long now.

Lincoln was readying the heavy crossbow that had come in on special request from the Academy's weapons department. He was all business tonight and he was a crack shot. I watched as he and Griffin carefully fed the cable into the bow's anchor that, once released, would lock onto its target. Coils of wire cable lay carefully arranged at his feet so when he fired, they wouldn't tangle or snag.

Lincoln checked and double-checked everything. Griffin, beside him, triple-checked. When they seemed satisfied, Griffin said something to Lincoln that I couldn't hear and made him laugh—a light, excited laugh by the expression on his face. One he never gave me. Not anymore.

My airways tightened as I crouched in the shadows, the Exile Scripture tucked securely inside my backpack, which had remained strapped to me since the moment it had been transferred to me two hours ago. Every day since we had acquired it, the Scripture had changed hands between Grigori—different partners responsible for keeping it safe for each twenty-four-hour period. Locking it away just hadn't been safe enough.

Spence moved up behind the others and Lincoln slapped him on the shoulder before covering up the guy-like gesture by giving him an awkward embrace. I could tell Spence was totally grossed out, but he played along. This was important.

Lincoln moved to the edge and aimed the crossbow that all of them had been drooling over since it arrived last week. He released the shot. It was good, clean. I followed the flash of silver to the Brighton building and smiled as it landed perfectly on point.

Right at Phoenix's unflinching feet.

The Brighton building was mirror height to the Maddox, but there was a great distance separating the two—Steph had worked out that it was over half a mile in a straight line. Lincoln had outdone himself to make such a perfect night-shot on the first go. Then again, he was just that good.

I tried to keep my eyes on Phoenix, just visible thanks to the small amount of roof lighting, as he hooked himself up to the harness and rolled the Scripture into a canister that he then raised above his head. I tried to look for something that would alert us to any sign of sabotage, since we knew he'd be planning something, but my eyes wandered of their own accord, drifting back to the Maddox, back to Lincoln as he stood on the edge of the building. He was magnificent. Even from this distance, I could feel the pull toward him.

He, of course, didn't look in my direction once. He knew not to. None of them so much as glanced my way. Spence was strapping himself to the cable, now taut at both ends, and I could see that Phoenix was ready to go.

It was almost time. Five minutes till eleven, and on the hour, both Phoenix and I were due to start the move toward the center.

I worried for the millionth time that this plan wouldn't work.

Spence was good; he was really good. Standing on top of the Maddox, he looked exactly like me, wearing not only my body, but my mannerisms and expressions, as practiced, as well as my real clothes—backup in case the glamour slipped at any time. Spence could conjure anything to complete his look, but having the support of real props only helped. He would have been able to fool anyone, even my father, but Phoenix was...Phoenix. He *knew* me, knew my emotions in ways no one else did. I was willing to bet they were very different from Spence's.

Lincoln and Griffin fussed over Spence—glamoured as me—careful to ensure they reacted to and treated him in the same way they would me. Everything they did would be scrutinized from afar as Phoenix and his crew tried to see what our reserve plan could be.

I held my position, hidden by the night, guarding the Scripture that we had no intention of handing over. That was my job. The Scripture had been given to me as a last resort—my condition to agreeing to this whole setup. There was no way I was going to sit back and let Spence dangle a hundred stories up in the air, sharing the high wire with Phoenix, knowing when Phoenix discovered it wasn't me at all, anything would be possible and the only guarantee was it wouldn't be good.

Griffin had agreed to let me be there. I was on top of the Atlantic, taller by five floors than the other buildings, giving me a slight advantage and better cover. I was equal distance from both the Maddox and Brighton, forming the point to the triangle. Obviously, I had to be far enough away that Phoenix wouldn't sense me unless I wanted him to, and I'd ensured I was at sufficient remove from Lincoln, so he wouldn't be distracted by me. Not that I was certain I distracted him like he did me, but just in case.

I checked my watch. One minute.

This is a bad idea. A very, very bad idea.

I'd half expected Steph to have called me. I'd told her if she did, I'd let her stay on the line as it all went down. I wasn't doing anything else.

Guess she's caught up with the research thing again.

Phoenix was right on the edge, and the Scripture was easily visible, as per the rules, hanging from a strap around his neck. Spence-as-me was on the edge too. Lincoln and Griffin had moved back into place, guarding the line and in position should something go wrong—as in, someone-cutting-the-line wrong.

11 p.m.

Phoenix dropped into open air, dangling from the high wire in his harness, looking like he did this every day. It was a basic zip-line setup, without the zip. Both he and Spence were harnessed but needed to pull arm over arm to make the distance. Spence dropped with a little less finesse. They both started to monkey forward.

Reaching halfway to the middle, they were moving at a similar speed.

My heart was pounding—I couldn't shake the feeling that something was wrong, very wrong.

Phoenix moved athletically, but was it with his usual fluidity? I looked closer, trying to figure out what had me so worried. But shielding myself like I was, I couldn't push out my senses. It was useless. It made me nervous that Phoenix's face was hidden by a hoodie. I wished I could speak with Lincoln or Griffin, double-check if anyone had actually seen it was him.

I turned my attention back to Spence. He was making good headway and I knew by now he'd be working hard on controlling his emotions, trying to neutralize them as much as possible in the way we'd practiced. The fake Scripture dangled from a leather strap, slung diagonally across his body, and he reached down a few times to adjust it.

I glanced at my phone again, my breath leaving light wisps of smoke in the frosty air. It had only taken them fifteen minutes to reach the center, which was impressive. I strained to see everything through the darkness. They each pulled their Scriptures from around their necks.

Everything was going according to plan.

So why is something screaming at me that it's time to panic?

Spence held out his Scripture. That was one of the other reasons why it had taken so long to agree on the exchange. We'd been stalling. It takes a long time to make a false ancient replica. In the end, we'd only had enough time to make the outside look convincing. When Phoenix opened the Scripture, he'd know, but that was the other reason why we'd agreed to this particular exchange—he wasn't likely to hang around in midair to check it. We hoped.

They made the swap slowly, as agreed. I looked over to the Brighton. The exiles Phoenix had brought were two of his best.

Diplomatically, one light and one dark. We'd been profiling his group for the last month, collecting information on them all, so I knew the two on the roof. Gressil, once a Power of Dark, had a particular strength in turning men against women, luring his male victims into impurity in exchange for luxurious indulgences. The other was Olivier, once an Archangel of Light. They'd both been there, in Jordan, but it was Gressil who we suspected had taken down Rudyard.

The two were an unlikely team. We had good intel that told us they despised each other, which was interesting, given their powers were so similar. Olivier's strength was in provoking mercilessness. The two of them working together made a very dangerous force. And they were now almost always at Phoenix's left and right.

My hand was itching to press the call button on my phone.

I had Lincoln's number up on the screen.

Something's wrong. Why is Phoenix hiding under a hood?

I was just about to make the call when Phoenix reached up and pushed his hood back.

Definitely him.

I sighed. I'd almost blown it, thinking they were pulling a similar stunt.

Spence and Phoenix both started moving back toward their buildings. Spence was making good time while Phoenix seemed to be taking things more slowly, almost lingering. Once Spence made it back to the Maddox, I let out a shaky sound of relief and checked my phone again: 11:45 p.m.

Why hasn't Steph called?

I knew she was waiting for us at Hades with Dapper, Onyx, Samuel, and Kaitlin. The rest of the Grigori were out patrolling, mostly in this area.

Steph had wanted to come and wait with me on the roof, but I'd talked her into staying at Hades instead, promising I'd give her minute-by-minute updates.

Phoenix finally reached the Brighton, easily slipped back onto the roof, and unhooked his harness. He walked to the edge of the building and pulled the canister containing the Scripture from around his neck.

He's going to check it.

The puffs of cold air stopped as I held my breath in panic, dreading his reaction. But then his demeanor changed. I couldn't see his facial expression, but somehow I could tell he was smiling. He held the unopened scroll in front of him, moved to the edge of the building, and—I was sure—looked right at me before…he set the Scripture on fire.

My eyes shot between the sight of the burning Scripture and Lincoln, Griffin, and Spence—himself again—standing together, stunned as they too watched what Phoenix was doing.

"Jesus, he knows it's fake," I said to myself, now standing up, getting ready.

My phone rang. "Move!" was all Lincoln bothered with before he hung up.

I didn't need telling twice. I made for the stairwell and then straight to the waiting elevator with the crate holding the door open. We'd planned for escape. Hell, we'd counted on it.

If Phoenix had known all along we were going to give him a fake Scripture, there was no way the one he'd given us was real. But why bother? Why set this whole thing up? Why follow through with it, do the whole cable act? All he'd managed to do was waste a couple hours of everyone's time and... *Oh.*

Oh! No... NO!

The elevator ride was torturously slow as I bounced up and down, only stopping when the back of my head banged against the mirror, cracking the glass. By the time I reached the bottom and flung myself out the fire exit, I was running faster than I'd ever run before.

A lot can happen in a couple of hours. We were all there.

I ran through the city streets, pushing past people, not slowing to be polite. A horrible twisting feeling raked its way through my insides. Four blocks on, I saw Lincoln sprinting toward me, Griffin and Spence following close behind. I felt like I was going to throw up. Lincoln slowed when he saw me, looking relieved. It just made me move faster. All the time we had spent on this stupid exchange and on keeping *me* safe—we were so stupid!

I kept going, running so fast it hurt but trying desperately to move faster. Lincoln must've realized because he was back at full speed within a second. I took the next turn, heading straight toward Hades. Dapper had repainted the entry door again. It was now fluorescent yellow, standing out like a beacon.

Lincoln was behind me. I heard him yell my name, but I didn't wait. I kept my eyes on the entrance and the bouncer who watched me approach. I yelled at him, "Door!" without slowing down. He swung it open just in time and I ran through.

Hades was heaving. It was after midnight on a Wednesday night and the place was sardined. I took a direct line, pushing past people so hard that some fell over. The music was loud, and though I could hear it, I was in some kind of trance, consumed by unfathomable thoughts so horrific they scraped through my mind like sharp knives against brittle edges.

I threw myself into the unmarked door at the side of the bar and bolted up the stairs, taking two then three at a time.

Steph should've called. She would've *called.*

I reached Dapper's door, which was ajar. I heard Lincoln pound through the door below. He was still yelling something at me, but I wasn't listening.

I went in.

chapter eight

> *"Since my people are crushed, I am crushed; I mourn, and horror grips me."*
>
> Jeremiah 8:21

When I was seven years old, Dad and I were driving home from a weekend away. I remember being so excited when we'd first set off, thinking Dad and I would have two whole days to hang out and go to the beach. The drive there had been three of the happiest hours in my childhood. I spent the entire time daydreaming about all the things we would do—the exploring, chatting, laughing. I really believed that weekend would change everything, certain that spending some real one-on-one time with Dad would make him realize...

But it wasn't like that.

It was me who realized.

We only went away so Dad could meet with some new clients. As soon as we got there, I was dumped with the hotel nanny and a bucket and spade. I didn't see him again until we were getting back in the car to go home.

I was devastated. Dad was oblivious. We were silent for the first two hours of our drive back. I spent the whole time trying to build up the confidence to tell him what I really thought of his so-called weekend away. I was just about to open my mouth when it happened.

We'd been driving on the freeway. You move so fast on those things, when something goes wrong, it's bad.

I remember staring at him really hard, trying to make him look back at me with the power of my seven-year-old glare when there was a loud bang, then another—like explosions. They were so close, immediately urgent, immediately dangerous. Before I could see anything, we went straight into a station wagon. My whole body jolted forward, the seat belt doing little to hold my slight frame in place. If Dad's hand hadn't been there to push me back, I would have flown right through the windshield. To this day, I don't know how he got his hand there so fast.

Our hood crumpled like a piece of paper. Steam and smoke rose from the car, melting into the heated air of that hot summer's day, rippling reality.

Dad screamed at me. At first I thought I was in trouble, until I realized he was just panicking. I nodded, frightened, and that seemed to settle him, the rigid tension in his expression easing slightly. Then we looked ahead.

We were not the main event. We'd barely caught the tail end.

Three, maybe four cars were in front of us, all in varying degrees of a compressed state. And in front of them, a truck was visible and maybe another car. I wasn't sure.

Dad got out and circled our car. I don't know what he was looking for, gasoline perhaps. Whatever he saw, he was satisfied enough to leave me there, ordering me not to move until he returned. I watched as he went to the station wagon we'd crashed into. The passengers were okay, I realized, because Dad didn't stay for long at each car, moving on up the line.

I heard sirens in the distance, but when I looked behind me, the traffic had been brought to a halt and it was clear it would be some time before an ambulance could make its way through the new parking lot.

People were starting to move around me, running forward into the disaster zone.

I found myself out of the car and caught up in the tide of people. I could see Dad running ahead. He was the first to reach the truck. I wondered if he had helped anyone out, but then I got closer and saw him through a gap in the cars.

He was bending over.

I hurried toward him, thinking he must be hurt. I hadn't even asked him if he was okay before he got out of the car.

I weaved my way between bystanders, dodging pieces of wreckage, but when I burst into the open space where Dad was standing, I abruptly froze.

He wasn't helping anyone. He didn't know how.

The truck had gone right over a small family car. It was completely crushed. The truck driver was alive. Still sitting in the front seat. He didn't look hurt at all. At least, not on the outside.

But I saw his face.

He looked right at me. Beneath him, there was no sign of life, and when he looked at me—even though I was only a kid—I knew he wished, desperately, that his fate had been the same.

It was his fault.

When Lincoln burst through the door behind me, I tore myself from the memory and saw only the scene spread before me. Dapper, on the floor by the minibar, covered in blood, mutilated. His apartment had been torn apart, as if a herd of elephants had stampeded the place and then come back for a second run, just to be sure.

I stood barely a few steps inside. Frozen.

Lincoln came in behind me and gasped. I turned my eyes to him and I knew the look I wore was the exact same one that truck driver had given me ten years ago.

It was my fault.

Lincoln didn't hesitate. He took one look at the scene, one look at me, and, just as my father had ordered me to stay in the car, he ordered me to stay where I was. And I did, for a while.

Dead. Dead. They're all dead. My fault. Phoenix knew. Knew me. My fault.

I watched as Lincoln ran to help Dapper, feeling through all the blood and exposed flesh, looking for vitals. The only way I knew it was really Dapper was his diamond-studded belt—it was wrapped around his neck, embedded in the flesh.

Lincoln carefully but quickly unwrapped it.

That's when I saw the thing that changed everything, something that truck driver never had the chance to see.

Dapper's fingers…moved.

"He's alive," I gasped. And that was all it took.

Maybe, just maybe. Oh, please, please, please.

I flung myself into action, bolting past Dapper and Lincoln, knowing I couldn't do anything to help there. I ran through the living area into the hallway, where I pulled up, almost falling over myself.

Onyx.

I crouched beside him. Like Lincoln had, I tried to ignore the blood, the massive swelling over his face. His shirt had been ripped off and he'd been beaten so badly that some of his ribs had broken outward, one poking through his chest.

I swallowed down the urge to be sick and I tried to breathe through my mouth. Now that I was more lucid, the senses were pressing down on me, demanding I know.

Apple poured through my mouth, giving the illusion that it was flooding my airways and that I couldn't keep swallowing so much. Regardless, it was better to breathe through my mouth—the scent of flowers was so overwhelming and had made the air so dense it was impossible to breathe through my nose effectively.

I didn't know where to start. Onyx was alive; I knew that much. He was breathing impossibly difficult, short, shallow breaths.

Not nearly enough, was all I could think. *That's not nearly enough air.*

Then I looked again at his ribs, puncturing the space where his lungs were.

I put my hands lightly on his chest. I didn't know what was better, keeping my eyes open or closed. It was practically impossible to concentrate over the blinding flashes of morning and evening—so strong, switching between searing sunlight and the darkest of moonless nights.

"Onyx," I forced through my strangled throat.

His puffy eyes opened to bloodshot slits. His arm moved slightly and I grabbed his hand.

"H—he..."

"It's okay. You'll be okay," I lied. Because looking at him, looking at what they'd done to him and Dapper, I didn't think they'd be okay at all.

My eyes flitted away, farther down the hall. *The bathroom and the bedroom to go. I need to look.* But I couldn't just leave him.

He gripped my hand a little tighter. I looked at him and then it occurred to me: Maybe he wanted this? He'd wanted someone to kill him. End it. He'd asked me to do it myself when we'd found him drunk and on the streets. He never wanted to be only human. Maybe this had all worked out for him.

He tried to speak again.

I bent forward, trying not to touch anywhere that would hurt, which was everywhere.

"H—elp me."

I watched his swollen eyes, trying to force themselves open properly, to show me the truth in his words. Onyx wanted to live.

My hand, still holding his, stirred. I put my other hand to his face gently. Then I let my power go, let it flow from me to him, wanting to heal him, to give him this chance at life. But I hit a brick wall, which almost made me black out.

I heard more people arrive, orders being shouted out. Griffin.

Spence came running into the hallway. "Jesus," he said.

I stood up. "I can't help him. I can't heal him." I shook my head. "He wants to live," I said. But my eyes were fixed on the end of the hall again, urgently.

Spence dropped down beside Onyx. "I'll help him. Go!"

I was at the end of the hall before he finished telling me to go. I don't know how long it had been since I entered the apartment, less than a minute maybe. Less than a minute for everything to change. And yet I knew, in a few seconds…everything could get so much worse.

Steph. Please, no! My fault, not hers.

The bathroom was clear. In the bedroom, I found Kaitlin and Samuel. Kaitlin was out cold, but her Grigori strength had protected her and, though bruised, she looked in a much better state than Dapper or Onyx. Samuel was already trying to get up.

I ran to him, putting a hand under his arm to help him.

"Samuel, Samuel! What happened?" I screamed, even though now I knew.

"There were eight of them that I saw. They caught us by surprise."

And I understood why. We'd expected to be dealing with all the action tonight, out on the rooftops.

Samuel looked over at Kaitlin and raised his fingers to a head wound dripping with blood before looking back at me.

"We should be dead." He was right.

But I couldn't focus. I couldn't concentrate on the other details right now. I heard sirens coming from out in the street. Griffin had called ambulances. Onyx was human and Dapper, although not altogether human, clearly needed medical attention.

"You should get her out of here. You don't want the ambulance trying to cart her away," I said in a daydream to Samuel. The last thing we needed was doctors getting their hands on a Grigori when she was in rapid-healing mode. Way too many questions there.

Samuel nodded, scooping Kaitlin up and heading for the door.

I followed him out. He didn't even pause to look at Onyx or Dapper. He had his job to do and right now that was to get Kaitlin to safety. He was a good partner.

Spence was still talking to Onyx, giving words of encouragement. Onyx was gripping his hand. There was a time, after Spence jumped him and beat the information we'd needed from him, when I didn't think those two would get within ten feet of each other. But that had been the beginning for Onyx in some ways—his true beginning, his human one. Spence had forced him to admit he valued his life, and now he was helping him keep it.

Griffin had taken over from Lincoln with Dapper, and when Lincoln saw me come back into the room, he looked at me with urgent eyes. Griffin turned too.

They'd obviously seen Samuel taking off with Kaitlin and Onyx down the hall. Everyone was looking at me for one reason.

I wanted to wake up. Or go back.

My fault.

I wanted to go back to that day I'd told her—convinced her that this otherworld existed, invited her to be a part of it. Why? Because I'd needed her. I didn't want to let go of my human world, lose her too.

My fault.

"Violet?" Lincoln prompted.

I started. He was right in front of me. I hadn't even noticed him walk toward me. He grabbed my arms. I thought he was going to shake me, but he didn't.

I should've seen this coming. Phoenix saw me coming. He knew I couldn't just hand over the Scripture to release Lilith. He knew me and played me and I…I walked right into it.

I heard the medics slam through the doors downstairs and their feet on the stairs. They were calling out, announcing themselves as they moved. I wondered fleetingly if people still filled the bar, dancing and drinking while above them…

I looked at Lincoln and then Griffin, still bent over Dapper. A similar guilt showed on their faces as mine. But not nearly as much.

Lincoln squeezed my arms, trying to bring me back to him.

I blinked.

"Steph's gone. They've taken her."

chapter nine

"And out of the darkness, came the hands that reached through nature, molding men."

Alfred Lord Tennyson

I don't remember much of what followed. The medics had come into Dapper's apartment and gone straight into damage control.

We'd followed the ambulances to the hospital in Lincoln's Volvo, but there wasn't much we could do and we were confined to the waiting room.

The doctors told us Onyx would be okay. His major internal injuries were to his ribs, which had also punctured his lungs, as I'd suspected. The main thing had been to plug the holes and get him breathing again, which they had managed to do. The rest was superficial. Painful, but he'd live.

Dapper was in worse shape. The doctors were amazed he was still alive. The injuries inflicted by the belt alone should have been enough to shatter his throat and airways, not to mention the damage caused by the internal bleeding from the vicious beating. They assumed he'd been attacked by weapons of some kind, as human hands simply could not cause this level of harm. We didn't correct them. To the doctors, Dapper was a medical miracle.

To *us* that meant we had been wrong about him too.

Dapper clearly had healing abilities. If he kept recovering at such a rapid rate, he was going to have some explaining to do in the hospital. None of us cared right now, but Dapper would. He was part of the community with his bar, so hiding his otherworldly abilities was all-important to him.

I went through the motions, helped by everyone but oblivious to anyone in particular.

Eventually, someone different moved in beside me, lifting me onto his lap. His arms moved around my waist, holding me close, as if his body would somehow power mine to life. And it could. My body, *my soul*, gravitated toward him in recognition, igniting something both marvelous and excruciating. He pushed the hair from my face and tucked it behind my ear. I breathed in the feeling of warm sun on my skin and felt the trickle of honey caress me from the inside.

When he leaned in to my ear, he whispered, just for me, "I promise you, she's alive. I promise you, we'll get her back." He swallowed deeply. "Unharmed."

I didn't respond. I wanted to believe him. Oh, I wanted to so badly. But how could I?

As if he knew my question, he moved closer, brushing a shaking hand down my hair.

"Phoenix won't hurt her because..." He faltered and something about that pause made me think he didn't say exactly what he was going to say. "He needs her to get what he wants."

That was all it took for me to snap out of it. I hadn't been thinking clearly. I hadn't been thinking at all, but Lincoln broke through the barriers, found me when others couldn't, and he was right. Absolutely right.

I pulled my head up. "This is the real trade."

He nodded.

Phoenix knew this would hurt me the most, knew I'd felt guilty about bringing Steph into this world. He'd expected it to hit me hard, but he didn't understand. Not fully. He didn't ever really get what Lincoln and I had, that Lincoln was my pillar of strength and that he was the only one who could bring me out of it to focus on what had to be done.

By the time we got back to Lincoln's place, I was no longer in such a fragile state of mind. When we'd left the hospital, I'd walked out without anyone supporting me.

Sure, I couldn't completely remember getting back to the warehouse, but that was because from that moment, only one thing held my attention: the choice.

Since I'd discovered my Grigori status, everything always seemed to come down to something like this. But usually it was a choice between letting someone else get hurt or letting myself get hurt. Like embracing to save Lincoln or facing Phoenix even though I knew the power he held over me. It wasn't that simple this time.

It was worse.

This time, the choice could have been anything—the answer would be the same. I wasn't going to stand by and let Steph die. The price was huge and I could feel the tension in the room. Griffin pacing; Spence hovering.

Lincoln didn't pace or hover. He went to the kitchen and made sandwiches. He put them in front of me. "You need to eat."

I did, chewing on autopilot. I needed my strength.

Samuel had called. He and Kaitlin were fine. They confirmed what we already knew, that the exiles had taken Steph. They had both tried to stop them, but they were taken down. The only thing that didn't make sense was why everyone had not been killed. It wasn't in an exile's nature to leave life behind. Especially when it came to Grigori.

Griffin had arranged for Beth and Archer to take the first shift at the hospital, waiting for Onyx and Dapper to come round fully. Dapper would have to be removed before anyone became too suspicious. Griffin was arranging a bogus hospital transfer through Grigori connections.

"I should get you home," Lincoln said from beside me. He seemed so calm, even though I knew he wasn't.

"I have to do it," I said, not daring to look at him as I voiced the very thing he didn't want to hear.

He sighed. "We can talk about it in the morning."

I jumped up. "What do you expect me to do? Just go home? Curl up in bed and get a good night's sleep? Steph is out there! With *him*!"

Lincoln just sat there, letting me yell at him. Spence and Griffin had settled down at the dining table. They were flicking through papers, Steph's research. I wanted to storm over and rip it out from under their noses. We needed to do something.

"There are too many of them for us to try and take them tonight. They'll be expecting something, and they'll be waiting for us," Lincoln said, knowing my thoughts.

I slumped back onto the sofa beside him, hating that he was right.

"I can't go home," I said. "Dad thinks I'm at Steph's tonight." Lincoln was silent for a moment, as if this one piece of news had caught him more off guard than anything else that had happened this evening. I felt the honey of his power stir.

Griffin stood up. "Violet, where is Steph supposed to be tonight?"

"At her place, with me." We'd expected to get back to her place after the exchange around midnight. I looked at my watch, realizing what Griffin was getting at.

As if on cue, my phone rang. All of us jumped. We'd been waiting for a call all night. But then I saw who it was and groaned.

"Oh no."

"Who?" Lincoln asked, still calm.

"Dad."

Griffin spoke quickly. "You have to cover this up, Violet. We can't have more humans involved."

He didn't mean it the way it came out, but I felt even worse.

Lincoln put his hand on my knee. "A party, out of town. Car trouble. Bad phone reception but you're staying at a friend's place. A girl's," he clarified meaningfully. "Someone I introduced you to through rock climbing."

The phone was still ringing. He held my eyes. My pillar of strength. I nodded.

"Dad."

"Violet, where are you? I've had Eliza Morris on the phone with me for the last half hour. You're supposed to be at her house tonight with Steph!" He was really upset. Steph's mom must have seriously let loose on him.

"Dad! Dad, don't worry. Listen." I took a deep breath. "I might get cut off—there's terrible reception here—but Steph and I are fine. We went to a house party outside the city."

"Violet! You never had permission to go out of the city! Where are you?"

"Dad, just listen. We're fine. We would've been home by now, but Steph's car broke down and our phones weren't working."

Lincoln nodded me on. I might get into trouble for going to an out-of-town party, but that was nothing compared to the alternative.

"I remembered a friend of Lincoln's lives nearby. I met her out rock climbing a few times and we had lunch at her place once."

Lincoln nodded again.

"And?" Dad prompted.

"Well, we came back to her place. We're staying here tonight and we'll be back tomorrow."

Lincoln gave me a look and tapped his watch.

"After we take the car to get fixed. We'll go straight to school and I'll be home after that," I added.

Lincoln gave another small nod. I'd bought us more time.

"Why didn't you call?"

"Lucy doesn't have a home phone and this is the first time my cell phone's had reception," I lied.

Dad sighed. It was working. It was time to drive it home.

"Dad, I'm really sorry. We didn't expect to be late back to Steph's."

"Well, Steph's mother is irate." He sighed again. "Give me the address and I'll come and pick you up."

My eyes almost popped out of their sockets. I'd expected him to leave it there.

I looked at Lincoln urgently. He pressed his thumb down a couple of times, telling me to hang up. I knew he was right. I needed to get out of this conversation and we needed to keep my phone free.

"Dad, we're already in bed for the night. Just call Steph's mom back for us. Steph's…already asleep. And don't worry if you can't get ahold of us. The phone drops out all the time. I'll call you as soon as we're on our way home."

I heard Dad yelling into the phone, insisting on more information. I waited a moment and ended the call.

Everyone in the room let out their breath as if they'd been holding it for the entire conversation.

"I don't think he'll send out any search parties tonight, but he knows something isn't right." This on top of the questions he had already been asking. I knew there would be more to come now.

Before anyone had long to consider this, my phone rang again. Everyone jumped again except me. There was no one left to call. It had to be him. I raised it to answer, but Lincoln stopped me and put out his hand.

"He'll be expecting you."

I didn't want to do anything to upset Phoenix. I didn't want to cause any more possible danger for Steph, but Lincoln held my eyes and they seemed to say so much. He was asking me to trust him.

I handed him the phone. He put it on loudspeaker.

Phoenix sighed languidly, the way he had in the past, knowing it unnerved me. "Ah, there you are, lover. I was worried you weren't going to take my call."

I didn't respond and instead closed my eyes and just concentrated on breathing.

"Put Steph on the phone," Lincoln said, calm as ever but with a hint of something else in his voice. Hatred.

"No," Phoenix said, not even considering it. But I could tell he was surprised to hear Lincoln's voice. "She's...busy."

"If you touch her, I'll kill you," Lincoln said, making his threat sound very convincing.

But Phoenix only chuckled lightly. "Will you?"

Lincoln was silent.

Phoenix thought he had this all figured out. As far as he was concerned, he was more than immortal; he was impenetrable. With the power he held over me, with our lives connected so inexorably, he knew no one would hurt him if it could be avoided.

No one but me, that is.

"*I* will," I said, ensuring that the full weight of my intention was clear in those two small words.

Lincoln gave me a resigned look and sank back in his chair.

"Now *that*, I believe. There you are, lover. It seems I now have two things you want very badly."

"I hate you!" I snapped.

He laughed again. "Yes, well, we can disagree about that later. Say tomorrow evening. Why don't we forget the elaborate design and just meet at our café. Just two lovers sharing a coffee and making an exchange."

"You'll give me Steph and the Scripture?"

This triggered a different kind of laugh from him. Darker.

"No. I'll give you one. You choose. Oh, and this time, if I don't get what I want, it will be Steph who suffers the consequences of your choices."

"She's not going to meet you alone," Lincoln said, the loathing dripping from his voice.

"Violet?" Phoenix said and waited.

Lincoln looked at me. "We'll find a better way than this," he whispered.

I glanced at Griffin and his truth leaked out of him.

Not if we want to get Steph back alive.

Lincoln was biased. I knew that. Griffin was concerned with retrieving an innocent, and we were Grigori.

"What time?" I asked.

I could hear the victory in Phoenix's voice. "Nine p.m. And Violet?"

"What?"

"Tell your friend Spence his services will not be required on this occasion." He ended the call.

He was never going to stop. There were no boundaries he would not cross.

I looked around the room. My friends and fellow warriors. I couldn't keep putting everyone at risk.

"I have to return him," I said, knowing it was true.

Lincoln jolted. "No! Not yet. Not until we know how to break the—" But I cut him off.

"We're not going to break it! Ever! As long as I live, he lives. It's like I'm a part of everything he does wrong. I can't do that anymore!" Then, I couldn't stop the final thought as I looked at Lincoln. "It will be better for everyone this way."

"And how is that?" he snapped, the cool exterior he'd worked so hard to maintain completely gone, his hands gripping the back of a dining chair angrily.

"He'll be gone. The Scriptures will be safe and I'll...You can get another partner, one less...complicated."

Lincoln shook his head as if he thought I was crazy. "Yeah. I can see all of that working out just swell. And I guess your dad and Steph will live happily ever after too?"

That stopped me.

"Violet," Griffin said, breaking into the discussion. "If it were our only option, we could consider it."

Lincoln spun on Griffin so fast it was clear it wasn't just a chair he was considering throwing into the wall.

"But right now," Griffin continued, unfazed by Lincoln's violent stare, "it is not a good option. If you make those kinds of intentions clear to Phoenix, he will hurt Steph—or someone else—to hold you at bay."

I knew what he was saying.

Dad. He'll go after Dad.

He was the only one left. And Phoenix wouldn't think twice.

"Not if he's gone," I said, but I'd lost my fight.

"Do you really think he will be that easy to return?" Griffin said, already aware he'd won the argument.

"I'm sorry," Spence chimed in, sounding agitated, "but I think everyone is missing the other option."

All eyes turned to him. Except Lincoln's—they were still fixed on me and fuming.

"What do you mean, Spence?" Griffin asked.

"I get that we all want to get Steph back, but there is no way you can really be considering making this trade. If you give that Scripture to Phoenix, he's going to bring the mistress of Hell upon us all. For the sake of one life, you will be forfeiting an unknown number of innocents."

"What are you suggesting, Spence?" Griffin responded.

"You want me to leave her there to die," I said, wanting desperately to hate Spence with all my heart. And I did hate him—for being the person who said it. For highlighting the price of my choice.

"Steph's my friend too. I want to get her out of there. But I think we should be trying to break her out."

"The trade is the only option if we want to get her out alive. We will try and make a plan. None of us wants to let that Scripture out of our hands, but if Violet doesn't turn up at that café with the real thing tomorrow..." Griffin didn't need to say any more.

Spence nodded. "You're the boss," he said, looking at Griffin and then to me. A backhanded statement. I knew he was insinuating that I was calling the shots, that even though I'd abdicated my rightful role of leader, I was in one way or another still driving the decisions.

It wasn't true. I hadn't forced Griffin into anything. That didn't mean I wouldn't do it regardless, wouldn't just take the Scripture and find a way to get Steph back on my own, but I hadn't made Griffin agree with me. I knew he'd done so for his own reasons, the reasons that set Grigori apart from exiles.

Collateral damage was not acceptable in Griffin's eyes after everything that had happened with Magda, the way she had betrayed us all for her own selfish desires. He wouldn't give on this issue, even though he understood Spence's point of view. Hell, even I understood it. It just wasn't going to change anything.

Spence, realizing it was a closed subject, took off for a shower. He'd set up home in Lincoln's spare bedroom and the two of them seemed to coexist quite well. Although Lincoln was always happy to have his home used as a kind of base of operations, he liked his private space, so I'd been surprised he'd been willing to have a housemate.

Griffin also made a move, heading for the door. "I'm going back to the hospital and then to check on Kaitlin. I'll see you tomorrow."

He was all business. Seeing there was nothing else he could do here tonight, there was no point in him staying. I was sure he had no intention of sleeping, though.

When Lincoln and I were alone, I stood up. "I should leave," I said.

"Where are you planning on going?" Lincoln asked, standing too. We both knew I couldn't go home.

"Maybe back to the hospital." I wanted to check on Dapper and, to my surprise, Onyx, plus no one would be suspicious of someone taking a nap in the waiting area if I could manage to close my eyes.

Lincoln shook his head.

"What?" I asked.

"You need to sleep. Especially if..." He was going to say, *If you have to face Phoenix tomorrow,* but he still didn't want to concede to that. "You can sleep in my room."

And then, despite all of the drama, despite all of my fears for Steph, I found myself staring into Lincoln's so-green eyes and the connection between us danced a dance of everything forbidden.

Spence came out of the bathroom wearing boxers and nothing else. He looked up at us briefly, not noticing that the tension in the room had risen even further. He threw one hand up as he crossed the hall to his room, ruffling his wet hair with his other. "Night," he said, before closing his door.

Lincoln disappeared into his room for a moment and reappeared with a towel, T-shirt, and lightweight sweats.

He shrugged, handing them over. "I don't think you have any more supplies here. If you give me your clothes, we can throw them in the washing machine for tomorrow."

I nodded, heading for the bathroom.

I had a scalding-hot shower, using the time to pull myself together. Steph needed me to be strong, needed me to bring her back. I could blame myself later—it wasn't going to help right now to theorize about all the horrible things they could be doing to her. Lincoln was right. They'd be expecting us to try to get her back tonight, and even if they did have her at the airport, which Phoenix still appeared to be using as his base of operations, that plane was too heavily guarded. We needed time to prepare. The titanium that lined the massive Antonov still affected our senses, hindering them so not only would we not know if Steph was in there, but we wouldn't know how many exiles were waiting either.

I dressed in the clothes Lincoln had lent me, comforted and

troubled at the same time. Even clean, they smelled of him, of his power, like sunny days and melting honey.

He was already in his bedroom when I opened the door. His eyes darted up. "Sorry, I'm just grabbing a few things."

I shrugged. "Take your time."

Of course, he didn't. He was straight out of there and into the bathroom himself.

I'd never been in his room before. Without him, that is. I'd certainly never slept in his bed. I found myself exploring, unable to resist, running my hands over the curves of his wooden bed, the softness of his cotton sheets. There was a picture of him as a child with his mother and one of her with someone I assumed had been his father. I picked it up, and from the back, another photo fell out.

My heart dived and my hand shook, holding a snapshot of myself.

He keeps a photo of me!

It had been taken months ago, just before my seventeenth birthday, just before I'd found out about everything. I looked so different, hanging midair in a rock-climbing harness, smiling. Young.

I heard the shower stop and hastily put the photo back. It didn't change anything.

I got into the bed and sat up. I heard him come out of the bathroom and then it was awhile before he popped his head around the door. Maybe he hadn't wanted to come back.

"Good night, Vi," he said, sporting a strained smile and careful not to cross the threshold.

"Linc?"

"Yeah?" he replied.

Stay!

"Thanks."

A look passed over his face, and he watched me for a moment before saying, "It'll all be okay."

I hoped desperately that he was right.

I slid between the sheets and rolled onto my side, listening as the door closed softly, followed by a lengthy delay before footsteps drifted away down the hall.

I spent the next hour biting my lip, half sitting up, wanting to go out and see him, then flopping back onto the bed, settling instead for burying my head under his pillow and breathing in the deliciously tormenting scents that were all him.

At one point, I actually made it out of the room and into the hall. But after a few steps, I could hear that he was awake himself, pacing around the living room, and I found myself sneaking back into his room, closing the door behind me, and cringing when it clicked. He'd know I'd been out.

I waited, half expecting him to come and confront me or something. But he didn't and eventually I stopped being a maniac and, exhausted, slipped into a much-needed few hours of sleep.

chapter ten

> *"No trumpets sound when the important decisions of our life are made. Destiny is made known silently."*
>
> Agnes de Mille

I woke Thursday morning to find my clothes, clean and folded, at the end of the bed. I knew he'd done it during the night and almost laughed out loud at how pathetic we were.

I got dressed and headed out to the living room. Spence was at the dining table "drinking" a bowl of cereal. Lincoln was on the couch, asleep.

"You want some?" Spence offered quietly, trying not to wake Lincoln.

There was a part of me that strongly suspected he was not asleep. The man was a warrior of warriors—I doubted he'd sleep easy with other people up and about around him. But I wasn't about to find out. He at least deserved that from me.

"No," I said. "I'm going for a run, and when I get back, we've got to go to school."

"Not me." He looked me up and down. "And not you, dressed like that."

"Yes, you are. I need your help. And I have a spare uniform at school." I wrinkled my nose at the thought of the uniform that was stuffed at the back of my locker. It probably smelled like old bananas.

Spence groaned. "Eden, school isn't for me, and right now, with everything going on, Griffin's hardly going to bother checking if I'm going or not."

"I don't care if you turn up. I just want to make sure Steph does."

Spence put down his spoon and looked up, the first sign of interest showing. He loved a plan.

"I need you to show up as Steph, walk around for a bit, and make sure people see her complaining of a headache. It'll be easier to cover for her that way."

"Won't they call her mom if she gets sent home sick?"

"Yeah, but if we're there before classes start, then she won't have signed in. People will just think she decided to go home and the teachers won't bother calling her mom. They're all scared of her mom anyway." It was true, and with the school dance coming up and Mrs. Morris one of the main contributors, they already had to deal with her more than they liked.

Spence considered this and, from the shrug and final two gigantic slurps of his cereal, seemed to agree it was a good idea. He nodded while still chewing. I rolled my eyes as I went out the door.

"Have I told you how much I love your devious streak?" he called after me.

I called Dad on the way to school and let him know Steph and I were back safe and sound and that we were going straight to class. He sounded relieved, but there was that something in his tone that I was hearing more and more—doubt. He ordered me straight home after school. I wondered if it was Caroline, if somehow she was pointing out to him that he seemed to be missing something fairly major. Caroline had always looked at me like she knew something was going on.

By the time we arrived at school, Spence was under a Steph-glamour. If I hadn't known better, it would have totally fooled me. He had everything down—her spritzy blond hair perfectly styled, well-fitting shorter-than-regulation-length uniform, even her low-slung backpack, worn that way to counter the fact it was always jam-packed with books.

Seeing Spence as her brought everything to the surface, and I couldn't help but throw my arms around him. I missed her so much. I had to get her back in one piece. Inside and out.

Spence seemed to realize and hugged me back. "She'll be okay. And"—he squeezed me a little tighter—"I'm sorry, Eden, I shouldn't have said those things last night. I've got your back—you know that, right?"

"I know." And I was counting on it too. If the time should come, Spence might be my best hope of taking Phoenix down.

The morning went smoothly, and after Spence had made sure a good number of teachers and students had seen Steph complaining of a headache and cramps—his own contribution, thinking it would piss Steph off—he bailed.

I stayed around, making sure the story stuck, telling people she'd gone home for the day. No one questioned it. Steph was one of the trustworthy ones.

I went through the rest of the day impatiently, frustrated that I couldn't be doing more. I knew Griffin and the others would be working on a plan, a way to get Steph back and keep the Scripture safe, and I hated that I wasn't being more helpful. Instead, I had to endure double English and Lydia Skilton's hyperactive response to beating me at track. After Spence's show-off tactics in basketball, I figured I shouldn't draw any further attention to our group.

My last two periods were free study, so I took the chance and left early. Kids did it all the time and teachers never really bothered to make a big deal about it.

I called Griffin and asked him to meet me in private. Hesitant, but clearly intrigued, he agreed. I waited for him outside school.

As Lincoln's Volvo came down the street, I thought for a moment that Griffin had brought him along, but when the car pulled up, he was alone.

I jumped in. "Thanks, Griff," I said, taking a look in the back, just to be sure.

I asked him to drive me home. I knew I had to see Dad and somehow find my way back out before tonight.

"So," Griffin said, when we pulled up outside my place, breaking the uncomfortable silence. There was so much to talk about but both of us had needed a moment. "What's going on?"

I played with the key ring hanging off the zipper of my school bag. "I need you to help me strengthen my defenses."

"More combat training?"

"No. Not those defenses. I…I need to be stronger around Phoenix. Keep him…out."

"Oh."

I couldn't look at Griffin. I was ashamed that Phoenix affected me the way he did and I hated to admit it. But for Steph's sake, I had to.

"I think that is one defense you're going to have to develop on your own, Violet. It's not that I don't want to help you; it's just that…well, your connection to Phoenix is unusual, as it was originally made by choice." He hesitated, like he didn't really want to go on.

"Griff, I need to know this stuff."

He nodded. "If you want to defend yourself from him, I suspect the key is in truly *wanting* to. There is a part of you, perhaps buried so deep that you're not even aware of it, that is choosing to let him in."

"That's not true—I hate him!"

"I believe that. But that's not all you feel for him."

I wanted to be mad, say something hurtful to Griffin in return. I didn't know if he was right, but I wasn't sure that he was wrong either. There *was* a part of me, a part I tried to ignore, that thought of Phoenix from time to time. I always shut it out but it was still there, longing for escape to that place no other living creature could take me. The bliss.

It wasn't real. It was completely fake. But that's also why I desired it, and as things got harder, even though it was him who was making them that way, I still felt lured by the prospect of escape. It wasn't *Phoenix*—it was what he could do.

Guiltily, I looked at Griffin. "Don't tell…"

"I wouldn't," he said, impressing truth into his words.

I nodded. "Does it ever get any easier?"

Griffin smiled solemnly. "We are soldiers in an eternal war," he said, as if that were answer enough.

"How are you doing, anyway?" I asked.

"You mean Magda?"

I shrugged, nervous to be raising the subject. No one had heard from Magda since the day she'd stormed out. It had been awful for Griffin to discover she'd been allying with exiles and deceiving him for so long.

He looked out the window, keeping his expression blank.

"What's done is done. Magda is no longer one of us. Looking back, I don't know that she ever really was. To be Grigori, you don't have to believe in God, you don't have to want world peace"—he sighed—"but…you have to believe in humanity, in our rights to exist and be free. Magda took that right from too many people."

"Do you think you'll ever see her again?"

"I hope not, because if I do, it won't mean anything good."

"Will you…?"

He looked at me now. "Find another partner?"

"Yeah."

His hands ran around the steering wheel thoughtfully.

"Theoretically, until one of us dies or makes a formal request, Magda and I remain partners." He sighed again. "I'll get a new partner, eventually. I believe in the system. There are some who choose not to, deciding instead to be part of the cleanup crew, be teachers, or be one of the Rogue, but none of that's for me. Anyway, I'm not ready yet."

I shifted in my seat to face him more directly. "Who are the Rogue?"

He hitched a shoulder and dropped his hands from the wheel. "Grigori who are not part of the system—they've either left their partners or not taken a new one after their partner has died, but for whatever reason, they choose to go out alone. Not part of any particular territory, preferring simply to roam, they work on their own set of…flexible rules."

I could tell Griffin didn't think much of the Rogue, but the concept fascinated me. The idea that there were Grigori out there just living their own lives. I wondered what they did if they were hurt, since they wouldn't have partners to heal them.

"So they don't answer to anyone?" I asked.

"Yes and no. Most of them work on a contract basis in return for income and other resources, but they don't consider themselves part of any team and are unreliable at best."

"Is that what my mother became?" I'd always wondered what her role had been after she'd married Dad and moved here. Griffin had been in the city by then, but he'd sworn to me he'd never crossed paths with her.

"No. From what I understand, your mother was always loyal to the Assembly, but after losing her partner and finding your father, she had taken...an extended leave."

I was still thinking about my conversation with Griffin when I opened my apartment door and saw Dad sitting at the dining table. With Caroline. He had papers strewn across the table and was tapping away on his laptop while she sat close beside him, passing him documents. I failed to hide my surprise. He'd said he'd be waiting for me when I got home, but I wasn't convinced he'd actually be there. And in as many years as she'd been working for Dad, he'd never brought Caroline home.

"Hi, Dad. Hi, Caroline," I said carefully.

"Hi, Violet," Caroline said, chirpier than usual. She played with one of her long, caramel curls, nervously picking up another piece of paper. She knew her being there said something.

Dad finished whatever he'd been typing, took the next document from Caroline, and looked up.

"You're early. Are you okay?" he asked, following textbook parenting and not acknowledging the fact that we had a guest, as if it were normal practice.

"Yeah, study period. I'm sorry about last night. We really hadn't planned on being home late and we did try to call," I said, following textbook daughter vagueness. Also ignoring Caroline.

Dad looked at me for a sign of deception, but I held his eyes—I didn't like it, but I could lie. I was my mother's daughter, after all. But just then, he glanced at Caroline and she gave a minute nod.

"Well, I want you around home more for the next couple of weeks. You've only got a short amount of school left and I know most of your exams are finished, but you still have a few subjects you need to concentrate on."

It was like I'd walked into the twilight zone.

Is my father actually practicing real parenting?

I couldn't help the small smile. It was just so out there. But I really couldn't afford this type of attention, so I explained, "I already have plans this afternoon *and* tonight."

"Change them," he said flatly, redirecting his focus back to his work.

I shot Caroline a look that told her I knew damn well this must be her doing. We'd always got on in the past, but she'd crossed a line.

"I can't!" I snapped, which got Dad's attention back and not in a good way.

"Yes, you can," he said.

"No," I said, thinking quickly. "I...I can't. It's...I have to go to the orientation night for the Fenton art course."

If anything would get Dad to back off right now, I knew that was it. But just in case, I gave him one more reason, realizing as I said it that this part was actually true. "And I was going to go to the cemetery this afternoon."

I hated myself instantly.

It might not have been a lie, but I shouldn't have told him just like that, and not in front of Caroline. A veil of darkness floated over him and whatever seemed to have changed in him in the last week changed back in an instant. He stood up, grabbing a pile of papers.

"We have to get back to the office," he squeezed out with an anguished expression.

Caroline moved quickly, slipping on her light trench coat.

"I'll wait downstairs, James." She smiled kindly at me as she opened the door, which just made me feel worse. "Stop by the office some time. We miss seeing you around there."

I nodded awkwardly.

Dad was close behind. I didn't expect him to say anything, but he surprised me by stopping at my side as he passed.

"Violet, I know you're hiding something. Just tell me you aren't in any trouble?" His voice had dropped and he was almost pleading.

I realized then that if something were to happen to me, there would be little to hold Dad to life or sanity. I had always thought I wasn't on his radar, not enough. Now I saw the true story—I was everything to him.

"Everything's fine, Dad." I swallowed hard. The deception now carried more weight. "I promise."

He gave a lopsided nod and left. I knew he wouldn't come out of the daze again today. Telling him I was going to see Mom had been cruel.

But necessary, a harsher voice within coaxed.

I didn't visit my mother often. I always felt like a bit of a fraud when I did.

Dad and I used to go to the cemetery together and it was awful—the silence of the car trip broken by awkward forced conversation. I always felt like an intruder on his—*their*—time. He deserved to visit her alone, not have to hold my hand. It was enough effort for him just to keep himself together, let alone carry the burden of having to include me and, worse, assure me somehow that he didn't blame me.

I knew he didn't, but I could always feel his uncertainties about how much reinforcement this issue required.

Dad loved her so much. Completely. No, more than that. It's a forever thing. He's a lifer. That's why now he's so lost. My earlier discovery that, if there were any anchor in this life for him at all, I was it made me sad for him and even madder at her.

I'm a poor man's substitute. Not nearly enough.

Dad loved me, I knew that, but he had planned on loving me *with* her. When that didn't happen...let's just say Dad doesn't specialize in the roll-with-the-punches department.

I knelt down before the headstone. My long hair fell forward and grazed the words I knew by heart.

Evelyn May Eden
"I will find you again, my darling."
Beloved wife to James—Mother to Violet

I cleared away the damp leaves that had stuck to the marble and laid down a bunch of white lilies that I'd picked up on the way. I always brought her lilies.

I didn't say a prayer. It wasn't my thing and I was pretty sure it hadn't been hers, either. I wished in a way I could cry for her, but I had never known her. I only knew of her lies. Well, that wasn't altogether true anymore. I knew some of her, maybe more than Dad ever would.

Like the fact that she held me for less than five minutes before she chose to leave us.

I closed my eyes, placed a hand on the headstone of the mother I'd never know or understand, and tried not to think, *How could you?*

Perhaps it was for the best that I never knew. I couldn't forgive her, but I still respected her in my own way. She was a Grigori warrior. She had faced down a rival mightier than most ever crossed paths with and survived. She was a legend among us. Any story I had ever heard hailed her as a champion, a savior even. As her daughter, I had little compassion to offer her, but as a fellow Grigori, I at least owed her this.

"I'm sorry. If it were you, I know you wouldn't do it."

She'd sacrificed herself. Her partner had died. She'd sacrificed me too. If she thought Lilith would return, I was confident she'd be willing to sacrifice Steph.

"But Steph…she's my family. So if you think I'm doing the wrong thing, just remember, you made me this way."

I shook my head, disappointed in myself. I took a deep breath and started again.

"I'm going to give Phoenix the key to releasing Lilith, and he'll do it too. I know he will. And it's going to be bad, really bad, because they will be here, together." Tears welled. "But I promise you, I'll do whatever it takes to make this right. I'll stop them." The enormity of the battles ahead swept over me and I considered the price of the promise I'd just made. I knew I would pay for it.

Walking away from her grave, I got the feeling it wouldn't be too long until I saw my mother again.

chapter eleven

> *"Why, O Lord, do you stand far off? Why do you hide in times of trouble?"*
>
> Psalm 10:1

I stood on the pavement outside my apartment building and marveled at how the world, ever unaware, continued to buzz around me even as I functioned in a seemingly doomed existence that was now dragging down the people I cared about the most.

I fidgeted as I waited, my hand nervously brushing the hilt of my dagger. It was 7 p.m.

Two hours left.

It felt like a small eternity waiting for the car to pull up. Lincoln was driving, Griffin was up front, and Spence kicked open the back door from inside. I jumped in, glad to get out of the cold.

"Hi," I said, including everyone but avoiding looking directly at Lincoln. I wasn't sure I would be able to stop myself from reaching out to touch him.

"Did you have any trouble with your father?" Griffin asked.

"He knows something's up. He'll leave it for now but"—I blew out a breath—"I don't know for how long."

Griffin gave me a nod. "We will have to give some thought to how we can manage him."

He was right, but I couldn't get into it now. I knew it would just involve more lies. "Let's just get Steph back," I said.

"Nice hair," Spence said with a smirk, causing Lincoln to glance back in our direction before he could stop himself.

Our eyes unwittingly locked and my chest felt crushed under the weight of his beautiful gaze. My hand went self-consciously to the hair I had pulled back into an unusually slick, high ponytail.

"I didn't want it to get in the way."

"You won't be fighting tonight," Lincoln said, quietly and seemingly in control. The white-knuckled grip he had on the steering wheel suggested otherwise.

"Just in case. Where are we going?"

"Hades," Griffin said.

I shifted in my seat, uneasy with the idea of going back there. Not only was it the scene of the crime, but without Dapper and Onyx, it felt wrong.

"Dapper's back there," Griffin said, as if reading my mind. "He's healed at a remarkable rate. I really would like to know more about what he is."

"So he's okay?"

"Bruised and battered but up and walking around."

I was amazed. That man looked like he'd been turned inside out less than twenty-four hours ago. No wonder Griffin wanted to know more.

It was a short drive to Hades, and we pulled up out front, in the no-parking zone. Clearly Lincoln wasn't in a law-abiding mood.

The security guy pulled open the door. "Any word on Onyx?" he asked as we passed. He seemed to care about him.

"Saw him today. Should be out of the hospital in a few days," Spence said, reminding me I hadn't even asked after Onyx myself.

It was a bit surprising to hear it had been Spence who'd gone to visit him. I wondered if they were becoming friends.

Inside Hades, the restaurant tables were filling up and the bar was just getting started for the night. Before long, the place would be heaving.

We went straight for the unmarked door that led upstairs and headed to Dapper's apartment. Griffin knocked on the door. It took awhile, but eventually we heard a voice on the other side.

"Who is it?" he called in his normal gruff tone, but there was something else too. Fear.

"It's Griffin, Lincoln, Violet, and Spencer," Griffin said, considerately ensuring Dapper would receive no surprise when he opened the door.

I heard his grunt and then a number of clicks as Dapper released what must have been at least eight deadbolts.

"Griff," I said, "maybe we should've gone somewhere else?" It didn't seem fair to keep dragging Dapper into all of this stuff, especially when he hadn't wanted to be involved in the first place.

"He insisted," Griffin said.

"Oh."

The door opened and Dapper stood aside to let us in. He wasn't alone. Kaitlin and Samuel were settled on one sofa, while Archer and Beth were sitting on stools at the minibar.

I felt a pang of guilt that, even with company, he'd still felt the need for locks.

He looked incredible. I mean, he looked like he'd been hit by a bus, with bruises over his face and sunken cheeks, but it was a more than significant improvement.

"I'm so glad you're okay," I said, holding back the tears that caught me by surprise. With everything else going on, I'd had little time to think of the others who had been hurt, but Dapper and I had become friends. He'd never admit it, but it was true.

"Might not have been if you hadn't got here so quickly. Griffin told me you were the one to figure it out and led 'em all here. Wouldn't have lasted much longer with that belt wrapped round my neck."

"Lincoln took it off," I said, needing him to understand I hadn't done anything good, hadn't helped anyone. It was my fault in the first place.

He shrugged. "Even so. I owe you one."

It looked like a big thing for him to say. Almost as if some kind of promise had passed between us. I looked at the others, settling on the free sofa and none the wiser.

"Should I ask?" I responded, wanting to know why I was so sure he'd just given me a very rare gift.

"Not unless you wanna collect," Dapper said, closing and bolting the door with his new security precautions. I didn't bother telling him those locks would hold off an exile for a total of zero seconds. I figured he knew it already.

"So," Dapper said, walking back into the living area with me on his tail. We both took a seat. "How you suggesting to get that girl back?"

No one answered. Obviously, the day of planning hadn't resulted in any bright ideas.

"I'm going to give Phoenix the Exile Scripture as a trade," I said, a flat resolve in my tone.

"No," Lincoln said from his seat across the room. "She is not."

"Actually, I am," I said, not wanting to have this discussion in front of everyone but willing to if necessary.

"I'm not letting you go in there on your own. He's too strong and he'll have exiles everywhere. You aren't strong enough to fight him. And he has too much power over you."

"Thanks for the vote of confidence," I said, holding on to my anger. It was the only thing that would stop me from absorbing all the put-downs he'd loaded into his speech.

"That's not what this is about," he said, still calm but not looking at me. He knew what he was saying was cruel, but he was playing to the room, destabilizing me and making everyone doubt I was the right person to do this. By the looks on some faces, it was working.

Fine. Two can play at this.

I controlled my breathing, took a moment, and then got to work. "You told me yourself, Lincoln, that Phoenix won't hurt Steph as long as he still needs the Scripture. It wouldn't serve his purposes to ambush me. I think you're forgetting he has been popping up around me for the past six weeks and hasn't tried to hurt me."

"But all that changes once he has the Scripture in his hands." Lincoln looked at me now. The man had determination in spades.

"True, but he'd know Grigori would be close. If he killed me in the café, he'd be fair game. He'd know you'd be out there and that you'd return him in an instant. I can't see him risking facing you one-on-one."

Ta da! He'd struck me with cruel criticism and I'd struck him with bitter compliments!

And now, I have the room.

"She's right," Griffin said, and I knew it hurt him to go against Lincoln like this.

Lincoln stood up and dropped his head. "Fine. But I want to be in her ear the whole time."

"What? What does that mean?" I asked, worried he was going to possess me or something.

"That's understandable," Griffin said to Lincoln, motioning to Samuel, who opened a large case that was resting on the minibar. He handed something small to Lincoln and then something else to me. I looked down. It was a tiny earpiece and a small silver pin.

Great, me and Phoenix in a conversation and Lincoln listening in. This is going to go really well.

"We'll have eight Grigori around the perimeter, plus myself and Lincoln in close range," Griffin continued. "If you see something that makes you think it's an ambush or setup of any description, you call us in. If, for whatever reason, you can't speak directly to us but you need us, say the word 'cherry.'"

"Christ," said Dapper, echoing my thoughts. "You people like to make things complicated. Just give her the damn thing—her bloodcurdling screams will let you know if she needs you." I couldn't hide the smile. Dapper and I had turned a corner.

Lincoln, on the other hand, didn't share our amusement.

Everyone gradually got themselves together, arming themselves with their daggers and anything else they felt appropriate. Samuel was like a walking armory. I wondered why he bothered, since Grigori daggers were the only weapon that really worked. I must have been gawking because he winked at me and pulled out his blade, angling it to the light. Running down one side were delicate grooves, like engravings.

"Our blades are very powerful—even the smallest splinter melted down and blended with plain silver can have a result." He shrugged. "Having this certainly doesn't hurt. Shavings from my Grigori blade have contributed to a good number of my weapons."

I also spied a few grenades on the inside of his coat. Guess they could come in handy in a pickle too.

I really do need a book on this stuff.

"But the stronger the exile," Griffin interjected, "the more likely that he would be immune to anything other than the pure force of a Grigori blade."

I nodded, my mouth now dry. Griffin didn't think Samuel's specialist blades would work on Phoenix. Samuel shrugged again, unfazed.

Dapper surprised me by sheathing an impressive-looking sword and slinging it over his shoulder before heading out. Two thoughts came to mind when I saw it. *Kill Bill*—and—*I'm going to have to broaden my weapon range.*

I guess I could understand Dapper not wanting to be left behind again, but he didn't seem like the fighting type. He gave me a semi-smile, sensing my concern.

"Girl's got some of my books to return," he said.

It was a lie. Steph had grown on him.

I pushed the thought aside quickly. I couldn't think about Steph. Not until I had her back.

Lincoln walked me to Dough to Bread, the late-night café Phoenix referred to as "ours." I'd told him he didn't need to. He'd been completely mature and ignored me.

"You can't go in there with me," I said after we'd walked most of the way in silence.

"I know," he said, sounding both resigned and worried.

"You think I'm doing the wrong thing, don't you?"

He was silent for a while. His breathing deepened. "On one side, yes, very much. On the other, no."

"Care to elaborate?"

"Not really. Only that I believe the choice is right. The trade. I just wish you weren't making it so impossible to keep you safe." He stopped walking. "We're here."

I stopped beside him. "I'd do anything for someone I love," I said quietly, not sure exactly what I was trying to say or what I wanted him to hear.

"I know you would," he said sadly. "That's just my point." He looked toward the café across the road. "How many can you sense?"

I concentrated for a moment. "Four." Then I decided to investigate further. "Hang on..." I delved into the well of my power, deep in my core, and connected to the senses.

I was still there, standing in front of Lincoln, looking right at him. But I was aware of a lot more too, and able to take that awareness wherever I willed it. I felt a surge of power, more than I was sure I could control if I ever let go fully. I moved my senses up so I had a bird's-eye view and took in the immediate area.

The exiles stuck out like pulsing hot spots. Three. One hidden in the alley behind the café, one on the rooftop, one at the back entrance. I could also see the Grigori, glowing in various shades, dotted around in pairs. I recognized Spence somehow. I wasn't actually seeing him clearly—I just knew it was him. He was blue. I sensed Griffin too, a kind of fuchsia, and near him something else I didn't recognize. Neither Grigori nor exile.

I moved my sentience inside the café through the ceiling. Phoenix was at the back. He didn't glow as red as the other exiles;

he was something else—soft orange, almost golden. A presence was beside him, but I couldn't see what it was. An illusion, maybe.

Phoenix's attention turned to the ceiling, as if he could see me watching from above. His gaze seemed to zero in on me.

Startled, I pulled back into myself and stumbled on the pavement.

Lincoln held my arm as I bent over and fought back the feeling that was somewhere between a killer flu and car sickness. I wanted to get down on the ground and rest, catch my breath. But I didn't. I forced myself upright and swallowed back the bile rising in my throat.

Get a grip! If I fall apart now, Linc will probably start yelling, "Cherry, cherry!" for Christ's sake!

"Are you okay?" he asked, his worry showing.

I nodded, somehow remaining upright. "Just dizzy."

He felt my forehead. "More than dizzy. Where'd you go?"

He was watching me closely. Looking for lies. Or maybe to see if I would self-combust.

"I…It's hard to explain." I concentrated on slowing my breathing, each breath grounding me further.

"Try."

I swallowed and wiped at the sweat on the back of my neck.

"It's like I can…I don't know—*use* the senses to see things far away. Go places, sort of…"

Lincoln's eyes went wide. "How long have you been able to do this?"

"Since the attack at Hades, but I didn't know how I did it then. It's happened a few more times since. It's how I knew exiles were at the airport, how I found you with Nahilius. This is the first time I've controlled it so much, though, pushed it out so far."

And now I'm paying the price.

He grabbed my shoulders, shaking me. "Listen to me. Don't do it again. Not for any reason. Not until...until we know what it is." Fear was rolling off him.

I nodded, alarmed by his fierceness.

He dropped one of his hands, running it through his hair.

"We should get you back to Hades," he said, starting to look around and digging into his pocket.

"Don't you dare pull out your phone. I'm going in there whether you like it or not," I said, pulling my arm out of his hold, almost losing my footing as I did.

We stared at each other. He knew I wasn't about to walk away from our one chance to get Steph back. Eventually, he sighed and I knew it was the only concession I'd get. But then he shook his head.

"You should've told me." He pulled his hand out of his pocket. Empty.

"I know. I'm sorry. But there has been so much, too much, that has happened and I just didn't want to admit there was another thing about me that I couldn't explain." And that was the truth.

"Does anyone else know?"

Kill me.

I considered making something up, denying it, but I couldn't so I continued with my stupid honesty streak.

"I think Phoenix figured it out. He called it a 'sight.' And when I was using it just now, I went into the café. I think he sensed me there."

Lincoln clenched his jaw and gave a nod. He put his earpiece in and clipped the mic pin to me. I followed suit and checked my watch. 9 p.m.

"I'd better go."

He nodded, which translated to *We'll talk about it later.*

I hitched my backpack, which didn't actually hold the Scripture but was a good decoy. The real Scripture was tucked inside my jacket.

"When you get across the road, talk into the mic, just so I know I have reception. Then wait to hear me respond."

"Okay."

I waited for a few cars and jogged across the road.

"Got me?" I asked.

"Got you." Lincoln's voice came through loud and clear as if he was right beside me. These things were good.

"I'm sorry," he blurted, catching me by surprise. "The things I said back at Dapper's. I was lying. You *are* strong enough to face Phoenix."

I bit down on my lip. He was regrouping, wanting me to believe in myself now in case it all went belly up.

I half smiled, not knowing if he could see me.

"You weren't lying, Linc. You were trying, and...I can live with that."

He didn't say anything else, so I made for the entrance to Dough to Bread after a quick brush of my fingertips over my dagger.

"Be careful," he whispered, just as I stepped inside.

chapter twelve

"Temptation is like a knife, that may either cut the meat or the throat of a man; it may be his food or his poison, his exercise or his destruction."

John Owen

Phoenix appeared relaxed, leaning back, legs extended and crossed at the ankle, as if he didn't have a worry in the world. It looked as if he was the only person at the table, but I knew there was something else there from when I'd scanned the café earlier.

I walked slowly but confidently, scoping out the other customers, getting a good look at the staff. Tonight, I didn't want any surprises.

Phoenix watched me draw closer, an amused look on his face that had me clenching my fists. I squeezed between a few chairs and finally reached his table at the very back. He'd already taken the seat with the best vantage point. I didn't sit.

"Good evening, lover," he said, smirking. His hair seemed almost alive, like black and purple flames with embers of silver. I wondered if normal people saw it the way I did and if they were as distracted by it.

"It's nice to see you." His smile widened. "In the flesh."

So he *had* sensed me earlier.

Well, good.

At least he'd know I was learning how to control it, whatever *it* was.

"Where is she?" I asked, keeping my emotions in check, only letting a little of my disdain for him creep out.

"Right here," he said, looking to his side. He patted the chair to his left. "How about you take a seat and I will reveal her to you." His eyes wandered, pretending to give a damn. "People are looking."

I sat down, not because he wanted me to, but because I was desperate to see Steph. "Show her to me!" I demanded and quickly regretted it.

He relished having power over me and it was enough that he'd already proved he could keep her hidden from my view.

"Please, Phoenix," I added, softening my voice significantly. My change in tone must have caught him off guard. He waved a hand through the air, as if disappointed things hadn't gone differently, and revealed Steph.

I gasped.

She was unconscious and had a large blue-green bruise on her cheek, while the blood in her veins showed prominently down the side of her face. I shot a look of hate back at Phoenix and was halfway to my feet with every intention of slamming my fist into him when he raised one hand, looked me right in the eyes, and said, "It wasn't me."

It stalled me long enough for him to add, "They did it before I got to her. I gave you my word I wouldn't hurt her, and from the moment she's been with me, she has not been touched or harmed in any way."

"Why is she unconscious, then?" I snapped. But I sat back down.

"Not unconscious—asleep. Just until we've made the trade. I thought it might be better for everyone that way." His eyebrows lifted. "She doesn't always know when to shut up."

"How? Have you drugged her?"

"Didn't need to." He leaned in a little and lowered his voice. "I'm much more powerful than you give me credit for."

The guy was as comfortable with lying as with telling the truth and history showed a bad track record, yet I found myself believing him.

But I can't trust my instincts around him.

He raised his eyebrows, reading my confusion.

"Is she going to be okay?" I asked, my strong exterior wavering a little even as I tried to shut my emotions down. Steph looked so fragile. Her small frame—usually held up with a whole lot of sass—was folded over in the chair. I fought the urge to go to her. I knew that wasn't in the cards yet.

"Other than the bruise on her face, she is untouched. She'll be fine."

Again, I wanted to believe him. Then I noticed something

strange. He wasn't influencing me, pushing his powers into me. I looked at him suspiciously.

"I just want this done," he said, again reading my emotions.

I nodded. But this time, I didn't have the same faith in his words. "Promise me you'll let me get her out safely."

He looked around the café, clearly uninterested in the conversation. "I have no use for her after this." It was as good as I was going to get.

Without him pushing and pulling at my emotions, I saw an opening, something that reminded me of who he used to be.

"Why won't you just give me the Grigori Scripture? You know it's not meant for exiles."

He laughed, genuinely amused, and shook his head. "I don't care about your stupid Grigori Scripture. I haven't even looked at it."

I scoffed in disbelief.

He shrugged like he didn't give a damn what I thought.

"It's true. Nor has any other exile. It is hidden well and I already know the names and faces of the Grigori I intend to destroy. I'm not interested in tracking down half-breeds for the rest of my life, but..." He seemed to relax and tense at the same time as he glared at me, like he wanted me to understand the importance of what he was saying. "I had to pay a price to get to where I am today. Those who follow me believe chasing Grigori is very important. I can't successfully go against them for no good reason. It is the way it is."

"So you *don't* plan on using it?" I asked, confused.

"Not if I can avoid it. Perhaps down the track you might find something worth trading it for." His eyes roamed over me in an intimate way. "I can think of one thing I would be willing to trade it for..."

"Son of a bitch! I'm coming in," I heard Lincoln say in my ear.

"That's not happening," I said quickly to both of them.

Phoenix smiled. "But until then, if it should become in my best interests to utilize it..."

He didn't need to finish. I knew the ending. Phoenix was self-serving first and foremost.

I waited with bated breath but Lincoln didn't burst through the doors.

"What do you expect to happen if you bring her back?" I continued. I'd seen the timeline from the exile records Griffin had managed to access. Phoenix had spent hundreds of years in human form before Lilith was returned, and he'd barely crossed paths with her. For all intents and purposes, it seemed likely one or both had disowned the other.

"Sometimes you don't know what you've got until you've lost it."

I had to look away. I felt a trickle of intense emotion I was sure he hadn't intended to leak.

"And anyway," he said, snapping out of wherever he had been, shutting whatever door had drifted open, "I was a different exile then. Confused. I no longer question my place."

"A little late in life to be seeking Mommy's approval, isn't it?"

"Careful..." I heard Lincoln whisper in my ear.

Phoenix's face hardened—a frightening determination that left me with no doubt. He would stop at nothing to bring Lilith back.

My eyes darted to Steph, who was starting to drool. I wondered if the sleeping state Phoenix had imposed on her was hurting her the longer she remained in it.

"Let's get this done," I said.

He jerked his head toward my backpack. "Is it in there?"

He was anxious now.

I shook my head. "It's inside my jacket."

I started to undo the zip, but he grabbed my wrists.

"Ow!" I said, before I could stop myself, then recovered quickly, twisting my hands to escape his hold but only managing to get one free. He kept a grip on my right wrist, the one that had bled into the chalice in Jordan, pushing my bracelets up and running his thumb firmly over the faint scar that remained there. I didn't know why that one hadn't healed fully—maybe because I didn't truly want it to. It was a reminder. I pulled my arm away from him again, and this time he released me so I could stand.

"Violet? Are you okay?" Lincoln spoke urgently in my ear.

"What the hell are you doing?" I snapped at Phoenix, keeping my voice down. People were looking.

"Sit down," he said, voice distant.

I did but pushed my chair back, increasing the space between us.

"I'm not an idiot, Violet. I'm not letting you reach into your coat to pull out something I cannot see. I have exiles stationed around the café. One on the roof looking in and one watching through the back window."

Both not lies.

He sighed, but I could see he wasn't altogether upset.

"If you pull something from your jacket, they will come in. If you want to do this trade, *I* will open your jacket and take the Scripture." He rested back in his chair.

Jesus.

"Violet, listen to me, he's playing you. Once he has his hands on you, he will have all the power. Don't let him do this," came Lincoln's hurried words.

"Promise me as soon as you have it, you'll release her and leave," I said through gritted teeth. "In that order, and through the back door," I added, wanting to give Lincoln a clue as to which area we needed to cover. With any luck, they'd take him down when he left.

"As you wish."

"Glad to see you're listening to me," Lincoln said, sounding pissed.

Oh well, I'd deal with him later.

Phoenix leaned in. "You're going to have to come a little closer, lover."

I could almost hear Lincoln fuming on the other end.

Note to self: next time, have Griffin on comm unit.

I moved my chair closer.

"Hands on the table," Phoenix said, enjoying himself now.

"Just hurry up," I said, reminding myself I could do this because it was for Steph. I cleared my mind and focused on keeping my guard up.

Phoenix unzipped my jacket, slowly. "From memory, you don't like things too fast."

I didn't respond. I didn't even look at him. One thing he *didn't* know was that this kind of behavior only inspired memories that fed my hatred toward him. Until, that is, his hands slid inside my jacket and I felt the familiar conflicting urges that always came when he was close—that urgent need at the same time as repulsion and hatred, causing an intense hunger. The Scripture was rolled tightly in a slim canister that sat diagonally across my chest.

He found it immediately but didn't remove his hand, instead sliding it down the canister to my hip, skimming my top and the band of exposed skin just beneath. The second his skin made contact with mine, a stampede of emotion, of intoxicating and alluring lust, rushed over me, impossible to escape and igniting the desire that I was trying so hard to ignore. A wave rippled through my body as sparks flew from his fingertips.

I didn't care what Griffin said about it having to be me *wanting* to stop him—nothing could have stopped this freight train.

I groaned before I could stop myself. All my worries, all the pain, lifted, to be replaced by something simple and blissful. It was both passionate and selfish.

Sensing he had the control, Phoenix inched his chair closer, his fingers moving around my back while his other hand cupped my face. His dark brown eyes swirled with a hunger that I could not describe but also…understood.

"Violet," Lincoln whispered in my ear. I couldn't answer.

"Violet," he said again, but no one was home. I was somewhere else. Somewhere easy.

"Violet, look across the table. Steph is there." His words melted into me.

Honey, he's like honey.

"Steph needs you, Violet," the honey voice whispered again. I could taste it in the back of my throat, like swallowing paradise. He was saying something important, but his words slipped away too quickly, sinking into the pot.

Phoenix was so close, his hair sparkling like a tiny fireworks display.

"You could still come with me," he said, as he bled more and more emotion into me. Canceling out all that hurt, replacing it with a desire—*his* desire.

It's so easy here.

"Violet!" Lincoln said, then sighed. "You don't love him. This isn't real. You know what's real and it's hard and it hurts and we can't...Damn it, Vi—we're real! Now snap the hell out of it and get your best friend out of there!"

Flashes of another type of desire burned through the lust. An awful, gut-wrenching, soul-deep need that would never be fulfilled, that was painful instead of delightful and much more difficult than anything Phoenix offered me. I felt a tear slip from the corner of my eye.

Phoenix was so close. I could see the bead of sweat trickling down his forehead. He was working hard to hold me. But my feelings for Lincoln were too strong and they kept burning through Phoenix's seduction, disintegrating everything he sent to me.

I bit hard on my lip and tasted blood. That helped too.

"Move back in your seat now or I swear to God, power or not, I will ram my dagger into your heart because I would rather die than be your prisoner."

Phoenix's eyes went wide and he moved back, taking the Scripture with him.

"That's my girl," Lincoln said in my ear.

Phoenix was evidently surprised by my reaction but seemed equally shocked by his own behavior. "I'd never force you to do anything," he said, as much to himself as to me.

"Every time you pull that stuff on me, it just makes me hate you more."

Phoenix regained his composure and slouched back in his chair, but he was out of breath and clearly caught off guard by my ability to push him away.

"Easier for both of us that way, don't you think?"

I glared at him. "You've got the Scripture. Now wake her up and get out."

He stood up. Steph stirred, groggy, her eyes starting to open.

Phoenix tilted the Scripture toward me. "I'm sure I don't need to check this one, though I'm also sure you've made a copy. I'll see you soon, lover." He left through the back door.

I scrambled out of my chair and over to Steph. I knelt beside her, pushing the hair back from her face.

"Exiles are on the move out here. Have you got her?" Lincoln whispered in my ear.

"Yes, yes—help me. Steph, sweetie, can you hear me? It's Vi," I said, trying not to cry. Failing. The door burst open and I looked up to see Lincoln bounding over wayward legs and chairs.

Steph opened her eyes fully and swallowed with difficulty.

"Vi?" she murmured.

"You're safe. You're back. I'm sorry, Steph. I'm so sorry."

She half smiled. "Less sorry, more water."

Lincoln reached the table. "How is she?"

"Thirsty!" I said, as if she had bleeding bullet wounds.

Lincoln smiled but was quick to grab a jug of water from the waiter's station.

He passed me a full glass and straw.

"Here," I put the straw in Steph's mouth.

"Thanks," she said after a sip. "I'm okay. Out of it, but okay." Then her head snapped up. "Dapper and Onyx? Samuel and Kaitlin?"

I exhaled. "Everyone's okay. Onyx is still in hospital, but everyone else is out."

"They…they tried to stop them. Fought for me."

"I know, honey, Samuel and Kaitlin are fine."

She gave a weak shake of her head. "Not just them. Onyx and Dapper too."

Wow. I wasn't surprised about Kaitlin and Samuel—they were Grigori—but Dapper and, more astonishingly, Onyx, who would have known better than anyone he didn't have a chance against their supernatural strength. I'd just figured they were caught unaware, not that they'd actually been standing in their way. It now made sense why Onyx had been in the hall—he was defending Steph.

"We have to get her away from here," Lincoln said. He was still standing, facing the customers, guarding us. To the other diners, Steph had just appeared out of nowhere and was clearly unwell—customers were more than just curious now.

"Steph, can you walk, just to the street?"

Lincoln nodded in agreement.

Steph started to get up. I supported her, putting an arm around her waist as gently as I could.

"How do I look?" she asked, once we were standing. I couldn't hold back the laugh—maybe it was delirium. Trust Steph to want a mirror straight away.

"Nothing a little foundation won't fix." Actually, it would take several bottles, but she didn't need to hear that right now.

We walked out, people moving aside for us.

"Is she okay?" a waitress said. "We didn't see her come in. Should we call an ambulance?"

"No, thanks, though. We're just taking her home now," Lincoln said smoothly.

Steph hobbled but was stronger with each step. Whatever spell they had her under was clearly lifting, and it appeared Phoenix had told the truth. Apart from the bruised face, she was in relatively good working order.

We made it outside and Griffin pulled up to the curb in Lincoln's four-wheel-drive. Lincoln grabbed the back door. Dapper was already in there.

"Good to see ya, girl," he said, looking at Steph, relieved. Steph crawled into the backseat with me close behind, and Lincoln jumped in the front before we sped off. Steph threw her arms around Dapper and he pulled her close, his hand gently smoothing the bruised side of her face.

"Thank you," she said, before slumping back against me. Dapper didn't respond, just righted himself and looked out the window as if it were nothing. It wasn't nothing, though. They'd been there and tried to defend Steph when I hadn't. I realized it wasn't Dapper who owed me one at all; it was *me* who owed him, big time. And Onyx.

chapter thirteen

"Generally it is the tortured who turn into torturers."

CARL JUNG

Steph fell in and out of consciousness during the drive back to Hades. I was nervous about taking her back there, but we needed to clean her up, and although my place was closer, with Dad around, it wasn't an option. Besides, Dapper insisted.

Griffin pulled up right outside the glossy yellow doors of the club.

"Where are Spence and the others?" I asked.

"They managed to take out one of the exiles at the café, but Phoenix was too fast. Just to be sure, they're guarding the perimeter. Nothing will get near here tonight," Griffin said, clambering out of the car.

That's something, I guess.

"Steph, are you awake?" I asked, not wanting to frighten her. Despite Phoenix's assurances, I had no idea how bad things had really been for her, but I did know, all too well, how awful the aftermath could be. I swallowed back the thoughts, needing to be strong for her, do whatever she needed me to do to help her get through this.

She hitched a shoulder. "Mmm…kind of…"

I opened the door. "I'll carry her in," I said to the others.

Lincoln took hold of the door, careful not to touch me. "I'll do it."

"No, I'm fine. I can do it!" I snapped, feeling the strain of everything that had happened earlier. I worked so hard not to be vulnerable around him and now, after what happened with Phoenix, I felt completely exposed again. It made me sick, the power Phoenix had over me, but at least it didn't grind into my heart and twist till I couldn't breathe.

Lincoln looked at the ground. "I know you can. But it might look a little strange—you carrying her through a busy bar. We'll have enough attention as it is."

I braced my hand on the car, pressing down hard. I was so angry now. With him, with Phoenix…with myself.

Steph stirred. "Vi, it's okay. Let him take me." She gave a faint smile.

I sighed and stood aside. Lincoln didn't look at me; he just kept his head down and reached in for my friend.

When we walked inside, Hades was, as always, full of activity. I had to do a mental count to figure out it was Thursday, one of the club's busiest nights. Once again, I worried coming here had been the wrong decision.

People were looking as we marched through the middle of the bar, not bothering with discretion for once. I saw someone moving quickly from a corner, then coming closer.

"Oh no," I said to myself. The floorboards suddenly felt like quicksand, sucking me down, holding me in place.

I hadn't even considered it. I should have, but with everything... I didn't think to check with Dapper if Steph's brother was working. He was pushing through the crowd, calling out our names. First Steph's, then mine.

"Steph, Jase is coming over here. We can't tell him what happened. We can't bring him into this too," I said urgently, all of my guilt at already having brought her into this world rising to the surface.

She looked at me, pausing to consider, and then nodded even though her eyes were still semiclosed. "I'll talk to him."

That was all we had time for before he broke through the crowd and was right there. Dapper melted back, obviously not wanting Jase to know he was mixed up in any of this. We weren't the kind of friends Dapper would brag about.

"Hey, man! What the hell are you doing with my sister?" he yelled at Lincoln.

His hands were balled into fists and he looked like he was getting ready to throw a punch. He shot a look toward me.

"Violet. Are you okay? What's going on?" But he didn't wait for my answer. "Give her to me!" he said, moving in on Lincoln, trying to get his hands under Steph and wrangle her away from him. Steph was trying to swat at him, but it just made him try harder. I could understand why. She looked completely out of it.

"Jase!" I yelled over the music. His head swung in my direction, eyes fierce.

I felt like smiling at him, proud to see he would step up like this for his sister. But a pat on the back was not going to help.

"Jase, she's okay!" I yelled again. "We're taking her upstairs." Then I remembered that Dapper wouldn't want any involvement.

"To the *staff* apartment," I emphasized, looking at Lincoln. No one else would have noticed the small nod he gave me.

"You're not taking her anywhere!" Jase yelled. "Give her to me!" He tried again to pull her out of Lincoln's hold.

Good luck with that.

Lincoln hitched Steph a little higher. "She's not as light as she looks. I've got a good hold on her. How about I get her upstairs, and then you can help her all you want?"

But Jase wasn't having it, and while his persistence was irritating, I felt a certain pride.

Griffin chose this moment to intervene. He put a hand on Jase's shoulder and looked right at him. I knew what he was going to do. Griffin's strength rests in his ability to find and deliver truth. If truth exists, he can see it in people and also give it to them wholly.

"We are helping her. We haven't harmed her."

I saw the shimmer, the slight dusting of Griffin's power as it moved from him and into Jase, whose eyes went wide and then, unable to deny the truth forced onto him, softened. Griffin nodded Lincoln on.

Lincoln led the way upstairs, taking Steph into Onyx's apartment and putting her down on the sofa bed.

Jase barged in behind them and sat beside his sister. He might believe they weren't trying to hurt her, but he needed to see for himself that she was okay.

"Steph, what's going on?"

Steph did her best. She was more and more lucid with every minute. I guessed in an hour or so, she'd be herself again. She pushed up onto the pillows and tried her hardest to keep her eyes open and smile.

"I'm fine. I just feel silly," she said.

"Where are you hurt?" Jase asked, looking her over.

"Just my face. I was at the library and was leaving to come here, but I fell down the stupid steps."

"Like I'm buying that!" he said.

"It's true," Steph went on, unfazed by her brother's refusal to get on board. "It was dark and I tripped and hit the railing on the way down." Her hand went to her face and she winced a little. "The librarian came out to help me. She gave me a pill, told me it would relax me." She feigned a sarcastic laugh.

It was actually very believable. Steph was spinning a wicked web while the rest of us remained silent, intently taking in the cover story so we could stick to it later.

"She gave you a pill that made you like this? The librarian?" Jase repeated. He had a pretty good bullshit detector.

"Yeah. Then Lincoln and his friend Griffin walked by and saw me outside on the steps."

Jase looked at Lincoln, who he'd met before, and then over to Griffin, who gave him a nod of introduction.

"They called Violet and brought me here because they knew you'd be here."

And there it was. The triple-twist, double-pike with a 5.0 difficulty and Steph had just brought it home with a perfect landing. Right in her brother's lap!

Jase's tough facade crumbled. He swallowed back what I was pretty sure was a big old dose of brotherly love and put a hand on her forehead.

"It's okay, you dope. I'll get someone to cover for me and take you home." He turned to me. "Thanks for getting her to me, Vi, and I'm...You know, sorry I was angry." He looked down, embarrassed.

Lincoln shifted in the back corner where he now stood beside Griffin, but when I looked over, he was watching the floor intently.

Steph started to fall back into a slumber.

"That's okay. I knew you'd want to help her. I thought this was a better option than just taking her home."

"Yeah, never know if anyone's going to be there these days. I take it she's told you Dad's taken a permanent sabbatical from parenting?"

Well, she hadn't said it exactly like that. I knew things weren't great and her dad was away a lot. That her mom was a bit of a...socializer and pretty erratic when it came to the mothering department. Which reminded me about her irate phone calls the night before.

"Kind of. Actually, that's the other reason we came to you. You see, Steph and I didn't make it home last night. We got stuck out of the city—car trouble."

Jase raised his eyebrows, a more suspicious look returning.

"Yeah, I know how it sounds, but it's true. Anyway, your mom called my dad and she was pretty worried. I think she'll want to see Steph soon."

Jase looked at his sister dubiously. "How soon?"

"Like after-a-cold-shower soon."

"Great," he said, checking his watch. "She's going to think I got her drunk or something and God knows what she'll say about her face!"

I took another good look at her and gasped. The bruised area was definitely smaller and the visible blood vessels had disappeared. If I didn't know any better...But that was impossible. No one could have healed her. Even *I* couldn't heal anyone other than Grigori.

I glanced at Lincoln. He was watching Steph curiously too.

"I could put a bit of makeup on her," I said, still staring.

"Nah, it's okay. Might be worth it for the look on Mom's face," he said, wearing a warm smile. "Kind of wish I'd been home last night to see her go off." When I didn't say anything, he quickly added, "I was working, you know, not...I did go home...Just late."

"Sure," I said, joking along. But Jase blushed.

From the corner of my eye, I saw Lincoln shift from one foot to the other again.

"You think you might be able to take care of that cold shower?" Jase asked me.

"Maybe you should have one too," Lincoln said out of nowhere.

Jase spun around, sending a particularly challenging look in his direction, the wrong thing to do. Lincoln was already in protector mode. I stood up.

"Why don't you guys go downstairs and we'll be down in ten?" I said.

"Won't you need someone to help you get her downstairs or whatever?" Jase asked.

Lincoln actually stifled a laugh.

What the hell has gotten into him?

"No, it's okay. I think whatever she took is wearing off, and after a shower, I'd say she'll be much better." Even if she wasn't, I could get her down the stairs more easily by myself.

Jase seemed unsure. Griffin walked toward the door.

"Come on, Jase. She's right. Why don't we go downstairs and find Dapper? He's a friend of mine, and I'm sure he'll give you the rest of the night off." He bled just enough truth into his words to get Jase on board. Lincoln was already on his way out.

Steph opened her eyes as soon as she heard the door close.

"You're awake?" I said, immediately looking for some way I could help her.

She slapped my hovering hands. "I knew it'd be easier if he thought I wasn't available for further discussion. So, we had car trouble last night, huh?"

"Yeah. I didn't know what else to say. Dad flipped and your mom was calling him, demanding to know where we were, so if anyone asks, we were at a friend of Lincoln's, in a bad cell reception area."

"Got it," she said, starting to sit up.

I helped her. "How are you feeling?"

"Better by the minute. I'll be much fresher after that shower." I turned on the water and gave her the change of clothes I'd stashed in my backpack.

By the time she emerged from the bathroom, Steph looked considerably improved and the damage to her cheek had faded further.

"Your bruises," I said. "They're getting better somehow."

"Did you…?" Steph started, prodding near her eye.

"No," I looked down, ashamed. "I tried with Onyx, but I can't heal humans."

"Oh. Well, you're right, I think. It's definitely feeling better."

"Steph, how bad was it?" I asked tentatively, petrified of what she might say.

"Other than the initial hit across my face, no one came near me. It all happened so fast. Samuel and Kaitlin barely had time to get me to the bedroom before they were here. Dapper tried to stop them at the door—he told them it would end the neutrality agreement—but they just kept coming. I heard them fighting him and Onyx, and one of the exiles yelling at the others, telling them they weren't approved for kills. Then they came into the bedroom. A European-looking one—dark hair and dark eyes—came for me, while the others went for Kaitlin and Samuel. He hit me and that's the last thing I remember before I woke up in Phoenix's plane."

I didn't know what to say, but Steph kept going.

"When I came around, I was upstairs, but I could hear Phoenix below. He was yelling." She swallowed. The memory frightened her. "I'm pretty sure he was hitting someone. It was weird. From what I heard, I think it must've been the exile who took me. Phoenix was mad that he'd hit me."

"You were his bargaining chip. He didn't want you harmed."

She nodded. "Figured it was something like that. He knew the exchange was bogus, didn't he?"

"I'm sorry, Steph." I could barely look at her.

"Don't be. It's not your fault, Vi." She gave me a hug and I held her so tight she had to start wriggling. "Easy on the human," she said, smiling.

"I never should've brought you into all this."

Steph stood up steadily. She really was doing much better, almost back to normal.

"We're not having this conversation again." And like that, she ended it. For now. "Come on. Big brother will get more suspicious if I don't get down there soon."

We headed for the bar, Steph letting me keep a supporting arm around her just in case. At the top of the stairs, she stopped.

"Did you give it to him?"

"Yes," I said, quietly.

"Did we get the Grigori Scripture?"

"No."

"Well, that's…"

"Yeah."

"I'll get back to the translation tomorrow. I'm getting close. A few more days and I'll have something."

I didn't say anything else. I wanted to argue. Tell her to stay in bed for a week or more. But there was no telling Steph what to do, and the truth was, now more than ever, we needed that translation because something was coming—something very bad—and Steph might be the best hope we had. A thought that made me hate myself even more. It was going to be harder to get her out of this nightmare world, in which I'd given her residency, than I'd imagined.

chapter fourteen

> *"But as for the good things of this life, and its ills, God has willed that these should be common to both."*
>
> Saint Augustine

My lungs were burning and I relished the feeling, wanting more, even though I was out of time. It had already taken two hours of running to feel the acid build up. Even doing so on empty—from lack of food and sleep—I still had super endurance. I'd wanted to hurt, needed the distraction. Anything rather than lying in bed contemplating.

Plus…I was avoiding Dad.

I still hadn't seen him since the previous afternoon.

Things were spiraling and I needed to take stock, refocus. I couldn't function otherwise. Phoenix had outplayed me and I couldn't let that happen again.

I was relieved Steph was okay. And baffled.

I just couldn't work Phoenix out. I was almost certain at times that a part of him hated doing these things and despised the other exiles. And yet—he was about to resurrect uber-exile Lilith. It didn't make sense. It was as if he wanted to force himself to become something he loathed.

I wondered if it was all just to kill me. If that *was* his ultimate goal, maybe it would be better if I just let him. I could end it all before he brought her back. But deep down, I knew the time for self-sacrifice had passed. If it were just about killing me, he'd had plenty of chances.

I got back to the apartment with just enough time to shower and change before school. But when I went into the kitchen to grab a quick coffee before heading back out, Dad was there, waiting.

Doesn't he work anymore?

"Morning. I didn't think you were…I just went for a run."

"Hmm."

He was dressed for work and had his drawing case in his hand. He was still raw with me. I just had to see through the speech and then he'd be gone.

"Sorry about yesterday," I tried.

"Violet, despite what you might think about me, I'm not completely ignorant. Whatever you have managed to mix yourself up in, it stops now."

I froze at the coffee machine. "I'm not mixed up in anything."

"Yes, you are. I don't know what it is yet, but I will. And until you decide to be honest with me"—he took a deep breath—"you're grounded."

I almost dropped the milk jug. "*What?*" I demanded, slamming the jug on the counter. *Has he been drinking?*

"You…You can't do that!" We just didn't have that kind of relationship.

"I just did. School and straight home every day. Study on the weekend can be here or at the library, but home by six. That's it. No more late nights. I'll be arranging to do some work from home for the next little while, so I should be here most days by the time you're due home."

I stood there, mouth open, stunned. I had a lot of things I wanted to say, but for some reason, nothing came out.

Dad took my silence, inaccurately, for acceptance and gave a curt nod before heading for the door. Before he opened it, he paused, shoulders slumped. "I'm sorry, Violet. But you left me no choice." He closed the door quietly behind him.

"I've been grounded," I said to Steph in history, after we'd finally made Lydia go away, swearing we would pass on her get-well wishes to Spence, who had decided not to turn up to school again. He was planning on stretching the mono excuse right up to graduation next month.

"It's like we've entered some kind of alternate reality. Your dad's all fatherly and my parents are completely losing it." Steph shook her head. Neither one of us could figure out what had happened.

The bruise on Steph's cheek was barely noticeable beneath a layer of foundation and she seemed back to her normal self in every other way, though I knew that didn't mean there wasn't residual damage lurking somewhere.

"How was Jase last night?" I asked, wondering if we had yet another problem.

"He doesn't buy the story, although Griffin did enough so that he's not jumping up and down too much. I think he figures you and I got ourselves into some trouble we don't want to admit to. The good thing is he got up to his fair share of stuff when he was younger and he talked to Mom, who's now decided I'm just acting out." She drew spirals on her paper. "And when she saw my A in chemistry, she switched back to not giving a damn."

"Well, Jase is worried about you," I said.

Steph raised her eyebrows. "Not *just* me. He asked after you a few times last night too."

"Oh. Well, I probably looked pretty freaked out."

"Yeah, I don't think that's exactly what it was. I think big brother has a crush…" She looked like she was on the verge of bursting out laughing.

A couple of years back, I'd had a bit of a thing for Jase. He's two years older than us and I used to think he was seriously cute with the whole music thing he had going for him. Then I'd met Lincoln.

"Steph, that's not funny," I warned.

"Is so!" she said, proceeding into a fit of giggles. Then she saw my face. "Oh, don't panic. He's into a different girl every week. It'll pass—just give him a wide berth for a bit."

I could definitely do that, now that I was grounded.

"Did your dad say I was banned from coming over?" Steph asked, a conspiratorial twinkle in her eye.

"No. Not yet."

"Well, research it is then. I know I'm close." She tapped her pen up and down on the desk. "We can go by Dapper's on the way. I'm sure he'll let me take that book I was using to your place for the night. I can feel a breakthrough coming on."

I smiled. What I really wanted to do was train or, even better, beat the crap out of something that really deserved it, but I guess I could make do with my makeshift studio gym and the rest could wait until tomorrow.

"Research," I agreed. At least it was something.

Dad wasn't happy when I walked into the apartment with Steph in tow, but he'd always had a soft spot for her and accepted that he hadn't stipulated that she wasn't welcome. I think he was just relieved to see that I'd come home at all.

Steph and I had made a speedy stop at Dapper's on the way. He'd reluctantly agreed to let her borrow a couple of books. It seemed their recent shared battlefield had earned her a little pull, which Steph didn't have any qualms about cashing in on. So, after making coffee, we closed ourselves in my room as far away from Dad, and his new inquisitive ways, as possible.

One good thing about the situation was that Dad was an amateur when it came to discipline. He had no idea how to implement a true grounding. I still had my all-important cell phone, so really he hadn't succeeded in cutting off my contact with anyone. And given my recent...stirrings of tight-leashed feelings, there was at least one upside to imprisonment—I didn't have to face Lincoln yet.

I'd been trying hard to shut it down. The influx of the very real emotions he had dragged out of me last night had my blood running hot and out of control. It said a lot that he knew my feelings for him were a key to pulling me out of Phoenix's thrall.

It's too cruel.

While Steph buried her head in books, I gave Griffin a call, followed by Spence, filling them both in on my homebound status. Griffin was already at Lincoln's, so I asked him to pass the update on to him. Spence promised to make himself available to train with me tomorrow after I agreed not to tell Griffin that he had been a no-show at school.

Once that was done, I did a short workout in my studio, and then, after a shower and a change of clothes, got comfy on the floor next to Steph and started to flip through the copies of the Scripture. Steph had made a number of them, using some to write on and others to be kept clean. Dapper, who seemed to be particularly erudite on all matters ancient, had a set too, along with Griffin and the Academy.

I stared at the first part and a section of writing, or maybe they were symbols.

"What language is it?"

Steph shook her head. "It isn't *just* a language. It's like a combination of language and numerical code. It's amazing *and* frustrating.

The language is old Hebrew, which is difficult to translate at the best of times, especially since I don't speak it, so I have to research every word. The numbers, which are basically every second word, correlate to the Hebrew alphabet but"—her eyes lit up—"this is where we have the breakthrough. Every sixth word. It reverses, changes the flow, and flips the alphabet. So the translation of one, for example, means the first letter of the alphabet for six numerical words but then means the last letter of the alphabet for the next six numerical words. It is actually quite simple but just confusing enough to throw someone off track."

"So what have you translated using this method?"

Steph licked her lips. "Okay. So, there are two main text works. From what I can tell, they're prophecies, kind of like guidelines to follow. So far, I think I have one of them down."

She handed me a sheet of paper. "Does this mean anything to you?" she asked, squirming.

If it weren't all pits-of-Hell information, I'd say Steph was in her element.

I looked at the piece of paper.

Awaken Tartarus and blanket day, to hide their eyes and Heaven's ray. Ash will fall as fire will rain, delivering to one, insufferable pain. Flames will roar and spear the skies, Igniting the view to the water's rise. A swell of death to deliver just one, resurrecting that, pardoned by none.

"It's a poem," I said.

Steph nodded. "Cheery, isn't it? And rhymey."

"Is that weird? I mean, should it rhyme like this if it's translated from another language?"

She looked at me strangely. "Yes, it's weird. It's *all* weird and I'm seriously concerned that this is your first question, but when did any of this stuff really make sense? I think from the way it's designed, it would translate to some kind of synchronicity and rhyme in any language. But, personally, I would have started with the 'Fire will rain' and 'insufferable pain' parts."

"Is the other one the same?" I asked, the translated words now churning in my stomach.

"Similar, I think. The code's slightly different, but I think I have it mostly figured out."

Steph and I theorized unsuccessfully for hours, stopping only to make toasted sandwiches for dinner and to occasionally reach over for a scoop of melted mint-chocolate-chip ice cream. I was surprised that, once she showed me how to work out the code, I wasn't altogether useless and actually managed to decipher some of the words myself.

By the end of the night, we had translated the first line of the second text.

At the southernmost point, the island hides a gate.

Which could mean a number of things.

After Steph had left, I went to the kitchen to make more coffee. I wasn't ready to sleep yet. Dad was in his room, probably still working, avoiding me. I went to my studio, closed the door, and did another caffeine-charged workout, stopping only to open the window and push out my senses. There were no exiles nearby tonight.

Unfortunately, it wasn't consoling—merely another reminder that Phoenix already had what he wanted. By not sending exiles after me, he was sending a smug message. Probably laughing, wherever he was.

My only hope was that it might take him some time to translate the Scripture too and, knowing Phoenix, he wouldn't trust the content to many, if anyone—so that could help as well.

Yeah, that's me—finding the bright side.

chapter fifteen

"You withered in heart, no peace shall be to you!"

Book of Enoch 6:5

I didn't sleep well. I couldn't get everything out of my head long enough to unwind. The few times I had drifted off, I'd woken with a start seemingly moments later. It was Saturday—girls my age were supposed to be at the mall, catching a movie, at worst, studying. My life would never be like that again.

Maybe...it never really has been.

Despite the early hour, I didn't expect to find Dad sitting at the breakfast bar. That is, until I remembered I seemed to be dealing with a whole new breed of parent, one I couldn't predict at all.

I could tell by the tie he wore that he was headed for the office. He probably had meetings planned. Dad didn't see weekends as any different from weekdays where work was concerned. I imagined two whole days in every week without work to concentrate on would be comparable to a death sentence for him.

"Morning," I said, rubbing my eyes. I was angry with him for choosing now, of all times, to start pushing into my life. I wanted to tell him to back off, outline that he couldn't start playing the hands-on dad role after relinquishing the position for the first seventeen years of my life, but…I needed out today. I couldn't hack another day without proper training.

"Morning, sweetheart," he said, taking a bite of his burned toast.

I decided to keep the peace. "I…um, I have a workout session planned today with my friend Spence." I swallowed my stubbornness and kept my tone free of challenge. "If that's okay with you?" I could barely look at him as I forced out the words.

Dad's mouth fell open. Any other time it might have been comical. But I didn't smile. I worried. There was a possibility that I was opening a door I might not easily close again.

"Be home by six."

I nodded, grabbing my bag. I had a lot to get done between now and then.

"I mean it, Vi. I don't want to have to review the grounding restrictions. But I will."

Hell, he's really getting the hang of this stuff. He's already advanced into threat territory.

I jogged toward Lincoln's place, stopping when my phone rang.

"Hi, Griff," I said, seeing his name on the caller ID. "It's early for you. What's wrong?"

"Where are you?"

"On my way to meet Spence," I said, sounding as relieved as I felt to be out of the Eden Penitentiary. I picked up my pace again to a light jog, wanting to keep moving as well as stay warm.

"Can you stop by the hospital on the way?"

"Sure." It wasn't much of a detour. "Why are you there?"

"Checking in on Onyx."

"Oh, of course. See you there."

I'd planned on dropping in on Onyx today anyway. I hadn't seen him since he was admitted and I knew I couldn't put if off any longer. The problem was, I wasn't sure what I was going to say to him.

I called Spence, who sounded like he'd forgotten we were training this morning, and put him off for a couple of hours. I could hear him pressing buttons in the background. He'd probably still be on the PlayStation when I got there.

I made it to the hospital quickly, and as I headed for the recovery ward, my anxiety intensified. I didn't know what to expect when I saw Onyx, how bad he would look or what I would say.

Will he remember what he said to me? Do I want *him to?*

Our relationship had changed and I had no idea what type of Onyx would be on the other side of the door.

I backed up a step and considered waiting for Griffin outside. But before I had a chance to do an about-face, the door swung open and Griffin stood there, phone in hand.

"I was just about to call you again."

I half smiled. "No need."

Beyond him, I could see Onyx lying in a bed, watching us. The unsure look in his eye, as if deliberating whether he wanted me to come in or not, disappeared quickly.

"Oh, superb," he said sarcastically. "Here she is. It's supposed to be meals-on-wheels not death-in-a-breath. You could've at least given me a chance to recover before you brought her in. Hell knows how many exiles are on her trail today!"

He flung his head back on the pillow and I couldn't help but smile. Apparently, some things didn't change. Not completely, anyway. I took another step into the room.

"If you insist on coming in, at least have them increase the morphine—I'll need it to get through the visit," he said, lacking his customary bite and his voice catching on the last words as true pain flared.

Onyx looked beaten up, his porcelain skin now antique yellow and his usually dark eyes faded and rimmed in red instead of his signature kohl eyeliner. He had bruises covering most of his face, and from his rigid position, I guessed his torso was bandaged tightly.

"I'm sorry you were hurt. I…I heard you fought them." I hadn't meant to stumble on the words, but I was still struggling a bit with the concept of "Onyx the protector."

He chuckled sardonically. "Are you insane?" An insane comment, coming from him. "Of course I didn't fight them! I just got in their way for a moment and not by choice. If I could've run, I would've."

I shrugged, unconvinced. "Either way, I'm glad you're okay."

He looked past me, toward the bare wall.

"Violet, we need to talk," Griffin said, glancing at the door. I nodded but then had a thought.

"Steph translated the first of the texts in the Scripture last night."

I focused my attention on Onyx. He tried to hide his interest, but his head jerked up and then suddenly stilled.

Like candy to a kid.

Griffin shook his head. "That girl is incredible. She has done what every senior Grigori at the Academy has being trying to do since we first got hold of the text. Amazing," he marveled.

I pulled the piece of paper from my bag and gave it to Griffin, sharing a quick look with him I hoped he'd understand.

"Onyx," I began, "do you think you might be able to help us figure it out?"

I knew I was taking a chance. And from Griffin's face, I didn't know if he was going to allow it anyway, but, despite what Onyx thought of us, I was pretty sure he'd know something that could help.

Onyx harrumphed, but it did little to hide his intrigue.

Griffin studied the paper and took a step toward Onyx's bed, reciting the poem.

"'Awaken Tartarus and blanket day, to hide their eyes and Heaven's ray.'"

"The sun," Onyx said.

Griffin nodded in agreement. "'Ash will fall as fire will rain, delivering to one, insufferable pain.'"

Onyx was silent.

Griffin went on. "'Flames will roar and spear the skies, igniting the view to the water's rise. A swell of death to deliver just one, resurrecting that, pardoned by none.'"

"Well, the end is obvious," Griffin said. "'Pardoned by none' is the damned."

"Lilith," I said, her name sticking like a splinter in my throat.
Onyx nodded, then grimaced. "Not only her, though. It can mean anyone. There'll have to be a way of selecting her."

"What hides the sun?" I asked.

"Darkness," Onyx said without hesitation.

"What about the other stuff?"

He shifted back in his bed. "I don't know yet. I'll give it some thought."

He knew more than he was saying, I could tell, and by the look on Griffin's face, he realized it too, but he didn't call Onyx on the lie, so neither did I.

"I'll walk you out," Griffin said. I nodded.

"Yes. Ta ta. Tell the nurse if she doesn't want me to hunt her down and rip out her heart once I'm feeling myself again to bring the damned morphine, will you?" Onyx demanded.

"I'll visit in a couple of days," I said, ignoring his comment and subsequent glare.

"No need. Dapper's discharging me tomorrow."

It seemed too early for him to be leaving the hospital and I shot a worried look at Griffin. He just shrugged.

"Dapper says he'll deal with him."

"If you really want to help, you could have a few bottles of bourbon waiting for my return."

I followed Griffin out of the room. "Never gonna happen," I said without looking back. But as I pulled the door closed behind me, I heard Onyx reply quietly, just so I could hear.

"I'm sure something will come up to convince you."

I wondered how much of that poem he did understand. Griffin was punching something into his phone as I joined him in the hall.

"I'm not sure if Onyx can be..." I started, but he cut me off, waving his phone for a moment.

"Already on it. I'll have Grigori posted here until he leaves and we'll monitor everyone who visits him. He won't do anything we won't know about."

I really hoped that would work. But we were both well aware that Onyx was still an unknown. He was with us because he had no better options at the moment, but if a more alluring offer came along...

Griffin started walking toward the exit. "The Academy called this morning. They're sending their Vice here," he said, making "Vice" sound dangerous.

"Who's that?"

"Josephine. She's second in charge at the Academy and on the Assembly. She's been around for a long time, is very powerful, and always gets her way."

I guess it wasn't a major surprise. With everything that had been happening, Griffin had had to keep the Academy up to date on developments. Now that we had given Phoenix the Exile Scripture, I could understand why they would send someone.

"Who's her partner?"

"She is currently partnerless. She has had four that I know of. They are all dead." Griffin wasn't exactly painting a rosy picture.

I slowed both my walking and my words. "Griffin, why *exactly* is she coming?"

"For the Scriptures, but also to…assess you."

"Why?" I asked, with an all-bad feeling.

We pushed through the exit doors to a cold wind blasting outside.

"Because they know something is going on. They've heard the rumors and though we haven't confirmed that your angel maker is one of the Sole, that won't stop them from investigating. You are potentially the most powerful Grigori ever to have been created. We still don't understand your capabilities, so they want you assessed and…monitored. They're going to decide if you need to be…" He stopped, looking worried and sorry for me.

"Griffin," I pushed.

"They think you need to be trained at the Academy. By them. Josephine will have the authority to make that decision while she is here."

I stopped midstride. "What do you mean?" I asked, louder than I'd meant to. "It's my choice! What are they going to do, lock me up?"

Griffin sighed and put his head down, but not before his eyes said *yes*. "They have ways to do almost anything they want. There are many Grigori within the Academy, all with varying talents that they will not hesitate to use on you if they believe it is in their interest."

I let his words sink in and didn't respond. What could I say? I was being told they were going to take away my choices, force me to move to the Academy. In that moment, I knew one thing for sure—I would never willingly allow that to happen.

"Violet, you know I'll do everything I can."

"When does she arrive?" I asked, unable to hold back my anger at him just because he was one of them.

"In five days."

We were both silent for a moment, then Griffin put a hand out but didn't touch me.

"Violet?"

I stepped back, glancing at him briefly. "I know," I said, turning to go in the opposite direction. "I have to go meet Spence," I said over my shoulder and then took off at a run.

Yeah, I ran. But with purpose.

It looked like Dad wasn't the only one who wanted me under lock and key.

Spence opened the door with the PlayStation controller in hand. "Where's the fire?" he asked, standing aside as I barged in.

I saw Lincoln coming out of his room and the feelings that stirred whenever he was near ignited, almost making me drop to my knees. It just amplified everything and I made a point of ignoring him, despite my body's screaming cravings, and beelined straight for the sparring area set up at the back of the warehouse.

"We have to train." I pulled off my sweater, kicked off my shoes, and started to stretch.

"Eden, chill. What's the rush? It's Saturday."

But I couldn't *chill*; nothing about anything happening in my life inspired an inclination to *chill*. I stood on the mats, hands on hips, and stared at Spence. Whatever he saw in me, it worked.

He put down the game controller and pulled off his shoes.

"Come to think of it, I was actually hankering for a pounding just before you arrived."

Out of the corner of my eye, I saw Lincoln move into the kitchen area. He didn't say anything and made himself busy, moving things around, but I knew he was watching.

Fine by me.

Two hours later, Spence was facedown on the mat again and I was dripping in sweat.

Griffin had arrived about twenty minutes after we'd started sparring and had insisted on acting as umpire.

"That's enough for today," he said.

Spence moaned and sat up. "Ah, ya think?" Then he lay back down, flat on his back.

"No, I'm not tired." I needed to do more. I needed to be stronger. I *needed* to be ready because it felt like there was no one I didn't have to fight in some way.

Lincoln was sitting on the couch and I saw him look over. He'd been silent the entire time. Occupying himself with things and never focusing on the session, but I had felt his eyes nonetheless.

"I'm wasted, Eden. Go hit a wall or something. I'm taking a shower." Spence crawled away on all fours to the bathroom.

Griffin laughed lightly. "You really are getting stronger," he said to me.

"No!" I snapped. "It's not enough! I've seen him fight. I've seen how fast he is. I've seen…" I dropped my head and put my hands on my hips, digging fingernails into my flesh, trying to hold back the scream that was clawing its way through me.

No one understands. I can't be responsible for any more.

Griffin stood up and I didn't look at him until he was standing opposite me. He'd taken off his sweater. And his shoes.

He didn't say anything, but his right hand went out with lightning speed, straight at my face. I dodged and hit him in his gut.

For the first time, as we danced around on the mats, Griffin and I sparred and I managed to take him down. He exposed my weaknesses—my tendency to go for the kick—and I worked out that he preferred distance rather than close-range fighting. But for every time I took him down, he took me down three more.

I was faster than he was and there wasn't much difference in our strength, but he was simply better, and I started to get frustrated.

"You've done enough for today," Griffin said.

Spence was back on the couch, showered, changed, and engrossed in his game again, but he paused long enough to yell out, "Girl's on a mission!"

I glared at him, but he just gave me a cheesy grin.

"Again."

Griffin shrugged and struck out. I dodged, but as I did, he leapt into the air and right over the top of me. I swung around to try and take him out by the legs but was too slow. He planted the exact same move on me before I had a chance to readjust my footing. I fell, then jumped back to my feet and fake swung at him with my left arm before hitting him with a jab from my right.

Griffin was calm, and though he moved slower than me, he kept taking me out—kicking me in my left side, then hitting me across the face without even changing position, while I was still looking for a way through. It was like he had eight arms, didn't move, and yet was never where I aimed.

I lashed out with my foot and made contact. Griffin kicked me square in the chest in return.

"For Christ's sake, stop wasting all your energy!" Lincoln yelled.

My head snapped up and over to him. He'd moved in closer when I hadn't been paying attention, and was now standing on the sideline, arms crossed, looking aggravated.

"Your arms are everywhere. You're flailing all about. If you insist on fighting, fight properly!"

Lincoln hadn't just been *watching* for the last three hours; he'd been judging me. Picking apart everything I'd been doing.

I felt desperate, but the anger was stronger and forced everything else aside. I couldn't do it. I'd felt him watching and that was bad enough, knowing he thought I'd been doing everything wrong.

It's too much.

The part of myself I'd been trying desperately to ignore, the part that was broken and constantly bleeding—that was always worse when he was near—exploded.

"Violet. You're doing great. Amazing, even. You can't expect to be perfect all the time," Griffin said, trying to baby-sit me.

I bit down on the inside of my cheek and swallowed the lump in my throat. I walked over to the side of the mat and put on my shoes, not bothering with my sweater, and headed for the door.

"Where are you going?" Griffin asked.

"For a run," I said, letting myself out and not quite managing to restrain myself from slamming the door behind me.

Who does he think he is, anyway?

I picked up the pace until I was running faster than humanly possible. I gave a sorry attempt at looking around. No one was watching me or yelling, "There goes the bionic woman."

Because no one cares. And why should I? Why does it have to be me *who chases angels who abandon their realm? Why do* I *have to give up everything? Everyone!*

And then more thoughts started tumbling, the ones that hurt the most. I heaved for air as my throat tightened.

Why is it so easy for him? How can he just go on the way he does? Why isn't he screaming or losing it like me?

It was unfair. I wanted to see him break down, damn it.

I kept running until I hit a small people-free park. I ran to the center and dropped to my knees, panting. Not because I was tired, which I was, but because my throat had closed so tight, I wheezed with every breath. I needed to escape.

But I can't escape from myself!

I dug my hands into the grass, my fingers strong, sliding into the dirt as I grabbed tight fistfuls of earth and tried to reel myself in, gain control. I ended up just throwing the soil and starting again, digging small holes until I was surrounded by a trench. My breathing got tighter and tighter and, when I couldn't force them back anymore, the tears started to fall. Soon my trench would be a moat.

The worst part was I could deal with all of it—the fighting, the risk, the pain, the responsibility, the sacrifices. All but one thing.

Why can't I just be with him?

Everything would be okay if I had him. If we could be what we were supposed to be, if I could let my soul open to him the way it yearned for me to do.

The vision of Rudyard's lifeless body forced its way into my mind. Then the sound of Nyla's final scream, her soul shattering. Forever lost.

I imagined what such a loss would feel like. It helped calm me a bit, the thought of how terrible I'd feel should Lincoln witness and then have to endure my death.

Not that I would actually see it. I'd be dead.

But he would be like Nyla. Forever trapped.

Lincoln thought the opposite. I knew when he saw these images, it was him who was dead and the sound of my scream that haunted him. Just like in Jordan, he would dive in front of any attacker to save me. But I also knew that Phoenix had a weapon Lincoln could not shield me from.

I felt him approaching, slowly moving in on me. He must've run to have caught up with me so fast. I closed my eyes tight, digging my fingers into the soil again, so hard my knuckles burned against the small embedded stones.

He stood silently behind me. He didn't touch me; he just waited while I cried.

It took me awhile to pull myself together, and when I turned to face him, the sun was beginning to lose what little warmth it had been giving. By then, he was sitting on the ground, looking out over the field.

"How many hours a day are you training?" he asked eventually.

"I...I don't know."

"I was right about your fighting. You're all over the place. You can't do this, Violet, not when you're so busy fighting yourself. You need to focus on beating your opponent. The only way you'll do that is if you rest, eat, and find the right mind space."

I grabbed a handful of dirt and threw it in front of me. "It's not that easy. Not everyone is like you."

His head snapped up then he shook it sadly. "You think this is easy for me?" He took a deep breath. "If you want to be better, you'll listen to me and do as I tell you."

Lincoln stood up. "Come on," he said.

I thought he wanted to drag me back to his place or take me home, but when I looked up, he raised his eyebrows, challenging me.

I wanted to keep digging my trench to somewhere else, somewhere happier, but I stood up and dusted off my hands.

"Stand still," he said. "Only move to strike. Take your time, watch me carefully, and when you move, move fast and with all of your power."

It sounds simple enough, but it's not. I like to move around and try and manipulate the fight. This went against my natural instincts.

Lincoln stood in front of me, arms loose by his side. I mirrored his pose, trying to keep myself still.

"Breathe," he said.

When he took a few steps to my right, I didn't follow. When he came back to my left, I stood still. He moved a few paces back to my right, close to my side and then, from the corner of my eye, I saw his hand flinch.

My arm went out so fast it caught his in midflight and my other hand, fisted tight, did not hesitate to go straight into his now-open body.

Lincoln stumbled back a few steps. "Good," he said, straightening. "Again."

I nodded and kept my position as he moved in on me.

He struck out at me occasionally from different directions. Each time, I managed to block him and get in a few more hits. But I grew impatient and moved from my position to try to finish him off. That's when he caught me off-balance and spun me into a death grip.

With my back against his body, we were the closest we'd been in weeks. He'd beaten me, but suddenly all I could focus on was his chest moving up and down against my back, mirroring my own. I couldn't stop exhaling with the relief that came from having him near me. It was as if my entire being, body, spirit, *soul,* needed him.

Lincoln rested his chin on the top of my head and we stayed like that for a moment, until he squeezed me and whispered, "I know."

He released his hold on me and we stepped away from each other.

"We should go," Lincoln said. "You'll miss your curfew."

"You don't trust me," I said. I didn't blame him. Right then, it took everything I had not to throw myself back into his arms and beg him to commit himself to an eternity of suffering just for me.

He backed up a few steps and closed his eyes briefly. "It's not you I don't trust."

chapter sixteen

"You hope for light, but he will turn it to thick darkness and change it to deep gloom."

Jeremiah 13:16

Over the next three days, I found a better stride. Partly because of Lincoln's words and partly because being grounded meant I wasn't out hunting every night. Instead, I brought out my paints for the first time in a while and realized just how much I'd been missing my art.

Dad, probably out of guilt, had bought me a new set of paintbrushes and left them in my studio. The strange thing was, everything I painted in some way seemed to reflect the image of a rainbow. It wasn't until I'd finished three canvases and stood in front of them that I noticed the unnerving pattern.

Griffin was right. There was still so much we didn't understand about my abilities. Exiles called me a rainbow, but what did that mean? The Rainbow represented a link between the realms. But what that meant for me was still a mystery, and I wasn't too keen on turning into some magical arch after a rainstorm.

I'd been doing as Lincoln said and, for the last couple of nights, even managing to get a few hours' sleep. I was eating meals and still training hard, but resting when needed. I could already feel the difference. My mind was clearer and I felt stronger in every way.

It was Wednesday and weekdays were proving difficult since I was supposed to be home straight after school, but I'd managed a couple of quick drop-ins to Hades on my way back with Steph to get more research supplies and check on Dapper...and Onyx.

Griffin still had Grigori posted at Hades around the clock. Officially, it was for security. Unofficially, it was to keep an eye on Onyx. So far, no trouble had been spotted, but Onyx had pulled me aside and told me he wanted to talk to me. I'd promised to return in the morning, which meant tomorrow I was going to have to break the rules of my grounding and skip school.

Yeah, well, "for the greater good" and all that.

Steph had been spending some afternoons, like today, at my place, and some working on the translation with Dapper, who seemed more willing than ever to share his expertise. I'd given up trying to help—Steph didn't come over for my code-breaking prowess; she just liked working on it from my home instead of her own. From what I could gather, she hadn't had a conversation with her mother in days, and the last she heard from her father, he'd had no immediate plans to come home. Steph had been working on the Scripture code constantly, trying to decipher what it all meant.

After giving up on my canvas, I returned to my bedroom where Steph was sprawled out on the floor. I could tell by the dark circles under her eyes and the fact she was drinking almost as much coffee as me that she hadn't been getting much sleep lately.

"Have you been in touch with Salvatore?" I asked from the doorway.

"A couple of days ago. Last thing I heard, he and Zoe were concocting some crazy plan." She threw down her pen. "He'll probably never come back."

I scooted down beside her and pulled her in for a hug. "Yes he will. And if he can't find a way to get here, we will." And I meant it wholeheartedly. Right now, my only opinion about the Academy was, *Screw their stupid rules!*

Steph hugged me tight, then pulled away and picked up her pen and empty mug.

"Coffee?" she asked, smiling. "I'm on the verge of getting this, I swear."

I rolled my eyes and snatched the cup. If anyone was on the verge of a breakthrough, it was Steph, but she'd been pulling that line on me for days, and I was sick of being her waiter.

On my way to the kitchen, there was a knock at the door. I opened it to find Jase leaning casually against the frame. He was dressed in jeans and a blue, patterned shirt. He definitely had the relaxed-DJ look going for him. Normal height, just a little taller than me, and a fortunate build so that even though I knew he didn't work out, he didn't look weedy. His best feature was his hair—the same pale blond as Steph's—and with his blue eyes and darker brows, it was striking.

"Hey, Jase," I said, smiling.

"Hi. Is Steph ready?"

I shook my head. "She's just in the middle of something. She asked me for coffee. Are you in a rush?" If Steph was really on the verge of that breakthrough, I wanted to give her a few more minutes.

Jase shrugged and stepped into the apartment. "I've got some time. If you're making me coffee too, that is." He flashed an easy-going smile back in my direction, headed straight for the kitchen, and took a seat at the bar. "So, how's school going?"

I started making the drinks.

"Good. Almost finished. Last exams next month and then I've got the Fenton course."

"That Fenton course is pretty exclusive from what I hear—you must be good."

I shrugged self-consciously.

"I guess you'll be glad to be finished with school. What's the plan after? College?"

His question completely stumped me. I'd stopped thinking about my future. Even when Dad had started harping on about it the other day, I'd just blanked on it. Jase must have seen the look on my face.

"Hey, don't stress. It's not a trick question. A lot of people take some time after school to figure out what they want to do."

"Is that what you're doing?"

"Maybe," he said, smiling again.

He didn't say any more as I finished making the coffee. I

passed him a latte, hoping that he liked his coffee with milk. He took a sip.

"So, Steph mentioned your dance is coming up next month."

"Yeah." I wasn't planning on going.

"She's still pining over that guy who was visiting a couple of months back. Some exchange student or something..."

Obviously her cover story to explain who Salvatore was. I nodded along.

"Anyway"—he took another sip—"I think it'd be a shame if she didn't go to the dance. You know what she's like. Only regret it, probably."

"Probably."

Steph had been dreaming about our prom for as long as I'd known her. The girl had about four dresses on hold for the event.

"So I was thinking, how about the three of us go together?" Jase suggested, his eyes darting away. "Unless you're already going with someone else."

Ah...

Why did I feel like he was asking me for more than just a helping hand with Steph? I meant to reply, open my mouth, and spit out words of some sort, but I couldn't think of one thing to say.

"Are you?" Jase asked.

Ah...

"Huh?" I finally responded, trying for confused in order to buy some time.

"Going with someone else?" Jase repeated.

"Oh."

Ah...

"No. I mean, I...I wasn't going to go." I looked back down and grabbed Steph's coffee. "I should..." I shuffled toward the hall and pointed to my bedroom. "I'll just...give this to Steph."

I went to my room and darted in, quickly closing the door behind me. "Steph!" I whispered urgently. "I think your brother just asked me to the dance!"

Steph was staring at a piece of paper.

"Steph! Help!" I said again, trying not to raise my voice. "This is serious!"

She looked up at me and I almost dropped the cup of coffee when I saw her face.

"I've done it, Vi." She held up the paper.

Suddenly, nothing else mattered. I put down the mug on my desk and sat beside Steph. "Is it another poem?"

She shook her head. "Not sure."

I took the piece of paper from her and read it.

At the southernmost point, an island hides the gate,
What once was of Atlas and also Kalliste,
The opening brews what will never cease.
Three to the water to entice the current,
Three to the fire to blast open their fate.
Three at the hand of the highest command,
Three at the hand of the heart of man.

Six to the ground, in return for one.
An offering of pain starts the rivers of fire,
And water stands high to cradle the course.
One can be beckoned,
When payment is made.
The Obolus red and blade,
At the hand of the admirer,
With only terrible desire.

"This can't be good."

Steph looked grave. "Well, we knew it wasn't the Scripture of Happiness."

We both sat there on the floor, staring at the prophecy that we didn't understand, until there was a knock at the door.

"Steph, if you need that ride home, we've got to go. I have work in an hour." Jase sounded a little unsure calling out from the hall.

"Oh no," I said, dropping my head into my hands.

Steph stood up. "Trust me, babe. You've got bigger problems. Just tell him we'll all go to the dance together, and if you're actually alive by the time the dance comes around, we'll deal with it then."

"Steph!"

"Just keeping it real."

Things definitely weren't looking good and Steph's remark was completely true, not to mention dire. But she stood by the door, one hand on her hip, and something in me clicked. Steph must have felt the same way or seen my eyes light up because, simultaneously, we both cracked up.

I'm not altogether sure if we were laughing or crying—both, maybe—but by the time we came up for air, we were gripping our stomachs, me on the ground and Steph half collapsed against the wall.

Jase knocked again. "Should I ask if someone's dying in there?"

Steph opened the door while we were still slipping into aftershock bouts of laughter.

"Sorry. It's just…Violet can be such a comedian."

Jase looked at me and put his hands in his pockets. *Damn.* He thought I'd been laughing at him.

"I…I hope you have a tux to wear," I said awkwardly.

Jase relaxed a little and reapplied his easy smile. "Naturally."

He was Steph's brother and a Morris, after all. Formal events were standard procedure in his world.

"So…" Steph said, sobered now too, "what did you want to do about this?" She held the translation up in the air.

"I'll take it with me tomorrow," I said, not elaborating. Steph knew I was skipping school and I didn't want to have to explain to Jase.

She gave me a pointed look. "I'll meet you in the morning then."

I wanted to argue—she hated missing school—but with Jase standing there, clearly knowing we were purposefully talking in code, there was little I could do.

I smiled uncomfortably. "Okay I'll see you then."

After I said good-bye to Jase and Steph, I collapsed on the couch. An hour or so later, my eyes were bleary. I'd read and reread the Scripture hundreds of times and could make little sense of it.

By the time I heard the front door and Dad quietly make his way through the apartment, it was late. No doubt he had a deadline looming.

"I thought you'd be asleep," he said, startled to see me still up, sitting in the silent living room. He made his way to the coffee machine, firing it up.

I shrugged.

"Nothing on TV?"

"Nah." I couldn't remember the last time I'd just sat and watched TV.

Dad took a deep breath and moved over to sit opposite me on the coffee table. "I know this grounding stuff is new."

My focus fixated on my hands, intertwining my fingers and hoping Dad wasn't going to try and have some kind of deep-and-meaningful with me.

"What's this?"

I looked up. He was holding the prophecy in his hand, reading it.

"Oh. That's nothing. Just…just an assignment for English."

"Hmm." He kept reading and I sat up straighter, fighting the urge to rip it from his hands.

"Dad, can I have it back?"

"Hmm," he said again, still studying the text. "Who wrote this?"

"I…I'm not sure, can't remember."

"I'm surprised they have you studying something like this at a Catholic school." Dad's brow furrowed as he seemed to absorb the words with something that resembled…understanding.

I tucked a few strands of hair behind my ear and tried for nonchalance. "Do you…know what it means?"

Dad smirked. "Are you trying to get me to do your homework?"

I played along with my own sheepish smile. "Poetry is not my strongest point."

"Your mother hated poetry." His smile deepened. "But I always enjoyed it. Let me see." He looked at the words again.

I crossed my fingers under the blanket I'd wrapped myself in.

"Okay…" he said eventually. "'At the southernmost point, an island hides the gate, / What once was of Atlas and also Kalliste.' This is a location, setting the scene. If you research the word Kalliste, you might find something there."

I nodded him on.

"'The opening brews what will never cease.' Things that never cease are the things that are fundamental to existence. You know—nature, life, death, good, and evil. It would be something like that, but 'brew' as a word is not usually a positive so I would guess the thing is not nice."

"Yeah, that makes sense," I responded, and then covered the remark with a light smile.

"'Three to the water to entice the current, / Three to the fire to blast open their fate, / Three at the hand of the highest command, / Three at the hand of the heart of man, / Six to the ground, in return for one.' This is about sacrifices to elements. It's almost like instructions. And then these parts—'the highest command' and 'the heart of man' describe who will make the sacrifices. I'm not sure, but 'of the heart of man' would imply something to do with love or perhaps…hate."

I nodded while biting hard on the inside of my cheek.

"'An offering of pain starts the rivers of fire.' This is about the emotion of the moment, the investments that will be made. 'And water stands high to cradle the course'—I'm not sure, but in history, water has always been the way for travel between worlds or lives. Water is like a passageway, so maybe it has something to do with change. Sweetheart, this is not a Catholic-school poem," he said, starting to look more suspicious. "Are you sure you've been asked to study this?"

"Yeah, we had to pick from a selection. Maybe I picked a bad one."

"Not bad…but definitely disturbing." He cleared his throat. "Okay, let's see. 'One can be beckoned, / When payment is made. / The Obolus red and blade, / At the hand of the admirer, / With only terrible desire.' This is talking about calling someone and a payment to be made by the admirer. Red…well, I'm sure you can guess that's some kind of blood offering, and the last line implies the admirer can have *only* bad intentions. It's almost as if…" He looked at me carefully and I held his stare as calmly as I could. "If I had to guess, I would say this poem is about invoking some kind of…evil."

I could feel the color drain from my face. I wanted to throw myself in Dad's arms and tell him everything. But at that moment, more than any other, I was also sure he *couldn't* know. I forced myself to breathe. I ran a hand over my face and yawned.

"Wow. Heavy." I stretched. "Maybe I'll choose a different poem." I stood up, trying to ignore my legs shaking under me. "Thanks anyway, Dad. I think I'll go to bed."

I felt Dad watching me as I walked toward my room.

I closed my door behind me, knowing there was no chance I would get any sleep tonight.

chapter seventeen

> *"This I will declare and point out to you, that he who created you will destroy you."*
>
> Book of Enoch 93:9

Wrapped in my long, black coat, which I'd buttoned up to conceal my lack of school uniform, I walked down the street from my apartment and around the corner before putting on my beanie, waiting five minutes, and then doubling back to head in the opposite direction. Dad was so unpredictable at the moment, I couldn't rule out him spying from the balcony and I really couldn't have him try and stop me from going to Hades.

I'd texted the translation through to Griffin and Lincoln during the night. It took about five messages for me to get all of the words to them and I hoped they'd managed to piece everything together.

They'd both texted back to tell me they would see me at Hades, and when I pushed open the heavy yellow entrance door, I found everyone already there, sitting around a few tables that had been pushed together in the center of the closed restaurant.

Dapper was passing around juice and there was a tray of cups and French press on the center of the table.

Spence threw me a croissant as I got close. "Hey, managed your escape from Fort Eden, I see."

I smiled. I'd been tough on Spence lately, mostly in training, but he never wavered; he was always the same. I went straight up to him and gave him a big hug.

"Ah, Eden," he squirmed. "I thought I'd made my position clear on this." He held me back at arm's length, smiling devilishly. "I just don't feel the same way," he said loudly and then feigned a "sorry" smile for me.

"And I was really holding out hope," I said, playing along.

"Most do," Spence said, shaking his head solemnly. "Most do."

I whacked him on the arm and took a seat beside him while Kaitlin threw half of her croissant across the table, landing it right on Spence's forehead and making us both laugh. Steph was standing to the side with Dapper, both speaking animatedly and over the top of one another. I got the feeling it was going to be a long day, so I poured a coffee and took a bite of my croissant while I cased out who else had been invited to the we're-all-going-to-die powwow.

Lincoln and Griffin sat at the far end of the table—of course I'd known exactly where he was from the moment I'd entered the building. Griffin gave me a look that translated to: *You should be sitting up at this end of the table.* I looked around my end—Spence next to me, a seat spare for Steph on my other side. Onyx had made himself comfortable a couple of chairs down, and I spotted him emptying something from a silver bottle into his coffee.

Typical.

The bruises on his face were almost completely healed. He had recovered at an impossible rate, not unlike Steph. I stared at him until he looked up and sneered at me.

Beth and Archer sat at the middle of the table, chatting to each other. I imagined they had seen a lot in their five hundred years. Today was just another day at the office for them.

I turned my attention back to the far end. Lincoln was beside Griffin. When I looked, he also glanced at me. We smiled at each other, just like any other friends would, but we both quickly looked away again. I was left breathless, as always.

Dapper was heading in the heavy-hitter direction and took the seat beside Griffin. Samuel and Kaitlin were next to Dapper and another pair of Grigori, Nathan and Becca, sat opposite. I'd only met them in passing. They worked on the outskirts of the city. Griffin had told me they were like border control, and from everything he didn't say, I had assumed it was a hands-on kind of job. They were young—about the same age as Lincoln—and I knew Griffin regarded them highly as warriors. He had told me before that if it came to a fight, we wanted to have them with us. The simple fact they were there spoke volumes.

That was it—everyone who had been invited to the insiders'

meeting. The most surprising attendee was definitely Onyx. I wondered what he'd done or said to get himself on the VIP list.

All in all, I was happy I'd chosen this end of the table—sitting between Spence and Steph was much easier than sitting between Griffin and Lincoln.

"You okay?" Spence asked, breaking into my thoughts.

I looked down. I was bent over in pain I'd been refusing to acknowledge, my arm wrapped around my waist.

"Um…" Was I? "Yeah, just not feeling great." I dropped my arm and sat up.

"Bad time of the month?"

"No!" I said, not bothering to protest at his jab while I tried to figure out exactly what the throbbing ache was.

Griffin started passing around sheets of paper, copies of the prophecy. I took one, even though I had the original folded in my pocket, and straightened myself out.

"Death in verse," Spence whispered in my ear as he waggled his eyebrows.

But despite Steph and I breaking into laughter the day before, now that I understood more of the content, I couldn't muster a smile and instead felt the blood draining from my face.

"Let's start from the bottom, people," Griffin said. Then he turned to Dapper and gave him a nod.

Dapper moved forward on his chair and pulled out a pair of spectacles. I was fascinated by how different they made him look. Dapper is a nightclub owner, not exactly slender, and his mannerisms are not delicate in any way. But with those diamante-studded frames, I was quite sure this was a side to Dapper he showed very rarely indeed.

"Right. Here's what we can decipher. Phoenix is the admirer with the terrible desire. There is no real hidden meaning in that. The Obolus is traditionally a silver coin that used to be placed on the eyes of the dead as payment to the ferryman for passage to the next world or afterlife. Phoenix will have to make a payment, probably silver, and 'red' I would assume is a blood-offering."

The explanation closely followed Dad's.

"Whose blood?" Spence called out.

"We're not sure. Griffin believes it will be Phoenix's own, but it could be another's. Once the payment is made, the one who is beckoned"—he raised his eyes to the table—"Lilith, in this case, will be released from Tartarus."

"Which is Hell?" Spence called out again.

"Yes," Griffin said, shooting him a "shut up" look.

Dapper studied the paper some more and pointed to it. "Then we have the verse above. This is about sacrifice."

I thought back to Dad's words. He really knew how to break down a poem.

"Six must be killed to bring her back. And this is where it gets difficult, but I believe three of a like kind, therefore exiles, must be returned in water and another three in fire, and"—he looked down and then back up, as if mustering bravery—"I cannot see a way for any of this to come to fruition if it is not at the hand of a Grigori."

Everyone bar Onyx looked stunned. Even Griffin, who I was sure had already heard this theory or even suggested it, was silent.

It was Steph who cleared her throat meekly and started to speak. "Exiles can kill other exiles but the only guaranteed return of an exile that could count as an offering to Tartarus must be made by a Grigori blade."

"Well, no Grigori is about to let that happen," Spence said.

But I never thought I would hand over the Exile Scripture to Phoenix.

Not until I did.

Griffin stood up. "There is still a lot that is unclear but we do have some time. Thanks to Stephanie, we have a translation that Phoenix would not have been able to interpret yet. And thanks to Onyx"—he glanced toward him and then quickly to me—"we have a location."

"You know where Kalliste is?" I asked, looking at Onyx.

Was that what he'd wanted to talk to me about today?

Onyx took a gulp of his "coffee," barely acknowledging my question.

"I want to come with you. I'll give you my knowledge and"—he looked at Griffin then me, smugly—"my word that I will share it only with you. Unless, of course, it is physically beaten out of me, in which case I will tell whoever has the fastest fist." He sat back, typical Onyx, smiling and waiting for us to give in to his demands.

"Why would you want to come with us?" Lincoln asked.

"I have my reasons. They are unrelated and do not concern you."

"Tell us about the location," Griffin said. Whatever Griffin had read in Onyx's request obviously hadn't worried him too much. Lincoln looked like he wanted to protest, but Griffin shut him down: "We have no other choice. We need that location."

Onyx gloated, leaning back and slinging an arm over the back of his chair, but I didn't miss the moment of relief he hadn't been able to hide. He moved into a dramatic presentation, relaxing his shoulders and stalling. I could tell he particularly enjoyed that he'd ruffled the usually impenetrable Lincoln. Onyx was one of the only people who seemed to irritate Lincoln. History does that.

"The first part of the poem almost told me, alone. There have been many stories over the years about...gateways. 'What once was of Atlas and also Kalliste.' Plato was one of the only humans to work it out—a city that was so great, it would've conquered the world. It was well before my time on earth, though I watched it from a different point of view. Maybe 10,000 BC. Of course, it is long gone now, somewhere at the bottom of the ocean perhaps, and what is left behind, a mere gravestone. An island that once held the name Kalliste—*the most beautiful.* What remains of it surrounds an opening to Hell, always waiting, never truly sleeping."

"Where?" Griffin asked evenly.

"It appears we will be taking a journey to the Cyclades Islands."

"Greece?" Steph asked. She paused, as if visualizing a map, which she probably was, before her head shot up. "Santorini! The most southern island. That's where the gateway is." And then, as if another thought sideswiped her, she blinked and paled. "Thera..." she breathed.

I looked around the table and a few other faces started to blanch too.

"What?" I responded. "What does that mean?"

Griffin swallowed. "The island of Santorini used to be known as Thera as well. It was an entire civilization built on top of an island, which was also…a volcano. In around 1650 BC, it erupted."

"Closer to 1630 BC," Onyx corrected. I had a feeling he'd been around for that one.

"The blast was so enormous, a great deal of the island sunk into the ocean and what is left now is just the outer rim. Some people believe it caused the destruction of the entire Minoan civilization on the neighboring island of Crete. And some," Griffin looked at Onyx as he finished, "believe that Thera was the home of the lost city of Atlantis."

"So the volcano sank?" Spence asked.

Lincoln stood up and moved away from the table as if he needed to do something. He stopped near the bar, still within hearing distance but facing away.

"Yes, it did," Onyx said, "but Hell does not stay down for long—it has been rising out of the water ever since. And that volcano is still very much alive."

"How did the volcano destroy people on another island?" Becca asked. "Even a huge blast couldn't send lava that distance."

"Tsunami," Steph said. Just one terrifying word.

"Can't fight that," Becca said, slumping back down.

"Yeah, 'cause a volcano on its own was going to be a piece of cake," Spence said.

I pulled out the first poem that Steph had translated. "'Ash will fall as fire will rain.' They're going to make the volcano erupt, aren't they? The volcano is the gate."

No one answered. No one needed to. Even Onyx was silent.

Dapper started cleaning, clearing away plates and cups. It was what he did when things were bad. The rest of us just sat there in shock.

Lincoln eventually rejoined the table. "When do we leave?"

Griffin took a moment to respond, deep in thought.

"Tonight."

I looked over at Steph.

She raised her eyebrows. "Don't even! I'm coming this time." She folded her arms.

"It's too dangerous."

"I'm sorry, Violet, but Stephanie is a part of this fight now. She has proved her value and there are still parts of the Scripture to be translated. There are some symbols she might be able to help decipher. If she is willing, and agrees to stay clear of the line of fire and follow instructions, she will be coming."

"What about school?" I asked, wishing once again I had never brought her into this world. How could Griffin do this? She had already been kidnapped once.

"We both know *I* can afford some time off school. And anyway, Vi, this is bigger than that stuff. It's not only important to you to stop him."

She was right, but… "I can't defend you."

"I never asked you to, and anyway, I have no intention of putting myself on the front line. How about you just do your thing and let me do mine?"

I could see nothing I said would change anything, and I could also see Griffin had no intention of letting me make her stay behind.

"I'll go too. We'll work on the Scripture together and stay out of the fight," Dapper said, taking off his glasses. His eyes locked with mine and he gave me the smallest nod, a promise. He would keep her safe. I nodded back—I'd hold him to it.

"Nine p.m. at the airport. Beth and Archer will stay behind and run the city," Griffin continued.

They both nodded.

"The rest of you are expected on that plane. It will be chartered, so bring your passports," Griffin said, putting his files away and digging into his bag.

I was about to speak up, explain I didn't even have a passport—I hadn't needed one for Jordan since we'd been smuggled in—when he pulled something out of his bag and slid it across the table till it stopped in front of me.

I picked it up—a passport and other forms of identification, including a credit card.

"Is this stuff legit?" I asked, looking at a picture of me I didn't remember having had taken.

"Yes." He smiled. "And no. It's standard documentation for all Grigori. We have it so we cannot be traced by government authorities. No one can ever track you if you are using these documents. Don't bring anything other than these and you'll be fine."

"The credit card?" I questioned, flashing Steph a quick smile.

"For emergencies," he said, giving me a don't-even-think-about-it look much better than anything Dad had ever delivered.

I slipped it all in my backpack just as Onyx cleared his throat.

"Yes, Onyx. I'll have documentation for you at the airport," Griffin said.

Onyx smiled broadly.

"Nine p.m., people," Griffin repeated before gesturing to Beth and Archer to follow him. There would be a lot they would have to go over before Griffin left the city in their hands.

Onyx slipped out of his seat and headed straight for the bar. "Keys!" he called out, when he stopped in front of the pull-down cage encasing all of the alcohol.

"Forget it," Dapper said, now wiping down the table.

"Oh, Dapper, *really*? Tell me you wouldn't like a large glass of something mind-numbing after discovering that Hell is about to play peekaboo via the most destructive volcano on the planet?"

Dapper kept wiping the table.

"Keys!" Onyx bellowed.

Sighing, Dapper tossed them through the air. Onyx caught them in one and had the cage open in moments.

Steph got up and started toward the door.

"Where are you going?" I asked, standing too.

"School. I'll get there for the last couple of classes, pick up the work for the next week or two, just in case, and tell them I'm going on one of Dad's business trips. I'll get your work too—unless, of course, you want to come with me."

I shrugged.

"Didn't think so." She hugged me tighter than usual. "I'll be outside your place at eight in a taxi."

I wanted to argue, to try and convince her to stay, but it was useless. "Okay," I sighed.

She squeezed me one more time and then took off via Spence. Whatever she said to him made him fall into hysterics.

Must have offered to get his schoolwork too.

I was vaguely aware of people starting to file out, but I sat back down at the table. I couldn't move yet.

How can Phoenix do this?

I'd seen a side to him that I was sure could never be capable of what he was now doing.

Is there any part of him that feels anything anymore? Maybe if I try to speak to him, find a way to reach him...

"Whatever you're thinking, stop."

I jolted from my mind-spiral and looked up. Lincoln was standing on the opposite side of the table. From the look on his face, he'd been watching me for a while and I'd been so lost in thought, I hadn't even felt him move closer

"This is all because of me. If I hadn't become involved with him in the first place...This is all because I couldn't love him." Something painful rippled over Lincoln's face and his hands fisted as if he needed to restrain them—as if he wanted to reach out to me. I felt the surge of his power, the flow of honey lifting from him and enveloping me.

Why is he using his power around me?

"The best thing we can do is stop him, but, Vi...I think you should consider not coming."

"Are you *deficient*? You think I'm going to let everyone else go there, even *Steph*, to fight the battle that's my fault?"

I shook my head in disbelief. Even knowing what was ahead—that I would have to deal with Dad first—not going was absolutely *not* an option.

"If you think that's ever going to happen, you don't know me at all."

"I don't think it's *going* to happen. But I do think you should consider it."

I stood up and laid my hands flat on the table to deliver him a fierce stare. "Well, it's been considered."

I grabbed my bag and stormed out before Lincoln had a chance to say another word.

chapter eighteen

"Two qualities are indispensable: first, an intellect that, even in the darkest hour, retains some glimmerings of the inner light which leads to truth; and second, the courage to follow this faint light wherever it may lead."

Carl Von Clausewitz

It was a bleak, drizzly day and the sun didn't seem to be offering any help. I shoved my hands into my coat pockets as I started to walk away. I didn't want to stop, just in case Lincoln decided to follow me. It was getting harder all the time. Just being around him caused reactions I couldn't control. From the moment I'd sat down in Hades this morning, something had twisted, wringing me from the inside out, and it had burned like dry ice. Now that I was away from him—all I felt was the lonely, trembling chill left behind.

I pulled my coat tightly around my waist and tugged on my beanie. I was so caught up in wondering how we were going to survive this trip—both the battle and the nearness—that I didn't notice Onyx until I was almost on top of him.

I stopped in my tracks. He didn't activate my senses in the same way as other exiles or cause that familiar buzz I felt when other Grigori were nearby. He felt like a memory, invoking the instinct to look over my shoulder—but more.

"What do you want?"

He pulled out from the shadows of the back doorway to Hades.

"My, my, we're touchy. I told you we needed to talk."

"What now?"

"Santorini is a small island—not like the city. It's not like anywhere else."

"What does that mean?"

He shrugged. "You'll soon find out."

"Forget it, I'm not interested in playing your games," I said, starting to walk away, still feeling empty and cold.

"You have to decide!" he called after me.

I stopped and turned back to him. The look on his face was almost genuine.

"The only person who will ever get close enough to him to make a strike is you. Lincoln has the capability, but we both know he will always hesitate..." His confident look morphed into one of fear. "She is...Trust me, Lilith is the epitome of evil. She will annihilate everything and everyone in her path. She was always demented, but after the time she has been...*where* she's been...she will have no intention other than destruction."

"As opposed to you!" I sniped.

"Oh, believe me, Rainbow—I had vision, right or wrong. But anything I have ever done will be a mere breeze in comparison to the hurricane she will unleash."

My breath was smoky in the cold air as it left my shaking body. "What are you saying?"

"She will be impossible to stop, possibly immune to our blades. The only chance we have is to kill Phoenix before he opens the gates and you're the only one who can do it."

Once again—great to be special.

"Why are you telling me this?" I snapped.

"Because…no one else is going to."

I bit my lip, absorbing his words, which seemed to provoke a small smile, or maybe it was a grimace, from him. He turned and walked into Hades, locking the door behind him.

I don't know how long I stood there, but it was long enough for the coldness in my body to turn to numbness.

It wasn't like I hadn't thought it myself—when Phoenix had taken Steph, I had had to accept it might be my only option. But Onyx, with his newfound need for self-preservation, was the first to say it aloud and somehow that made it different, more real.

The truth was—I didn't want to die.

But that doesn't mean I won't.

No wonder Lincoln wanted me to stay behind.

I sat on the couch where I had been waiting for the last two hours. I'd expected Dad home right after school hours and thought we'd have time. But Steph was due to be outside in less than half an hour, and I was still waiting. I had no idea how we were going to get through this conversation. There would be no elaborate manipulation this time; there was no way to make this easier. I couldn't just lie.

My duffle bag was packed and by the door, my backpack beside me on the couch. I flipped through its contents once again. I'd done as Griffin had instructed and replaced all of my forms of identification with the ones he had given me. My wallet was now filled with a membership to a library I didn't recognize, a new student card, driver's license, and passport—all of which identified me as Violet Eden, age twenty-one.

When I tried, I could pass for nineteen, maybe twenty, but twenty-one was a push. I guess the Academy figured such precautions would make things easier for everyone.

I pulled out my mother's wooden box and tried to ignore the wave of senses that always overcame me when I touched it. I opened the now-familiar letter she had written to me seventeen years ago and wondered if I would ever be able to think of her without resentment.

Unlikely.

I picked up her wristband and felt the senses build within me like an orchestra before I dropped it again. No one knew what had happened to the other one, but I could tell Rudyard had had his suspicions before he'd…I didn't like touching the leather; it always felt wrong. Twisted. Like it was generating some kind of energy of its own, even now, all these years after she'd died.

The door clicked open and Dad walked in. Finally. He was saying good-bye to someone on his phone. From the smile in his tone, I was willing to bet it was Caroline.

I wondered if it was planned or just fortuitous that he had her now that it looked like he might lose me. Not that he knew that yet. I scrunched my hand, digging my nails into my palm to stop myself from thinking about it. The idea of angels, both light and dark, messing with my dad was more than upsetting.

"Violet!" he yelled as soon as he was off the phone. He hadn't even made it into the living room, but I could see him standing by the door, looking at my bag.

He stormed into the room.

"What's going on? And why weren't you at school today?"

I wasn't surprised the school had called—I'd made no attempt to cover up my nonattendance when I realized what was happening. I didn't get up and I didn't raise my voice. Instead, I looked at him, honesty in my eyes—and love.

"I have to go away for a few days. I've been waiting for you to get home so I could see you before I left."

"And just where do you think you're going?" he barked incredulously.

"Dad..." I stood up and wiped my hands up and down my thighs anxiously. I didn't want to hurt him like this. "I wish I could tell you everything but please trust me when I say I'm doing the right thing. I know you think I'm part of some cult or something—but I'm not. I'm a good person and I wouldn't do this to you if I didn't have to. Dad..." My throat tightened, but it was the only chance I had of helping him understand. "I'm doing what Mom asked me to do."

He stumbled back.

I glanced at my watch anxiously. "I don't have much time. Mom wasn't...she wasn't always honest with you, but I know she loved you and that you loved her. I...I don't want to lie to you like she did, so...I'm giving you this." I held out the wooden box. "It's time you read the letter she left me, and when I get home, I promise I'll try and answer your questions...if you want me to."

Dad didn't take the box. Instead, he stood, immobilized, his mouth open, eyes darting between mine and the box. "You have no right to speak about her like that," he said in a low voice.

I smiled sadly. "Actually, I have more right than anyone." I walked to the door and opened it, realizing that trying to explain everything to him like this wasn't going to work.

"You are not walking out that door!" Dad ordered, taking strides across the room to intercept me.

"This goes beyond you and me, Dad. I wish it didn't. I wish I could just be your daughter and be who you want me to be, but I...It doesn't matter what you say or what I want. One way or another, I'm going."

I reached down and picked up my bag, but Dad got there at the same time, grabbing my wrist, desperately trying to force the bag free.

"Dad, stop!" I said, trying not to resist him. "Please," I begged, "I don't want to hurt you."

He didn't let go, pulling harder, confusion at my ability to block his efforts showing in his strained expression.

"Let go of this bag!" he roared.

I heard a car horn from the street. Steph was here and I had no more time.

"Dad." I held still and looked at him. "Dad, I'm sorry."

He returned my gaze for an instant, desperation flooding his eyes.

"I love you, Dad." I pulled my arm out of his hold using a physical strength he couldn't possibly comprehend, leaving him holding only the bracelets that had covered my markings.

We both gasped, looking down at the otherworldly patterns that started to churn and swirl, reflecting different—impossible—colors and then, as if rising from beneath, outlines of the feather-tip markings that matched those on the carved box and my mother's wristband. All of it entirely inhuman.

I pulled down my sleeve in shame.

"What *are* you?" he said in a daze.

My eyes welled. "I'm your daughter, Dad, but...I'm her daughter too." I picked up my bag.

"Don't blame this on her!"

"No," I half laughed and took my bracelets from his still-suspended hand. "Of course not."

I walked through the door, snapping off the handle when I closed it, locking him inside. I got into the elevator to the sounds of Dad pounding on the door, screaming my name.

I'm sorry, Dad.

I didn't know if I would ever get the chance to make things right again.

Steph didn't talk much on the way to the airport. She could tell things hadn't gone well with Dad. I should have just lied to him. Steph clearly hadn't had any major drama getting away from her place, though it hadn't left her in the best mood either. Her mom had helped her pack.

The taxi pulled up outside the terminal. Spence was waiting for us.

He hoisted our bags under his arms.

"You're being awfully helpful," I said, attempting to shift into a better mood.

"Hey, we might be on our way to Death Island, but I've always wanted to go to Greece." He shrugged, almost dropping a bag. "And it beats another desert."

"True," I said, agreeing wholeheartedly. I never wanted to see another desert again.

My phone rang and I pulled it out of my pocket.

Home.

I pressed end and turned it off.

"Where is everyone?" Steph asked, keeping the conversation moving as she brushed a hand over my arm in silent support.

"Waiting for our plane. It just landed," Spence said, weaving through the crowds.

"Whose plane is it?" I asked, following him past the maze of people checking in.

"The Academy's," he answered, shooting me a sideways glance.

I stopped midstride. "Spence, is Josephine on the plane?"

His worried look deepened and he nodded.

Perfect. This day just keeps getting better.

I'd forgotten all about the Academy sending in their pit bull.

"Where do we check in?" Steph asked, looking around.

"We don't—private flight. We just have to go through passport control over there." He pointed to a small tunnel with a sign above saying "Private Aircraft."

We presented our passports and I snuck a peek at Spence's. It looked just like mine, a blank cover that didn't say anything on it.

"Why didn't they ask why our passports look different?" I whispered when we'd gone through.

He smiled devilishly. "Because they're all under a glamour. Wherever we are, they will present as if they're passports of that country. No matter where we go, when we arrive, someone will say, 'Welcome home!'"

It was genius.

Then I saw something else. "Spencer *Gregory—that's* your name?"

Spence took his passport back and put it away. "Don't have a reason to be anything else. No one knew my parents' last names and I'd always been Spencer Smith before that—or whatever my foster parents made me call myself. When I found out who I really was, I made it my official name." He pushed through the door at the end of the corridor. "Here we are."

Despite the easygoing explanation, I felt a history in the weight of his words, the loneliness that lurked behind them, and I had a sudden urge to wrap him up in cotton wool and keep him safe always. Instead, I gave him a gentle shoulder nudge, which he ignored, as we entered the holding room.

Everyone was there, wearing casual, easy-to-fly-in clothes. I didn't need to look to know Lincoln was in the far corner, but I couldn't stop my eyes from traveling to him. He was leaning against a glass wall, looking out over the airstrip. He didn't turn my way, but by the tight set of his shoulders, I could tell he knew I'd just walked in.

Samuel and Kaitlin were sitting in a lounge area with Nathan and Becca. After acknowledging our entrance, they went back to their conversations.

"Violet," Griffin said. He was standing with Dapper, and whatever file they were looking at was quickly closed. "You're here," he said, sounding relieved.

"Said I would be," I replied, wondering if Lincoln had mentioned something to Griffin about me not going.

Onyx was sitting at a small table with more than a dozen tiny bottles of alcohol, several already empty. He waggled a few fingers at me and then drank another one.

I shot a look back at Griffin. He just averted his gaze as if there was nothing he could do about it.

Dapper, though, walked over to Onyx and started to pocket the bottles. "I'll portion them out."

Surprisingly, Onyx shrugged and put up little fight.

A long, sleek jet rolled along the tarmac, and we all watched as it pulled to a halt. I'd seen that plane before; when we arrived back from Jordan, the Academy had had people waiting to take Nyla and Rudyard. Griffin had carried Nyla aboard.

By the haunted look on his face, Griffin was reliving that memory too.

The plane's engines shut down and men dressed in dark blue overalls ran toward it with fuel hoses.

"We board in ten minutes," Griffin called out. Everyone nodded and started gathering their bags.

"Violet," Griffin said quietly. I followed his lead and moved toward the back of the room with him. "You've probably already figured out…" He looked at the jet.

"Josephine's on that plane?" I asked rhetorically, but when he kept looking at me, I realized it was more than that. "She's coming with us." I thought at least she might be staying to rest for a day or so.

He nodded. "Listen," he said hurriedly. "I promise you I will do everything I can to stop them from forcing you into anything. More of the Academy will meet us in Santorini. If things get too… if Phoenix is successful, we will need all the forces we can gather. There are fifteen thousand innocent civilians living on that island." He looked down.

"What do you want me to do?" I asked, putting a hand on his arm but dreading what he was about to say.

"I have to go to mainland Greece. There are Grigori there who need to be informed and complications that we must prevent. It's the way things are done there and since I'm still officially the leader, it is my responsibility, unless we hand over the entire case to the Academy…which we won't." He emphasized the last words. "I'll take Nathan and Becca with me, but it might take a couple of days to sort everything out. The Grigori there are hard to find—few in number and overrun by exiles. Josephine is of a Seraph, so while I'm gone, she will automatically assume control over any Grigori who answer to me. Technically, I can nominate someone to speak in my absence, but Josephine will ultimately have rank."

"What does that mean?"

The doors leading out to the tarmac opened and a small vehicle drove a set of stairs up to the jet door.

"Do what she says," Griffin said, looking increasingly nervous. He put a hand on my back and guided me forward.

"She is very good and you can trust that she wants to stop Phoenix, but Violet…" He leaned in close, whispering now. "Lincoln told me how your senses have developed. Don't tell her anything about your powers that you don't need to. And *don't* defy her. She prides herself on being the most powerful of us all."

"But you said she was the Vice?" There had to be someone above her.

"She is." He squeezed my arm, too tight for comfort. "By *choice*." And then he let go and powered ahead of me, leading our pack.

We left the holding room and walked onto the tarmac. Lincoln moved quietly, loading our bags into the baggage compartment. I passed him mine, trying not to look at him, but when our fingers brushed, our eyes met. I didn't know what to expect, maybe that he would say something about me not coming or maybe nothing at all, but instead he gave a crooked smile and I felt a little of that warmth that only ever came from him seep into me like a ray of sunshine. I smiled back and his stunning green eyes lit up for me, and I knew, though they weren't nearly as spectacular, that mine did the same.

Despite everything else, I let myself soak in the warmth as I climbed the stairs behind Steph. Until, that is, I walked straight into the back of her.

"What—" I started to say, but Steph's yelp drowned me out.

"I can't believe it!" she cried, now running up the steps two at a time.

I leaned to the side to see what she was looking at and there they were: Salvatore and Zoe.

Before I knew what I was doing, I yelped too and followed at Steph's pace, bounding up the steps.

Steph was already in Salvatore's arms and he was speaking quickly in Italian to her. I grabbed Zoe and we hugged like the friends we now were—friends who had fought and suffered loss together.

"You came back!" And I realized then that I'd started to doubt they ever would. At least not for this, not when they knew it was such a lost cause.

"We told you we would, didn't we?"

I pulled her tight. Someone coughed behind me.

"Ah, Eden, you might want to let her go now."

"Oh," I said, releasing my grip and actually looking at Zoe

properly. Her spiky, short hair now had pink tips, which somehow still managed to look dangerous. She was wearing a dark gray camouflage-pattern sleeveless dress. Only Zoe would pull the overall look together so well, finishing it off with heavy leather boots and her dagger hanging from her waist.

Spence lifted her into the air.

"Let's move the reunion into the plane, people," Griffin said, coming up the stairs behind us. But he was beaming too. We'd all needed some good news.

I moved past Zoe into the cabin, and Salvatore and Steph broke their embrace long enough for him to say hello. I could tell instantly that his English had improved even more and that I would be able to understand almost everything he said.

Everyone shook hands and hugged as we moved inside. I reached the main cabin area first and spotted the small entourage already seated at the back.

A woman who must have been Josephine sat with her legs crossed. She had long brown hair with auburn streaks that were highlighted by her tight ponytail. She wore a figure-hugging scarlet wrap dress, more feminine than most Grigori attire, and was clicking the top of a pen in her hand as she stared directly at me with aqua-blue eyes.

Six Grigori flanked her and it was clear to see why: dressed in similar black clothes and with their eyes not on me so much as on everything, they were definitely bodyguards.

The woman, who looked about thirty, was older than any Grigori I had met. I had no idea of her real age but knew, perhaps by her frighteningly superior air, that she was significantly ancient. She stood up, taking her time, making a point. This woman rushed for no one.

I felt Lincoln move up behind me, his hand lightly touching the small of my back, cautioning me as much as he was supporting me. I could feel his worry through our partnership, and this time, I didn't step away from his comfort.

The woman looked toward Lincoln and gave a tight smile. "Lincoln Wood."

"Josephine," Lincoln said calmly. "It's good to see you. Allow me to introduce you to my partner, Violet Eden."

Her eyes briefly cast to me as if I were a fly she had just swatted, though she couldn't help but pause when her gaze reached my wrists, despite the fact they were once again covered.

"Yes. Violet…Eden. I've heard so much and yet…" She looked me up and down. "Well, let's just say I was expecting something else."

Oh. We're going to be great friends.

She pursed her lips and looked right through me as if I were no longer there at all. "Is that you, Griffin Moore?" she called out, and waved a hand in the air. It was odd to hear everyone's full names, like once she said them, a certain command was assumed. I didn't like it.

"Take your seats, everyone," Griffin said, not rushing but heading in our direction. It was a sweet power play and I liked that Griffin made her wait. "Stephanie, perhaps you can do that from a sitting position," he said, squeezing past her and Salvatore in a lip-lock.

"And far away from me," Dapper grumped, pushing the two of them into a set of seats at the front.

I don't think Steph noticed or even came up for air.

"Oh come, Dapper, let them have their young love," Onyx teased. "It makes the buildup to tragedy so much more entertaining." He glanced in my direction and raised a hand. "Exhibit A."

"Onyx, it's not too late to throw you off this plane," Lincoln muttered under his breath, but Onyx heard and shut up, sitting down next to Dapper, who passed him one of his alcohol miniatures.

"Isn't this interesting?" Josephine said, looking at Onyx in disgust as he sipped on his drink. "Is he mentally stable?" Intrigued by him, she had difficulty hiding her contempt.

Griffin reached Josephine and graciously gave her a kiss on each cheek. My mouth almost fell open.

"It is so good to see you, Jossie. It's been too long."

Jossie? She does not *look like a Jossie!*

Josephine blushed, but it looked as though she did it on purpose. Why was I suddenly sure that nothing she did was ever *not* on purpose?

"It has been too long, old friend. I've told you too many times your place is at the Academy—not out in the wild. After everything that happened to Magdalena—tell me you have come to your senses."

Griffin took Josephine's hands in his. "Perhaps you were right. Maybe it is time to give it some thought again."

Josephine smiled. "You're teasing me, Griffin."

Griffin turned back toward us, now aligning himself beside

Josephine. Another strategic move, I suspected. The eyes of the black-clad Grigori surrounding Josephine were immediately fixed on him.

Josephine laughed lightly and turned a less friendly eye on them. "Please, relax. We are all on the same side on this plane. Except, perhaps, the human exile and his…intriguing companion," she said, making sure we were all aware she'd noticed Dapper wasn't just human. She flicked a hand at two of her bodyguards. "Go sit near them."

They scooted to the seats behind Onyx and Dapper.

"Oh, splendid," Onyx said, sounding drunker by the second. "Company by way of assassin."

"The rest of you can relax and enjoy the flight," Josephine said to the others. But none of them shifted their eyes from me, so I didn't think those were their real orders.

"Why don't you take a seat with Lincoln, Violet? Josephine and I have much to catch up on." Griffin steered Josephine toward the back of the plane while I felt Lincoln's hands on my hips, spinning me on the spot and pushing me toward the front seats, the farthest possible from her.

"You know her?" I asked, keeping my voice down, as soon as he was sitting beside me.

"I spent a couple of years at the Academy, remember?"

I nodded. Lincoln had spent time there, completing mandatory training before taking a position under Griffin and waiting for his partner—me.

"How old is she?"

"No one knows."

He gave me a quirky look and held out a hand. "If you want to ask her, go right ahead."

"Got it."

His smile widened, and I had to look away before it hurt too much.

I twisted my hands in my lap and played with my bracelets.

"Dad saw my markings."

Lincoln's eyebrows shot up. He knew how major this was. "Are you okay?"

I tucked loose strands of hair behind my ear. "I hate her, Linc."

"No you don't," he said, quietly, knowing who I was talking about.

"I do. And now Dad will never forgive me. Even if I make it through this alive, I…I saw the look on his face when he saw my wrists—it was like he was scared of me. I don't know if I'll have a home to go back to."

We were both silent for a while. I had started to close my eyes when I felt him, so tentatively, reach over and brush a strand of hair away from my face. His touch left a searing trail in its wake.

"You'll make it through this and…you'll always have a home to come back to."

I closed my eyes tight to hold back the tears. I wished he hadn't said it. It felt like my heart might explode. If possible, in that moment, I loved him more than ever.

chapter nineteen

"To die and part is a less evil; but to part and live, there, there is the torment."

George Lansdowne

I drifted off, letting the motion of the plane lull me to sleep. Lincoln stayed silent beside me.

Eventually, I woke up to the sound of voices.

"Oh, get over yourself. You've been guarding her for hours. If she knew you weren't letting us talk to her, she'd hit you in the face," Steph said, sounding pissed.

I kept my eyes closed, listening to Lincoln's laughter, and fought the urge to open my eyes.

My own personal sentinel.

"Probably," he said.

"She's my best friend, you know. I could just yell at her to wake up."

"You could try," Lincoln said, and from his tone, I could imagine the challenging look plastered over his face.

Steph made a huffing sound. "We're landing soon enough anyway." I actually heard the flick of her hair. "And don't think I can't see you gawking at her all doe-eyed."

Lincoln didn't say anything else, but he must have done something because I heard Steph quickly shuffling away with a high-pitched, "I'm going, I'm going."

I waited until I heard her chatting with the others.

"That was mean," I said, opening my eyes.

He glanced at me but looked away quickly. "You needed rest."

"Are we landing?" I could feel the plane descending.

"Gotta refuel."

I sat up urgently, looking out the window. "In the *ocean*?" Lincoln laughed and leaned over me, his arm going around my body, his chest pressing into my back. He pointed out the window to a massive ship. It looked like a navy boat, all flat on top, and as we got closer, I could see helicopters and other small aircraft lined up. I couldn't speak and neither did Lincoln, as if he'd acted before thinking and now we were so close, touching, that neither one of us knew what to do.

The burning that always came when we were near each other reached fever pitch and I fought for breath. My heart beat so rapidly, I considered the chances of a heart attack. It wasn't me; it wasn't some stupid crush; it wasn't even love. It was more—much, much more. It transcended anything he and I could ever be individually and was all about what we were together. My soul was screaming for him, demanding that it have his.

And I want to give it. Oh so much.

Lincoln moved closer, his body shaking, and I couldn't stop from leaning back, letting myself melt into his arms.

I have to turn around. I have to kiss him. I have to…

I shifted, starting to turn, but his hands, now firm, held me still. He spoke right into my ear.

I can smell him. Sunshine and honey.

"Put up your guards."

I knew what he meant, but I just inhaled again.

Mmm…more honey.

"Do I taste or smell of anything to you?" I murmured.

"What do you mean?" he asked, but I knew he knew what I meant.

"You smell like hot days at the beach, the sun—like you're the sun. And you smell sweet, like honey, when you use your power, creamy honey when it's melted onto toast—I can taste it." He faltered, the pads of his fingers kneading my arms, sending shivers through my body. But he recovered, clearing his throat. "Violet, put up your defenses."

"You're not going to tell me, are you?"

"That's not what you need from me right now. Put up your barriers, trust me."

I wanted to argue, to fight against his hold so I could face him, but when that man asked me to trust him—what else could I do? I started to put up my defenses.

It was like what I did to keep Phoenix at bay but different.

Phoenix's power seeped into me like poison. Using my power to block Lincoln was like bricking up the windows and boarding the doors. It was hard work and it felt…wrong.

I'm blocking out the sun.

Every fiber in my being, my soul, begged me, told me this was wrong, that there had to be another way. But I didn't know what that way was, and neither did he, so I forced my defenses up and pushed the sun away.

After a few minutes, I started to become aware of my surroundings again, heard the air-conditioning whirring and voices chatting behind us. Lincoln's hold on me softened, and when I didn't move, he released me slowly and moved back to his seat.

"I'm sorry, Vi," he said, so softly I almost missed it.

"Me too." I wrapped my arms around myself, rubbing them, trying to adjust to the lonely chill that was now creeping over me.

He nodded. "I'll sit with Spence on the next flight."

I took a steadying breath and tried to speak without my voice shaking. "How long have you been using your power against me?"

"Since the night in the park with that exile you hunted. I… when we healed each other, I didn't think I'd be able to make my legs move away. I pulled into my power, not really knowing what I was doing until I'd put a wall between us."

I nodded. "It's good."

And terrible.

Griffin, Nathan, and Becca were the only ones to get off the plane on the stopover. They had another jet waiting that was going to take them directly to Athens.

Before he left, Griffin called Lincoln and me back to him and Josephine. Lincoln stayed close to me but not too close, and we tried our best to keep everything as normal as possible.

Josephine watched us with a glint in her eye, as if she knew just how difficult it was for us to be close to one another, as if she got some kind of satisfaction out of it.

"Josephine, I have explained to everyone that you will be leading the operation while I am in Athens."

"And after you join us in Santorini," she said sweetly.

Griffin gave a nod. "Of course."

Yeah, right. Once Griffin's back, there is only one person any of us will be taking orders from.

"We should only be a couple of days behind, but hopefully I will gain the support of the Greek Grigori and find some soldiers for our cause."

"I have every confidence you will deliver in spades, my friend," Josephine said.

Griffin smiled. "Thank you, and in my absence, I would ask that Lincoln speak on my behalf both to my Grigori and before the Assembly." But he spoke as much to me as Josephine. Was he asking me to let Lincoln lead me?

"Well, well, Lincoln—how far you've come," Josephine said snidely, like she was talking about something else altogether, but then quickly added, "I'll look forward to receiving your counsel."

"Thank you," Lincoln said.

Griffin kissed Josephine on the cheek, shook Lincoln's hand, and hugged me, positioning himself to whisper, "Be careful."

I took my seat again, and after Lincoln walked Griffin off the plane—I assumed for some final instructions—he stayed away, sitting with Samuel and Kaitlin. Once back in the air after the refuel, I squeezed in next to Spence and for the next few hours we played Bullshit, our favorite card game. Zoe banned Salvatore from playing after the first game. Unfair advantage.

Eventually Spence figured out how Steph kept winning—counting cards—and took her hand too. She wasn't upset; she was happy to move to the other seat and cuddle with Salvatore.

"So how did you guys manage to get away from the Academy?" I asked Zoe, after looking around and making sure we had some privacy.

Zoe hitched a foot onto the seat in front and popped a few M&M's, her candy of choice. "Turns out it's handy to have a lie detector on a mission. The things that boy can find out when he puts his mind to it. Let's just say, it was a mistake telling him the review of our case had been delayed indefinitely. Romeo found a wicked sense of determination."

"Mr. Carven?" Spence asked.

Zoe smiled. "My lips are sealed. But…if it did have something to do with Carven, it probably also involved Ms. Trindle."

"Oh!" Spence laughed while scrunching his face. "I'm going to have nightmares for weeks." He lowered his voice and turned to me. "Trust me, you don't want me to paint this picture."

"It's okay. I think I have enough. Bottom line, how long can you stay?"

Zoe slumped down in her seat and played her thighs like drums. "With Sal on the case? I'd say we have an open-ended ticket."

I smiled, looking over at Steph and Sal. They were both beaming. She was showing him the translations now, speaking animatedly but in hushed tones, bringing him up to speed.

"So you guys are…?"

Zoe shrugged. "Since Jordan…you know." She started flicking her fingernails. "We're partners. I'll understand him one day, and till then, we've got the important things, like each other's backs, covered."

Nyla had been right.

She'd always said they'd figure it out. I remembered the last time I saw her. Vacant—as if her soul really wasn't with her at all, as if it was completely lost to her.

"Have you seen Nyla?"

Spence went dead still beside me. I knew it had been the hardest thing about not going back. He loved Nyla. She and Rudy had been the closest thing to a family he'd had.

"The same," Zoe said.

We left it there and went back to some more Bullshit. That is, until we figured out Spence was pulling a glamour over half of his cards.

chapter twenty

"A fool's paradise is a wise man's hell."

Thomas Fuller

Santorini glowed like a crescent moon floating in the sea.

We circled the island before landing on the small airstrip, and I wasn't the only one glued to the window. The view was breathtaking. It was the most beautiful place I'd ever laid eyes on. The low-level buildings on the cliff scaled the heights, practically on top of each other, and all sparkling white—like snowcaps. In the dusk, lights shone from the houses, illuminating the island with gold.

Then I saw a small, dark circle of land in the ocean near the island and I felt something else, not as magical but definitely powerful.

Josephine stood up and walked to the front of the cabin, stopping right in front of me, to address us all.

"Look out the window. The peak you can see emerging from the ocean is the caldera, volcano. It has two main parts, each with its own name. Palea Kameni and Nea Kameni—the old and the new burned islands. The latter of the two will be our focus. Nea Kameni has a number of craters but only one we believe has the potential to erupt. Once we get to the hotel, everyone is to stay inside until we head out in the morning. This is not a request. Anything you need until then will be provided within the walls of the hotel. Santorini must be viewed as hostile territory until we have secured favor with the Athenian Grigori and…the Keeper of the island."

"*That* should be interesting," Onyx said. Even from halfway down the plane, I could smell the alcohol on his breath.

No one else said anything or asked who this Keeper was, so I kept my mouth shut.

Santorini looked so beautiful from the air, but I was quite sure, thanks to Josephine's speech, that once the plane touched down, we would not be welcome in this particular paradise.

Paradise built on top of a volcano!

Whether it was Josephine's words or just the dark, we all worked quickly to collect our luggage, move through passport control, and find taxis.

Lincoln stayed close to me, though far enough away. I didn't tell him to leave me alone or to come closer, despite wanting both. Griffin had given me an order on that plane: he wanted me to follow Lincoln's lead and I was going to respect that. As much as I could, anyway.

I beelined for a taxi. Salvatore and Steph, along with Spence and Zoe, were slipping into the one in front, while a pair of

Josephine's bodyguards were traveling with Onyx and Dapper in the one behind.

I'd just pulled the door open when I heard the click of high heels behind me.

"Violet, be a dear and ride with me. I have a matter I'd like to discuss with you."

"Oh," I said, still holding the taxi door. "I...um..."

"I'm sure Violet would love to travel with you, Josephine," Lincoln said, putting a hand on my shoulder and easing me away from the taxi I was already halfway into. "You won't mind if I escort her, though? She gets quite sick in the back of cars. We've found it safest if I'm nearby to send her some healing if needed."

He moved between Josephine and me so it was clear it was not a request. Lincoln rarely challenged other Grigori so forcefully; usually he preferred to bide his time and let things go. I liked this side of him. A lot.

Because I really need another side of the guy to adore!

Josephine studied him for a minute and then broke into a soft laugh. "Of course. I was going to ask you to join us anyway. This matter concerns you too, I imagine."

"We'll grab the next car," Kaitlin said, quickly removing her and Samuel's luggage from the trunk as one of Josephine's black-clad ninjas loaded heavy bags on top of ours. When the ninja girl started to get in the front seat, Josephine put up a hand.

"We will see you at the hotel, Morgan."

Morgan looked at Josephine like she didn't know if that was code for something or not. I imagined it was a pretty tough job keeping up with all of her games. Josephine flicked her hand out. "Away."

Once we were moving, Josephine rolled down her window, letting some night air into the car. I did the same on my side for equilibrium. Lincoln had strategically placed himself in the awkward middle seat, a gesture I was sure wasn't lost on Josephine.

She sat up straight, knees together, a black patent briefcase that caught the moon's reflection resting on her lap. "This is only a short drive, so I will get to the point. I mentioned earlier that Santorini has a keeper of sorts. The Grigori from the mainland tried and failed many times to keep their people stationed on the Cyclades Islands, but they were always found, usually washed up. One exile, very old, very powerful, claimed ownership of the islands. He made it clear to the Grigori that our type were not welcome but struck a deal: in return for us staying off the islands, he agreed to ensure exiles would not be permitted here either."

"Is he killing?" Lincoln asked.

"Perhaps. We can never know for sure, but nothing significant enough to create anarchy."

I was horrified.

"Yes, Miss Eden, I can see the look you are giving me, but when you are ready to get off your high horse, you might consider that Grigori numbers are not endless and exiles have populated Greece for so long without a strong force of resistance that their numbers have grown to potentially devastating levels. This agreement keeps the islands free of roaming exiles in dangerous numbers. It is not perfect, but the Keeper has always stayed true to his word and Santorini continues to have one of the lowest crime rates in Greece, with violent acts almost unheard of."

"That doesn't mean they aren't happening," I said stubbornly.

"No, but the Keeper, though dangerous and motivated by intense greed, of course, leads us to believe he is not prone to malicious brutality like most exiles. His attentions delve...elsewhere."

"How so?" Lincoln asked flatly.

Josephine seemed to deliberate for a moment before smiling secretively, making it clear she was not going to say any more.

Lincoln remained calm as if nothing she had—or *hadn't*—said upset him. "We can't be on the island," he concluded.

"Correct. That is also why Griffin has gone to Athens. The Grigori there will be upset we are breaking the terms of the truce. But I intend to settle this problem tonight." She peered around Lincoln's broad shoulders at me. "With a little help."

"You want us to return him?" I asked, but Lincoln wasn't nodding or chatting now. He was dead still.

"No. That, I'm afraid, is not an option. But the Keeper has particular weaknesses and very particular...tastes." She opened her briefcase and turned it so its contents faced Lincoln and me.

"Jewelry?" I asked.

The case held a number of stunning pieces, mostly diamonds. In the center lay a necklace so big it looked like any normal person would collapse under its weight, then a number of bracelets, all dripping with pea-sized diamonds but also the occasional colored stone. Finally, there were the rings: six of them, all made of silver inlaid with solitary gems—three diamonds and the others red, yellow, and emerald. Seeing the stones made me nervous.

"Are these some kind of payment?"

"Yes," Josephine said, admiring the bounty.

"Is there…" My mouth had gone dry and I licked my lips. "I can't see any sapphires in there."

Josephine laughed. "I can tell Magda's antics have left a mark on you all. No, there are certainly no sapphires or any other stone that could potentially cause Grigori any trouble. That, you can be certain, is not on my agenda."

Great to know you have an agenda at all, lady!

"What do you want us to do, Josephine?" Lincoln asked, taking back the conversation.

She sighed and closed the briefcase. "I would do it myself, or ask another if I believed it could work, but unfortunately, the Keeper has very specific prerequisites. If we are to present him with this payment, it will have to be by someone to his liking, and his *liking* is young with long, dark hair, substantial…" She looked at my bust then changed her tack. "And with a power that intrigues him and, believe me, he has seen a lot."

"No," Lincoln said.

I had clammed up completely and couldn't speak. The only thing going through my mind was, *Please don't make me do this.*

"We will find another way," he carried on. He emphasized his point without raising his voice and was all the more forceful for it.

"And yet, there is no other option. Since Phoenix has the Scripture..." she said, tilting her head so we both understood her meaning—*Since Violet* gave *Phoenix the Scripture*—"we must expect that he will be on his way to the island by tomorrow, if not already. This is our only chance to gain the upper hand." She pouted, a show of false pity. "I'm sure Violet understands that, Lincoln, and while I appreciate you're protective of your partner for...various reasons, we must put the cause first tonight. Naturally, I do not expect Violet to be unescorted. You will be with her the entire time, and she will only be expected to deliver the jewels and allow the Keeper to take possession of them."

I watched Lincoln's jaw clench so hard it looked like his temples would explode. I turned my attention to the window and focused on the night outside.

"No," he said again.

I closed my eyes momentarily and tried to push everything else aside. I had to be strong, not give in. *Not* run.

"Linc," I said, keeping my gaze on the scene outside the window. "It's okay." I didn't need to look at Josephine to know she was smiling, but Griffin had given me clear instructions not to go up against her. "As long as Lincoln can come with me and I'm not expected to—"

"Of course not," she cut me off. "Lincoln will be with you the entire time. I have already stipulated that in the arrangements."

I nodded.

"It's already arranged?" Lincoln replied, his calm now wavering.

"Yes, I put everything in place as soon as I knew our destination. I just didn't know who we were going to send—until I saw how beautiful Violet is."

So, why am I so sure she doesn't think I'm beautiful at all and that she planned this whole thing before she ever laid eyes on me?

The taxi pulled up outside a white building that looked like all the others we'd passed on the drive. We were much higher up now, though.

Did someone say…cliffs? Joy.

"Welcome to Fira," Josephine said, getting out of the taxi. Samuel and Kaitlin pulled up behind us and everyone else was already waiting at the foot of a winding staircase. Onyx was sitting on top of his bag and looked utterly wasted as he fanned himself.

Samuel walked past us, pausing briefly to glance meaningfully at Lincoln, who gave one of his own glances in return.

"It is not a large hotel, and since we expect more Grigori to join us shortly, we have booked it out. I will have the main suite. You can work the rest out among yourselves, though I require my staff to be in the rooms surrounding my own, for practicality's sake." She gave a tight smile and then started for the stairs, leaving her bags for her ninjas.

Steph came up to me, a spring in her step and a childish smile on her face. "Are we sharing?"

"Sure, but maybe you should hang out with Sal and the others until I come and get you. I have to go out and I don't want you on your own here."

Steph's smile vanished. I knew she would freak if I told her what Josephine had asked and that she wouldn't refrain from giving the Vice a piece of her mind. I patted her on the shoulder and started walking up the stairs so I didn't have to look at her while I lied. "Don't worry, Steph. Just recon. I'll be with Lincoln the whole time."

"Really?" she responded suspiciously.

"Absolutely."

"But Josephine said no one was allowed to leave the hotel."

"Yeah, I know, but she asked us to make a delivery or something. No drama. It will probably only take an hour or so."

"Okay then. I guess I'll drop my bags in our room and catch up with the others. I wanted to get their take on the prophecies anyway. I think there's more to those symbols than just the sacrifices."

I looked over my shoulder at her, grateful that the light was only dim, and flashed a big, fake smile. "Great idea. I'll find you after."

Then she ran up a couple of steps. "Vi, can you believe he's back? And he looks so incredible! I don't know how, but it's like his hotness level has doubled!"

My smile became more genuine, and when we reached the top of the staircase, I put an arm around her. "I'm really glad you're happy."

"You will be too, you know. It might not be right away, but I know you will. Some things are just written in the stars," she said, looking up at the twinkling sky, drunk on love.

I hitched my bag higher on my shoulder and opened the hotel door for her. "Even the stars can't change *some* things, Steph."

chapter twenty-one

"Every sweet has its sour; every evil its good."

Ralph Waldo Emerson

The Academy had been around for a long time. Among other things, the organization clearly had money. No doubt it didn't hurt that we were traveling with prima donna Josephine. I imagined she wouldn't do anything on a shabby-chic scale. With no Grigori permanently inhabiting Santorini, there was no safe-house hotel—like there was in Jordan—for us to use.

The hotel where we were staying assumed an elevated—and therefore defensive—position above Fira, the main town on the island. It looked down over hundreds of white buildings, the only color besides a sporadic blue or golden-domed rooftop, their architecture following the natural curves of the landscape. I tried not to look for long, tried not to think about Dad. But it was hard not to be mesmerized, the town so startling above the water.

My attention drifted beyond the immediate, out to the night sea and the volcanic crater. It looked so harmless, a tiny little island, nothing lighting it up, no towering peak giving it strength—it seemed completely, deceptively, lifeless.

Steph had taken off already, and I had an hour until Lincoln and I were due to meet downstairs. I stared at my phone wondering if I should turn it on and call Dad before putting it away in my bedside drawer. Then I collapsed on my bed with no intention of moving for the next fifty-five minutes.

I had just kicked my shoes off when someone started knocking on my door.

"Go away!" I called out, assuming it was Spence or one of the others.

"Josephine sent me," a girl's voice called back to me.

I sighed and stared at the ceiling before rolling off the bed. I really needed sleep. I schlepped over to the door, and when I opened it, Morgan stood there with a large, black box resting in her outstretched arms and the briefcase Josephine had shown us earlier.

She smiled courteously then pushed past me, carefully placing the box on the bed and the briefcase beside it.

She turned to look at me and screwed up her face. "You do realize you have less than an hour to get ready?"

I looked down at my outfit. I looked pretty average in my jeans and tank top and I still had my baggy sweater tied around my waist. After however many hours it had been since my last shower, even I didn't welcome the armpit test.

Morgan shook her head, belying her blank expression, breaking into a quirky smile that made me wonder if the ninjas were really that bad.

"Josephine sent a dress and shoes for you." She bit her lip. "You'd better get in the shower while I sort out your clothes and makeup. Where is everything?"

She almost fell over in horror when I showed her what I'd brought cosmetics-wise. I don't know why she was surprised. I hadn't planned on getting dressed up. Luckily for Morgan, Steph's bag contained a veritable "what's what" of beauty essentials. I couldn't help but laugh and relax. I'd had Morgan pegged as an emotionless go-fetcher, but this girl was more like Warrior Barbie.

I did as I was told, too tired to argue, and had a quick shower, following instructions not to get my hair wet, since we didn't have enough time to start from scratch.

When I emerged from the bathroom cocooned in the snugly, white hotel robe, which only made me want to sleep even more, I found that Morgan had transformed my room into a beauty salon. All of Steph's cosmetics were laid out in some kind of color-and-type sequence, with brushes that she must have found in Steph's bags too, straightening irons, nail polish, and, hanging from the open wardrobe, a dress that made me first gasp and second lunge for my dagger.

Morgan shot up in the air, hands out defensively. "What's the matter with you? Haven't you ever had your makeup done before?" she asked, sounding like I'd actually hurt her feelings.

"Where did that come from?" I demanded, jabbing the point of my dagger toward the dress and then back to her. "Answer me, now!"

"Okay, relax! It was loaded on the plane when you boarded; Josephine ordered it online. She said, I don't know…she said it was perfect. And can I just say, if you don't like it, you don't need to attack me over it! I'm not even armed!"

I looked at Morgan, standing opposite me in a defensive position holding a tube of lip gloss. If she had done this on purpose, there was no way she would have come in unarmed. She looked like she had been caught completely off guard and I instantly felt bad for her.

I threw my dagger onto the bed. "Were you really planning on fighting back with lip gloss?" I asked, letting a smile spread across my face.

Morgan looked down, aware of her pose for the first time, then back at me, still unsure, but realizing where I'd thrown my dagger—closer to her than me—she relaxed and smiled back.

"Remind me never to go dress shopping with you," she said, walking toward the most divine gown I'd ever seen. "What's wrong with it, anyway?"

I stepped up beside her and ran my fingers down the black silk. "I…I've seen it before." I didn't want to tell her I'd seen it with Phoenix—that he'd offered to buy it for me. "I just…It caught me by surprise. I thought it might be someone playing a joke on me."

Morgan moved behind me and started yanking at my hair with

a brush. "I can promise you this much—there isn't anything funny about tonight."

I spun to face her. "What aren't you telling me? Why am I getting so dressed up?"

Morgan directed me to the designated makeup chair and started slapping foundation on my cheeks. "Josephine knows what she's doing. I know she seems…unfriendly, but you'd be better off just doing what she says."

She went to work on my eyes, and I had to close them. After a while, accepting she wasn't going to say any more, I decided to try and find out some more about the ninjas. "Are all the people at the Academy like you guys?" From what I'd seen of Spence, Zoe, and Salvatore, Josephine's uniformed Grigori were different.

"In what way?"

"All ninja-ish and guard-like."

She raised her eyebrows. "I'll take that as a compliment. Grigori are in high places all around the world; we have to be to access the exiles who get there too."

"So that's what you're going to do after you leave the Academy?"

"Everyone takes a different major in final year. Max, my partner, chose Ghosting." She shrugged, grabbing the mascara wand and blotting it on some tissue. "It's not really my thing, but Max really wanted to do it. Ghosts always get to work closely with Josephine and he thought it would help us get good placements."

"So you *like* Josephine?" I asked carefully.

She smiled and I could see she really did resemble a Barbie doll, with her long blond hair and perfect white teeth. "No one *likes* Josephine. But then, that's not her job."

She turned my chair toward the mirror. I almost didn't recognize myself. It seemed like ages since I'd actually felt girly…and well, this was even more. The way she'd done my eyes, made the corners so dark and smoky with the slightest glimmer of silver at the top was amazing. I looked like a woman. All of a sudden, I couldn't wait to see what the dress looked like on.

I hadn't been out in public without my bracelets since I first received my markings. I felt exposed and was fiddling so much that Morgan had resorted to slapping me on the hands. Which hurt.

"Stay still," she said. "It's hard enough doing this in the elevator, let alone with you twitching like you're having some kind of seizure."

I tried to stop bouncing on the balls of my feet as she clipped the last piece of jewelry on, the necklace with four rows of teardrop diamonds, each one—Morgan told me about a hundred times—a perfect three carats. I placed a flat palm across my collarbone, which was now home to seventy-two carats' worth of diamonds.

I'm a walking Tiffany's.

I looked down at the rest of my glistening ensemble in the elevator mirror. Three rings on each hand that miraculously fit perfectly, apart from the one with the ruby that was a little loose. Looping, diamond-studded earrings, a glittering bracelet on one wrist, and opposite, a platinum armband in the design of a snake curling its way around my upper arm, encrusted with smaller diamonds. Then there was the ankle bracelet, which was the most dainty of the pieces and held matching, though significantly smaller, teardrop diamonds to complement the necklace—and was my favorite.

Finally, I pulled back my dress at the slit to reveal the web of delicate chains holding an arrangement of vibrant green emeralds in the pattern of a spider—its eight legs stretching around my thigh. Though it was bizarre, it was also…kind of hot.

But the jewelry paled in comparison to the dress.

I remembered staring at it in the shop window, thinking it was the most stunning gown I had ever seen, but now—it was more than I could have imagined. It fit perfectly, as if it had been specifically designed for me.

Black and strapless, the fitted bodice was finely detailed with black crystals, while the rest of the fabric floated down elegantly, and the high slit at the side showed flashes of skin when I walked.

The elevator doors opened while I was still staring at this unknown version of myself in the mirror.

"*What* are you doing with that?" Morgan asked, pointing to my hand, which held my sheathed dagger.

"I didn't know where to strap it."

"You are *not* putting a dagger on that outfit," she said, extending her hand to stop the elevator doors from closing.

"Well, I'm not going anywhere without it." I'd made that mistake once before and experienced the full force of Onyx at his worst as a result. "Where I go, my weapon follows." I spun toward the open doors and froze, the force of his power hitting me first.

Honey. Everywhere.

Lincoln was standing on the opposite side of the tiny foyer, looking straight at me, his hand gripping the table he stood beside, wearing the hungriest expression I'd ever seen on…anything—animal or human.

Oh.

It's the dress. Breathe.

It's just the dress, maybe the jewelry.

I closed the short distance between us, hoping I wouldn't trip on the way, and saw that he looked amazing. He wore a tailored suit, which sat on him, like my dress, as if it had been measured perfectly to his body, with a black shirt, open at he collar, sending me all the right—no, wrong—messages.

"You look great," I said, since he hadn't said anything.

His eyes glanced down before he could stop them, and once he pulled them back up, they seemed to drag their own way back down again before he realized. I felt a wash of self-consciousness. Suddenly, I couldn't tell if he approved or not.

"Well, you're clearly in capable hands." Morgan rolled her eyes like a pro. "I'll have the car come around. Max is going to escort you there, but he has to stay in the car. Okay?" she said, holding my eyes to be sure I'd heard and understood. She put out her hand. "Give me the dagger."

I didn't move. "No."

She gave a frustrated sigh.

"I'll carry it," Lincoln said, opening his jacket a little to reveal his own dagger. I trustingly passed it to him. He took it carefully, ensuring he didn't make contact with me at all.

"Here's the car," Morgan said from the entryway when she heard a horn beep. She pulled open the hotel door. "Josephine said to remind you, you have to present the jewels and allow him to take possession of them—those are the terms."

I nodded, my short-lived excitement fading fast. I turned to ask Lincoln what he thought that meant, but he'd already disappeared outside.

Way to make a girl feel pretty.

chapter twenty-two

"An angel can illume the thought and mind of man by strengthening the power of vision."

Saint Thomas Aquinas

I made my way down the spiral staircase, hoping I wouldn't trip and have some spectacular fall. I really didn't care that much about being pretty. Not like Steph, anyway. But now that I was all glammed up, I didn't want to make an absolute fool of myself. I mean, how many chances was I really going to have to wear a dress like this?

Halfway down the stairs, I felt the shift. "Oh no," I moaned. "Not now." I put a hand on the railing to steady myself as gravity lightened its hold on the world and something else, something that shouldn't have been there, moved around me. Last time their realm had touched with ours, we'd been in Jordan, so it didn't seem so strange to see sands rolling in. But on Santorini, a volcanic island, seeing desert sands start blowing toward me was just plain unsettling.

I tried to back up a step, but my legs were cemented, like last time. I took a deep breath and concentrated on restoring my barriers. I couldn't be this defenseless when Nox, or Uri for that matter, arrived.

Gradually, like waking a sleeping limb, I started to feel the prickle of nerves coming alive. Wiggling my toes was good but not enough. I kept my focus, my grip moving along the railing again, and then, willing more, I found myself taking that step back up the stairs.

Okay. We have movement!

The sands drifted in and then rained down on the steps, a few grains falling into my hand. I started trying to reach for Lincoln through our link, but barely managed the thought before someone else was standing in front of me.

"Uri?" I asked, fairly certain but still slightly confused each time I saw one of my identical guides. Uri was an Angel Elect. He looked disheveled and dirty—not in the way someone who was kind and all good could shun material possessions and survive with the barest necessities. No, he always looked like he was coming off the biggest bender ever. Sandy blond hair, tangled, cupping his face; a tailored white shirt, unbuttoned at the top and hanging loose at the bottom; black pants that looked like they were in need of a wash; and…no shoes. All topped off with a three-day growth.

I stared. There was something about him. I couldn't decide what it was, but I found myself more unnerved around him in many ways than I was with Nox.

Nox was simple. His motives were wrong; he wanted wrong; he

was wrong. Uri…Uri was something else, but something altogether more frightening.

He watched me as I watched him, and I could see he was having thoughts of his own. The look of disgust was unmistakable, but I'd learned to expect that. Angels who have not chosen this life may be intrigued by humanity, but they also see us as lower beings—it's almost as if they don't want to get too close in case it's catching.

"Good evening, Violet," Uri said, his voice dry.

I stood tall and put my hand out to shake.

His eyes went wide and I couldn't help but smile. I'd just had a double score. First, I knew he didn't particularly want to have to touch me—but hell, he'd made me shake his hand once before so it was only fair—and second, I'd shown him I was strong enough to move.

Go, me.

He moved forward, taking the step up to me as I took the step down. This time, he kept his expression neutral.

Taking his hand was like holding something unnatural—my mind boggled. His grip was firm—all man—but his skin was so soft, like a newborn baby's. These two sensations—strength and innocence—are not supposed to go together. And there was something else—a spark, crackling between us.

I flinched at the sensation. Uri's hand steadied me, and his eyes lifted, amused. "First, you touch the human, then the spirit, then…the angel."

I was about to ask what that meant but, like he had done once before, just as I'd seen my angel maker do, his face dropped what minimal expression it held and became vacant. Still holding my hand, still there, but…not.

No crackle. Not even a snap or pop.

And it felt strangely familiar.

"You look…superficial," he said suddenly, moving back as soon as I released his hand in shock. It had only been five or six seconds, but he had definitely gone somewhere momentarily and returned just as quickly.

I shrugged, trying to regain my voice. "Not by choice, though I'm not complaining."

"Clearly," he said, judgment rolling off the word.

Whatever.

He looked at me as if he'd read my mind, one eyebrow twitching slightly. Of course, that was about the most I'd ever seen from Uri. Unlike Nox, he didn't smile much.

"You do not fear me as much as you should," he said, a question in the statement.

Damn angels—whether exiled or not, light or dark, they were all creatures of pride.

"If I spent all my time fearing the things I should, I'd never stop screaming."

Uri tilted his head. "True."

Oh, comforting.

"What are you doing here, Uri? Is this another 'You need to surrender' conversation? Because I'm kinda in a hurry." Not that that mattered—right now he was stalling time. I looked past him to see Lincoln standing by the black sedan. He had one hand on the roof of the car, eyes closed and his head bowed as if he were praying. He looked like he'd been trapped in some state of torture. Another cheering thought.

"I believe you're going to see one of our fallen?"

He didn't "believe" anything. He knew. Angels always *know.* I nodded.

"He's called the Keeper. That's all I know. I have to give him payment, so we can stay here. Apparently returning him would cause more harm than good."

"Perhaps," Uri said. "Though you would be wise to keep your eyes open."

"What does that mean?" He wasn't just telling me to be careful.

"The Keeper is a collector. He has many things that were never intended for this world. But some, in the right hands, would be more…appropriate."

"Okay…" My hand planted itself on my hip. "But you're going to have to be more specific. I have no idea what you're talking about," I said, feeling once again the frustration of talking to these otherworldly beings who seemed to know so much and have so much control, yet at the same time just didn't get it. "If you want to help, Uri, help!"

His interest in me grew, making me want to calm myself, hide my anger from him.

"It is not for us to take action and not necessary for us to have the desire to…help, as you put it. Already with you, we walk a fine line."

I was about to snap back but caught my breath when I saw something moving behind him. It was like when I'd seen Nox in Jordan. Something, like sunspots or heat waves, floated in the background. Something...living.

"What...what are those things?" I asked, fighting back a shiver.

"Reflections," he said after a pause.

"I don't understand."

"No."

Irritated didn't cover it. I hated the way this worked—no information when I wanted it, only when they deemed it appropriate. Who the hell gave them so much control?

"So is this like last time? You have some message for me and one from Nox or something?"

"Nox does not trust me to deliver his messages," he said, bitterness in his tone.

I couldn't figure them out. They had some kind of understanding and yet a mutual disdain for one another.

"Are you two really brothers?" I asked, unable to stop myself.

"Do we look like brothers?"

"You look like twins, exactly the same," I said.

"Then, we are the same."

I didn't know why I'd bothered. "Just say what you came to say," I said, crossing my arms.

"I have."

"That's it? Surely you can give me something more to work with. You do realize what's happening here, don't you? Phoenix is going to bring back Lilith." And I don't know why, but at that moment, I was quite sure he'd be successful.

"Trials will come and they will go. Those that are left standing must evolve. It is the way of the universe."

"More tests? You're supposed to be good, an angel of light!" I snapped.

"Girl, all existence is a test. Some just get challenged in more obvious ways. And I do not give myself that title. I am an Angel Elect. Humans have decided elect must be light, malign must be dark. You also gave us wings and halos." Uri looked over his shoulder toward Lincoln and I felt the urge to redirect his attention—to protect Lincoln. I took a step toward Uri.

"Don't. Leave him alone."

"And what is it you think I can do to him that has not already been done?"

With that, he turned back to me. We were now close, too close.

"Is it all decided?" I asked, my voice quivering at the thought. I needed to know.

"You have choices, as always. Consent remains yours to be given freely. But you have certain inclinations firmly embedded, so your path will not be altered easily. Though there are those who believe otherwise and are determined."

"How do I stop Phoenix?"

"You cannot. Only he can stop himself. He must choose, as must you. For him, the right choice has not yet crossed his path."

"Will it?" I asked, feeling a faint spark of hope.

His head tilted to the side, a finger twitched. Normally I wouldn't notice the minuscule movements on an ordinary person, but Uri was not ordinary and he did not move at all unless encouraged. Something about my reaction fascinated him. I quickly set my mind and face to blank, which only captivated him further, earning me a small up curl at the corner of his mouth.

"Look for what is old, not necessarily alluring to the eye, but certainly beguiling to the angel within. Good-bye, Violet."

I swallowed. Question time was over.

"Good-bye, Uri," I said, my eyes drifting again to his surrounds and feeling the urge to reach out and touch—no, more. Those floating things behind him, and even the shadows that seemed to hover below them, were so lifelike and disturbingly beautiful—shimmering under unnaturally luminous light. I wondered if they were angels, perhaps in their true form. Whatever they were, I felt a sense of protectiveness toward them and a desire to be near them. I was drawn to them.

Uri turned his curious gaze from me, and the sands started to whirl around him. Even though it was amazing, it wasn't dramatic; it just had to be. I felt the change as normal gravity returned and my stomach lurched with all that was not human about what had happened. Why was I the only one who could see these things? But then I opened my tightly clenched fist and stared down to find grains of sand that had remained behind.

Well, that's new.

I started making my way slowly down the rest of the stairs, trying to readjust my movements and slow my breathing. The entire visitation by Uri had left me on edge. He was certainly an unwanted surprise, but although he left me more unnerved than Nox had ever done, at least he didn't make me feel like he was trying to ensnare me.

When I joined Lincoln at the car, he held the door open for me and looked at the ground. I could feel his power, the silken honey flavors thickening all around him. Nothing had changed for him—he hadn't witnessed the conversation with Uri; he'd been halted in time and space like everyone else.

"Are you okay?" I asked, as I slid into the backseat. Because despite what I knew, he looked different and seemed as if he was out of breath too.

"Are you?" he replied, his voice shaky. "I swear I could've...Did you just use your power or...I think I had some kind of déjà vu."

He felt it too.

When I'd tried to reach out to him through our link, he had registered something. I bit down on my lip and considered telling him everything. But right now, I didn't know if he'd believe me. Crossing the realms like this was not normal for Grigori and I hadn't told anyone about my encounter with Nox in Jordan. At the time, it hadn't seemed like something I needed to keep secret, but so much else had happened since then that I'd started to wonder if it had been just another trick of the mind. Now...well, it felt like I'd become a radar for all things wrong and weird. People already looked at me strangely. I didn't want Lincoln to become one of those people.

Before I knew what I was doing, the words came out. "Everything's fine."

He nodded, still holding the door open, *still* not looking at me. I was certain he knew I was lying.

"Max will ride with you in the back. I'm going to sit up front."

"Oh. Sure."

I sank back into my seat, telling myself it was better this way. Reminding myself that if he were sitting beside me now, looking the way he did, any progress I'd made in the steady-breathing department would have flown out the window. Breathing while wearing the bodiced dress was already challenging enough. But still, the knot in my stomach—the one that wasn't about being Grigori or making good decisions and was all teenager—twisted.

"You're Morgan's partner, right?" I asked the perfectly groomed black-clad guy sitting next to me.

"Yes, I'm Maximilian," he said. "Or just Max," he added with a small smile.

Wow, another ninja who's almost normal.

"Did you arrange the car?" I asked, anything to break the tension that was riding along with us.

The sedan was a significant improvement on the earlier taxis—not quite a limo but large and black and equipped with a suited driver.

Max cleared his throat. "No. The car was sent courtesy of the Keeper."

"Oh," I said, realizing it would probably be better not to ask any more questions with the Keeper's chauffeur listening in. I looked at him again and my curiosity grew, mostly because…he was human.

Thankfully, the drive was not long. Santorini was a relatively small island, so even though we had probably driven half its length, the car soon pulled to a halt outside what I was sure—from the bright, roaming light I'd been watching on our approach—was a lighthouse.

We all got out, Max giving me his arm to help me keep my balance on the gravel in my extreme high heels. He walked me to the door, Lincoln following a few paces behind.

"Where are we?" I asked, nervously pushing back the power I could feel emanating from the place.

"Akrotiri Lighthouse, the bottom point of Santorini. I'll be outside with the car," Max said, stopping at the foot of the stairs leading to the front doors. "This is as far as I'm permitted."

He moved back to the car, beside which the chauffeur still stood. It was disconcerting that the driver too obviously didn't want to move any closer to the lighthouse.

Lincoln had approached so silently that his words startled me.

"Are you ready? We can leave right now if you'd prefer?" Something in his voice sounded hopeful.

But I had to go in there and give this exile the jewelry. Josephine said that would be all.

How bad could it be?

Yeah! 'Cause dealing with exiles is always straightforward! And Josephine can definitely *be trusted.*

A wave of nausea washed over me.

I knew, deep down, something was very wrong.

Despite my intense desire not to believe anything that came out of her mouth, Josephine had been right about one thing—Phoenix would be on his way by now and this might be our only hope of staying on the island.

Just show him the jewelry and let him have it.

I could do that.

Before Lincoln, with that concerned look on his face, had a chance to say anything else, I reached out and knocked on the door.

chapter twenty-three

"But the wicked are like the tossing sea, which cannot rest, whose waves cast up mire and mud."

Isaiah 57:20

Words failed me when the door opened and I found myself staring at a faceless man. If that's what he was. My stomach churned. I was torn between squinting to see if I could see anything in the shadows of his hooded cloak and turning on my heel to make a run for it.

The last time I'd stood before a faceless figure, I had done something that would stay with me forever. Suddenly, everything I had been telling myself a moment earlier seemed ridiculous.

We need to go! We need to go!

I started backing away and looked over my shoulder. Max was standing by the car watching us, straining to see who had just opened the door.

"We need to go," I hissed urgently, under my breath.

But Lincoln didn't take his eyes off the doorway. His power was swirling around me, so intense it was like swimming inside a beehive. He was standing rigid and pale, looking beyond the cloaked figure.

"It's too late for that."

I followed his gaze and clapped a hand over my mouth. Another eight figures, all cloaked, all faceless, stood behind the one at the door. The weirdest part—I could sense only one exile nearby.

These...*things* were hollow, but they were smiling—I could *feel* it. The nauseous sensation returned tenfold. I was quickly regretting my decision to go through with this.

The figure at the door spoke—not out loud—but inside my mind.

"Welcome. You will follow me. The Keeper is waiting."

Holy hell.

I almost dropped to the ground it was so invasive, like dozens of cockroaches clawing their way out from inside my head. Fear intensified and I retreated another step, but Lincoln's hand was there, flat on my back, pushing me forward. He had heard the words too.

I looked at him, panic making my pulse fly into overdrive, but he just nodded me on. I knew he was right. You couldn't run from exiles, and whatever these things were, I didn't think running from them would be smart either.

I shook my hands, hoping it might throw off some of my terror, and walked into the lighthouse ahead of Lincoln. Once inside, the chill from the cold, stone floor spread through me, claiming me.

The figure at the door gestured for me and Lincoln to follow. The others, standing shoulder to shoulder, made no move to join us, but as we moved past them, I heard voices.

Screams.

Deathly howls of men, women…children. Hundreds. Thousands. And just like when the figure at the door had "spoken" to us, every sound was amplified within my mind so that it was more than just hearing—it was *experiencing*.

I didn't realize I had stopped, lost in the horror, until Lincoln took my hand, the warm honey of his power soothing me, reassuring me that I was okay. Only his voice could break through the shrieking.

"Keep walking. Remember who we are. Use your will."

My eyes focused on Lincoln and gradually I took back control of my mind. The screaming faded until it stopped altogether.

I swallowed, my throat dry and scorched. "It felt so real. Like *I* was screaming."

He kept an anxious eye on me and squeezed my hand before releasing it. "You were."

Oh.

The faceless figure was still moving ahead. We hurried to keep up with him and his long, fluid gait as he took us down a narrow, winding staircase until it opened up into a more cumbersome version, as if one had been added to the other. It looked as if the lower staircase was the older of the two.

Weird.

After what felt like, and probably was, over a thousand steps, we reached the bottom and a hallway.

Too low, no air.

I'm not normally claustrophobic but this was extreme. I half expected to stumble across a door with a sign over it saying, "Hell (Staff Only)."

I tried to focus on my surroundings to stop the feeling that the walls were moving in on me and clear the blotches floating before my eyes. The hall was completely wooden—floors, walls, and ceiling lined with heavy boards, almost red, polished so much that they reflected the beams from the modern downlights that were everywhere, making the place look like some kind of starlit dungeon.

At the end of the long walkway, the faceless figure pushed open a heavy set of double doors and I noticed a long corridor to the right. Whatever space existed down there was obviously big, and since I didn't appear to be able to sense the faceless…things, I instantly worried there were many more of them lurking.

"Violet?" Lincoln spoke quietly, picking up on my unease.

I turned my attention back to him, and, despite the fear in his eyes, they were still his eyes and they made me feel better, stronger. Together, we walked through the doors, which closed behind us with a thud. I would have spun around…if I hadn't been so mesmerized by what was in front of us.

Living harmony.

A grand room with a stone floor and more wood-lined walls,

but this time with a combination of light and dark shades working together to give it…life. The paneling was incredible—some parts so dark, it was as if the wood had been burned before being molded to the walls, other parts so light, the wood was almost green with youth. Combined with the shades of the polished stone floor and the flickering candlelight from the wrought-iron lanterns, it was as if the room had its own spirit. We walked toward the far wall, and I was certain we were somewhere that was entirely, gracefully balanced and also entirely, unnervingly otherworldly.

How long has this place been here?

After carefully taking in our surroundings, Lincoln moved to the corner and melted into the shadows, the best vantage point. Watching his accuracy, I suspected he had spent some time Ghosting at the Academy himself.

I stopped at the far wall, which was almost all glass and showcased a sweeping ocean view. The reflection of the full moon glistened in the water, rocked by its continuous motion. We were deep beneath the lighthouse, the glass exterior obviously hidden from human eyes and embedded in the cliff face.

"Beautiful," a liquid voice rang out from the corner of the room.

My breath caught and I looked for the owner of the voice. Someone had appeared behind us while I'd been gawking at the view. I hadn't even been paying attention to the senses, which had been growing stronger. As with my art, I had allowed myself to be absorbed by the design of the room, a potentially perilous oversight.

I had not even heard the door open, a thought that brought on a shiver. I shot a look at Lincoln, but he didn't move or even seem to look back at me.

To my relief, the stranger—obviously an exile—had a face. The hollowness of the horrors that had greeted us was still with me, tugging at buried feelings that I did not want to resurface. Strangely, this being was not as striking as most exiles. He *was* handsome, but in a softer way, despite his imposing height. Hazelnut hair fell in gentle waves around his face, kind lines were etched into his tanned, olive skin, and his mocha eyes were warm but dangerous at the same time. He was broad and muscled, yet the delicateness of his features somehow kept everything balanced. He looked like a friendly giant. But he was an exile.

I concentrated on my senses, letting them paint the truth. He tasted of powdery red apples, like fruit that has been frozen and later thawed. He smelled more like herbs than flowers—thyme and rosemary. The sounds of birds' wings flapping, crashing into trees, was not too different from usual, along with the conflicting sensations of warmth and chills that flowed through both my blood and bones. But when I looked for the flashes of morning and evening that came whenever I was near an exile—there was nothing.

He closed the distance between us and stopped in front of me.

"Incredibly beautiful," he said, looking me up and down. He glanced at Lincoln, who had become so still in the corner even *I* barely felt his presence.

"I am being spoiled tonight." Desire flashed behind his soft eyes.

I cleared my throat nervously. I knew, as the one who had been called upon to do this job, that I had to do the talking if this was going to work.

"We're here to give you the jewels in return for your permission to stay on Santorini." My mouth was so dry, I had to swallow between the words.

"We'll get to that in a moment. Would you not like to stay for dinner first? At least a drink?" He smiled dangerously, which helped me start to see beyond my first impressions.

I didn't know what we were supposed to say—but Josephine hadn't told me we would need to stay for a meal.

"We would prefer to make the exchange and be on our way."

He tilted his head. "Your name?"

I could feel my palms getting clammy. "Violet."

"And your shadow?"

"Lincoln," I said, sounding as nervous as I felt. It would not help any of us if I lost control of the conversation so early. I stood a little taller. "And you are?"

"Many simply call me the Keeper now. Before that, I was known as Irin. You may call me whichever you prefer."

"Okay, Irin."

A faceless figure entered the room carrying a tray with two flutes of champagne. He stopped in front of Irin, who gestured for me to take a glass. But I couldn't stop looking at this strange form, who caused echoes of torment to ring in my ears. Not nearly as bad as the orchestra that had sounded when we entered but still distracting. And disturbing.

Irin cleared his throat.

I looked back at the tray. "Oh. No. Thank you, but I'm okay."

"Please, one drink will not hurt and I would be offended if you did not accept my hospitality." He took the glass and held it out to me.

I wanted to look at Lincoln, ask him if he thought it was poisoned. But I didn't, scared of appearing weak. There was no way he could know, anyway.

I took the glass. Irin smiled and took the other, clinking it against mine and then drinking slowly, waiting for me to follow. I did.

Just champagne—as far as I could tell.

And delicious.

I'd never tasted expensive wine like that before.

"Now, Violet, please turn around and show me my payment."

I blushed and took another, larger, sip of champagne, noticing as I did that my glass had somehow been refilled.

Imagination.

I took another sip. Same thing.

Probably not even real. Tastes good though.

I started to turn around on the spot awkwardly.

"No," Irin said. "This won't work." He moved closer to me and took the glass from my hand. "Your hair, though beautiful down, would be better away from your neck for the moment. Would you mind holding it up as you display the…offering?" I noticed he didn't say jewelry and I felt a tingle of fear at the base of my neck.

I bit my lip, increasingly uncomfortable. I held my hair up with both hands and started to turn, taking my time so he wouldn't make me do it again. I tried to steal a glance in Lincoln's direction, but I couldn't see him at all, despite feeling him and his power in the room.

When I had made a full turn, Irin seemed satisfied.

"Stunning," he said and passed me back my champagne. I took another sip.

I started to feel something strange and wondered if it was the champagne. But it wasn't like being drunk or even a reaction to a poison—it was almost…emotional. I pushed it aside.

"Do you like Santorini?" Irin asked, moving to the window.

"It's beautiful. Is that why you live here?"

He laughed lightly. "Originally, perhaps. But now I cannot fathom being anywhere else. I once built Utopia on this island, overflowing with wealth and sustenance—everything exactly as we…" He trailed off and his eyes honed in on me. "I will never leave. Though I do sometimes desire something new."

"What rank were you from?" I asked, unsure if I'd gone too far.

Irin took it in stride, showing that no offense had been taken by my question. "Originally? A Principality, then I was sent to this world. The first of my kind. Now, I am the last." He seemed sad for a moment but snapped out of it quickly. "And I have discovered a way to survive."

"By killing," I said softly.

"From time to time, but my tastes rarely venture there for more than survival's sake. I am not as lurid as my exile brethren, nor have I suffered the same mental derailment. A physical form was something that I was intended for, and as a result, I assimilated with more ease…however"—his expression shifted to somewhere between conniving and forlorn—"I must admit, it has also left me with…needs."

"What needs? What *are* you?" I asked, taking another sip of my drink, noticing that each time he did, I automatically felt the desire to do so too.

"My dear, 'Irin' is just another name for Grigori."

chapter twenty-four

"Wherefore have you forsaken the lofty and holy heaven, which endures for ever and have lain with woman; have defiled yourselves with the daughters of men; have taken to yourselves wives…and have begotten an impious offspring?"

Book of Enoch 15:2

I backed up a step, stumbling.

"Do not fear," he said, moving with me and clearly satisfied with my reaction. I put a hand out to the dining table I'd backed into, experiencing the same offbeat sensation I had felt earlier, losing my strength for a second, as if it was being drained.

"Violet?" Lincoln said from the corner.

He was offering to step in, but we both knew that wouldn't end well. At best, we'd return Irin, but there were still nearly a dozen faceless unknowns waiting for us upstairs. Plus, I was quite sure there were other beings lurking around us now.

"You…you all died—in the flood," I said to Irin, knowing

Lincoln would wait. I'd heard the stories enough times by now. When the floods came, they had destroyed all the exiles and the then-angel Grigori had turned on their duties, seeking vengeance and power and...women instead.

He smiled wryly. "A few always survive. Some of us were fortunate to have been underground already when the waters came. This room you are standing in, and some more that lie below, was originally created as a basement for our palace."

I looked at him, sure he was insane. We were so far beneath ground level, it couldn't be the basement of anything, and I was pretty sure that at the time of the floods, civilizations were *not* building palaces.

"My wife and I stayed here until the waters receded, though I admit it was a dark world for a while."

Another shock. He had a wife?

"Yes," he smiled, as if reading my mind. "My wife was the reason I lived here at first and abandoned my elect duties. She was a queen to her people. It was they who pulled a small group of us to safety and kept us beneath the ground.

"When we surfaced, we shared our knowledge and showed the people how to build a world more incredible than anything they'd ever seen. Alas, it was a simpler time—easier to dazzle with the basics of water delivery and drainage—but we also showed them how to build towns and castles. And"—he pointed in the direction of the volcano—"we were in the perfect location. Hidden as well as any place could be from the eyes of prying angels." These last words spoken with raw hatred.

"You know the volcano holds the gates to Hell?"

"Of course. But"—he shook his head—"in the end, that was their demise."

"Whose?"

Irin's voice dropped so I had to strain to hear him.

"The exiles who survived with me grew tired of living on the island. I tried. I sent them to Crete and told them to build their own kingdom there, but I knew it would be a short-lived solution. Eventually they grew so restless and desperate for their old army, they tried to open the gates. But they only caused destruction."

"The eruption," I said, remembering Griffin explaining that it had abolished an entire civilization on neighboring Crete.

"Hmm…" he said, from somewhere far away. "The wrath of Hell moves quickly. The fury of angels merciless. The exiles were destroyed along with everything we had created. Thousands of humans killed."

"How did you survive?"

"Once again, we went to ground."

"You and your wife?" I was actually starting to get excited, caught up in their love story. "You both survived?"

"No. She…sent for us. But there was so little time. When I got down here and realized she had gone back up in search of me, it was too late. The wave had already hit."

"That's why you'll never leave," I said, genuinely sad for him.

"This island was once hers. I could have sustained her mortal life force and had an eternity with her. Instead, I suffer her absence every day, the effects everlasting, but…" Pulling himself out of his memories, his expression shifted back to his previously amused state. "I have discovered new indulgences to occupy my time." He gestured to the cabinets that held shelf upon shelf of jewels and artifacts—ancient weapons, coins—and paintings on the walls above. I did a double-take when I spotted a Van Gogh and beside that, what I suspected was a Rembrandt.

My eyes settled on a silver necklace. I was struck by its simplicity in comparison to the other more gaudy and elaborate pieces. I couldn't take my eyes away from it, as if something was drawing me toward it.

Uri. This is what he meant. Why?

"Do you like it?" Irin asked.

I nodded. "But I don't understand how it is in this collection." He went to the cabinet and removed it. I shouldn't have been surprised that it wasn't under sensor security and behind locked doors, yet I was. He held it toward me and I took it in my hands, feeling the buzz of its presence immediately. The necklace held power.

"What does it do?" I asked, handing it back, just in case.

"It was my wife's. It holds a piece of the angel realm and helps to prevent illusion caused by anything or anyone angelic to the wearer. Of course, it is of no use to you or I as we do not need such things, but to a human, it is very valuable indeed." He slipped it back carefully into the cabinet. "She never adored this piece like others I gave her—she had lavish tastes—but our sons have always insisted we keep it," he added.

And that's when I stopped feeling sad for him. Sons.

"Those...the people who let us in?" I asked, that small twinge becoming a prickling sensation shooting up my spine.

He nodded. "Our surviving progeny."

Ancient Nephilim.

Fear coursed through me and I felt the pinch again, like something being pulled from me. Irin smiled.

He clasped his hands together. "Now, to our arrangement."

I swallowed, my mouth still dry as I struggled to absorb everything he was saying. He was *Grigori.* Not part human, part angel like us—one of the first all-angel Grigori. One of the ones who sided with exiles. Was the city he talked of Atlantis? Did that make him *more* dangerous or less? And I had no idea what he meant by his "way" of survival.

"You have presented the jewels quite beautifully," Irin went on. "Now, I will take possession of them."

I nodded, eager to proceed, and started to pull at the ruby ring that was already slipping off my finger.

"No, Violet," he said softly, taking a step toward me. "*I* will take possession."

Oh.

I pressed my lips together to stop them from quivering. Give me a fight any day, but this? All I could think about was the emerald spider with its many clasps around my upper thigh. I hadn't even let Morgan fasten it.

I took another step back but hit the glass wall. Irin smiled, closing the distance and putting his hands on my shoulders, pushing down steadily until I fell to the window seat. I was a fish in an aquarium and trapped with a shark.

"If you are quite comfortable..."

I couldn't talk, but the second his hand took mine, my body seized, knowing that his touch intended more.

"Violet?" Lincoln called again from the shadows, his tone controlled but somehow forced.

"I'm okay."

Then, I just shut down. Years of practice kicking in.

I retreated to that place where I'd long ago taught myself to go to block everything out, like removing myself from my body, to find somewhere safe and light, somewhere I wanted to be, always.

I smelled food cooking. And basil, lots of basil. Lincoln's warehouse.

Irin's hands wrapped around my wrist, one sliding up my forearm and then back again before he started to undo the clasp to the first bracelet, slipping it off slowly, so I could feel the chain trail against my skin.

I looked out the window, dead still, then thought about basil and focused on the light that cascaded through Lincoln's great arch windows every morning.

Hands slid across my collarbone to my opposite arm and the silver snake. He started to uncoil it, his fingers sliding up and down from my elbow, finally removing it.

Two down.

I went back to thinking of the belonging I'd always felt in my core when I was with Lincoln. I ignored all the problems, the reason why we would never be together, and clung to all the things that made us right and made me feel so safe.

Then Irin's mouth closed around the ring on my index finger and I flinched. I had to look. He was awaiting my reaction.

"Enough!" Lincoln's voice charged.

Irin smiled and stood up, letting my hand go.

Lincoln stepped out from the shadows. "You will not touch her again."

I wanted to speak up, tell him I could handle it, but I didn't, relieved just to have him in my sights.

"A deal was made. The stones are only part of the arrangement. Unless, of course, you have something better to offer?"

The way Irin spoke…the cat that got the cream.

Lincoln's hands flexed by his sides and I wondered if that "something better" Irin had in mind involved a dagger. Just when I thought Lincoln might make a move, he spoke again.

"You're an incubus, aren't you? Some exiles discovered they could sustain themselves and increase their power by feeding on human emotion. But not many could and even fewer dared to because it was so…addictive. Just one more reason you don't belong here. After you lost your wife, you became one, didn't you?"

What does that mean?

Irin shrugged. "The need she left in me was great, yes. I never cared to control humanity like the others. I simply wanted to enjoy its offerings." He moved to take my hand again. He was still smiling. "Speaking of which…"

"Do that again and I swear to you she will be the last thing you ever touch." Lincoln had his dagger in hand and had already moved closer.

Irin didn't appear concerned at all, which worried me. We had no idea what he could do and I didn't think it would be an easy fight.

"You feed on emotion..." I said, trying to defuse the moment while putting all the pieces together. "No wonder you like me."

"Oh, my dear, don't get me wrong—you are simply delicious and would be even more so if you were not so efficiently damaged, but you're a mere appetizer compared to your partner."

Lincoln didn't look at me. I was relieved; I didn't know if I could bear to see those eyes right now. No one had ever called me damaged out loud before. Well, no one other than me.

Irin paced slowly, watching as I no doubt displayed my shame as well as confusion at the second part of what he said. He was feeding off Lincoln.

He sighed, wistfully. "Like opening the cork on an aged wine... On an island where most emotion is that of honeymooners in love, which, while ripe for my purposes—ah." He shook his head in awe. "You two are like lobster in a world of mudfish."

I braced myself for him to continue removing the jewelry, but Lincoln took another step toward us, lowering his weapon.

"I'll do it," he said, as if subjecting himself to corporal punishment. "I'll take off the jewels."

Irin paused, considering the offer. "Why would I give up the feeding you provide me by being forced to watch?"

"You know it will cause just as much...if not more this way."

"Bringing you so close to your forbidden?"

Lincoln swallowed and nodded once.

Irin grinned and swept a hand from Lincoln to me. "Very well. In return for a kiss."

"No!" I wasn't kissing anyone.

"Not me," he said.

"No," I said again, which seemed to please Irin even more.

He retreated to the large dining table in the center of the room.

Lincoln moved to me, and his green eyes burned into mine.

"I will not force her to do anything, ever."

And though he spoke to Irin, his words were for me—a promise that I was safe with him and the apology for what we both knew we had to do. He knelt in front of me, a look of pain and fear covering his face.

"It's him or me." Then he leaned in close to my ear and whispered, "Put up your guards."

I felt an outpour of Lincoln's power around me. Could taste and smell the honey flavors unique to him overlaying the ever-present feeling of warmth and sunshine.

He started with the ankle bracelet, taking it off slowly, giving Irin the show he demanded, but without the creeping fingers. I tried to keep my barriers up, trying to put the pieces together like a wall of Lego, but I was not in Lincoln's league when it came to harnessing my strengths this way. Even visualizing a heavy steel fortress, I could still feel his fingers moving against my skin and it put a match to something inside me I was powerless to contain.

Lincoln moved to my hands and closed his eyes, as if praying for a moment, before his mouth closed around my finger and removed the ring. He did it so gently, with an endearing respect. It didn't surprise me that he used his mouth as Irin had. He knew that Irin would expect no less. But then he went to the second ring, and the third, and by the fourth, my cheeks were flushed and the small spark within me had started to blaze. Lincoln's touch had grown more sure and his contact more constant.

I tried to sing nursery rhymes in my head, to chant the alphabet, but when his mouth closed around the final ring…I had to hold on to the skirt of my dress with my free hand to stop myself from grabbing him.

Irin wheezed a chuckle like he was reading my mind.

I'm going to kill you. If not today, one day, I swear, I'm going to come back and kill you. Read that, you creep!

Thinking it might be best to direct Lincoln to the necklace and earrings next, I stood up but almost fell back down, my legs were shaking so much. Maybe it was the champagne finally hitting me—I'd been subconsciously sipping from the ever-filling glass.

I tried to keep my defenses up, but I wasn't doing a great job and was becoming increasingly unstable on my feet. I felt every minute movement as Lincoln unclasped the heavy necklace, releasing me of its weight. He followed with the earrings.

"Is that everything?" he asked, his eyes downcast and his voice so rough it barely sounded the words.

I stepped back, the slit in my dress parting to reveal the emerald spider on my thigh. I saw his eyes widen and caught the sound he couldn't contain.

It sent a shock wave through me.

Wordlessly, he dropped to his knees and started with the clasps at the back, but he struggled to work around the fabric of the dress. I pulled it back for him, leaving my whole leg exposed, hoping to hell that it meant he would get it done faster because I was burning up.

Don't think about how every time he takes his hand away from you, you want to scream.

Finally, Lincoln stood and turned to Irin, placing the emerald masterpiece on the table in front of him.

"I want your word that once this is done, we will have no opposition to our stay on the island, and in addition, I want your assurance that you will not assist any other exiles coming here—for any purpose."

Jesus Christ. He is seriously some kind of warrior god to have been so quick thinking. I was still stuck on the "champagne is magic and your fingers feel sooo nice" part.

Irin laughed heartily. "Oh, my boy, I would do almost anything for the finale. I give you my word on both, though I will not refrain from imposing a similar arrangement to grant these exiles abode."

Lincoln seemed to realize this was as much as he was going to get and nodded, before walking back to me. But it got me thinking.

"Wait!" I said louder than I'd intended. Everyone stopped. "I want something else."

Damn it. These angels are going to owe me.

Lincoln looked at me, "don't" written in his eyes.

But I did anyway.

"I want the necklace. You said yourself, you have plenty that are more special and more valuable. If you want me to do this, then I want the necklace." Right at that moment, I was sure it was important.

Irin's easy expression changed and he slammed his fist down on the table with such force that the whole piece jumped up before thumping back down. But I saw the look in his eyes—the greed, the hunger—and knew any promises he'd made to his freakoid children came second to his own needs.

His smiled returned. "I suggest you hide it well until you are clear of the island. I will not be held responsible if my sons discover its whereabouts."

I shrugged in casual agreement even though my heart was pounding. Lincoln started toward me again, looking relieved I hadn't just blown everything. And maybe a little impressed. Definitely curious.

"But," Irin added sheepishly, "you will both need to lower your defenses for the kiss."

My heart stopped thudding and skipped a beat instead. We thought we'd one-upped him, but really he'd walked us right into his trap. Lincoln lifted his luminous green eyes to meet mine and we stared at each other.

The worst thing, as awful as it was, was that part of me was dancing inside.

My entire being wanted this, and while I knew we'd made the decision, for all the right reasons, never to let this happen, I wanted him to kiss me—desperately. Before I knew what was happening, eagerness overruled and I'd dropped my defenses. A wave of pure need crashed into me. I took the closing step toward him.

"Violet," Lincoln said, straining against his emotions, but that was all we had time for before I felt the honey of his power melt away, replaced by only him. For the first time in ages, it was just us. His hand went to the side of my face and then to the back of my neck as he drew my so willing body toward him.

As we kissed, I felt him pull me closer, tighter, but not tight enough. Never close enough. His mouth molded to mine and I felt his soul reach out to me as mine did to him. *Almost* touching—desperate.

Mine, mine, mine.

I was surprised my hands didn't go wild, trying to get to all of him—but they didn't. I just held on to him for dear life. In that moment, I was quite willing to take down anything that ever tried to take him away from me again. Lincoln held me in the same way, his arms gripping me so firmly that my back arched in perfect agony as we kissed. I could feel it now, Irin feeding from us, the tiny tendrils of my feelings for Lincoln being pulled from me, but there was so much more, he barely touched the surface. When Lincoln's lips broke from mine momentarily, I cried out to him frantically, "I love you!" as if this might be my one and only chance to say it again.

The words snapped something between us. Lincoln stiffened and pulled away, stumbling back, even though I'd held him with all my strength.

I was breathless.

And broken.

My arms wrapped around my waist as I tried to hold myself together.

Lincoln kept moving back, a stunned expression on his face. I felt his power start to swirl as he leaned over, bracing his hands on his knees, and put the barriers between us back up. I attempted to follow suit.

"More than I could've *ever* dreamed. Soul mates," Irin slurred, drunk on our emotion.

I wanted to stab him in the eye, which helped bring me back to myself a bit. He stood up crooked and walked lazily to one of the cabinets.

He threw me the necklace, and without thinking, I stuffed it down the front of the dress.

And if Uri thinks he's getting it, he's got another think coming.

"We're leaving," Lincoln said.

"Feel free, payment has been more than sufficient. I have only a parting question," Irin said, following us dreamily.

We headed for the double doors. Lincoln pushed them with staggering force and held them open for me. We charged through the hall and started up the stairs with no intention of stopping until we reached the ground level, where the faceless exiles still stood as if they'd not moved the entire time. In front of the door was the one who'd shown us in, blocking our way to freedom.

I spun around, my whole body shaking. Irin was right behind me.

"What?" I roared, finding my voice.

"How did my hauntings reveal themselves to you?" he asked

calmly, gesturing a hand to the Nephilim. "What do you see when you look at my sons?"

"Nothing," I said, earning a flash of the eyes from Lincoln. Irin smiled knowingly. "They're empty, hollow, except for the sound."

"Yes, they accumulate those. The screams of all who have laid eyes on them before. Put a few together and it's quite the symphony." He walked us a few steps closer to the door and nodded to the Nephilim, who moved away at his command.

"And Lincoln, what about you? I should warn you, I can see every form my children take."

Lincoln served up death-in-a-stare. "Then why ask?" he growled.

I knew he would take Irin down if he felt he had a good shot. But after the feed Irin had just gorged himself on, it would probably be suicide. And we had our orders.

Irin closed his eyes in some kind of delight. "Dessert."

Lincoln's nostrils flared and his jaw clenched. "I saw Violet." When Irin's eyes opened, his face flooded with pleasure.

"Each one, *exactly* as she is tonight. Quite a beautiful sight, though"—he winked at me—"for your partner, more torment than he could imagine."

"Torment?" I repeated, starting to feel sick. "That's what they show us?"

"They show us exactly what we most dread to see in ourselves." Irin opened the door and held out his hand for us to leave. "Please, *do* stop by again."

chapter twenty-five

"Whatever fate ordains, danger or hurt, or death predetermined, nothing can avert."

Theognis of Megara

Lincoln sat in the front on the way back to Fira. I was in the back, next to Max, trying not to suffocate in the overwhelming amount of power Lincoln was pulling on. No one spoke.

The chauffeur dropped us back at the hotel and Lincoln was out in an instant, bounding up the steps three at a time.

I followed, less enthusiastic.

By the time I reached the foyer, I could hear him yelling. I followed the sound into the hotel bar where Josephine sat comfortably, surrounded by four of her ninjas.

When Morgan saw me standing in the doorway, her expression dropped a little. She shifted in her seat like she wanted to come to me, but I shook my head. It wouldn't help her to leave her post.

"You had no right! An *incubus*!" Lincoln bellowed. It was the third time he'd yelled those words since I'd walked in. "Do you have any idea how much you are risking?"

Josephine smoothed down her skirt and looked uninterested. "Lincoln, calm down. I sent you in there to do your job. The Keeper called after you left him to tell me we are welcome to stay on Santorini. You have both returned unharmed. I don't understand the problem." But the way her look had morphed from one of boredom to one of challenge said she understood exactly.

"You played us! This had nothing to do with Violet's power and everything to do with our…connection," Lincoln, still furious, yelled, but without as much volume. Since when had he downgraded our relationship to a *connection*?

Josephine stood up. "Yes. It was the easiest way. I knew once the Keeper laid eyes on the pair of you, it would guarantee our stay. I have a job to do and nursing you and your partner's feelings is not part of it." She brushed past him toward the way out. "Really, Lincoln, all this soul mates business is tiresome. It's no different from a forced chemical reaction and has nothing to do with your *real* feelings for the girl. You need to learn how to control the effects at some point unless you aspire to an end like Nyla's. I still have high hopes for you. Consider this your first practice session." Josephine went out the door, but not before floating a look in my direction. She knew I'd heard everything.

Lincoln stood still, hands fisted by his sides. As soon as she was gone, he dropped his head and let out a ragged breath.

"Is it so terrible to be close to me?" I asked softly.

His head flew up and he spun around. *He* hadn't realized I was there, which in itself was a sign of how distracted he was.

"Violet, you...should go to bed." His shoulders tensed and he moved to the bar, pouring himself a glass of wine from the bottle that must have been Josephine's.

I leaned against a stool and took off my shoes, which had cut into the backs of my heels. "You could've at least said I looked pretty. Or...I don't know, *something*." Because for some reason, out of everything that had happened tonight, that seemed to grate on me the most.

He took a gulp of wine and shook his head. "You don't want me to start saying *something*. Trust me."

I felt a sting in my eyes and blinked back the tears. "Am I really the thing you dread to see in yourself most?"

He collapsed onto a stool. "Is nothingness really the thing you dread to see in *yourself*?" He looked so pained that I decided to give him an honest answer.

"Yes. Since I embraced and killed that image of myself...I've always feared that a part of what I'd done was true, that I really did kill a part of myself. It felt real. At first, I thought it was my soul, but then you and I...Well, things wouldn't be like this if I didn't have a soul, right?"

He held his glass up as if in agreement.

"But I'm still frightened by what I've become, am *becoming*, and about..."—I looked at the blue carpet, avoiding his eyes—"the things I've given up." I still couldn't look at him, but when I heard the stool creak, I quickly added: "Now you answer me. Am I the thing *you* dread the most?"

He started to move, finishing his drink and taking a few steps toward me. But I needed to know. "Answer me," I insisted.

He stopped and sighed. "Yes. That's what I dread."

I closed my eyes and nodded, my jaw and neck aching with the awful truth.

I'm such a fool. Leave. Now!

"No wonder tonight was so horrific for you. Good night then," I said, barely getting the words out before rushing for the stairs.

"Violet!" Lincoln called after me.

But I didn't want to stick around for an encore. Was Josephine right? Were Lincoln's feelings for me only there because our souls were somehow chemically drawn to one another? Did *he* believe that if it weren't for that, he wouldn't care for me?

I ran up the stairs, suddenly feeling ridiculous in my outfit. Instead of going to my room, I kept running, not able to stop until I stumbled out onto the rooftop, gasping for fresh air.

The view over Santorini was breathtaking, and even through my blurred vision, once again, I was awestruck by its beauty. But now it just made me cry more.

Everything beautiful is tainted.

To prove my point, I looked out to the ocean and the volcano's silhouette.

How can I do this? How can I be this person who fights these battles?

All I wanted was to get into my flannel PJs and eat a tub of ice cream while bawling my eyes out. Everyone wanted me to be someone I wasn't. Even Lincoln.

"Me and my big mouth," I muttered to myself. "Stupid, stupid, stupid." There he was, in the middle of his dreaded nightmare, and I was telling him I loved him.

Leaning my back against one of the small barrier walls, I slid down to the ground. Once there, I realized just how tired I was. I cried and cried even though I knew I should go to my room. We were expected up early in the morning to start our investigations. But all of my strength had faded and now my anger too.

As I drifted off to sleep on the hard concrete of the rooftop, a cool breeze carrying musk and jasmine swept my hair across my face. Something was telling me to do something, ringing some muted alarm bell, but I felt numb and ignored it, soon deep in slumber.

The ground was uneven and something was digging into my back. I started to open my eyes, then I felt him. He had obviously been here for some time. The senses were well-established within me, not like when first sparking.

How did I sleep through that?

I tried to stop my body from tensing and suppressed my instinct to leap up, on the offensive. If he had come to kill me, he could've done the job by now, easily.

My hair was covering my face, so I took the chance to open my eyes. He was sitting on the barrier, feet up, back against one of the higher pillars. The sun was in its first soft moments of rising and provided the perfect backdrop lighting.

He was looking out at the horizon but I could see his eyes.

Tired, lonely…lost.

"I know you're awake," Phoenix said.

I wasn't surprised. He didn't move or say anything else, so I sat up, stretching out the kinks in my body as I did.

I stood and found myself moving toward him, marveling at how comfortable I felt around him at times, despite knowing how much he hated me and that eventually, he would kill me. Perhaps there was some kind of peace in that. Maybe he felt it too, knowing I would take him with me if I could.

"I told you that dress would look ravishing."

Then he did the strangest thing. He reached behind his back and revealed a to-go cup, passing it to me. The coffee aroma wafted over me.

I took it, staring at the cup, completely dumbfounded.

"Drink it. I don't need poison to kill you," he said plainly.

Sadly true.

It was hot and yet I knew he'd been here for a while. Had he come and gone? Known I was stirring and left to get it? I took a sip and almost choked.

"Our definition of poison is a little different," I said, holding it back out to him.

"Drink it."

I resisted the urge to spit. "What is this and how much sugar is in there?"

"Coffee and ginseng, and a lot. Drink. You need it."

I eyed him suspiciously. "Why?"

"Because the Keeper fed off you last night." He glanced at me briefly. "And he fed well."

"How do you know?" I asked, wrapping an arm around myself, remembering the uncomfortable feeling of Irin's eyes on me.

"Just the look of you tells me enough, but…I also can't feel you the way I normally can."

That was interesting. "And you care why?" He didn't answer. I half laughed. "Just like Jordan," I said, as much to myself as to him. "You need me. Jesus, you're just fattening me up for the slaughter!" But I took another sip anyway. If it was going to help bring back my strength, I wasn't about to refuse it.

He smiled, but the smile disappeared quickly.

"So you figured out the Scriptures."

Our hopes of a few days' lead on him were now over.

"Naturally."

I looked around, wondering how he'd managed to get through a hotel full of Grigori. "Did you fly here?" I asked, sure I would have heard the distinctive shriek if that stairwell door had opened.

"No. I was traveling across rooftops. It was a leap to this one—but when I'm moving that fast, momentum carries me."

"Huh. Makes sense." Nothing could stop Phoenix when he became the wind. A thought that made me shiver.

We stood and looked out toward the horizon and the volcano. I knew he must be there for a reason, which couldn't be good. But he was with me, where I could see him, not attacking my friends or sneaking up from behind, and in a way, that made it easier.

He looked me up and down again and shook his head. "No wonder the Keeper hasn't requested our payment yet."

I couldn't contain the small lift at the corners of my mouth.

"I'm sure he'll love you."

For the Keeper to have someone like Phoenix, who could feed him emotion, would probably be his ultimate pleasure.

Phoenix shrugged. "Which is why he'll never see me."

"Why not?" It seemed like a no-brainer.

He smiled a smile I had not seen since before…everything changed.

"I'm like emotion on a drip for his kind. And after the feed he's just had, he's very strong. He'd try to never let me go."

"Good to know," I said.

His smile broadened and he jumped off the wall to stand uncomfortably close. "Try," he emphasized.

I wasn't sure if we were about to fight, or if more of his exiles were soon to arrive. In the same way that Phoenix's awareness of me was off, I was sure I wasn't operating at a hundred percent either. Regardless, I found myself increasingly relaxed. I wondered briefly if he was making me feel that way.

"I know you healed me. Back in Jordan, when you saw Magda coming for you. You healed me in case she returned you."

He wiped a hand over his face as if tired, hiding his eyes. "I needed to be at full strength. Wouldn't have made any difference to you if she'd gotten to me, anyway," he said, downplaying his admission to healing me.

He was partly right too. If she had killed him, I'd be dead.

"Why do you hate me so much?"

Phoenix shot a dangerous look in my direction. "I had a life before you. It wasn't perfect but I had it in hand. You made me want things, want to belong. Now I won't stop until I do."

"Do you really think bringing her back will give you a place in this world?"

He smiled again. Not warm anymore. I'd gone too far; the tone of our conversation had changed.

"She will take the world for her own—and I will be the son who made it all possible."

"Yes, you will. Can you live with that? Because I know that the person who was once my friend would never have been okay with bringing that kind of evil into the world."

He leapt back up onto the wall. "I was never your friend. And anyway, that person is gone. All that's left is the exile. I have arrangements to tend to but I'll return. Meet me up here tonight at midnight."

"And why would I do that?"

"Because I'm not inclined to take your life yet, but some of your friends are more expendable. I don't just have exiles here, lover. There are still a number at home, watching over your father."

My hand flew to my mouth.

"He's safe, don't worry. I know you won't let him down." With that, he leapt off the roof, his last words only just reaching me. "Only you, Violet."

He called me by my name.

I couldn't keep sight of him, he was so fast—only the wind remained. I realized that he hadn't tried to use his power on me, hadn't pushed those feelings of lust or seduction into me, which made me even more nervous.

Phoenix was right. The exile was the one in charge now. The human in him seemed almost fully extinguished.

And the games were over.

chapter twenty-six

"And to every man has been assigned a good and an evil angel; one assisting him and the other annoying him, from his cradle to his coffin."

Voltaire

By the time I made it back to my room, Steph had already gone, leaving a note on my bed:

Call me ASAP otherwise am raising alarm. And if you are okay, expect lengthy explanations ahead!
Steph xx

I sent her a text:

All okay. Back in room. Catch up after shower. Vi xx

Three seconds later, she replied:

God Squad meeting downstairs 2hrs. In Dapper's room if looking for me. S xx

I tried not to think as I showered, but it was impossible. Phoenix had given me an ultimatum, and no matter which way I looked at it, I couldn't see a way out.

After getting dressed in a pair of shorts and a yellow tank top, I collapsed on my bed, staying there until I heard a knock at my door. I wondered if it was Lincoln but quickly discarded that theory. I'd be able to feel him.

I opened the door to Spence, who, in his uniform of faded loose jeans and a T-shirt—green today—looked altogether too happy to see me.

"You alone?"

"Yes..." I said suspiciously.

"Up for a little bit of information gathering?"

"No. I'm up for a little bit of sleep gathering, actually." I motioned for him to move back so I could close the door.

"You've lost your spirit, Eden!"

When I didn't respond to the challenge, he added, "Josephine's having a meeting with the Assembly at the moment, and your partner was invited. They've been in there all morning, since Lincoln hauled in some guy."

"What guy?"

"No idea, but Lincoln seemed pretty determined to keep him under wraps. I only got a glimpse, but if I had to guess, I'd peg him as Grigori, though…He didn't seem too happy about being here." Spence raised his eyebrows and looked down the hall eagerly. "Aren't you interested to know why you weren't told about it?"

He was good, I'd give him that. Spence knew exactly how to spike my interest. I contemplated for a moment before pulling my hair into a ponytail, grabbing my room key, and heading out with him.

"So what's the deal?" I asked.

"They're planning something, but we're just the foot soldiers. That's the thing with the Academy. They aren't like Griffin; they operate on a need-to-know basis and even then…"

"We *don't* need to know?"

"Well, I definitely don't. I'm on their shit list for all eternity, but you? I'd say they're keeping you out of the loop on purpose."

I heard the implication but threw it out there anyway.

"And so is Lincoln?"

Spence shrugged. "He's sharing my room. I've only seen him once, but he's…busy and not in a talking mood. Then this guy turned up. Something's going on."

"Okay, where are they?"

"I followed one of Josephine's crew until he went into the bar. I'd say that's where they are now."

I nodded. "There are two entries to that room," I said, remembering the scene in there after we'd returned from seeing Irin. "Which one did he go through?"

"The one near the elevators."

"Okay, we'll go to the other one then—hopefully they won't be watching it as closely."

"Nice to be working with you again, Eden. You missed a great night last night, by the way. Got Zoe so drunk we almost talked her into doing a naked knock-and-run on Josephine's door."

I smiled when I saw the twinkle in his eye. "Sorry I've been so moody lately."

"It's okay. You're a chick. I get it," he said, laughing. I swiped him playfully on the shoulder. "Still can't keep your hands off me, I see!"

"Yes. I don't know how I make it through the days." I fake swooned.

We bantered that way, letting off some steam, all the way downstairs. I realized how much I'd been missing hanging out with Spence. Apart from Steph, he was one of the only people who offered no added complications to my life. Just a friend.

Who might get me into a little trouble every now and then…

A thought that had me smiling even more.

We were right. The other door to the bar was still ajar and all the Grigori inside were sitting around a table at the far end. But Spence and I could hear just fine.

I could make out five Grigori. Josephine, two of her ninjas who had been on the plane—I hadn't bothered to get their names yet—someone I had never seen before, and Lincoln. They were talking to each other across the table, but I could hear additional voices and noticed a speakerphone in the middle of the table. They were on a conference call.

"We need to decide on acceptable casualties," Josephine said matter-of-factly.

My eyes narrowed as I looked back at Spence. He just raised his eyebrows as if to say, "Well, that's Josephine."

"It's too early to be talking about acceptable casualties!" Lincoln said, and though I could hear his conviction, I could also sense the weariness. He was exhausted. "We should be focused on defusing this situation. There are a number of plans we can make for all stages of this process that we should be concentrating on."

"And what plan would you suggest, Lincoln Wood?" Josephine asked, condescendingly. I had half a mind to barge in there and show her a close view of my fist.

Lincoln turned to the man I didn't know. I got my first good look at him as he leaned to the side, idly resting his chin in his hand, all but yawning. Dressed in faded black jeans and a T-shirt, he also had a long, leather jacket that was hanging off the back of his chair. I almost scoffed—we were hardly in leather-jacket climate. But then I caught a glimpse of what it concealed. The man had more weapons than I'd ever seen one person carry—strapped inside were more than a dozen silver blades.

Are they all Grigori blades?

The stranger looked at Lincoln through dark eyes. He had such sharply defined cheekbones, he looked like he could do with a few extra pounds, and his jaw was in dire need of a shave. His hair was buzz-cut short, and I could see the scars that read like a road map over his scalp. I swallowed hard. Even though I had my own on my wrist, generally Grigori didn't scar. Whatever had inflicted those wounds had done so before this man became Grigori, before he was even seventeen.

"Oh, this'll be grand," he said, watching Lincoln as he kicked out his feet under the table. "Let's hear it, then."

"You have people who are near. Call them. Get them here."

"Not bloody likely, mate."

"Gray, you and I both know you're lucky we showed up when we did. You had no permission to be on this island and no way of getting off without the Keeper discovering you. It's a miracle you survived as long as you did. That's why you came groveling to us. How did you end up stranded here for over a month?"

"Someone's sick idea of a joke." Gray flashed a cold smile. "I'm not one of your troopers. I made that choice a long time ago. I don't answer to you or your bleedin' Assembly."

"Fine," Lincoln said sharply. "Then leave now. But we won't be taking you off the island when we leave, and since the Keeper and I are now so friendly, I'll be sure to let him know where to find you."

"Christ, you don't waste time with negotiations, do you?"

"We're out of time," Lincoln snapped. "How many can you have here by tomorrow?"

Gray sighed, "Some. A fair few more if you give me a couple of days."

Lincoln turned back to Josephine, a steely determination on his face. "With Rogue and Academy forces, our numbers should rival anything he has."

"And, again, your plan is?" Josephine responded, feigning lack of interest.

I was quite sure I wasn't the only one fully aware that Lincoln had just taken over as commander in chief. I felt a swell of pride for him, but the anger wasn't far behind. He was having this meeting behind my back. Surely, I would be a part of one of those potential plans when it came to stopping Phoenix?

Lincoln strode across the room confidently, but I could see how much he was straining. He started to open his mouth to go on but halted midstride, a look of fury passing over his features for just a second before he returned to his previous stance.

"Excuse me," he said to the group, pulling his phone out of his pocket. "I have a call I need to take." He walked out the back doorway.

I looked quizzically at Spence, who shrugged. I hadn't heard his phone ring.

We stayed where we were, listening as Josephine went on. "He's gone. There are too many unknowns here to be sure of anything, Drenson. Griffin has kept his team close; they will be loyal to the end. He'll be back tomorrow, if not tonight, and we have no new information about the girl other than that the meeting with the Keeper was successful—the pair are indeed kindred in soul. This doesn't help us in any way."

While Josephine spoke, she passed an assessing eye over Gray, who was displaying no curiosity in her conversation. Her final look—and message—was nevertheless received clearly: he wouldn't repeat a word of it.

"Well, Lincoln appears to have a plan. Let's get through this mess they've created first, then we'll deal with the girl," said the male voice on the loudspeaker.

"Hmm," Josephine contemplated. "Her power is unknown, and those who have some concept of it are tight-lipped. It's only a matter of time. We can't afford to leave it for too long."

"No," he agreed.

A hand clasped my upper arm and spun me around. Lincoln—a very, very angry Lincoln—snapped his other hand over my mouth before I could speak. Spence jumped up.

"Shh!" Lincoln mouthed.

We both nodded and let him drag us into the stairwell. Once the door had closed, he turned on us.

"*What* are you doing?"

"I...I...They were talking about me."

His eyes flashed menacingly in the direction of the bar.

"Violet, you can't be here," he whispered sternly, and then, as if deciding something on the spot, he started pulling me toward the stairs.

"Hey, Linc, come on, man. We just wanna know what's going on," Spence tried, but it was a lost cause: Lincoln was fuming.

"Spence," he growled, keeping his grip on my arm, "I guess I should be grateful you didn't just make yourself invisible and come right on in. Go for a walk."

We so should've done that.

Spence stood tall.

Good for him.

"Eden?" he asked, and I appreciated him letting me decide. Most guys just go ahead and do the macho thing.

I looked at Lincoln, who was not about to calm down in a hurry.

"It's okay. I'll catch up with you in a bit."

Spence hesitated a moment, then sighed. "Only 'cause I know you, man," he said to Lincoln. "But"—he gestured toward the hand still gripping my arm—"go easy." And with that, he spun on his heel and headed for the foyer doors.

Lincoln's hold on me loosened instantly, but he didn't let go. Instead, he led me up the stairs and toward my room. "Key?" he demanded, stopping outside my door, hand out, not looking at me. I took out my key and handed it to him.

He unlocked my door and dragged me inside.

"Stay in here. We're going to the volcano in an hour. Until then, don't leave your room. Can you manage that?"

"You can't just order me around, Lincoln!" I said, ripping my arm out of his hold.

"Actually, I can. Griffin left me in charge. Right now, you have to accept that there are people here who know more than you do, have more experience than you do, and might have good reason for not involving you in certain things."

"What? So you want me to pretend I didn't just hear you talking about launching some kind of army? Stop treating me like a child!"

"Violet, I just caught you spying on a private meeting. If you don't want to be treated like a child…" He clenched his jaw for a moment and looked away from me. "Stop acting like one."

I was speechless. He had never spoken to me like that before. Lincoln was understanding; he included me in things, encouraged my opinion. He'd never told me to stay away before, even when it meant I could be in danger. And he'd *never* called me a child. It was almost as if he had deliberately said the one thing he knew would upset me the most.

He went back to my door and didn't turn round to face me when he stopped to say, "Just stay in your room…please."

I wanted to tell him to go jam his head up his ass. I *wanted* to fight back and stand up for myself, but I was so stunned, I couldn't manage anything more than the meek "Yes" that fell from my lips.

After pacing the room for a few minutes, I collapsed onto my bed and put a pillow over my head. I had an hour until we were supposed to meet downstairs.

Of course, the minute I stopped seething about Lincoln and closed my eyes to finally get some rest, I felt the room change, like it had lifted off the ground. I was so tired, my body lethargic, wanting to stay still. This time, it was easier for me to break the hold of the spell, but it was also physically draining. I just didn't have the energy, which wasn't good, considering I'd already had a visit from Uri. It had to be Nox on his way, distorting my reality to make room for his.

I pushed the pillow off my face and tucked it under my head.

Okay, so not the most defensive move, but an improvement.

This time, the sands cascaded down from the tops of the walls until Nox appeared, standing beside Steph's bed.

He looked the same and yet different. There was the smoothness he always had—the easy look of someone inviting but with an ulterior motive, always working an angle. Then there were his clothes. Unlike Uri, he enjoyed the material aspects of humanity, and today he was indulging in a to-the-ground, slim-fit black tunic that was tapered at the waist and had a raised collar.

Please. I rolled my eyes.

"It is very *Matrix*, don't you think?" he asked, not coming any closer, displaying the same repulsion toward me as Uri had done.

I wondered fleetingly what he'd do if I sneezed on him.

Probably run screaming.

"If you're going to offer me a pill that lets me live in ignorance, I'll take it."

This earned me a smile, though not a very warm one.

"I'm tired, Nox. I'm sure you have something completely messed up to tell me, but honestly, I don't care."

"You do look below average. Even for you."

I pushed up onto an elbow. He was eyeing Steph's bed.

"You know what? You suck."

Not my strongest ever comeback.

I could see the same movements in the background behind him as I saw each time he or Uri visited. They were so delicate—translucent forms like jellyfish—but when my eyes focused on one spot, they seemed to dissolve and re-form in another place, still moving as if trying to go somewhere.

Searching.

Nox watched me and followed my gaze. "You see them?" he asked, trying to hide his interest.

I nodded.

"Do they call to you?"

"I…I don't know." And yet I did feel a distinctive pull toward them. "What are they?"

"If you are meant to know, you will."

"Like I said, you suck."

He raised a single eyebrow and then motioned to Steph's bed. I collapsed back onto mine as he slid down onto the other, lying on his back and carefully positioning himself in the middle.

Weirdo.

"I have never been told that before," he said, preoccupied with testing the springs.

"Well, you do. All of you, actually, angels in general—suck. We'd be better off without you."

He laughed lightly and it was a clear warning. I felt his presence terrifyingly close to me, despite the fact he hadn't moved an inch.

"Without us, you would be nothing more than lowly beasts. It is only through us that your dim minds have the faculty of higher intelligence. Without us, you would still live in trees until the larger, more territorial creatures wiped you out."

I didn't have a response for that and from the way he said it, I was fairly certain one would not be welcome anyway.

"Would you get off my best friend's bed?" I settled for.

"Did you like my gift?" he taunted, not moving.

"I'm sorry?"

"Oh, I know. It was a shame I could not be there. Uri insisted on taking the first visit this time and I missed my chance to talk to you in the dress, but I watched. I believe I made a significant improvement. Would you really have attacked that girl?" he asked, smiling.

The dress. It was him.

"How...? Josephine arranged the outfit."

"Yes, but coincidence is my specialty. You didn't really think it was only by chance that the dress you swooned over while in the presence of darkness would not come to show you its favor?"

"I..." I sat up.

He raised his eyebrows, watching how easily I was now able to move in this twisted reality.

"What does that mean?" I asked, starting to panic. "Why would darkness favor me?"

He chuckled. "Fear not." He sat up too. "Remarkably comfortable," he said, marveling at the bed.

I glared at him and he flicked a hand to one side, bored with giving explanations.

"You are so easy to influence, Violet. Really, it makes working with you so entertaining. Especially when I have the pleasure of wondering just where that will of yours might take you next. How *was* Phoenix by the way?"

"You think I should go with him?" I whispered, afraid of the answer.

This seemed to bring more joy to Nox than anything.

"The better question is—if you thought it *was* what I wanted you to do, would you do the opposite simply to prove a point?"

"Get out!" I hated the way he twisted everything, made me feel guilty when I hadn't done anything wrong. Nonetheless, his words struck a chord. I didn't want the favor of darkness, nor did I want to walk right into its traps.

"Certainly." He stood in a fluid, graceful movement, though as he did, one of the many small buttons on the front of his jacket popped off. Instinctively, I caught it before it hit me in the face. Nox watched, perplexed by this new imperfection in his outfit, but recovered quickly. "Before I go, I wonder…if you could have something you desire greatly, something that has been denied you… if that were available—would you consider opening the gates of Tartarus yourself?"

"No."

He smiled knowingly and left, the sand melting back into the walls and the indent from his weight on Steph's bed disappearing completely.

I opened my hand. Just like the grains of sand, the button had stayed behind.

I can keep things.

Nausea stopped any further thought. I rolled over and closed my eyes, but then had to keep going, rolling off the bed. I made it to the bathroom just in time. The combination of fatigue and realm crossings was not kind to my stomach, and I felt like there was nothing left of me after the third time I had thrown my head over the toilet.

Eventually, I crawled back to bed, wondering if I should tell someone about these otherworldly visits. But then I remembered the way Lincoln had spoken to me, his orders to stay put, and my stomach lurched again, so I settled my head onto the pillow, kicking my shoes off, and decided, spitefully, to tell someone.

Later.

chapter twenty-seven

"What does not kill me, makes me stronger."

FRIEDRICH NIETZSCHE

I sat at the less crowded, front end of the boat. I was grateful for its size, even if it was just another display of excess by Josephine—it made it easy for me to escape from everyone. Well, everyone but Steph, of course. She hadn't bought my story about just being exhausted, though it was true. Mostly.

Kaitlin and Samuel had seen us off at the marina and, after their initial shock at discovering that Josephine had sent Lincoln and me to an incubus, explained what they knew.

"Irin must have fed on your emotion and energy, which is very dangerous in the hands of an inexperienced incubus," Kaitlin cautioned.

At least I knew that Irin was definitely *not* an amateur.

"Direct contact with them is really dangerous, Violet!" Samuel snapped. "You two should have told us."

I gulped and refrained from sharing the fact that he'd barely touched me. Lincoln had made sure of that.

Had he known? Was that why he stepped in last night?

Lincoln had looked fatigued this morning. Now, sitting on the boat, I tried to look over my shoulder discreetly, as if taking in the views from the bow. He was talking to Max while leaning against the side railing, as if resting. But when I looked more carefully, I could see he had a white-knuckled grip on the railing and his brow glistened with sweat. He was working hard just to stand. When Josephine beckoned Max over to her and he had walked away, Lincoln's relaxed face contorted, briefly exposing his agony, and his body folded over before he could stop it.

Irin had said Lincoln was the best source of emotion. I didn't know why, but he'd fed off him severely.

My shoulders sagged and I groaned. I wanted to be mad at Lincoln for all the things he hadn't done last night, for the things he'd said last night *and* this morning, but seeing him this way, all I could do was worry for him.

Lost in my thoughts, I didn't realize I was staring until he caught my eye and straightened. I could tell he was about to come over. I looked away and quickly jumped into conversation with Steph, who'd insisted on staying glued to my hip today. I didn't look back again and he didn't come over.

It hurts too much to be close.

And it did. Literally. The pain encompassed my entire body.

Maybe I was losing my mind, but I was sure that the sharp spasms I was feeling intensified whenever I was near him.

The boat was an old-style wooden vessel, highly polished so that it gleamed under the morning sunlight. With its three crisp white sails, it was perfect and made me want to point it toward the horizon and let it take me wherever it so desired.

I laid back and closed my eyes.

"Are you going to tell me what's going on?"

I lolled my head to the side and squinted to see Steph. "What do you mean?"

She pushed her sunglasses up onto her head. "Is this the brightest place you have ever been or what?" she asked, looking directly into the sun. She didn't wait for my response. "I know you didn't come back to our room until this morning. Max told Salvatore that you got back with Lincoln just after midnight. I get the whole Keeper thing, which is just wrong, by the way." She threw a severe look in Josephine's direction. "You should've told me, you know, but either way, you were still missing for a long time. What gives?"

I closed my eyes again and felt the warmth from the sun.

"Nothing gives. I was upset after having to see the Keeper and didn't realize he had taken so much of my energy. I went up to the rooftop to clear my mind, but I fell asleep. When I woke up, it was already morning and I came back to our room. I see you weren't alone anyway," I added, raising an eyebrow. I'd noticed the extra pillows and blankets.

"He was on the floor," Steph said with false dignity.

I smiled. "Yes. But was he always there?"

Steph elbowed me but then I felt her slump beside me.

"Actually, yes. He was paranoid all night that you'd walk in at any moment and accuse him of stealing your best friend's honor."

That made me laugh out loud. Steph too.

"Where is your Italian stallion, anyway?" I asked between snorts.

"Josephine sent him to collect Academy arrivals. A plane is due in about now."

"I don't trust her. There are too many things going on we don't know about." I cast a worried glance in her direction and then toward Lincoln.

As we neared the volcanic island of Nea Kameni, the boat dropped its sails and everyone moved to get a better view of what at first just looked like a large mound. When you think of a volcano, you expect something dramatic with a gigantic peak, but this... this was desolate—ashen, black, and rocky, the only signs of life coming from the fine carpet of red moss, bleeding from the barren earth. I shivered at the sight, knowing what secrets lay beneath, and fought the urge to scream at everyone to leave this place.

When I walked past Lincoln, I stopped, pulling out a bottle of Coke from my bag to which I'd already added a few extra spoonfuls of sugar at the hotel. Finding the ginseng had been more challenging, but an accommodating kitchen hand had gone on a mission and returned with something that smelled about the same. The syrupy coffee in the morning had worked wonders, and I'd already had one of my concoctions since then, so was feeling better again.

"Here," I said, holding it out to him.

"No thanks," he said, looking at me strangely. Lincoln didn't usually drink fizzy drinks.

I pushed it toward him again. "It helps."

He took the bottle and studied the bottom, where a clump of sugar hadn't dissolved. "What's in it?"

"Sugar and ginseng." He gave me another odd look from beneath a furrowed brow. "It works."

"Who told you that?" he asked, his eyes fixed curiously on me.

I froze, trying not to give away my surprise at the question. "Kaitlin," I said after barely a pause.

He considered the bottle for a moment before taking it. "Thanks," he said.

I nodded and moved on, avoiding his eyes. I hated lying to him.

As we got off the boat, I saw him sipping the drink. He wasn't enjoying it, but he took another gulp.

"Can you ever forgive me?" Morgan asked, surprising me from behind. I'd been concentrating on Lincoln and righting myself on land. That and trying to comprehend the fact we were now not only on top of an active volcano, but also…the fiery gates to Hell.

How did they end up in paradise?

I turned and cocked an eyebrow. "For the part where you dressed me up to pimp me out? Or the part where you knew what you were sending me into and didn't tell me?"

She actually took a moment to consider the question. "The

second part." She smiled guiltily. "You have to admit, you looked hot. So I won't apologize for that but I *am* sorry I didn't tell you."

I pulled on my once-black, now sort-of-gray cap. "It's okay. I figured you were under some kind of Josephine gag order or whatever. Just promise me she doesn't have anything else like that in store for me."

"Not that I know of..." Morgan let the sentence linger.

Up ahead, Josephine was walking with two of her Grigori flanking her and Lincoln not far behind. I'd half expected her to say something to me this morning, but thus far, she hadn't even looked in my direction.

"What's their deal anyway?" I asked Morgan, gesturing toward the other ninjas. They hadn't acknowledged any of us, nor left Josephine's side.

"That's Hiro and Mia. They've been at the Academy for four years now. Josephine's had them working with her for the past two. They're the head Ghosters and take their position very seriously. Don't be offended if they never speak to you. Unless Josephine orders them to, they'll see it as a distraction."

I watched them walking behind her. Josephine wouldn't even need to see or hear them to know they were there, always reliable. The way they moved, positioning their bodies between her and any object or person of question, was indisputably accurate and silent but deadly.

"So no after-work drinks, then," I joked.

"No after work, period." Morgan *wasn't* joking.

I guess there are people like that in all professions, the first-in, last-out types. I couldn't help but think of Dad. I dug into my pocket and pulled out my cell. I'd been trying not to think about home, but I had to know: Had Dad already cut me off?

I turned my phone on, and when it finally came to life, I was frustrated to see that there was no reception.

One more reason to get off this rock.

Josephine had somehow convinced the Greek authorities to consider closing access to the volcanic island until further notice, citing seismic activity. Spence had moaned he was going to be stuck all day following up what she had started, having to talk to local government to persuade them it was necessary. I thought he was joking, but apparently he was the best choice since he could use his glamour skills to look the part. I also suspected Lincoln liked the idea of keeping Spence and me separated.

The third pair of Josephine's ninjas walked ahead of us and held notepads. They talked quietly and waved their hands around a lot. I didn't know what they were pointing at. The whole lava-charred island seemed the same to me—dead. But they must have seen more. Steph had noticed too and was not so subtly inching in their direction, eavesdropping.

"What about them?" I asked Morgan and Zoe, who was lagging behind with us.

"Oh, they're the Conductors," Morgan answered.

"Conductors?" Once again, I felt naïve that I didn't know all the terms. It was hard to fit in history lessons around the fight-for-your-life practicals with exiles trying to kill me all the time. Luckily, Morgan didn't seem to mind explaining.

"You have to think of each Grigori as a type of instrument. No two of us are exactly the same, so when we need to come together in a battle against exiles, the Conductors are called in. They work out everyone's strengths and how they can be put to best use in different scenarios."

Zoe kicked a black rock toward a pile of other larger black rocks. "Just like baseball. Fielders, pitchers, basemen." She threw me a cocky grin. "I'm a batter."

Of course.

"What are you?" I asked Morgan.

She shrugged. "It really depends on the fight, but I usually stay in the outfield with Max," she said, continuing with Zoe's analogy. "We're both forms of shields. My strength allows me to send out pulses of confusion. If people come across the field I'm working, they lose clarity and usually go back in the direction they came from. Max performs a type of glamour."

"Like Spence?"

"Same theory, different results. Spence glamours himself, people in close proximity, and small objects to assist. Max can glamour large spaces. Say we end up in a fight with exiles in a populated area—as long as he's familiar with the space, Max can keep us hidden so passersby just see the area as if we're not there."

I nodded, impressed. It now made sense that Max was being so attentive to every detail—he was making blueprints.

"And together," Zoe said, sweeping an arm toward Morgan, "they make a wicked diversion. Morgan keeps them away, and those who slip through see nothing out of the ordinary."

"But can people pass through Max's barrier and see what's really happening then?"

"It can happen if it were just his shield, but no one gets through the both of us," Morgan answered in a way that left no room for doubt.

I wondered where they'd want me.

"On the bench if it's up to Josephine," Morgan said before she slapped a hand to her mouth. I realized I must've spoken aloud.

"What?" Zoe spat, saving me the effort. "Violet's our best damn hope!"

Morgan held her hands up in defense. "I don't know anything, I swear."

Zoe stepped closer to Morgan, formidably so. "Out with it."

Morgan squirmed under the weight of Zoe's glare and spoke quickly. "I overheard her talking to the Conductors on the boat. She said to make sure the plan wasn't dependent on Violet in any way. When they tried to argue that her gifts were pivotal if we were outnumbered, she cut them off. I couldn't hear what she said, but whatever it was, it shut them up because they didn't argue again."

Why does she not want me involved? Does she think I'm just going to stand back and let my friends fight for me?

Maybe it was something else. Maybe she thought I'd already be dead by then.

Is this what they were discussing this morning? Does Lincoln know?

I walked silently at the back of the group, taking a few moments to think. I still hadn't told anyone about my run-in with Phoenix or his request—he'd already proved when he took Steph that he was willing to hurt those around me to get what he wanted. If I told Josephine, who clearly had ulterior motives, that Phoenix wanted me to meet him tonight and she stopped me from going, someone I cared about would suffer. No. The risk was too great.

The Conductors called Zoe over to them and I went with her—I needed to find out as much as I could. Although they regarded me with little interest when I approached, somehow I knew it was a pretense. I had to hold back my cynical smile. It was all games with these people.

Griffin still wasn't altogether sure what the Academy knew about me. After Jordan, he had requested—with a side of "demand"—that no one speak of Phoenix's revelation until we had more information. Of course, that didn't stop the theories.

It wasn't comforting that Griffin was so worried about what the Assembly would do if they knew for sure. Obviously, it would not involve a red carpet.

My orders were not to go against Josephine, and I'd had every intention of following them, but hearing Phoenix's politely delivered threat changed things.

Ahead of us, on the gravel pathway that snaked around the island, Lincoln was walking with Josephine. He was looking better, nodding as they talked in hushed tones and pointed to different parts of the volcano. He had his hands full trying to deal with her. She had already accused him of being too caught up in his "connection" to me.

And, Phoenix had said, *only* me.

Phoenix would not stop. He would hurt me, hurt everyone I loved. He'd done it to Lincoln when he brought back Nahilius, to Steph by kidnapping her, and now he had threatened Dad.

It will never end.

A tear fell from my eye, and I quickly brushed it away.

No time for that.

There would be no good in telling Lincoln. He couldn't change my mind, and it would only make it harder for both of us.

I needed to work out the best way to let everyone know that Phoenix and countless exiles were already here without revealing that I'd actually seen him.

chapter twenty-eight

"And the fifth angel sounded, and I saw a star fall from heaven unto the earth; and to him was given the key of the bottomless pit. And he opened the bottomless pit; and there arose a smoke out of the pit; as the smoke of a great furnace."

REVELATIONS 9:1–2

"Zoe, we need to get a sense of the water depth around the island. Can you manage that?" the female Conductor said, as if she barely had any faith in her abilities.

Guess she missed the part where Zoe made an entire mountain rock it out in Jordan a few months ago!

Zoe shot her a smartass smile. "Already done. It's deep all the way round, but definitely deepest on the western coast. And"—she looked uneasy and rolled her shoulders—"there's something moving in the water. It's creepy."

"What is it?" I asked, refocusing on the conversation.

She made a sour expression like she'd just eaten something bad. "Don't know, just that there's motion deep down that isn't a fish, you know?"

The Conductors nodded, wrote down the details, and got back to business.

"How many yards to the bottom?"

Zoe balked. "Do I look like a tape measure? Deep, as in no one needs to go that deep. Easily hundreds of yards."

"And what about the volcano? Can you sense the energy coming from it, sense what is below? Do you think you could influence it?"

Zoe shifted her weight then closed her eyes for a moment before reopening them, grim. "I can't sense the volcano at all. It's almost like it isn't even here. Maybe...maybe if it erupts, I'd get a better handle on it..."

Oh, well, there's something to look forward to.

The Conductors nodded and walked off without another word.

Steph joined us as Zoe muttered, "Damn pencil pushers. Wait till everything goes wrong, then we won't see them anywhere."

"What do you think they're planning?" I asked, watching as they moved farther away, now talking with Josephine and Lincoln.

Zoe shrugged.

"I think they're trying to work out a way to control the volcano. Maybe to disable it or something," Steph said.

We shared a grave look. Even with Grigori skills, controlling a volcanic eruption seemed unlikely. Before any of us managed to put this doubt into words, there was a thundering explosion from where the Conductors had just been. The three of us hit the ground in time to see the showering of what had once been a very large boulder into thousands, *millions* of tiny pieces, raining down on us like grains of sand.

Josephine stood tall, and as we watched in shock, she dusted off her hands and walked ahead.

"Well," she said loud enough for us all to hear, "at least we know my power is not affected here."

What in holy hell is her power?

I stood up, ruffling rock dust out of my hair.

"Show-off," Zoe sniped between coughs as she got up.

"More like homicidal maniac," Steph said, looking at her now not-so-cute shorts-and-tank-top combo after I pulled her up. Morgan, who had been a little farther away, seemed to escape without too heavy a dusting of sand.

Ahead of us, Lincoln grabbed hold of Hiro's shirt, pushing him back a few steps while exchanging a number of heated words that I didn't catch. Max and Mia had to step between them to pull them apart. After that, Lincoln appeared to calm down, eventually resuming his conversation with the Conductors.

We spent the next couple of hours scoping out the volcano. Every now and then, Josephine would blow something up, never giving any warning. By the time we were ready to return to the boat, we looked like we'd been rolling around in a dirt bath, though nothing had come as close to us as the initial blast.

Josephine, unsurprisingly, wasn't marked at all, apart from wearing a smirk of satisfaction.

Zoe, Steph, and I broke away from the pack on the walk back to the boat and Zoe filled us in: "She can separate atoms. She isn't actually exploding anything so much as pulling things apart with her mind. She explained it to our class once, saying she can look at any natural object and see its billions and billions of atoms. Once she sees them, she can move them. Apparently, though, as dramatic as she made it look today, it has its limitations. *She* can't move anything larger than a pencil. So unless she wants to just separate something into pieces on the ground and have it fall to dust, she's relatively useless on her own."

"So how did she make the rocks move?" I asked, watching Josephine as she walked ahead.

Zoe smiled ruefully. "Hiro's specialty is gravity. He can remove it for short periods of time in isolated areas, but only enough to lift an object to hover level. The combination of her power and his causes the explosive reaction, a kind of double effect. There are other Grigori who have well-developed telekinesis too—Josephine always keeps one of them close."

I shook my head. "She had him raise the rocks so she could make as much impact as possible." I totally agreed with Zoe and Steph—she was showing off and it did seem homicidal.

I wondered if it was Hiro or Josephine who had decided to let the explosions' residue come down on us, but didn't deliberate for long. Hiro would have been under orders.

Steph cast a suspicious look my way. "And since everyone else knew this stuff, I guess it was mostly for your benefit, Vi. The question is, why?"

I already knew the answer. It was a warning.

I was relieved to be back on the boat and rushed to take my same position at the bow, facing into the wind. There was little I could do on the volcanic island, and being stuck over there had brought my old escape instincts to the surface.

Despite Kaitlin and Samuel's efforts, when we disembarked at the marina, we had to push through dozens of tourists demanding to know why they were not allowed to visit the famous landmark, especially angry now they'd seen us sail in from that very place. We just put our heads down and walked through, spotting Salvatore waiting for us halfway up the steep path that would take us back into town.

I had sensed exiles as soon as my feet hit land.

So many people surrounding us made me nervous. Looking at all the faces, knowing I could sense the exiles but not being able to pick them out clearly was disconcerting.

"Steph!" I yelled. She was hurrying ahead, trying to get to Salvatore, and didn't hear me over the people traffic.

"Violet?" a voice came from behind.

I closed my eyes briefly, partly in dread and partly in pleasure, soaking up his presence—sun first, then melting honey. Of course, Lincoln didn't need to hear me to know something was wrong—he would have felt the spike in my anxiety.

He came up beside me. "What is it?"

I shook my head to tell him now was not the time to discuss it. "Back at the hotel."

He nodded and I was grateful he didn't push. "How about I walk with Steph?" he suggested, giving me a look of understanding that made me want to cry. My recent anger with him slipped away. He didn't need me to explain I was worried for her safety here; he didn't need to ask for answers. He just knew, knew me.

Unable to manage words, our eyes lingered on each other, sending my heartbeat into overdrive before he broke contact and hurried on to catch up with Steph. He whispered something in her ear that made her look back at me and make a show of linking her arm through Lincoln's.

I lagged, staying where I could keep a good watch on things. I thought I was the only one who had fallen so far behind until Josephine appeared by my side as if she'd always been there. How she managed that I had no idea.

"Violet, is there anything you would like to discuss with me?"

I looked straight ahead. "Nothing I can think of."

"I expected you to say something about last night," she said, but that wasn't what she was really asking.

"I heard enough last night. You had a job to do. You did it. Right?" I glanced at her and then looked ahead again. Her lips were curled.

"I'm glad you understand. It gives me hope that we might be able to get along after all."

No chance of that.

I forced a tight smile.

"Given your abilities, I assume you are aware of the increased presence of exiles?"

I nodded, wondering what her sense was.

"When did you plan on alerting us to this?"

I fought the urge to put distance between us and held my steady pace. "I only just felt them. I might've been able to sense them earlier, but I wasn't myself this morning," I said, unable to resist the dig.

She stopped walking, taking hold of my upper arm as she did. I froze, doing nothing but staring at the hand restraining me. Lincoln had grabbed me in the same way this morning; he'd been rough even, but Josephine's hold was different. Cold, rigid fingers and sharp nails dug into my skin, eager to break the surface. Yeah, she wanted to...badly.

"I am not one of your devoted recruits, Violet. I have no intention of bringing my people into this mess you have created and risking their lives simply to save yours. I am fully aware that the lost opportunities to eliminate Phoenix are predominantly due to efforts to protect you. I won't suffer such hesitation for my people." She squeezed my arm, assuring me of her strength. "If I find out at any stage that you are lying to me, I will have you detained and removed from the island."

Her fingers tightened, nails now cutting into my skin, and she pulled me close to herself, adding, "*And* from Lincoln."

I clamped my jaw shut and fisted my hand. I kept my head down but lifted narrowed eyes to meet hers. "Are you finished?"

"Quite," she said, holding my arm for another few seconds before letting go and proceeding up the path before me. Mia and Hiro quickly appeared by her side.

I don't know how long I stood there, people moving around me as I watched Josephine hike back up to the hotel. She had just drawn the lines and I was now more certain than ever—I couldn't risk involving anyone else in my plans.

chapter twenty-nine

"Thus saith the Lord God; An evil, an only evil, behold, is come."

Ezekiel 7:5

Dapper came to our room that afternoon. He'd been confined to the hotel with Onyx, and he and Steph had just come back from reporting their latest opinions on the Scripture to Josephine and Lincoln. I left them to the braniac business, locking myself away in the bathroom for a shower, where I noticed Josephine had been successful in her mission, crescent moon–shaped cuts from her nails remaining as evidence on my arm.

I considered trying to cover them up, but I'd spent enough time trying to conceal such things in the past and I was damned if I was going to protect her. When I emerged from the bathroom in cargos and a black tank top, Onyx was sauntering into our room, carrying a bottle and two glasses. Dapper didn't even look up as he poured them each a drink. As odd as their weirdly synced, alcohol-fueled friendship—which I suspected might be a little more—seemed, it was becoming comfortable. Onyx had changed. Not only did he show fewer signs of his previous insanity, but it was also becoming apparent that he wasn't as immune to us as he would have us believe. Onyx and Dapper, unlikely a pair as they were, had unwittingly become my allies. I trusted them more than some of the Grigori.

I leaned on the bathroom doorframe, drying my hair with a towel.

"You're looking better," Dapper commented.

"On top of the world," I replied sarcastically. "What's the latest?"

"Shouldn't we be asking you that?" he countered, a lilt in his voice.

I rolled my eyes. Of course, that explained why no one had been very chatty with me when they first got in. "Josephine told you the exiles are here," I deduced.

"And that you knew it," Steph added, voicing her disappointment. "That's why you sent Lincoln to walk me back to the hotel. I don't need a bodyguard, you know."

I decided to ignore her comment—nothing I said would make it better while she was in a mood.

"Has anyone seen them yet?" I asked casually.

"Nah," Dapper said. "They're being sneaky. Staying out of almost everyone's range. But she assumes they're all here, Phoenix included."

The way he said it, he was clearly looking for my reaction, which I ensured remained completely neutral. "Probably," I hedged. "So where are we with the Scripture?"

Dapper put several pieces of paper down on the coffee table and then put on his glasses. "We have the majority worked out. The first prophecy is fairly clear. 'Awaken Tartarus and blanket day, to hide their eyes and Heaven's ray' basically means just that; when the volcano erupts, it will bring the attention of Tartarus and deliver a cloud of ash that will cover the sky. 'Ash will fall as fire will rain' requires no real imagination. It's the next line we're stumbling over. 'Delivering to one' is very general. Perhaps it means the one who opens the gates or is somehow responsible for them. In short, we don't know. The rest...well, flames, death, water, and resurrection—that's all to be expected, given the ultimate goal."

"And the second one?" I asked, tucking a strand of hair behind my ear. This might be my last chance to absorb this information.

"Aren't we keen?" Onyx quipped, as I noticed Steph watching me pensively.

Dapper picked up the next piece of paper. "The first two lines hold no surprise. It was the location. The next part is the instructions. Our best guess is that this is a description of sacrifices—three to water and three to fire—but it also has requirements for whom should perform those sacrifices and clearly describes more than one person."

"So who, then?"

Dapper shook his head, frustrated.

"We don't know," Steph said, taking over and keeping it simple. "We all have different theories—powers, angelic ranks. But the thing that really stumps us is the 'Three at the hand of the heart of man.'"

"Why?"

"Because exiles are not men. Not truly. Humans are."

When none of us said anything, Dapper resumed speaking.

"The rest seems to relate to Phoenix's direct role as 'the admirer.' Basically, if he ensures the sacrifices, one will be delivered from Hell. With an offering of pain, the gates will open, and such an offering at Phoenix's hand—most likely his own blood—will guarantee his desire is fulfilled."

Because otherwise, any one entity from Hell could be released—Phoenix and his stated desire was the key to ensuring it would be Lilith.

"What about the water line?" I leaned over his shoulder. "'And water stands high to cradle the course,'" I read.

"Water is always the path between one world and another. It resembles the crossover. It could be as simple as that," Dapper said, but there was something else, a tone in his voice that implied he had another theory he wasn't sharing.

"What about the symbols?" Onyx asked.

"Actually, it was Josephine and the Conductors who figured that out. They think they're coordinates, using the constellations with Nea Kameni as the anchor. They've worked out that it marks six points around the volcano's center."

"If you're about to say it maps out a star, I think I'll laugh," I said, giving up on drying my hair and tying it up in a ponytail.

"No. But maybe just as odd," Steph said. She opened her notebook to a blank page and passed it to me with a pencil.

"Draw a circle." She waited.

I sat beside her and did as she asked.

She nodded. "That's the volcano. Now, inside it, put a dot here, here, and here. Then, outside the circle, put a dot here, here, and here," she continued, pointing to each marker.

"Okay..." I stared at my spotty creation. "I don't get it."

"Join the dots with straight lines, first inside, then outside."

I stared at what was a large inverted triangle surrounding the circle and a much smaller upright triangle in its center.

"Why does that look so familiar?" I asked, trying to work out where I'd seen something similar.

"Because circle within triangle," Onyx said, who'd been watching as I drew the symbol. He snatched the pencil from my hand, flipped the drawing upside down, and added streaks running from the edge of the circle out to the larger triangle. "*That* is the Eye of Providence."

"Huh?"

Steph smiled. "The All-seeing Eye."

"Oh. Right." I looked around, confused. "Isn't that meant to be good?"

"Heaven be damned, girl!" Onyx said, standing up hastily and spilling some of his drink. "Haven't you learned anything yet? Nothing is simply good or evil. If all your human fantasies were true, *I'd* be good!"

I just blinked at him. That put things in perspective.

"If there is a place for this symbol in righteousness or salvation, it's possible there is a place for it in destruction and damnation," Dapper said, shaking his head at Onyx's outburst. "And since that circle you drew is the mark for our anchor, the volcano, it seems likely it is more a mark of great power than simply good or evil. Also, the use of the triangle is an unmistakable—perhaps more relevant—link. In history, the inverted triangle represents water; the upright, fire; and the two combined, a symbol of divine union and in some religions…resurrection."

"Jesus," I mumbled, staring at the sketch. "All that from a triangle?"

But no one smiled.

Onyx slumped down with a refilled glass. He was starting to slur his words. "Who do you think is responsible for *evil*?"

"You," I snipped.

"A generous compliment." He bowed his head. "But no, if there is one who could create all things in this world, that *one* must be capable of creating both the greatest good *and* the greatest evil. It *must* be one and the same, just as angels are both and humans are some form of disturbing subbreed."

"Onyx…" Dapper warned.

I glared at Onyx. "You know the one good thing that might come out of Phoenix opening the gates to Hell?"

"Pray tell," he said, waving his fingers in mock anticipation.

"I'll know where to drop you off!"

Onyx smiled and we were suddenly all on the verge of laughter.

But before we could fully relax, I stiffened—I could feel Lincoln was nearby, and unable to stop myself, I tapped into his heartbeat, which was increasing with every step as he moved closer. I concentrated furiously on slowing down my breathing and shutting myself off, but it was too late to stop the gouging feeling in my stomach and chest.

There was a knock on the door. Lincoln and Spence walked in.

"Thought we'd find you in here," Spence said, collapsing on my bed. Lincoln stayed by the door. "Honestly, after the day I've had, the whole *day-from-hell* reference has new meaning. I've spent the last three hours glamoured as a science geek, pretending to be a volcanologist. Do you have any idea how hard that is when I don't know the first thing about volcanoes? When I don't even speak Greek?"

Dapper and Onyx chuckled, taking another drink.

"Why have you been doing that?" Steph asked.

"Josephine's orders. She wants the Greek officials to consider stopping tourists from coming to Santorini, but this place is a major draw. Griffin's trying as well, but without more evidence, they won't raise an alarm. I think they were getting pretty suspicious when I couldn't answer any questions actually relating to the volcanic activity. Did you know those things release sulfur or something?"

Dapper laughed some more and I saw Steph smiling now too.

"You spoke to Griffin?" I asked hopefully. "Is he on his way?" Since getting back to the hotel, I'd already noted the large number of Grigori there. They had obviously been arriving throughout the day.

"I spoke to him," Lincoln said flatly. "He'll be here by morning."

I couldn't understand why, but he seemed put out by my question.

"Oh," I responded, unable to hide my disappointment. With

Griffin not getting to Santorini until tomorrow, it confirmed my decision.

"So what now?" Steph asked, slumping in her chair.

"There's not much else we can do tonight," Lincoln said, pushing away from the wall. "The exiles are here, but Mia and Hiro just called in from the airport—there's no sign of Phoenix's plane, so we think they're hiding out in one of the smaller towns. We've got more arrivals getting settled and we've divided up the night watch with running patrols, but wherever Phoenix and his exiles are, they're in hiding for now. Apart from what Josephine"—he turned to me—"and *Violet* sensed, no one else has felt them moving around."

The penny dropped. He was angry I hadn't gone to him too.

I stood up, suddenly uncomfortable sitting while he held the higher ground. "Josephine knew as soon as I did, and I knew she'd tell everyone." I felt a pang of guilt for lying, but I wasn't going to risk everyone's safety just to share my burden. At least it was partly true. After getting back from Hell Island and my encounter with Josephine, I'd beelined straight for my room.

"You said you'd explain when we got back to the hotel," Lincoln went on, his tone not only hurt but also accusatory. "Is there anything else we don't know?"

If the question wasn't loaded enough already, his glare made up the difference.

It raised my defenses. "I guess I just figured you'd be having another one of your secret meetings and she'd tell you there," I answered back, regretting it instantly and dropping my eyes. He was meant to be holding the fort for Griffin until he got here and the bottom line was—I'd let him down.

And I'm about to again.

"I'm sorry," I said, meaning it for so many reasons.

"Well," Spence said, jumping up with renewed faux-energy, "since it seems like there's nothing else we can do tonight, I'll be assuming the position of cruise director." He swept out a hand and took a bow. "How does a little last supper sound?"

"Apt," said Onyx.

Dapper smiled, resigned, and Steph was already up, sifting through her luggage for something to wear. I glanced at Lincoln, his intense green eyes looking for something.

"Sounds great," I lied, turning my attention to Steph, trying to break the tension.

"That's the spirit, Eden," Spence said.

"Got something I can wear?" I asked Steph as everyone moved toward our door.

Steph threw me a shorter-than-I-liked red dress. "You know, next time people complain I pack too much, I expect you to remind them it is because I have to pack for you too!"

"I'll spread the word. Meet downstairs in fifteen," Spence called, already out the door.

Five minutes later, I was ready to go with shoes in hand and impatiently waiting for Steph. All I had bothered to do was put on the dress, some mascara, and lip gloss. Fidgety and unable to stay still, I called out to Steph that I'd wait for her downstairs. I grabbed my phone and went out into the hall. As soon as it registered reception, it began beeping. I tried to ring my voice mail, but only got some recorded message in Greek, so I looked at my texts.

Twelve from Dad. All saying "Call me," the first six ending with "now!" the last six with "please!"

There was also a message from Jase. I wondered why he was texting me instead of Steph.

> Gig's up! Can only hold off Mom 4 so long. Whatever beach u 2 r baking on u better get home pronto!
>
> And call yr Dad!
>
> Looking 4ward to yr dance. Jase.

I had no idea where to start dealing with that, so I just closed the message and called Dad's cell. It barely rang once.

"Hello?" his voice answered quickly.

"Dad?"

"Oh, thank God, Violet! Are you okay? I've been looking everywhere for you! Where are you? What's going on? I've checked all the hospitals, the airports…"

But of course, he wouldn't have been able to find me. I was traveling under a passport that hid all my details as fast as I used them. Dad sounded so panicked—his voice was shaking. He was petrified.

"I'm in Greece, Dad," I said, instantly feeling relief at telling the truth.

"What? How? *Greece?* The country? Who's with you? Is Lincoln there? I went to his place. I know he's not here."

"Yes, to all of it. I'm sorry, Dad. I'm sorry for everything."

"No, Violet, that's not good enough! Is Stephanie there? I've tried to get hold of her mother but can't get past her son!"

I owe Jase.

"I…I can't talk for long. Things here are…Well, I'm okay."

There was silence on the other end of the phone.

"Dad?"

I heard his ragged breathing. He was crying. "I'm here," he said, trying to hide it. He took a deep breath. "Violet, I read your mother's letter. I don't understand."

"I know, Dad. Sometimes I still don't either, but I promise you, when I get back, I'll tell you everything and if…I promise I'll make sure you know the truth. About both of us."

"Violet, just answer me this: if your mother were still alive, would she agree with whatever it is you are doing?"

Now I was the one trying to hold back the tears. I sat down at the top of the stairs, not wanting to risk the call cutting out in the elevator. "Yes, Dad, this is exactly where she intended me to be."

His breath caught.

"Dad, do you love Caroline?" I asked, not sure if I was ready for the answer.

He paused for a moment. "It's not that easy, but she's a good woman and…I'm trying."

"You deserve to be happy."

"Come home to me, Vi. As soon as you can. I know I…I can do better, be a better father, if you just give me a chance."

"It was never about that, Dad. You're a great father." I held off the tears, looking at the ceiling, and sniffed. "I love you." And then I hung up before I could hear whether he said it back or not.

"You heard?" I said, already knowing Lincoln was close.

He sat down beside me. "Don't ask me what you're about to," he said, an edge to his voice.

I half laughed through the sobs. "I don't need to. I know you'll tell him everything if I don't make it. And anyway, that's not the thing I need to hear you say yes to."

Lincoln stood up and moved to the banister, putting distance between us. He looked away as well, focusing on his shoes. I let my eyes slide over him. He was in dark jeans and a black T-shirt that clung perfectly at the seams to his bronze, muscled arms. I took a mental picture but it wasn't right; it wasn't enough.

"Linc?" I asked softly.

He looked up, my tone catching him off guard, his eyes, green as ever, glistening in the bright light of the hall.

There. Perfect.

Then they narrowed, but I had my picture now.

"Violet, what are you planning? I know you're keeping something from me."

I stood up, pulling myself together. "I want your word that if the time comes and Phoenix needs to be taken down, you'll do it."

"Violet," he said through gritted teeth, "please, don't do this. There is a way to sever your connection to Phoenix. We can break it and then I'll take pleasure in finishing him off."

I bit my lip. "Do you hope you can break ours too? It's just another *connection*, after all. If one can be broken, why not the other?"

He shook his head. "You think you have me all figured out."

I opened my mouth to respond but he put a hand up.

"Stop trying to change the subject, anyway. You know you didn't give me a chance to explain last night."

"And you won't get a chance tonight either until you promise me. In fact"—I stood and started stomping down the stairs in my bare feet, still holding my shoes—"you won't get another conversation out of me until you do. There's no more time, Lincoln, and you and I both know you're the only one strong enough to beat him in a fight."

"Well, that keeps it simple then, because I won't do it!" he yelled after me.

I halted, my back still to him, and closed my eyes.

"You wanted to know why I hit Phoenix the other night?"

He didn't say anything.

I sighed. I knew this would hurt him, but I had to do it.

"He killed Rudyard on purpose. He did it so we'd know we

could never be together. It's my fault, Linc. Rudyard. Nyla. And he's just getting started." Now I turned to face him, my eyes wet. "Josephine's right. We've let a connection—something that's out of our hands—control us." My chest tightened, each word like another brick weighing down on my struggling lungs, but I kept going. I had to. "If you knew me at all, like I should know you, you would accept that deep down, letting that connection control us isn't something either one of us would really want."

I saw it.

I dropped my gaze and turned to start back down the stairs. He didn't say anything, didn't argue, didn't follow me. But I saw his shock at hearing about Rudyard, his hurt at understanding it was true, we were to blame, and…I saw his surprise at my final words.

chapter thirty

"Everywhere the human soul stands between a hemisphere of light and another of darkness; on the confines of the two everlasting empires, necessity and free will."

THOMAS CARLYLE

Lincoln didn't come to the restaurant for dinner. Josephine told us that he'd decided to patrol Fira with Mia and Hiro. It was the only time that evening that she actually acknowledged my presence, and she watched for my reaction, enjoying baiting me. I didn't give her the satisfaction—everyone was taking turns patrolling. Lincoln had clearly decided to add a shift in order to avoid me. I was relieved, even if I couldn't fully ignore the way my entire body ached for him.

It had been happening ever since we'd grown closer in Jordan. Maybe even before then. The pain of being near him was intensifying all the time. But sometimes, like now, separation was even worse. I felt so much yearning that I'd swear I had internal injuries.

I worked hard at keeping up my barriers, and I knew that wherever he was, he would be doing the same. But I doubted that anything could ever sever our "connection." If nothing else, at least our earlier conversation would keep him avoiding me for the rest of the night. And that could only be good.

I played with my food and nodded along with the conversation, even laughing when Spence dropped half his grilled octopus down his shirt. I acted normally, if a little distant, but no one noticed. Even Steph was too busy chatting with Salvatore in the corner of the table, slipping into Italian to share sweet nothings.

When dessert arrived, I picked at my gelato and almond shortbread as I looked around the table and convinced myself I was making the right decision. I had brought no one else into it, had left no one to face the blame for my actions. I resolved to face Phoenix, and if I could stop him before he opened the gates to Hell, I would. Most importantly, he wouldn't hurt my friends.

I checked my watch again, and when I looked up, Onyx was staring as if he could see right through me.

"You still have some power, don't you?" I asked him. I'd suspected it for some time, but now I was sure he was seeing things that a mere human could not.

"Surrounding myself with those who carry power does seem to revive a certain strength in me, but no, I'm not becoming powerful once more. Not nearly."

"That's why you wanted to come, isn't it? To stay close?" When he didn't answer, I went on. "Did you heal yourself after the exile attack?" I still hadn't figured out how he'd recovered so quickly.

His hand went to his now-healed face and neck as if he too marveled. "I'm afraid that's a mystery to me as well." He hitched a shoulder and I realized he wasn't telling me the whole truth.

"What you're sensing is time. So much time and so many things that I have seen. Not many looks or thoughts have escaped my view."

I nodded—it made sense, but I didn't want to admit that to him so I kept my expression neutral.

"Too late." He gave a toothy grin.

I glanced around nervously. My instinct was to move away from him, but for some reason, I couldn't respond.

"You're in pain—and not just in your mind."

"Just muscle aches," I said, concentrating on my gelato again.

"The soul." He raised his eyebrows when I looked up. I stopped breathing.

"What about it?" I stabbed at my dessert repetitively.

"It can be like a beast within us—calling to us, feeding us, leading us. But the beast is savage, and if it has found and tasted its mark, it will not quiet until it has what it desires. Your soul is fighting you, Violet. There is only so long you can hold it at bay before..."

I shook my head, cutting him off. "I know what you're saying and you're wrong. We never...My soul hasn't joined with his." We had fought it, had stayed away from each other.

"When denied for long enough, souls can take on a mind of their own. Sex is the obvious form of joining, but if a connection is strong enough, it can find its way through other things. A look, a kiss, a touch, words, declarations. The soul can reach through anything if it is stirred by them. You may not be fully joined to him, but the process has begun and your soul is clawing at you from the inside out."

I bowed my head as tears slid silently and plentifully down my cheeks. He made so much sense.

"If I die?" I barely got the words out.

Onyx considered the question. "No, he would survive. To join completely, you would need to consummate bonding fully and willingly, but until then, expect to experience more and more pain as your soul's demands increase."

At least that was something. I checked my watch again.

"Going somewhere?"

My head snapped up and my next words surprised me as I realized my final decision had been made. "I need to make sure no one follows me."

Onyx shrugged, but I could see the shock in his eyes that I was trusting him. "Diversions are my specialty."

I nodded in thanks. He leaned into me, grabbing my hand, his grip not just tight but oddly compassionate.

"I shall be disappointed if you do not prevail."

"Careful, Onyx. That sounds like you might actually care."

"Would you prefer I said that I hope you fail? That Hell is

unleashed upon us all as your friends mourn for you and blame themselves? Or perhaps that, if it was me in Phoenix's position, I'd use every advantage I have and then kill you and all your friends anyway?"

It took a moment to recover from his honesty, but I surprised myself once again by actually smiling. "Maybe just 'good luck.'"

His eyes scanned the table quickly, as did mine. No one had been watching our hushed discussion.

"How about this?" He dropped his tone so that it was barely audible. "*You* are from the Sole."

"Nothing new there, Onyx." I started to lean back in my seat but he tightened his grip.

"The Sole *is* the highest command."

Yes…they are.

Why hadn't I seen that before? Wishful thinking…

At least now I know why Phoenix needs me and…when he'll be finished with me.

Onyx stood up, grabbed a bottle of wine from the table, knocking another one over in the process, and started swinging it around wildly, feigning drunkenness. I wondered how often he'd used that decoy.

When he moved toward Steph and flicked the bottle so that its contents flew into her lap, I slipped from the room. Onyx had played his part perfectly. Steph was the most likely to notice my absence; this would keep her busy for a while.

Once outside, I ran. Through the narrow cobbled streets of Santorini, I ran from the truth, ran from my soul, and—even worse—ran from my heart. I could never hide the truth from myself. I wasn't *connected* to Lincoln. It wasn't that we were chemically soul mates and fighting some offhand pairing. Now Onyx had explained it to me, I could feel it so much more.

My *soul* raking at me from the inside, pining for what it not only craved and desired…but for what I loved.

It was painful to consider that it may not be true for Lincoln, and that maybe that was for the best. But for me, the pain of being without him would never pass, would only increase. We could stand beside each other for eternity, but if he wasn't mine in every way, it would make no difference.

I made it to the hotel and caught a glimpse of myself in the foyer mirror and realized I hadn't stopped crying.

"In a rush?" a voice spoke out. I spun to see the leather-clad Grigori from the secret meeting leaning against a wall.

"You're Gray, aren't you?" I asked, trying to pull myself together quickly.

He raised an eyebrow. "At times. And you're the one who has this lot's panties in a twist."

"You're one of the Rogue, aren't you?"

"I'm just like you, sweetheart. I just read the fine print. Where're you off to, anyhow?"

I wiped away the tears. "Have you been following me?" I half asked, half accused.

He took a step toward me. "You look like someone headed for trouble."

"No. I just have somewhere to be." I needed to shut him down. "I'm sure you do too."

"That your way of telling me to sod off?"

I glanced at my watch then back at Gray. I was out of time. "Would you rather me tell you in another way?"

He threw his head back and laughed. "You think you could take me? Sweetheart, oh, that's priceless. But, like you say, I have somewhere else to be, so we'll have to pick this up another day." He took another step toward me, so we were almost touching. "And, just so you know, I'll be looking forward to it." With that, he gave me a wide grin and sauntered out of the hotel.

I bolted for the stairs.

By the time I reached the rooftop, I was doubled over in pain. I stumbled to the edge of the building.

Dad would be okay. Phoenix would keep his word and not go after him. And even if I didn't make it back...maybe he'd be better off without me, the constant reminder of Mom. He was finally showing his first signs of moving on—maybe he and Caroline would work out.

Steph had already endured too much because of our friendship. I couldn't ask any more of her. It was time for me to be the smart one. I'd left her a gift under her pillow before leaving the room tonight. She'd know my wishes and, if not, at least it would help to keep her safe.

Then there was Griffin. Poor Griffin, he would blame himself, think he should have been there to stop me going. But he was our leader and he would do his duty to the end. If something happened to me, Griffin would help stop Phoenix.

Onyx already understood, which was stranger than anything else. Dapper would pretend he had never cared until he actually didn't. Spence would be angry with me, so angry that he'd be okay.

And Lincoln. A cry escaped my lips. He'd look for me. But I had to accept that he was more of a victim in this than any of us. I would have loved him anyway, even without the soul thing—but he…he dreaded me. If Phoenix ended things, ended *me*, Lincoln would be allocated a new, better partner. He could be what he really wanted to be—a great warrior. And he would return Phoenix.

Phoenix.

I grasped the barrier at the edge of the roof and looked down. I could deny it all I wanted, but it didn't stop me from being scared. Then I reminded myself of what it would be like if I didn't go with him.

He'll be maddened, take it out on the people I love.

I could feel them now. Both of them moving toward me. I'd let my barriers fall with the pain; my soul had broken out and my power had extended. Lincoln was racing, I could feel his heartbeat. Somehow he knew I was at a crossroads, but he was too far away to help. I wondered where he was, why he had traveled so far. Phoenix was closer, moving at speed, lightning fast.

I took hold of my dagger to give my shaking hands something to do, but it didn't help much.

My mind was racing. Phoenix would be here any second, with Lincoln only moments behind.

Lincoln will be caught off guard. Phoenix will have the advantage.

"Whatever are you doing, lover?" Phoenix's voice was low. He was close but not close enough. I still had the upper hand as I held my dagger, point raised.

"Don't move, Phoenix."

He didn't. Which alerted me to just how much he needed me for his plan to work.

Gressil and Olivier, his exile generals, leapt onto the rooftop behind him. I hadn't been expecting backup and I wasn't the only one surprised by their appearance. Phoenix covered his reaction quickly and put a hand out to stop them where they were. Both did as ordered, but Gressil struggled, his hunger clear. He wanted to fight.

I forced my eyes back to Phoenix. "You'll kill everyone on this island if you make that volcano erupt. Last time they tried to open the gates, it destroyed everything."

Phoenix held his hands up, palms out. "I don't want to fight you yet, but I will. I need you, yes—but I've healed you once before. I can do it again."

"There are children here, Phoenix, babies, thousands of people and their homes. Whether you admit it or not, I *know* that the human in you knows that, and I can't let you do this."

His eyes narrowed and darted in Gressil and Olivier's direction.

Is that look meant for me?

It almost seemed like a warning.

"How about a compromise?" he offered, his eyes now boring into me.

I could feel Lincoln's determination, his power growing, searching me out. He knew where I was; he would be here in moments.

"Fast," I said.

Phoenix didn't hesitate. Perhaps he also sensed Lincoln nearing. "I will help minimize the destruction. I can't promise to save everyone, but I *can* prevent the masses from going down with the volcano. I'll save thousands *if* you come with me."

Something in the way he said it made me think he was pleased with me.

I couldn't think straight.

He's offering me a deal: if I go with him and help him open the gates, he'll save lives in return. But if it works and he brings Lilith back, would thousands more not die anyway?

Phoenix took a step toward me.

"Don't," I warned. He was smart enough to stop.

The stairwell door blasted open and Lincoln launched himself through it, freezing at the sight of Phoenix in front of him. Three of the most lethal exiles in existence were standing just yards apart.

"Well, aren't we the perfect triangle?" Phoenix mused.

His words struck a nerve—I'd just been looking at triangles, drawing them.

Lincoln assessed the scene fast. With Phoenix, Gressil, and Olivier all present, we had little chance to overcome them, given Phoenix's power over me.

"Violet, don't...don't..." he said quietly.

I could see Gressil from the corner of my eye. His expression was wild; he was barely restraining himself and now also sending a deadly stare in Phoenix's direction. Phoenix would not be able to contain him for long.

"I have offered Violet a compromise: to help preserve the human lives on this island, she will come with me."

"If I don't go with you, you can't make it work anyway!" I argued, still struggling to comprehend all the angles of this choice.

Phoenix's eyes narrowed enough for me to know he was losing his patience. "I can awaken the volcano without you, and if you don't come with me, I'll release the Grigori Scripture to Gressil and Olivier to do with as they please."

Gressil smiled.

A shiver ran down my spine. I knew he would take great pleasure in hunting down and eliminating any human destined to become Grigori. I remembered how frightened I had been when I first met Phoenix and discovered he was an exile. I couldn't imagine being faced with someone as violent as Gressil.

"Violet," Lincoln said calmly. "Look at me."

But I couldn't. It was taking all my strength just to hold off the intensity of pain. Being this close to him had never hurt so much.

"I'll go with you," Lincoln said to Phoenix.

Phoenix laughed. "Afraid not. It's her or nothing, but I'll give you every chance to get her back in one piece..." He paused. "Though I cannot control her actions. Or yours. I've made my offer; I have more than enough witnesses to that effect," he said, turning to Olivier. Then he looked back at Lincoln, something else showing in his expression, before turning to Gressil. "*I* will not be the cause of any long-lasting harm to her." He turned back to Lincoln, and I was sure something passed between them.

Lincoln nodded.

I dared another glance in Lincoln's direction. Sweat was dripping from his brow and his face was contorted in what looked like agony. Did he feel it too? No, he'd run all the way here from wherever he'd been; he was just exhausted. Even more reason for me to go—if he had to fight Phoenix now, it would not be good.

"No. No, Violet, listen to me!" Lincoln could tell where my thoughts were going. "Come over here. You need to come to me." He stood still.

It was all up to me. Lincoln needed me to move closer to him before he could try and defend me, and Phoenix wouldn't move closer to me until he knew I would cooperate.

"Please, Violet. This isn't your responsibility. Please look at me." Lincoln sounded so tired, but that one glance had already hurt too much. I couldn't look at him again without crumbling.

He sighed, a sound so sad it felt like a knife in my heart.

"It's okay. I…I understand. Just listen, then. You, Violet Eden, do not do this. *You* don't take the easy option and that's what this is. You never stop fighting. *We* never stop fighting. We'll find another way to stop this. Vi, I can't—" But he was cut off when once again the door to the stairwell flew open.

Gray.

"Decision!" Phoenix demanded.

Gray paused, assessing the scene. His eyes settled on me, and I could tell he would not interfere here.

He led Lincoln to me.

I suddenly realized he was working with Lincoln—I just didn't understand what their plan was.

Gray took a step back, hand reaching out casually to the stairwell door and bracing himself against it.

Sly.

He was barricading it.

Lincoln was right. I don't run. Violet Eden doesn't quit. And she doesn't dream silly dreams that end like a storybook. I adjusted my grip on my dagger. Time was up. I needed to decide and really, I'd already achieved more than I'd expected. Phoenix was an empath. He could sense my emotions more than anyone, even Lincoln. He'd have known for a while that my choice was made and how I felt about having to make it. And yet, he'd taken my bait, offered a deal, almost as if he'd wanted the same thing all along…

That's exactly it! He just wants Lilith. He'll do whatever he has to in order to bring her back. But he can't tell the others he isn't excited by the idea of mass murder. Going with him is my only option.

"Gressil, you may stay if you desire. Olivier, I need your presence," Phoenix ordered, smiling as he felt me make my decision.

I turned to Lincoln. "I'm sorry," I whispered, as I sheathed my dagger and held my arms wide.

They both moved, but Phoenix had me in his clutches before Lincoln had barely taken a step.

I closed my eyes and didn't fight. When his face nestled in my hair and his voice murmured softly into my ear, "Sleep," I knew I could resist it, but instead, I forced back the impulse and allowed myself to fall into slumber.

chapter thirty-one

> *"It was like something lurking in the darkness within him... There it remained in the darkness, the great pain, tearing him at times, and then being silent."*
>
> D. H. Lawrence

Phoenix

I double-check the locks again before falling into the heavyset armchair on the far side of the room. Locks can't stop them physically, but not one of them would risk breaking my door.

Having her so close is...distracting.

Almost everything is working out as I'd planned, yet still I feel the gnawing in my chest. It never lets up, but when she is around... It's worse than having a cursed conscience.

I try not to watch her, but it's impossible. My eyes have barely strayed from her since I swept her into my arms.

I wonder if she knows her markings swirl while she dreams. I grind my jaw. I hate myself for this, but it's not easy—not when I could just reach out and touch her. She's luminous, even in the dark—like a light shines from within her. A light that is burning me alive.

"Christ," I mumble to myself.

Thinking back to the first time I laid eyes on her at Hades on her seventeenth birthday, I still wonder: Why her? Why me? I've been around for a long time—there were many women before her. I'm a creature of lust and have always taken what I wanted—the guilty, the innocent, the coveted, those with promise, and those without. All of them lured so easily by the otherworldliness they could never understand. They found me impossible to resist. Even when I treated them poorly, then abandoned them, they still came to me.

I can't explain why everything changed the second I saw her, only that it did. And I can never go back.

She floated through her surroundings that night, unaware of the attention she drew to herself. Lincoln was with her, watching carefully as she drank too much. I could tell just by the look on his face that he loved her. I could feel it too—and was surprised how much it irritated me, that he leaked so much pure adoration and devotion to her. Perhaps that's why my interest in her stirred. Perhaps.

Now...she's ruined me.

I should have killed her that night, saved myself the heartache from knowing what it was like to hold her in my arms and feel that forbidden hope. Did I truly believe she could have found love with me? That perhaps redemption was not unreachable?

Fool!

I planned just to have fun, entertain myself for a spell and then do away with her. I should've known I was in trouble when I found myself unwittingly smiling, unable to take my eyes away. The clincher had been when Lincoln ran from her advances.

He could be such a pansy.

But taking her in my arms, knowing a Grigori made of a Power lurked nearby was madness, even for an exile. Powers are territorial. If ever there were a Grigori to avoid, it would be them, almost impossible to beat for most exiles.

The moment I touched her, my suspicions of her power were blown out of the water. Raw power.

I should have dropped her and run, but by then it was too late. Decision made. I was going to have her.

I laugh bitterly as I watch her sleep.

I think of all that has happened since finding her. Barely a blink in my existence, but everything has changed. Partly my fault, but partly hers too, and I refuse to punish myself when I can focus all my energy on retribution. We love the ones we hate.

And I hate her with all my heart.

I never believed anything could be worse than being cast out of the angel realm...but being cast from her life has been agony. Now, my hatred makes me do things I never thought I'd be willing to do, whatever my potential.

I hear another fight break out down the hall and try to ignore the sounds of flesh ripping at flesh. I don't care. If I didn't need exiles, I'd kill them all myself just for the therapy. But I've lost my patience with too many lately, serving them up to the Grigori on platters. My forces are already thinning and some of the exiles are becoming suspicious.

Competent exiles are few and far between, and unfortunately, the most proficient are also the most ruthless. Gressil has been one of the best, but having him so close…I have barely been able to make it through the days without killing him. Olivier isn't much easier.

A loud crash, like glass smashing. More fighting. At least right now, they won't expect me to step in. They think I'm in here beating her…or worse. Ironic then that I'm too damn terrified even to wake her up.

I jump to my feet when she rolls over, then remind myself she is under my illusion. She can't wake without me knowing.

An exile's deathly scream comes from the hall. I smile. It sounds like Justin. It is only a matter of time before his heart is torn apart. Judgment will not go well for him. Then again, it won't fare well for any of us. Especially me. Especially now. But suffering consequences is something I am used to, a result of never belonging in any one place, never holding any true value despite my power.

Well, that is about to change.

Despite my efforts, I have been neither angel nor human enough. But I will rule as an exile.

I give in, stand up, and move closer to her.

"I never knew," I whisper, unable to stop myself.

She can't hear me. It is bad enough I can hear myself. Admissions of guilt are not my thing, and now I've opened myself up to that one particular memory, the hardest one to push from my mind.

My skin burns even now, remembering how every touch she graced me with that night in the wilderness felt like a gift I was not worthy of.

I brush a few strands of hair back from her face, and my fingers ache to touch her again. I move away for fear of doing just that.

Why did I ever let that connection form between us? I hadn't planned it but still reveled when the power surged through me, masochist that I am.

Thrilled by the knowledge I had power over her, I promised myself I would never use it because I loved her. But even so, already, quietly, my dark mind had begun plotting ways to ensure she'd always be mine.

I should have told her straightaway. Maybe she would have forgiven me. Maybe she would've even understood why I didn't heal Lincoln. I knew that if she didn't embrace, didn't become the power she was destined to be, then one way or another—exiles or angels—they'd destroy her.

I couldn't stand by and watch that happen.

Looking at myself in the mirror, I pick up the hotel vase with its fake flowers and throw it at my reflection.

Think about the future! Remember the look in her eyes when she told you to leave and not come back!

I grab a fragment of broken mirror and run the point down my arm, drawing both distraction and strength from the pain. Don't forget the sight of her falling into Lincoln's arms the moment I released her from the bond—as soon as her true nature was once again in her control.

I take a deep, steadying breath and watch the wound heal. Good as new.

And now, more than ever, I must rise from the ashes—that's what a Phoenix does.

I have a purpose now. Soon I'll have Lilith. Finally, I will be the son she always wanted me to be. She will give me a place to belong in this world. I've fought our relationship in the past, rejecting her ways, thinking I could be better.

I have been wrong.

I look down at the Scripture before me. Releasing the scrolls had relied upon the existence of light and dark, but it had also required Violet. Carrying out these instructions will be no different. I glance at her again.

One girl, so much power.

She still doesn't realize what she is, what she could be to either side, though I have always suspected which one is grooming her. She is key to so much. It all revolves around her. Something her Grigori have yet to work out or accept. They carry the knowledge of angels but also our pride. They are so preoccupied protecting their world, they are too caught up to see that, in her, they already have the tool to do it.

I look at Violet. It's her fault. She did this to me.

I don't need these people. Once I have Lilith back, we'll have no need for them. We'll go away, start again. No longer forsaken, I will belong.

I feel the energy in the room spark. The compulsion is fading. In a few minutes, she will open her eyes. Will she show fear at the sight of me? No. She grows stronger every day. Soon she won't think twice before ending me. Maybe I will talk to her. Let her speak to me.

I glance at the map lying on the coffee table. We will leave soon. Everything is arranged.

There are three stages, water first. She'll hate me after making her do this, but there is no other way. It is for the best and it is easier for me when I see the flashes of hate in her eyes. It keeps me focused—and after this, the other flashes, the ones that show she knows me in a way no one else does, will dissolve altogether.

Fire comes next, forming the second point of the triangle. The way it has all come together makes me wonder if this is all some game, some twisted mark of fate that the three of us are so entwined.

Doubtless.

Fire will be easy. Lincoln will do what he has to do to save her. He'll do anything for her, except the one thing they both want—I've seen to that. I let her think I had Rudyard killed on purpose. I wish I had been strong enough to give that order, but in reality, the exiles had broken rank and acted themselves. I had lost my control over them for a moment while I made sure Violet survived.

I'd called them out as soon as I could, but I was too late to save the one called Rudyard. And his mate.

I'd beaten Gressil to within a breath of his life for that. It is a miracle the exiles don't get away from me more often. Soon I'll be finished with them and can leave them for the Grigori to finish off.

After fire comes my part, the third point of the ultimate triangle—not within the diagram but drawn into the words—this is the only part about which I'm not one hundred percent sure. The prophecy requires my pain, payment—blood, naturally—and desire. I have no problems with any of those, but the line about "insufferable pain" troubles me. Who? Of the three of us, who must suffer the greatest pain?

I notice Violet roll from her side to her back. Her hand moves out before she can stop it—good girl—searching for her weapon. Of course, it is far away from her for now. She pretends to sleep even as someone knocks at the door.

It is Olivier, with two enforcer exiles behind him. I like that he is too afraid to come to me alone. He asks after Gressil and I try to hide the smirk on my face as I explain I have not sensed him since he chose to remain and fight against Lincoln.

Even before the door closes, I can feel her emotion. She has worked out the arrangement I made with Lincoln: her safety in exchange for ridding me of Gressil. She is so confident Lincoln has succeeded, so certain of her faith in him. I want it to make me hate her, but it does the opposite.

Damn it—she's so frustrating.

I would give anything to make her mine, but I will never be enough for her.

I sit beside her while she lies still, keeping her breathing steady, even though I sense her heart rate jump at my nearness. And then I realize—the line I have fretted over so much in the prophecy is really the only one I needn't worry about. I run my hand over her forehead, allowing my fingers to move down the side of her face.

"Love will kill us all."

And it is entirely insufferable.

chapter thirty-two

"Violet, the amethyst, signified love and truth; or passion and suffering."

Anna Jameson

The first time I woke, it was to a loud banging. I was lying on a bed. I moved my hands and feet, which were bare, and felt silk sheets beneath me. I could sense an overwhelming number of exiles nearby, but only one actually in the room with me—Phoenix. I felt for my dagger. It was gone.

How many exiles were here? Too many to count.

I heard noises of movement and a door opened.

"Where is Gressil?" a voice growled.

"I cannot say for sure. I left him to fight, at his request. I have not felt his presence since."

I could hear the satisfaction in Phoenix's voice. Gressil had obviously become a problem. Phoenix had left him behind to fight Lincoln. That was their exchange. Phoenix's oath he wouldn't kill me, and Lincoln's word he would destroy Gressil in return. Gressil was gone.

Good.

After the door closed, I heard him come closer. He knew I was awake, but he let me pretend to be asleep. Maybe so he could pretend too. Leaning over me, he pushed the hair back from my forehead. His fingers lingered on a strand of hair and then trailed lightly down my face.

"Love will kill us all," he said sadly. "First, it makes us lie furiously so we can be what we must in order to appear deserving. Then, it tears us apart with raw truth. Whether we are man, exile, or angel—it doesn't matter. For us all, the nature of truth is unforgiving."

I could hear the regret, could feel it flowing from him to me like a confession, and my chest tightened for him.

"Sleep, my love," he compelled me to do so again.

And, like the last time, I let his power overrule my own, finding solace in the silence.

I woke to find Phoenix carrying me, cradling me confidently in his arms as he moved on foot. I could feel other exiles hovering, hungry to reach me. My face was stiff and sore. I heard them arguing behind us, but I was too groggy to make out exactly what they were saying. He spun around and the sound that came from him was terrifying. I half expected him to crush me in his arms, but he kept the same controlled hold on me.

"If any of you come near her again while she is in this state, I give my word that your fate will match Aiden's!"

I sensed the exiles moving back, uncharacteristically cowering from Phoenix's unquestionable power.

I assumed Aiden, whoever he was, had been responsible for the throbbing pain on my face—I wouldn't be surprised if my cheekbone was broken.

Aiden was dead.

I'd seen Phoenix take down an exile before, ripping his heart right out of his chest. No wonder I could taste the aniseed flavor that signaled their fear. None of these exiles questioned his power.

It should have frightened me too. But it didn't. If nothing else, Phoenix had honor in battle. He wouldn't let them beat me without a fair fight, just as he'd never allowed exiles into my home when I was asleep. He wouldn't even use *his* powers over me unless I could stand and fight—there was no challenge in that.

I opened my eyes the little I could, wincing at the sharp pain. Dawn was coming, lighting the sky only just. I had a feeling more than one night had passed.

He was watching me.

I shifted—the slightest angling of my body toward him—into his hold. I knew I was safe with him even though he held me in this coma-like state. It didn't mean he wouldn't hurt me later or let one of them kill me. It didn't mean he'd stop me if the time came for drastic measures. But for now, I was safe.

I saw something in his eyes as the corners of his mouth lifted, a look that was not exile but…*human.*

"Bliss," he whispered, followed softly by, "sleep."

His power—jasmine and musk—blanketed me and I closed my eyes once again.

The next time I woke up, I was lying on a narrow vinyl bed opposite a galley—I could tell by the sound and movement that we were on a speed boat. It took a while, but this time I woke fully. I could sense Phoenix somewhere above. There were no other exiles with us, but I could feel their distant presence nonetheless, an awesome number, unlike anything I'd ever sensed before.

The boat started to slow. He knew I was awake. My hand pushed out and knocked something cold and hard—my dagger in its sheath. He'd left it for me.

I wasn't going back to sleep this time.

I took inventory. My legs were wobbly but working. My face was bruised, but already I was healing, so I knew some time had passed since I'd been hit. The pain that I'd been experiencing internally, thanks to my soul, seemed to have lessened, though I didn't know how long that would last. I could still feel it lurking inside me, like a clever snake waiting to strike.

Phoenix had left a change of clothes, and while I didn't want to give him the satisfaction of putting them on, I didn't want to have to fight in the red dress I was still wearing. I quickly changed into the pants and tank top and was relieved to find a pair of sneakers too. I shivered—it was creepy he knew all my sizes. I secured my dagger around my waist and quickly scanned the small cabin to see if there was anything else that could help me, but everything was bolted down. I searched in vain for a radio but it was futile—Phoenix had been thorough in his preparations.

Looking through the small porthole, it seemed like mid-morning, but again I felt certain another full day and night had passed since I had last woke. I had no idea how long I'd been under Phoenix's spell.

After waiting as long as I dared, I made my way up to the deck. Phoenix was sitting on a plastic bench that wrapped around a square white table fixed to the floor. A large sheet of paper was spread out in front of him. A map. Drawn on top of it, a carefully plotted, large, inverted triangle with another smaller one within.

I took in my surroundings, squinting into the strong sunlight. We were offshore, but I could still see Santorini in the distance and its white cliff tops reflecting the sun. The ocean was an amazing, rich blue—the type you usually only see in the movies—except for the water encircling the boat, which was as dark as tar and uninviting. It lapped against the hull menacingly, hiding something awful deep below.

"Where are your exiles?" I asked, my voice croaky and my throat sandpaper dry.

"Busy drawing straws." He glanced up at me, a small look of amusement in his eyes, then, just as quickly, went back to his papers.

"Not many of them like the water. Drowning is uncomfortable. Being immortal and trapped at the bottom of the ocean even more so."

"How long have I been asleep? Why am I here?"

He picked up a jug that was at his side and poured what looked like water into an empty glass, sliding it in my direction. "This is your fourth day with me."

"How have I not starved?" I asked, subconsciously patting myself down. I was definitely slimmer but thought that was more a general result of the past few months.

He hitched a shoulder. "While you're under, your body conserves its strength and resources. Now drink," he commanded.

I took a step toward the water glass before shaking myself out of it. "No. I let you bring me here, but don't think you can influence me without my permission."

He shrugged. "If you're thirsty, you know where it is." He studied the map again and tapped his pen on the table. "I need to know what they're planning, Violet. I'm sure Griffin will try to launch some kind of attack as soon as we arrive at the volcano. What are they going to do to stop me?" He pushed as much compulsion as he could into the question.

I laughed briefly. "Well, I really was the wrong person to take! I wasn't even invited to the war room. I have no idea, only that it's not Griffin calling the shots at the moment. But if I know Lincoln, I'd have to agree with you."

With any luck, he'll be waiting for you with a great big welcoming party!

Phoenix studied me for a time. "You really don't know."

It wasn't a question—he'd been trying to read me and seen I wasn't hiding anything.

"Let me guess. That was Lincoln's doing?" he said, frustration leaking from his tone and showing in his snarl.

I blinked. "What do you mean?"

He threw his pen down now and sat back. "Leaving you out of the loop was smart. I'll give him that."

"Why am I here, Phoenix?" I repeated, not needing a reminder that Lincoln had been keeping secrets from me yet again.

"I need your services."

"Well, you know what, you can go stuff yourself!" I said, suddenly having serious second thoughts.

He just smiled. "I could. But I don't think so."

Had I made a huge mistake coming with him? Maybe I had—to think I could stop him from the inside. Plus, being on this small boat was making me feel claustrophobic. I started looking for a way out.

"I'm leaving," I said, searching my pockets for my phone before remembering he'd taken it. I stormed to the edge of the boat, leaning over the railing.

"More dramatic threats?"

I glared at him and started to climb the steel wires. "I'm a good swimmer."

Santorini didn't look *that* far. I'd have a better chance of survival trying to get back to the island than staying out here with him.

"That may be, but there are things in this water that move much faster than you today, especially if you're bleeding."

The threat was loud and clear.

I spun, but he was already right there. Before giving it any more thought, I kneed him in the groin and moved myself into a better defensive position. I knew he was right about the water, but with him and I alone like this, it might be my only chance. We were both awake now, both strong. He wouldn't hesitate to hurt me if it served his purposes.

Phoenix folded over in pain, even though he tried to laugh it off.

I held my position.

"Okay then," he said, straightening. Then, like lightning, he hit me across the face.

Fighting on a small boat is challenging. Every time you move, you bump into something hard. But I kept my focus. I was strong and tactical and I used everything I had—Lincoln's training to stand still and wait for the attack was particularly handy in the confined space.

Phoenix was cocky to start with, lazy in his defense. He thought he'd have me easily. But I dodged his strikes cleanly and returned hits, making contact. When I finally managed a kick to his gut, forcing him hard into the railing and giving him a good view of the dark waters, his expression changed. He'd come dangerously close to taking a bath and the exile in him raged, fueled with a sense of pride and superiority. Now, the fight really began.

He delivered a full-force hit to my stomach, which threw me back as he grabbed my arm and swung me around so that his next kick went into the small of my back and made me fall on my face. I got up fast. My back was spasming in horrific pain, but I didn't stop. I moved forward, knowing he would try to finish me with his fists, but I ducked in time, hitting him as I came back up, then stepping away from him enough to ensure my next kick caught him in the side of his ribs. When he moved to protect the area, my knee went up, without thinking, to strike his face. But Phoenix was too fast. He caught my leg, pulled it out, and spun me so hard, my entire body pretzeled until I lay twisted on the ground, one of my feet in his hold.

He crouched on top of me, straining my leg backward at the knee before dropping it. Then, he sat on top of me.

"Well," he marveled, as if perplexed. "That…took longer than I expected."

I squirmed under his weight, but I was pegged facedown.

"And that…" He slammed his fist down on the boat decking.

I flinched.

"Wouldn't be the wisest thing to do right now!"

I could feel the tremor running through him as he held me down. I waited for him to do something, go on the attack. I was his captive and he clearly wanted to prove it. I stayed still, barely breathing, and closed my eyes.

Waiting can be worse than anything else in the world.

To my surprise, a few minutes later, he seemed to rein himself in and his breathing settled. When he spoke, his voice was even.

"Now, here's how it's going to go. In about fifteen minutes, three exiles will be brought before you and you will return them as and when I instruct you. Do you understand?"

"Never!" I spat out, grimacing under his weight.

"And if you don't, not only will I be forced to hurt you, badly, but I will finish what I started with Steph." He leaned over me until his body covered mine and his mouth was at my ear. "I give you my word on that."

I clenched my jaw. Phoenix might not, for whatever reason, want to kill me yet, but he would kill Steph and anyone else I cared about if he had to.

"Do we have an agreement?"

"Yes."

Another speed boat appeared shortly after, pulling up alongside us. Olivier was on it, plus half a dozen exiles, three bound tightly in lashings of metal chains. Phoenix tied their boat to the back of ours but didn't invite them to climb aboard. I wondered if they were really that afraid of the water or if that was just an excuse for why he'd been keeping them away. I suspected he was either protecting me in some bizarre way or staking his claim on me.

After being curtly instructed, Olivier pushed the first exile into our boat and over to Phoenix, who yanked him closer. The way Phoenix handled him was...strange—with a kind of contempt, as if he was pleased to be destroying him.

"These are three of our strongest. Are you sure you want these ones?" Olivier asked.

"Absolutely," Phoenix said with a growl.

Why is he destroying their most vicious? Is that a requirement of the sacrifice?

I didn't think so. In fact, the more I thought about it, Phoenix seemed to take every opportunity he could to destroy an exile. He needed them, but he also despised them. Even now.

Does that mean there's still hope?

He hauled the exile toward me, forcing him to his knees.

"Return him and throw him to the water before he is gone." I took my dagger in my hand, wondering why it hadn't occurred to me to use it when I'd been fighting with Phoenix. I hadn't even considered it.

"I can't just execute him!" I pleaded.

But Phoenix simply pushed the exile closer to me, moving nearer himself at the same time, and speaking quietly, so the other boatload could not hear.

"He kills women only. None older than twenty. He rapes them until there is no life left in them and then he burns their bodies, roasting his dinner on the flames."

Phoenix held my eyes, making sure I understood that he was telling me the truth.

When I drove my dagger into the exile's heart, I didn't feel as bad as I thought I would. In fact, I felt almost entitled. I pulled it out and threw him to the water as instructed, not willing to risk Steph's life with another delay.

Whatever lurked within the shadows pounced quickly, wrapping itself around the exile like silken evil, pulling its catch deep before disappearing entirely. Without another word, Phoenix started up the engine and took us in a straight line to the second sacrificial site. I looked at the map again. We were traveling to the points of the outer triangle.

Three at the hand of the highest command.

The second exile targeted children, taking them from their parents for ransom and then delivering them back afterward. In pieces.

I killed him fast.

The third one, from the look in Phoenix's eyes, was the worst. He didn't tell me what this one did; he just appeared envious that I was the one who got to return him. That was enough for me.

Each time we stopped, the waters darkened around us until I threw overboard the dying exile and something sinister moved in their depths, swallowing its victim whole.

I felt little remorse for returning these monsters. No fate could be too awful for them. But still. With each thrust of my dagger, I hated Phoenix for making me do this, forcing my hand to bring about their ends and using their demise to help unleash something even worse.

When the last exile had been taken and Olivier's boat was headed toward land, I turned on Phoenix and hit him across the face with the hilt of my dagger. He stumbled back. I hadn't expected to injure him, not that way, anyway. I had hit him so he'd know.

"It will never be you. You will never break me!"

He stood up straight. "Oh, believe me, Violet, I know that." He shook his head, more to himself than me. "I feel you…All the time, even when you are not near. I know where your emotion is vested and who has the power to break you. I know it is not me. But thank you for the reminder." He wiped a drop of blood from his lip.

"I'll do it again if you like," I said, wondering if this would be it, if this would be the moment his intentions changed. I'd done as he had bidden, made the sacrifices. My worth to him was quickly diminishing.

"You could try."

I made a quick decision—I wouldn't get another opportunity. If I could stop him now, they still had a chance. Six sacrifices were needed. Three had been made, I couldn't change that, but there were still three more.

Three at the hand of the heart of man.

With the full force that my power could bring, I urged it forward with all my will to stop him—amethyst mist surrounded me instantly. But Phoenix was ready and swift.

I didn't even see what it was, fist or weapon—it could have been the entire boat he brought down on my head. I dropped to my knees and struggled to hold on to consciousness.

"Who is the heart of man?" I whimpered as my vision blurred.

"A man in love," he said.

And as my eyes closed, two things happened: I moaned Lincoln's name, and I saw a tear fall from Phoenix's eye.

He was right.

Love will kill us all.

chapter thirty-three

"Our acts our Angels are, for good or ill, our fatal shadows that walk by us still."

John Fletcher

My angel maker walked to his window. My art studio felt different, and I realized I wasn't sure if this was *my studio—my home—at all anymore. The same dismal rain that always fell in my dreams pattered against the glass.*

My head hurt from where Phoenix had just belted me.

"You need to help us," I said, disoriented and out of place. "You need to stop him!" I reinforced, bracing a hand on my workbench.

"We cannot intervene," he said simply.

I felt a wave of anger toward him. Did he even care what happened to us?

"But he's yours! You made him!"

"Did we?" he responded, now looking at me. "I believe that right falls to more than one."

"What do I do?" I begged. "I don't know how to stop him. He's stronger than me."

The angel was fast, faster than I could follow, but he was now in front of me and in his eyes, a golden fire blazed. "You are *me! He is not stronger than you!"*

My entire body shook with pain and fear. He was not just frightening; he was so much more—like life, death, and everything beyond. I could not fight him in any way.

Then, just as fast, he was back at the window, expressionless as he studied the beads of water running down the glass.

"Your mother..." He paused, caught in a sudden memory. "You are quite like her. Difficult. Daring to demand that which cannot be. At least she was wise enough to have something to bargain with."

"What are you talking about?"

"Semangelof should not have entrusted such a task to just one. He was reckless, but...she prevailed nonetheless. Her worth became great and her sacrifice lent her further strength. If it were not for these things..."—he looked at me oddly—"her child would not have survived receiving an essence such as mine."

"You needed her," I said, coaxing him on despite my increasing dizziness.

"Yes. She was unique on her own and her child showed signs of being even more so."

"I was her bargain!" The truth was unforgiving as it sank in. I hadn't believed I could think less of my mother until this moment.

"What did she trade me for? Heaven?"

"She had two conditions. One to hand over her life; one to hand over your fate. An agreement was made."

"What were they?"

"I cannot reveal them, only what I requested of her—that she wear one wristband at her end. One, she left to you; the other stayed with her in death."

"That can't be true," I said, not wanting any part of this conversation to be real. I would have known if she had worn a wristband when she died—Dad would have said something when he saw the other one she'd left for me.

"And yet, it is. Once she passed, the band stayed with her spirit, not her body."

"Why tell me this now?" I asked, frustrated.

"Because I believe that now might be the time to prepare."

I shook my head and almost laughed—he wasn't going to tell me.

"Whatever, I don't care what my mother did. She's gone and as far as I'm concerned, good riddance."

My angel looked at me, his eyes still blazing with golden fire. "You feel you have nothing." It wasn't a question.

I put a hand to my head, which was burning under his scrutiny. My other hand went out wide.

"Take a good look, angel-I'll-never-know-the-name-of! Do you see lots of happy thoughts surrounding me?"

"Perhaps you have everything and simply cannot see it."

I took a step toward him, a fire of my own now blazing in my glare.

"Yeah. And what would you know? You have no idea what it means to be human. If you did, you'd do something." I was challenging him.

Something passed over his face, prompting me to follow his gaze. I gasped. Blood was seeping through my top. I couldn't feel it, yet it was real.

"He's killing me."

"Killing, yes. But not you."

He started toward me, this time more slowly. Before I could stop myself, I'd taken a step backward. I knew better than to show that kind of weakness in front of him.

He took another step—this time I didn't move. The corners of his mouth twitched. At first I thought I'd amused him, but it was something else—intrigue, perhaps, or even…pride.

"We gave humans a mantra, a long time ago. I give it to you now because, child of soldier, child of man, child of angel, it is not necessary to win the battle if, in the end, you can win the war."

"Then help us!" I pleaded, my hands shaking as I looked at the blood. I didn't understand.

His hand moved to my stomach, and he coated it in dripping blood, pulled my dagger from its sheaf, and smeared my blood down the blade before returning it to my side.

"I already have," he said, reaching out again, his arm now the paw of a lion. He struck me across the face before I could react, the blow so fierce that as I flew toward the back wall of my art studio, I braced myself to go right through it.

*Instead…*I opened my eyes.

chapter thirty-four

"No one will be released from prison until he has paid the last obolus."

Luke 12:59

The pain was severe but I held back the scream lodged in the back of my throat. It would only make things worse.

I was in his arms again, cradled like a child and wearing something different. A knee-length silver dress. I could see why—it made a dramatic backdrop for the blood. Even in my battered state, I felt a surge of rage that he'd taken the liberty.

Dizzy, I tried to focus on my surroundings. We were outside. The sky was still blue, but I reasoned it must be afternoon by now. We were somewhere high. I could sense exiles. Many, too many. But Grigori too, also in great numbers. I could hear the ocean sounds, could smell, almost taste, the salty sea water and something else—sulfur.

We were on Nea Kameni. *The volcano.*

"Stop bleeding her!" a voice hollered, from far away. "You're going to kill her!"

My head ached and my body felt limp. When I strained to see who the voice belonged to—it sounded so familiar—my arm fell heavily to my side, dangling.

Not good. How long has he already bled me?

We were on the rim of the main crater. I could sense exiles directly behind us, but only a few. I concentrated for as long as I could to find the rest. They seemed to be hovering at the base of the volcano. Already fighting.

We are at war.

"Then I suggest you do not delay!" Phoenix called back. He held his arms out with me rag-dolling in their grip. "She doesn't have long left."

I looked up at his face. His eyes were so dark, so sad. "I'm sorry, Phoenix." I winced.

He jolted, surprised I was awake. Then he shook his head. "Someone's been busy."

Phoenix wasn't talking about me. He knew my angel had interfered.

"Too little, too late!" he hissed back at me.

I let my head fall back again and that's when I saw them—the dark smoke lifting from the crater cleared enough for me to get a glimpse. Lincoln stood before an exile, chained and bound just like the three I'd sacrificed, dagger in hand. To my left and right, two other exiles were positioned in the same restraints, completing the triangle.

A man in love.

Not just a soul connection but love. Was that possible? Or had Phoenix just made a vital mistake?

Lincoln drove his blade into the first of them, throwing his victim quickly to the volcano. The smoke rose up and pulled down its catch, just as the ocean had engulfed my earlier offerings.

Three to the water, to entice the current,
Three to the fire to blast open their fate.

"No!" I tried to scream, but I was too weak.

Does he realize I've already completed the first half?

I looked beyond Lincoln. Griffin stood on the edge of the crater, Spence by his side, their faces grim.

Why aren't they stopping him? They should be stopping him!

But, if anything, they seemed to be helping him, guarding him.

"Do you have any idea what you are doing?" I asked softly, through the pain, knowing he'd hear me.

"Yes," Phoenix responded.

Lincoln returned the second exile and fed him to the volcano, which breathed a cloud of darkness from deep within, high up into the sky.

Awaken Tartarus and blanket day.

I followed the dark cloud as it plumed like smoke from a

nuclear explosion and then spread outward, blocking out the sun completely.

To hide their eyes and Heaven's ray.

"I'm creating a new world. One where I belong," Phoenix continued, as if reminding himself, reinforcing his beliefs.

I reached out to him, my hand covered in blood. He flinched when I touched his cheek, my fingers slipping away weakly. "You already do," I breathed.

Lincoln moved to the third exile, pausing to turn toward us, but I couldn't see his face clearly.

"I know you won't kill her! Do you think I'm so stupid, Phoenix? You love her!"

Phoenix looked stunned. "He's right, of course." His shoulders dropped as he spoke to me. "But you already knew that." And then, louder, he called back, "Are you so sure you'll take the chance?"

Lincoln returned the last exile, kicking him into the volcano. The ground vibrated, the smoke increased, and then small flakes like gray snow shot out of the opening and floated back toward the ground. It was now as dark as night.

Ash will fall.

"Phoenix!" Lincoln roared.

I saw him start to move, but the crater was large and he was on the other side. Griffin and Spence started running toward us from the other direction.

I struggled to hold on to consciousness. "I'm willing to die to stop you, Phoenix. Once I'm gone, Lincoln will return you."

He smiled. "I know. But somehow I don't think that's going to happen."

With that, he put me down on my feet and withdrew my dagger from its sheaf. I stumbled, unsteady, and blinked at the sight of my blade when I saw it was red.

From where my angel maker smeared my blood.

I could feel the moment he started to heal me again. The wound was closing and the pain receding, but I was already so weak, it felt as if I had no blood left to give. He kept hold of my hands and swung me wide, leaving me hanging over the crater and its billowing hot smoke.

"Phoenix! No!" A desperate cry sounded. Lincoln.

I dangled over the mouth of the volcano while beneath me, Tartarus stirred with anticipation.

"'Six to the ground, in return for one,'" Phoenix said, reciting the prophecy. He knelt and placed my hands on the rocky edges of the crater, making sure I had a good enough grip. "'An offering of pain starts the rivers of fire.'"

"Don't do this!" I panted, the toes of my sneakers grappling for a foothold.

His sights paused on me for a moment. "Hold on!" He ran my dagger down his arm, slicing it open and covering it in his own blood. Then, he threw it into the volcano, screaming, "Your payment has been made by my hand! Deliver her!"

He crouched down to me, adjusting my hold on the rocks, though I was still slipping. It was so hot with the smoke that my hands were wet with sweat, and I wouldn't manage for much longer, but I had a good enough grip for now—my rock-climbing experience paying off.

"My word stands. Tell your nature wielders: I'll do what I can—wind will be at their side. Hold on, Violet; he's almost here."

"You think the human is gone?" I screamed at him with a sudden burst of strength. "You're so wrong. Exiles only want to destroy and take power, but I know you sent them to us so we would return them. You control them even as you used them! Everything you've done, you've done to belong."

Phoenix's eyes were wide as he stood up, looking over the battlefield he had created.

"That's human, Phoenix! It's not the human in you that's gone at all!"

I could almost hear his heartbeat stammer and then pause.

His mouth opened, and he looked at me with utter surprise.

Then he took off, moving like the wind, disappearing into the darkness, but his whispered words, and their sadness, lingered: "It's too late."

I could hear them coming. Lincoln was faster than Spence and Griffin; he'd reach me first. I could sense the exiles moving around, and I let myself slip into my other sense.

My spirit lifted from my body and I looked down over the

mouth of Hell. Exiles were everywhere. We were at the top, around the crater, while everyone else fanned out around the base, already fighting. I could sense signatures—some awful, some unknown, many frightening.

Then I felt the warmth of my people, Grigori, some fighting on the volcano and many at its perimeter and farther afield. At least a dozen boats surrounded the island, and I saw the glimmer of something linking each one, surrounding the volcano. A shield. They were protecting the rest of the world from this site. But would they be able to hide the smoke and the darkness or what was still to come?

There must have been more than a hundred Grigori.

Where have they all come from?

I came back to myself. The use of what Phoenix had called "sight" had only taken a second or two, but my hands were starting to slip.

Phoenix had to be stopped. He had proved to me time and time again that I could not fight him. He had too much power over me.

"Violet!" Lincoln yelled, sliding to the ground above me. He leaned in over the lip of the volcano, arm outstretched. "Take my hand!"

The volcano roared.

It will be easier for them all. Especially him, in the long run. This is the only way to stop Phoenix.

I felt the blast below. The volcano was preparing to erupt.

A breath of fire shot up, and I couldn't hold back the scream as the flames raged up the back of my legs and body, searing my flesh. I was so weak and so tired. I screamed again, but before I could let my hands slip from their rigid hold on the edge, Lincoln stretched out his own badly burned arm and grabbed hold of one of mine.

I looked up, my eyes pouring with tears of pain and understanding. I had to look away. I let my other hand slip from the rock and hang loose.

"Don't, Violet!" Lincoln's voice was strong and unwavering. It caught me by surprise. "Don't. You. Dare. Look at me!"

It wasn't compulsion, but I still couldn't stop myself. I had to see him one last time. I opened my mouth to tell him good-bye, but he didn't let me speak.

"If you let go, I'm jumping in there after you!"

My hand slipped in his hold and I did little to stop it, but he clung on.

"It's better this way, Linc! You can fight him without me and then you'll be free!"

He looked at me like I was mad until his jaw set with determination.

"You smell of winter dew at the first crack of dawn and when you use your power, it feels like being submerged in the most intoxicating vanilla cream that I lose myself in it every time and…and you *were* beautiful," he blurted out, catching us both by surprise. But he went on, ignoring the fact my hand was still slipping. "So stunning in that dress the other night, I could hardly look at you it hurt so much. You *are* the thing I dread the most in myself,

Violet, because…I love you so much that I can't trust myself. I'd die for you, give up all my power for you. I'd give you my soul in an instant, even if it meant I had to spend eternity in torment—just for one moment with you as mine. Wanting you consumes me. I dread you because I know the risk, but I'm so selfish, I want you anyway. I'd take you even though it could kill you."

I cried out again, the pain now so much worse, inside and out.

My hand continued to slip as I looked into his eyes, intense with want, and I knew he was telling the truth. He would jump in after me. I forced my loose arm up and he grabbed it, leaning farther into the opening.

He lifted me out and as he did, the severity of my burns became apparent. I couldn't hold back the screams and he placed me belly down on the ground.

"Fuck."

It was bad. Lincoln never used that word.

"Oh, fuck."

Or Griffin.

"Fuck."

Spence said it quite a bit, but it was that third one that tipped me over the edge. I started trembling uncontrollably.

Honey and cream. Not as trickly and warm this time. No, this time it enveloped me, then washed through me like a flood. I felt the worst of the pain ease. Lincoln was working his power over me as fast and hard as he could.

"We don't have time!" Spence said urgently. I could hear him panting. He and Griffin had been fighting off exiles while Lincoln tried to heal me. "This thing is about to explode for real, and we do *not* want to be up here!"

Feeling returned to my legs, intensifying the pain from the burns on the backs of my thighs and calves.

"She needs to be able to fight!" Lincoln yelled.

But I knew he'd keep going no matter what. I pushed myself to my knees, trying unsuccessfully to hold back the tears.

"It's okay. I can fight, but I don't have a dagger."

He cupped a hand around my face; his eyes seemed to say so much—hold so much love.

"Stay next to me. Like old times."

He meant when I couldn't use my dagger. I'd fight them; he'd return them. I nodded.

Lincoln helped me up, being careful where he touched. Then he pulled off his T-shirt and started easing it over my head. When I looked at him quizzically, he simply shrugged.

"Most of your dress has melted to your back."

Splendid.

chapter thirty-five

"Black as the devil, hot as hell, pure as an angel, sweet as love."

Charles Maurice de Talleyrand

Spence moved ahead to intercept the exile approaching us. It was like *Night of the Living Dead*, everyone covered in ash and blood. Not a pretty sight.

"Griffin," I said, my voice catching I was so glad to see him. "Phoenix said to tell the nature users that wind will be on their side, though I don't know what that means exactly."

"We can't believe anything he says," Griffin dismissed.

"Yes, we can," Lincoln said. "It was part of the bargain. He will hold to it."

I nodded, Lincoln supporting me, carrying most of my weight as I leaned into him. "He doesn't want everyone dead; he just wants her back."

Griffin was talking into a two-way radio. I heard Josephine respond, and he relayed the message.

"There's something else," I said, trying to hold my own weight. "I sacrificed the three to the water. If three to the volcano makes it erupt, three to the water can't be good."

Griffin smiled. "We're ready for that. Come on. We need to move."

It was an order and we followed. Behind us, the volcano started to rumble. It was about to erupt.

We picked up the pace, and when we neared the battle scene at its foot, I turned back to see a bolt of liquid fire launch from the volcano's opening into the afternoon sky that was dark as night.

"'Flames will roar and spear the skies,'" I said.

Lincoln looked over his shoulder, but urged me on.

We leapt into the mix of exiles and Grigori, and I don't know where it came from—adrenaline, Lincoln, my angel maker—but I summoned a reserve of strength. Side by side, Lincoln and I battled, taking down exiles who stood in our path, flanked by Griffin and Spence.

We maneuvered our way to the center of the battlefield, finding Samuel, Kaitlin, Nathan, and Becca all fighting hard. When we saw each other, we quickly converged, forming a circle and putting our backs to one another to gain the advantage over our opponents.

Lincoln absorbed the brunt of the attack, and I managed to bring down those who made it through before he stepped in to return them. A couple of times I tried to use my power to stall them, but only succeeded in holding the odd one until Lincoln took over.

Every movement tore the flesh on my back and I fought the building need to pass out. All the while, I could see lava rolling down the volcano toward us. We didn't have long.

I looked everywhere to find him, knowing that even though my choice was to live, it did not come before my decision to destroy him. But Phoenix was long gone. This entire battlefield had been arranged to mask his escape.

"We need to move, people!" Griffin called out the instruction again.

It was then that I noticed that all the other Grigori had boarded boats except for us.

"Let's go, let's go!"

As a team, we held our circle, fighting off raving exiles. They saw the lava coming too, and, like us, I was sure they could sense something else brewing, but still they fought savagely, needing the kill, needing to be the most vicious and believing they would prevail.

"Go!" Lincoln yelled at me, as we neared the boat. But I didn't move from his side. He shot glances at me, between hits with the exile he had well in hand.

"Griffin!" Lincoln called out. "We're on board!"

He grabbed the exile he was fighting, drove his dagger into his chest, then spun round, lifting me up in the same motion, ignoring my cry of pain, and running onto the boat. When he put me down, he smiled. "Must you always be so difficult?"

I was breathing hard and working to stay upright, but I couldn't help smiling back. We both turned and watched as the last of our group, Griffin and Spence, leapt aboard and we pulled away from the shore, leaving exiles clambering toward their own vessels.

Josephine pushed ahead to the bow, hands raised. Seconds later, one of the boats exploded, casting exiles into the water, arms flailing, drowning.

"They hate the water," I said as Josephine walked back past us. A woman on a mission.

She glanced at me briefly, a small smile betraying her steely exterior. "I know."

Our boats were now positioned in a row between the volcano and Santorini. The other boats, presumably filled with the remaining exiles, sped toward Santorini.

I hated that they were getting away, but then I saw the line of people on the shore. Not people, Grigori—waiting for them.

"Who are they all?" I asked in disbelief.

"The Rogue," Lincoln answered.

"Here she comes!" Josephine called out and, in a domino effect, one person from each boat repeated what she said to the next, ensuring everyone heard.

Lincoln wrapped an arm around me. I cried out as it pressed the cotton of his T-shirt into the raw flesh on my back, cutting into it like blades of fire.

"I'm sorry, but we have to move back," he said.

I nodded, crying with every step. Now that I'd stopped fighting, the pain was only getting worse.

"What are they going to do?" I asked once we stopped moving and I could breathe again.

"Just watch. It will either be the most amazing thing you've ever seen or the last."

"You did this."

He looked at me, something new in his expression. "You knew?"

I rolled my eyes and tried to pull off mock surprise. "Which part? That you purposely didn't let me know what the plan was because you knew I'd go with Phoenix? Or that you knew 'the highest command' meant me and 'the heart of man' meant you?"

Lincoln's expression changed from surprise to respect and he nodded. "Actually, it wasn't all me. After you left with Phoenix, I told Steph you had to be the highest command and she worked out that I might be a candidate for the other. Griffin confirmed it."

"And the rest?"

"I couldn't be sure of Phoenix's intentions. But I knew he'd come to you." He paused. "And I also knew it wasn't Kaitlin who told you about the ginseng drink."

I grimaced, but he just smiled.

"It wasn't until that night on the rooftop that I figured out he wasn't after civilian kills—we know any other exile would consider that a priority—but when he asked me to kill Gressil, I knew it couldn't be just to protect you."

"And you were so sure I'd go with him?" I asked.

He moved to pull me closer, but hesitated when he saw my body contort in pain. "I know you. And Phoenix knows you too.

Your reaction to him taking Steph was enough for him to realize he could use that threat over you again. You'd do anything to protect the people you care about."

"So, why didn't you just tell me?"

"Because he would've found out everything, even if just sensing it through you—we couldn't take the risk."

I remembered Phoenix's fury when he couldn't probe more information out of me.

"If he knew what we were planning and it didn't agree with his own plans, he could've taken it out on you or Steph or anyone else, and you would've never forgiven yourself. This way, you didn't know anything that could be used against them, anything that you'd blame yourself for later. But..." He dropped his head, running his hands through his hair. "I had no idea he'd take you for so long. I...I looked everywhere, Vi. Nearly lost my mind searching. I'm so sorry...I can't even begin to imagine—"

I put a hand on his bare chest, cutting him off. "I was asleep almost the entire time, until the sacrifices. He didn't touch me—except for when I attacked him."

Relief flooded Lincoln's face, and his hands wrapped around mine and squeezed. Beside us there was more commotion, people running up and down the deck. He motioned toward the volcano that was now erupting violently. We wouldn't be safe here for long, though I didn't think escape was an option now either.

He squeezed my hand again. "Here we go."

While we watched the volcano, I considered the fact that Lincoln had been controlling this whole situation from the moment we arrived in Santorini. Griffin had been right to leave him in charge.

The volcano lit up the sky, blood-colored fireworks detonating from its top, fire raining down as it continued to leap from the rim, lava surging down the slopes. The entire island was now almost covered in rivers of fire, while beyond, a power just as great had surely been building since I'd made those first three sacrifices. Now we could see its prize: a swell in the sea so enormous it looked not like water but as if the very edges of the world were closing in on us.

I gripped Lincoln tight, despite the pain. "'A swell of death…' A tsunami!"

"Now!" Josephine screamed.

Zoe threw her hands wide, her head back. On the boat beside her, several other Grigori I didn't recognize did something similar. In the water around the edges of the island, whirlpools started to swirl. Other Grigori started tossing something into the vortexes.

The tsunami drew nearer, building in size.

If this thing hits, we're all dead.

"Griffin!" Josephine yelled.

Suddenly the whirlpools exploded, fountains of water forced up from the sea's depths in succession from left to right, creating momentum and a new tsunami.

When I looked at Griffin again, I saw he was holding some kind of remote control. They'd been using explosives.

The new surge sucked in the water surrounding Santorini and

moved out toward the open sea and the oncoming tsunami, which looked like it could eat our man-made wave for a snack.

Something flashed with lightning speed behind our wave, moving back and forth so fast, it was just a blur. The wind picked up, lifting the ridge of water even higher.

"Phoenix," I whispered. But it wasn't enough.

"Hiro!" Josephine yelled.

I watched as, just as the others had done, he and two other Grigori started coordinating their powers to move large boulders from the backs of their boats, sending them flying toward our wave, now headed on a collision course for both the melting island and the oncoming tsunami.

The volcano, as if sensing the threat, roared with another explosion, lava now flowing into the boiling water, turning the ocean floor red.

The tsunami crashed over the volcano effortlessly, like it was no obstacle. I gripped hold of Lincoln.

This was it.

When our wave—so tiny in comparison—was yards away from impact, Josephine called out again, "Now!"

The boulders flew one by one into the wave as the tsunami crashed over it. And, like a perfectly conducted climax, Josephine exploded the rocks into billions of atoms, forcing the entire tsunami up and into the sky.

Our feeble wave—David to a mighty Goliath.

At that moment, the wind came again, this time from Santorini.

It blew hard and fast, Zoe and the other nature users adding to its strength until it picked up the rain clouds that would have surely drenched the entire island, blowing the tsunami back out to sea, swooping low to silence the volcano, turning its remaining red glow to smoldering black on its way.

The sun broke through the darkness as we stood in the downpour. Griffin looked up, watery soot coursing down his neck. "I think all eyes are wide open now."

"No wonder they're crying," I said quietly, because I could already feel it. Something else, something that didn't belong, was with us.

But also, I couldn't deny it: Phoenix had helped us save Santorini.

chapter thirty-six

"Destiny has two ways of crushing us—by refusing our wishes and by fulfilling them."

Henri F. Amiel

In the aftermath, our boats returned to assess the damage. Groups of Grigori used their various powers to help put out the hot spots and contain the gases coming from the site, while others started preparing notes that would be handed anonymously to the Greek authorities later.

I felt relieved that the fight between exiles and Grigori had been successfully hidden from the outside world. It had been a massive group effort and now that everyone was starting to converge, I could see more than a hundred Grigori on the volcanic island and in the boats, and the same again back on Santorini.

Some, however, had not survived. Though they had fought for the cause, I couldn't help but feel the weight of responsibility as I watched Grigori carry the lifeless bodies of their partners aboard the waiting boats.

Lincoln explained to us that Griffin had brought large numbers of extra Grigori from mainland Greece, along with the Academy arrivals, to build our army. The Rogue had taken up position guarding Santorini from incoming exiles and placed their nature users strategically, some sent as far as the surrounding islands to guard against any flow-on effects from the tsunami.

Lincoln had left no stone unturned.

I hobbled off the boat, despite his objections. He wanted me to stay aboard so he could heal me, but I insisted so he followed, only to be bombarded by Grigori, congratulating him on a stellar attack. Lincoln shrugged off the compliments, redirecting credit to the Conductors and Josephine instead.

I left him to do his thing as I saw another boat sailing in—Steph, Dapper, and Onyx all aboard. They must have been behind the firing line. I was relieved to see them safe and returned a wave to Steph.

"Vi! Are you okay?" she yelled out.

I nodded, not really feeling up to hollering, and pointed in Salvatore's direction when I saw her eyes scouring the island. She smiled in relief. I noticed she was wearing Irin's necklace that I'd left under her pillow. Nothing had been shielded from her today. I hoped it was a good thing.

As I waited for their boat to anchor, a sound made the hairs on my arms stand on end. The roar was unmistakable: my lion. The same one that has visited me in my dreams and first awoken my angelic essence. And suddenly I understood even more. This was not just my lion—this was my angel maker. They were one and the same and somehow I knew—when he was in animal form, he was there to help me.

I followed the sound until I found him. Larger than any normal lion, almost as tall as me, his mane was fiery bronze, like his eyes in my dreams. He stalked me and I knew I should be afraid. He moved closer, hesitating as he took those final few steps, a wild beast trying to control his ferocious nature.

When I could almost reach out and touch him, he stopped and lowered his head. I looked back over my shoulder. Lincoln was still encircled by Grigori, Steph and the others still stuck on their boat. I returned to face my lion, noticing that the ground where he stood was red hot and yet he remained still, patient.

I took a cautious step closer, grateful Phoenix had at least left me with my sneakers, and slowly reached a hand toward his mane. Just as I was about to make contact, his head snapped up, the look in his eyes a clear warning. I dropped my hand.

Got it. No patting.

He shook out his mane, his tail swishing from side to side, and stood tall as he roared, his breath blasting over me. The relief that caressed my injured body was instant.

He shook his head again and began padding back around the foot of the volcano, not bothering to avoid the hot spots. He stopped and looked up toward the peak before disappearing out of sight.

I didn't need to lift Lincoln's T-shirt to know all my wounds were healed. My angel maker had just interfered. Again.

I looked up to the peak of the volcano, wondering why my angel maker had taken the time to make such a pointed stop.

What is up there?

Something caught my eye behind the still-billowing smoke—something glinting in the sun. Silver. No, surely not...No one would go up there. I squinted again until the smoke cleared enough for me to be sure: I was staring at a figure, blackened by soot and ash, and as I watched, it fell to the ground at the edge of the crater.

I was moving before I realized, heading up toward a place I never wanted to go again. My feet kept slipping into patches of lava, but I kept going. Someone was up there.

"Violet!" I heard Lincoln yell, but I didn't stop. I had to get to the top; I had to see. A strange energy propelled me forward—not just my own, but also my angel maker's. He wanted me to go there, demanded it.

I picked up my pace, stumbling every few steps.

"Violet! Wait! It's not safe!" Lincoln shouted.

He was so fast, he soon caught up to me, but he stayed behind a few steps, cautious. Maybe he thought I was going to finish what I had started earlier.

"I'm okay," I said, not stopping. "I saw something up there."

"Violet, no one has gone up there; it's too unstable. We have to go back down. You're hurt—we need to heal you."

I stopped and lifted the back of his T-shirt, exposing my flesh. He gasped.

"How?" he asked, taking in the fact that all of my injuries had gone.

"My angel maker."

"That's...that's not possible."

I held my hands out. "And yet...Do you trust me?"

"Yes," he said without hesitation.

"Then understand that I need to be up there."

He wanted to argue, to get me to safety, but instead he sighed and nodded.

When we reached the top, I walked quickly around the crater to the place I thought the person had been. At first, I couldn't see anything and started to doubt myself, but then, just visible against the smoldering ground, I saw the silver glinting in the sunlight that had caught my eye from below. I ran over, dropping to my knees.

It was a woman, clothed only in a thick layer of ash and with dark hair so long, it covered her. On her right wrist, something silver. I picked up her limp arm. She barely moaned, but it was enough to know she was still alive.

Just.

I rubbed my fingers over her bracelet.

Lincoln dropped to his knees beside me, pushing the hair back from the woman's face. "She's not an exile. She feels like...Can you sense her?" he asked, starting to wipe some of the ash from her face.

"She's Grigori," I said, feeling distant, fighting the woozy sensation that was building inside me.

One wristband.

"Where could she have come from?" Lincoln asked, baffled.

"She came from the volcano," I said, knowing I was right.

Lincoln paused, partly at my answer and partly because he'd wiped away enough ash from her face to see her. "She looks... Violet, she looks like you."

Griffin chose that moment to stumble over to us. "Heard you'd decided to venture up here again." He was puffing—obviously he'd run the whole way, worried we were in trouble.

"What? Were you feeling nostalgic?" he joked uneasily. Then he saw the woman. "Oh, who's this?" He crouched down beside us. Then he saw the wristband, took another look at the figure before him, then turned to me, questioningly.

I sat back on my heels in total disbelief.

"She's my mother."

chapter thirty-seven

"Here, then, I have today set before you life and prosperity, death and doom."

Deuteronomy 30:15

Lincoln carried the woman down the volcano, Griffin and I following, dazed.

My mother.

"Did anything else happen when you were with Phoenix?" Griffin asked.

I thought back. "No, no…I don't know. He kept me asleep through most of it. I remember being on the boat, we fought, then he made me sacrifice the exiles and knocked me out. I woke up on the volcano."

But then I realized I didn't *just* wake up. "Wait! There's one thing. I had a dream and my angel maker was there. I…I asked him to help us and…" I shook my head. "He took my dagger and wiped my blood on it." I looked up at Griffin, who was also figuring it out. "Then he told me he had helped us."

"The same dagger Phoenix threw into the volcano?"

I nodded.

"Phoenix wasn't the only one who made an offering. Your blood was on that blade too."

I looked at the woman in Lincoln's arms.

Have I done this? Brought her here?

"But I…The prophecy said it could only deliver one."

"Only one to the person with terrible desire, but maybe this was something else?"

I shivered—a sudden chill running through me—and noticed that I wasn't the only one feeling it. Everyone seemed to have sensed something and we all looked toward the headlands of Santorini.

From such a distance, the only things visible were two figures. One had long hair, almost to the ground, that was blowing wildly in the breeze. Orange. No—gold. Hair of gold, just like Phoenix had hair of opal.

The woman, my mother, stirred in Lincoln's arms. I froze, watching as her eyes opened. They were not like mine. I had Dad's eyes. Hers were electric blue and striking. She looked in the same direction we all had, but now my eyes were fixed on her.

"Lilith," she whispered before passing out again.

"God help us," Griffin said from my other side.

I started walking down the slope toward Steph.

"Don't you want to go with your mother?" Griffin called behind me.

I stopped and looked back at them. "Why would I want to do that?"

I carried on until I reached Steph, who pulled me onto her boat, where I buried my head in her shoulder and cried all the way back to Santorini.

I waited for the numbness to set in, but as everyone returned to the hotel, all I felt was anger.

Steph helped me to our room with Salvatore, refusing to let me out of her sight. She had already packed our things, but we needed to shower and change. The Academy had ordered us all off the island. Apparently, Irin had started to cause problems, threatening to attack us if we were not gone by midnight, which gave us only about two hours. Sure, we could use our forces to overwhelm him, but there would be inevitable repercussions that no one wanted to consider right now.

I started to wash away the dried blood and ash. Thanks to my angel maker, underneath, I appeared unharmed, a thought that made me laugh and cry at the same time. Some things could not be changed, though. I was desperately weak. The blood loss would affect me for days, and I looked gaunt.

I got out of the shower and studied myself in the mirror, wondering if it would ever end—the fighting, the pain, the sacrifice.

How could my angel maker punish me by sending her back? The person she cared so little about that she abandoned me the moment I was born.

And what of all the rest of it? What about the Academy? I had no idea what they planned to do with me. Josephine had proved what she'd said at the beginning was true—I no longer had any doubt she wanted to defeat exiles. She hadn't been corrupted like Magda, but that didn't mean she wasn't dangerous, that she wouldn't take me down in a heartbeat.

And as for my soul...Since waking up in Phoenix's arms, it had quieted. I had been near Lincoln since, but I hadn't felt the same physical pain at being close to him. Maybe my weakened physical state had also lessened my soul's ability to fight me. Whatever it was, I was grateful for the reprieve.

There was a polite knock on the door.

"Sweetie, Lincoln's here," Steph said. I knew she'd tell him to go away if I asked.

"Okay," I said, throwing on a pair of jeans and a white V-neck T-shirt. Steph went straight into the bathroom and closed the door behind her, turning on the shower to give us privacy.

I sat on the edge of my bed, trying not to look like I needed to.

Lincoln sat down opposite.

"Salvatore went to get his things," he said.

I nodded.

"Umm...Everyone is loading up the cars downstairs. Griffin has spoken with Josephine, and for now, the Academy has agreed to you staying under Griffin's guidance."

I nodded again. I heard the "for now" but at least that meant I could go home.

"She threatened to split us up," I said, trying to hold down my anger at the world.

Lincoln was silent for a moment, then answered, "I'll never let that happen."

I breathed a sigh of relief. I had been scared that he might agree with the idea.

He stood up, came over to me, and put a hand on my shoulder. "She's okay. They've cleaned her up, and she's in and out of consciousness, but they expect her to be fully awake soon."

I nodded.

"Do you want to see her?"

I shook my head, keeping my eyes focused on the carpet.

"Okay," he said, before giving my shoulder a squeeze. "I've got to get to the airport. Josephine insisted I have the pleasure of seeing off the Rogue since I brought them here. But I'll see you there."

I didn't look up, didn't say anything, just nodded. It was all I could muster.

I took a seat up front, as far away from Josephine as I could get. Apparently, our large number meant planes were hard to come by, and so she had offered to let us use the Academy jet, which meant she was escorting us home.

Great. I would rather have swam.

When we got out of the taxis, Spence was waiting for us. I felt like such an invalid, which only fed my anger. I was glad Spence took over, though. I felt like he understood.

Onyx and Dapper were sitting together, already with drinks in hand. Dapper smiled when he saw me; Onyx raised his glass.

Steph and Salvatore settled into the seats behind me, and Spence sat across the aisle, leaving me room to spread out.

Josephine had her crew around her, though I noticed they were slumped now, not worrying so much about staying at full attention—even Hiro and Mia didn't seem to care, though I suspected they would act at a moment's notice if one of us tried to jump Josephine.

I gave Morgan and Max, my favorites of her crew, a nod and felt the comfort of my people as they piled in behind me, each one stopping briefly to place a hand on my shoulder. I didn't turn around, afraid they would see the tears welling.

This is my family.

Even if I did miss Dad desperately, the thought made things a little easier. Until, that is, I heard the bathroom door open and turned in time to see Max leap to his feet and help *her* walk to a seat behind Josephine.

My mother didn't even spare me a glance, not that I'd waited before ducking into my seat.

Why the hell is she on our plane?

I felt the panic rising in my throat. My knees bounced up and down. I couldn't do this, be trapped here with her. My eyes darted around and fixed on the still-open door. I was so close.

Five steps and I'll be out.

If I could make five steps on my own without passing out. I bit down on my lip and considered my options. Spence would probably come with me and we would find another plane. But I really didn't want to cause a scene, draw attention to myself only to be dragged back on board. Josephine would just love that. But I couldn't, simply *couldn't*, be here. With her.

Just as I was about to make a move, Lincoln's silhouette darkened the entrance, and the second I saw him, I started to shake all over. He took one look down the plane, then back to me. Griffin appeared at his side and looked at me, seeing I was a cowardly mess, before putting a hand on Lincoln's shoulder.

"I'll sit at the back. You take a seat down here," Griffin said in a soft tone that conveyed more than his words. Protectiveness.

Lincoln didn't hesitate and sat down beside me, almost pulling me onto his lap. I heard Griffin stop and speak, quietly but loudly enough for those around us to hear: "No one comes down this end of the jet."

First Nathan, "Not a problem, boss," then Becca, "Our pleasure." The strongest fighters in earshot supporting his order, making sure I knew I was safe.

Lincoln held me tight and brushed my hair back, combing it through his fingers and behind my ear until eventually the shaking stopped and I eased back into my seat.

I stirred at the sound of conversation drifting from the back of the plane.

"I see you're awake again," Josephine said.

"Yes. I'm feeling better all the time. Sleep seems to help rejuvenate me," came a somehow familiar voice, even though I'd never heard it before.

"Do you have any memory of what happened?" Josephine asked.

The speaker hesitated, but then responded clearly. "No. Other than that it seems some time has passed."

"Indeed. It is more than seventeen years since you were last thought to be with us, Evelyn. You've been greatly missed by many."

I looked over to see Lincoln watching me carefully. I turned toward the window but kept concentrating on the conversation Josephine was making no attempt to keep private.

"Do you know why you're here?" she continued.

Evelyn paused again before she answered, making me distrust her.

Not that I don't already.

"I can tell you this much—if I'm here, you can be sure Lilith is back."

"Hmm," Josephine said. "That's quite correct."

"Well!" Evelyn snapped. "How the hell did you let that happen?"

I could hear the contempt dripping from Josephine's voice as she answered. "Her first son, Phoenix, discovered a lost Exile Scripture from the time of Moses. He found a way to open the gates to Hell and resurrect her."

"Wait!" Evelyn said. I could tell she was now standing. I was sure all eyes were on her. Except for mine, and Lincoln's, whose gaze I could feel was still fixated on me. "Phoenix? No, that's not possible. We watched him for decades. He wasn't ever inclined toward Lilith's ways; he was more human than exile. Powerful and malicious at times, yes. Greedy and possessive too, but generally sane. Something must have made him change, brought out his darkness. What happened?"

I couldn't take it anymore. Lincoln put a hand on mine, but I pushed it away and stood up. All eyes quickly moved in my direction and there was a collective holding of breath. Evelyn's electric-blue eyes took me in, sensing a challenge.

"*I* happened. Phoenix is the way he is because of me," I said, putting my hands on my hips, refusing to show how weak I was feeling.

My mother's glare intensified and she took a step toward me, throwing a hand up in the air as she did. "Well, congratulations! You just brought Hell to earth."

I stared right back. "Oh, believe me, I know."

She flinched and resumed walking. When she reached the halfway mark, Nathan and Becca stood up on opposite sides of the aisle, their threat clear. Evelyn stopped.

"Let me pass."

Griffin stood too and looked at me, waiting. I gave a small nod.

"Let her by," Griffin said.

Nathan and Becca took their seats again but stayed perched and ready.

Evelyn absorbed all of this, taking a few more steps. I stiffened at her nearness and Lincoln was up in a shot and standing behind me.

"That's close enough," he said.

Evelyn looked him up and down, assessing this new threat. She stopped as requested.

"Your markings?" she questioned, motioning to me to reveal them.

I held out my arms, inner wrists exposed. She saw the scar that had never fully healed after Jordan.

She gasped. "What's your name?" Her voice quivered.

I didn't answer.

"Violet?" she whispered.

But I wasn't going to let that fool me. I stood tall. I'd had practice at this, at blocking everything out. I knew the rules, despite my earlier desire to escape.

I don't run. I don't quit. I don't believe in fairy-tale endings.

And it helped knowing I had a kick-ass warrior at my back. "It's the name my mother gave me—before she handed me over to an angel, sealed my fate, and abandoned me and my dad, leaving us with no answers."

Evelyn just kept staring, so intently that I struggled to hold eye contact. She glanced at Lincoln again, then back to me.

"Phoenix fell in love with you," she said finally.

I froze at her words but recovered quickly, turning my back on her. "I don't owe you any answers."

I dropped back down into my seat, knowing I had no energy left and not wanting to pass out in front of her. I heard her walking away. Lincoln stayed where he was for a while and then sat down beside me again.

He didn't say anything. He didn't touch me. He knew I couldn't have handled it right then. I turned toward the window and pretended to sleep while trying to ignore the hundreds of thoughts bombarding my mind, fighting for attention.

It wasn't long before I felt him move away, and the first twinge of my soul stirring within, warning me.

"Let me by."

"I'm sorry, Evelyn. I'm sure there is a lot that needs to be discussed, but right now, she's exhausted. You have no idea what she's been through." Lincoln's voice caught, but he covered it, clearing his throat. "She needs to rest…and so do you, I imagine."

"You're her partner?" she asked confrontationally.

"I am."

"You're from a Power?" It was an odd question.

"How did you know?" Lincoln asked.

"At least some things were done right," she mumbled. "I suppose if I were to make a point of passing you now, you'd be willing to use force?"

"A fair assumption," he said, and I could tell he wasn't joking.

My soul stirred again.

"Would you die for her?"

I almost stopped breathing. I could feel his eyes on me.

"I do. Every day."

chapter thirty-eight

"What is done out of love always takes place beyond good and evil."

FRIEDRICH NIETZSCHE

We landed in a thunderstorm and the turbulence was too much. I felt sick by the time the plane drew to a standstill—though more so at the thought of what would happen now we were home.

As we began to taxi toward our terminal, Griffin and Josephine moved to the front of the plane. Dealing with everything else, I'd almost forgotten she was there, probably enjoying the show.

The pair stopped in front of Lincoln and me.

"Violet, Josephine will be returning to the Academy immediately. We have no idea where Lilith is headed, but we can assume she will be in control now, so it is unlikely she and Phoenix will return here. Josephine will mount an investigation and put out feelers to all Grigori worldwide until we get a hit on them. In the meantime, the Assembly will be...reviewing your unique situation."

I nodded. No doubt that wouldn't mean anything good, but there was little else to say for now.

Griffin cleared his throat. "Also, Josephine will be taking your moth—" My look cut him off. "Sorry—Evelyn, back to the Academy with her. Given the circumstances of her return, she will need to be fully debriefed and monitored."

I looked up, seeing in Griffin's eyes what his words only touched upon.

They were going to imprison her, just like Josephine had threatened to do to me. I glanced over my shoulder at Evelyn. She was standing at the back, leaning casually against the wall, arms crossed, as if unconcerned. But she wasn't.

Could I stand by and let them take her? Why should I bother trying to stop them? She would never help me. She'd probably handcuff me for them if the roles were reversed. And I already had enough troubles with the Academy.

I looked at Lincoln. He was glancing around too. I knew what he was thinking.

Even if we wanted to do something, we have no chance.

We could fight, but that would be bad, bad, bad. Plus, even though I'd be happy to punch Josephine, I didn't want to fight the Academy Grigori; I liked most of them.

I turned back to see Josephine looking smug.

"Violet? Are you okay?" Lincoln said loudly.

I looked up at him in horror. He knew better than to draw attention to me when I was like this. He put a hand over my face.

"You look like you're going to be sick. Spence! Take her to the bathroom!"

Spence moved quickly, helping me up.

What is Lincoln doing?

I wasn't going to be sick. He knew why I was panicking.

As Spence pulled me down the aisle, I caught Lincoln giving him a small nod.

What the…?

Spence opened the door to the bathroom and, to my horror, stepped in with me, a finger to his lips.

I mouthed, "What's going on?"

He shrugged. He didn't know either. All we knew was that Lincoln had sent us down here on purpose. Why?

Because Spence must be able to do something no one else can.

I dropped my face in my hands and then looked up at our reflections in the mirror. I wished Spence could glamour me into looking better.

Glamour! That's it.

I put my mouth to his ear. "Lincoln's giving us the chance to get her out of here. I can't just let the Academy imprison her. If I clear the way, can you hold a glamour that no one out there will see through? Can you help me get her off?" And all the while, my soul churned, loving and screaming for that man more and more.

Spence grinned. "Don't need to ask, Eden. I've already told you I've got your back."

I squeezed his shoulder gratefully. "And I've got yours. Whenever. Whatever."

I stumbled out of the bathroom. "Linc," I breathed.

He bounded up the aisle to my side. "Hey! You okay?"

I glanced at Evelyn and let her see my eyes dart toward Spence. It was the best I could do. She didn't react at all.

I hope this works.

"Yeah. Just dizzy. Can you help me off?" I asked.

Lincoln wrapped his arm around my waist. "Everyone, clear the aisle."

And it was as easy as that. Everyone moved back, watching me, the poor invalid who needed to be helped off the plane by her soul mate. I was grinding my teeth the entire time.

Lincoln knew, of course. My asking for help was a surefire way to tip him off. Griffin too, who actually looked like he was enjoying the moment as we passed him and Josephine.

"We'll be seeing you soon, Violet," Josephine promised as we passed.

"I'm sure," I said, wishing I didn't have to look so pathetic in front of her.

"Hey, Kaitlin!" Griffin called out, standing on one of the seats. "Throw us a couple of bags."

Heavy bags started flying through the air, providing the perfect distraction, keeping prying eyes away.

Lincoln and I kept moving, keeping up the pretense of my

weakness until we'd disembarked. Once we were off, we made a beeline for the terminal, only stopping when we were surrounded by other people. I turned around. Spence was right behind us and dropped the invisibility glamour instantly. He was alone.

"Where is she?" I asked, suddenly sick at the thought we'd been caught.

Spence shrugged apologetically. "I had her until we hit the terminal, but as soon as there were people, she just took off into the crowd."

I put my hands on my hips and let out a breath. What had I expected?

"Whatever. Let's go."

chapter thirty-nine

"And the angel said, 'I have learned that every man lives, not through care of himself, but by love.'"

Leo Tolstoy

There was so much to do, but not one of us knew where to start. Somehow, we all ended up back at Hades. By the time Lincoln, Spence, and I walked into Dapper's apartment, everyone else was already there.

The conversation ebbed and flowed as we reflected on the past few days, Griffin telling us how he'd managed to recruit so many Grigori from the mainland to help our cause and Lincoln filling in the gaps, explaining that he'd been back to Irin to request their and the Rogue force's safe entry to the island. I wondered if Irin had fed from him again, but Lincoln, as if reading my thoughts, assured me that the Keeper had simply agreed, still on cloud nine from whatever payment Phoenix had sent him.

That was where Lincoln had been coming from the night I left with Phoenix. I could see the regret in his eyes now, how much it pained him that his delay in reaching me had enabled Phoenix to take me away with him.

Theories were thrown around about what Lilith would do, now that she was back, where she would focus her destructive energy. The only thing everyone agreed on was that it wouldn't take her long to resurface.

I made my way to the minibar, where Onyx was handing out drinks like a pro.

"You asked me once if I was willing to make the big choices," I said, grabbing a Coke.

"And?"

"I am. Are you?"

He downed a large gulp of whiskey and cast his eyes around the room, filled with enemies of old. "I believe I already have."

I nodded. "You're welcome to stay close to us," I said, giving him my word. "Thank you for helping me."

He shrugged. "I'm not good, Violet."

"I know that, Onyx, but you're not evil either."

He gave a brief nod. "You saved a lot of people on that island, myself included."

Tears welled and I shook my head. "It was my fault. I helped Phoenix bring back Lilith."

He waited until I'd composed myself.

"If you hadn't brokered the deal, it would've happened anyway, just differently. You did the best you could. I'm amazed you managed what you did."

I really hadn't thought of it that way.

Dapper joined us at the bar. "I need you to work tomorrow, Onyx. Trisha said a couple of staff have called in sick."

I could see Onyx was tempted to tell him to get stuffed, but then he surprised us both by simply passing Dapper a full glass. "I can do that."

Dapper sipped his drink to hide his shock and nodded, with a raspy, "That's good."

Onyx harrumphed and moved away. Once we were alone, I leaned in to Dapper. "I know it was you who healed Onyx and Steph."

Dapper fixed his gaze on me.

"I won't tell anyone," I offered.

I saw the tension leave as his shoulders and mouth relaxed. He cleared his throat awkwardly. "Thank you."

"Ah-hem."

We spun round to see Griffin. "Except I already know and would prefer not to have to pretend otherwise."

"Me too," Lincoln said, now walking toward us.

"Didn't anyone ever tell you it's rude to listen in to other people's conversations?" snapped Dapper.

"Afraid I'd already worked it out, my friend. Lincoln had too, I expect. There weren't many alternatives once we ruled out Violet's abilities," Griffin said, lowering his voice now.

"Just humans?" Lincoln asked.

Dapper grunted, apparently resigned. "Anything mostly human."

And then I couldn't help myself. "Dapper, what *are* you?"

Dapper picked up his cleaning cloth and started wiping down the bar. "Just a barman. That's all I bloody well wanna be, anyway."

With that, we let it go, melting back into other conversations. If Dapper wanted to keep his business private, that was his call. I was glad Griffin and Lincoln seemed to agree.

Settling on my barstool, I looked around the room and smiled. My friends, *my family*, were home and safe. We had big problems and the safe part wouldn't last long, but for now, we were okay.

Steph found me a bit later on, hiding in the bathroom.

"You okay?" she asked.

"Yeah. You?"

She sat beside me on the edge of the bath. "Yeah. Thanks, by the way," she said, fingering her necklace.

"Sure. I'd prefer that you didn't have to be around this stuff at all, though."

She shuffled closer to me. "I know, but this is exactly where I want to be, Vi."

"I know." I stood up and took her hand. "Come on, Salvatore's probably sent out a search party." That earned me a smile. "Yeah, yeah, I know…You love him."

She followed me out, still holding my hand and bumping my hip. "I really do."

We linked arms and walked out laughing—right into a silent living room.

"What's going on?" Steph asked, still laughing.

But she stopped when she saw her brother standing in the doorway.

"Someone said they saw you come in here," Jase said, realizing he'd interrupted something.

"Jase! Hey! Yeah, I just got back," Steph stalled, not sure how much to say.

I suddenly remembered the text he'd sent me. I squeezed Steph's hand.

"Yeah. Some crazy getaway. We…um…we got stranded up the coast and just grabbed a lift back. Someone…working downstairs told us you were here, so we came up to look for you."

Oh my God, this isn't going well.

Jase snorted. "And just *happened* to find Lincoln and his friend Griffin? Along with *my* boss, who has also been mysteriously absent for the exact same amount of time as the rest of you!"

Damn. He is observant.

"Jase…I…I…" But she had nothing.

Neither did I.

"She was with me," Salvatore said from behind, coming up and putting an arm around Steph. "In fact, we were all together, doing things very important. I am apologizing, Jase, but Steph is not able to tell you where she is been or what she is doing. Can it be enough to know she's with people who care for her, just as you? That now she is being home and safe and maybe one day she tells you more?"

Jase looked completely gobsmacked.

He wasn't the only one. I'd never heard so many words come out of Salvatore's mouth in one go.

Griffin chose that moment to step in. "Salvatore is right, Jase. We wish we could tell you more. But everything he has said is the truth, and it is your choice what you do with that."

I could see Griffin's power swirling, using his ability to instill truth. A layer of mist moved over Jase, penetrating him with this honesty. Steph's wide eyes told me her necklace was working well too, as it broke down the illusions that would normally hide human eyes from such things.

Jase looked around the room. He was still for so long, people started leaving—first Samuel and Kaitlin, then Nathan and Becca, and eventually, Dapper too, who put a consoling hand on Jase's shoulder on the way, "You'll be all right, man. Sometimes it's better not to know everything. Damn well wish I didn't!"

He was followed by Onyx, who seemed revived with a bounce in his step. He smiled broadly at us. "And I thought you people didn't mess with humans."

Steph squeezed onto the sofa with Salvatore, beside Spence and Zoe, and waited nervously. Lincoln and Griffin made themselves comfortable at the minibar while I was left in no-man's-land.

Finally, I went up to him. "Jase?"

His eyes focused on me. "Something really big is going on here, isn't it?"

I smiled sadly. "Yes, but believe me when I tell you it's better if you don't know."

He looked at Steph. "She's safe?"

I wished I didn't feel like I was lying. "Yes."

"And you?"

I saw Lincoln shift from the corner of my eye. "Yes. I'm fine."

He threw a hand toward Salvatore, who was watching nervously. "So he and my sister…?"

I smiled. "Yeah. He's a good guy."

Jase nodded as if he'd figured that much out for himself.

"So, I just pretend you were off sitting on a beach up the coast?"

I put my hands in my pockets. "Better than us lying to you."

"True." The corners of his mouth turned up mischievously. "So…if Steph is going out with him, I guess that means it'll just be me taking you to the dance?"

Lincoln stood abruptly. I felt his fury building and had to force myself not to look.

Jase, however, did, and whatever he saw made him stubborn.

"Saturday night, right? I'll pick you up at six and we can get something to eat on the way."

"Oh." My mouth was dry. All I could concentrate on was feeling Lincoln's rage. "Oh," I said again. I really didn't want to hurt him.

Steph jumped up. "Why don't we all go together? You know, as a group."

"Yeah. A group would be good." But I could still feel Lincoln behind me so I added, "Jase, I'm not really available…like that." I swallowed hard, unsure if I was doing the right thing. I didn't want to lead him on and, more than that, I didn't want to hurt Lincoln. Just because we couldn't be together…

"Oh," Jase said, flashing another look in Lincoln's direction. "I didn't realize you were seeing someone."

"I'm not…It's just that…" I took a deep breath. "It just wouldn't be fair to you, Jase. I'm sorry."

He stepped toward me and put a hand out toward my face. I grabbed it before he made contact. "Jase. I mean it," I said, surprised by my reaction.

Lincoln must have felt it too because I sensed him relax. I knew he'd understand what I said next. "The dance will be fun—if you're okay with going as friends?"

Jase glanced in Lincoln's direction again, then back to me. He took a step back. "Steph, I'm leaving in twenty and you'd better come with me if we're going to figure out something to say to Mom."

Steph nodded. "I'll meet you out front."

Jase headed toward the door, stopping to look back at me. He smiled a killer smile that would have blown most girls away.

"Friends is fine, Vi." His hand braced the doorframe as his smile widened. "For now."

Either he was well practiced at pissing other guys off or just had really good intuition, because he was out the door in a flash.

Good God.

Spence broke the awkward silence. "Come on, Zo. Let's get you settled at the hotel. You can pout about Music Man later. Can't believe the Academy is paying for your accommodation!" He pulled her up from the sofa.

"Well, you will when I tell you the dirt we have on Mr. Carven. And anyway," she said, throwing me a foul look, "I'm pretty sure I already called dibs on Music Man."

I'd forgotten that Zoe had hit on Jase a couple of months ago. I gave her a worried look, but her annoyance morphed into a light smile.

"No biggie."

I breathed a sigh of relief—I couldn't take on anyone else right now. Seeing my chance, I jumped at the exit opportunity.

"I'll walk out with you guys," I said, grabbing my bag.

I stood in the middle of the footpath, immobile. Getting away had been all well and good, but once I had said my good-byes and loaded Spence and Zoe into a taxi, I found I had no idea where to go. I couldn't face Dad yet—I knew there would be endless questions that I would have to answer. Before that, I needed to get my head straight.

I felt his presence when Lincoln neared. I started to speed up—it would be better to stay away from him right now—but he was beside me within moments. He pulled his coat off and wrapped it around me.

"Come on," he said. "I'll sleep on the couch."

I let him walk me all the way to his warehouse, and we settled into a perfect silence that somehow conveyed more than anything we would dare say aloud.

"I'll run you a bath," was all he said when we got there.

I soaked for as long as I could before my hungry soul dragged me back out to him.

While Lincoln disappeared to have a quick shower, I picked up my paintbrush and pulled back the drop sheet from a section of my wall. I hadn't thought about the mural much lately, and I still wasn't ready to tackle the whole thing, but now, down one side, I felt inspired and outlined something that felt right—a single lily on a long stem.

Lincoln made dinner. Pasta. I asked for extra basil, which made him smile for some reason, and I soaked up every note of its aroma as it cooked.

Mmm...Home.

We sat in silence while we ate and until I made coffee. I dosed Lincoln's with sugar, knowing if I asked, he'd say one, so not bothering and instead just adding the two I knew he really preferred. He smiled as he watched.

"He likes you," he said eventually. I knew he was talking about Jase. When I didn't respond, he added, "I wanted to rip his throat out."

I couldn't hold back the smile. "I'm glad," I said, saying exactly what I knew I shouldn't.

He started to laugh but covered it quickly with a cough.

"You should get some sleep," he said, clearing away our plates.

I didn't want to sleep. I wanted to grab him, make him all mine.

I followed him to his bedroom, where he stayed standing in the doorway. I went straight to the bed, sitting on the edge.

"Are we going to talk about your mom?"

I shook my head. "No. She's gone."

"You don't think she'll come back?"

"I hope not." I flicked my hair so it curtained my face. "I never want to see her again."

"We'll see," he said under his breath, but he let it go and I was grateful. I wasn't up to contemplating the hows and whys of her return. Or anything else for that matter. At least I could rely on the fact she followed a consistent pattern when it came to me. Permanent absence. Whatever she was here for, I hoped she would stay away from me. And Dad.

"There's...an extra blanket on the end of the bed if you get cold."

I nodded, my mouth dry.

"Good night, Violet."

He turned to leave, pulling the door behind him.

"Stay!" I said, before I'd had a chance to think about it. But I didn't want to take it back.

He opened the door again, just a fraction, something new stirring in his eyes. He clenched his jaw and braced a hand on the doorframe, as if restraining himself, and I felt his power flare, guarding him.

"I can't," he said.

"I know. But stay anyway. Just till I fall asleep."

I heard his swallow from across the room. "That's...not a good idea."

"Well, I can't be alone," I said, looking at the floor. "I can't close my eyes. I can't…" I started, not realizing I was crying until I saw the tears fall onto my leg. I kept my head down so he wouldn't see. I knew I was being unfair, knew it would make things harder for us, but I didn't care. Or maybe I didn't believe things could get any harder.

It was silent for so long it became unbearable. I wasn't going to force him, so I lay down and rolled over, turning my back to him, giving him his chance to escape. I figured he'd gone, but a few minutes later, I heard the creak of floorboards and felt the blankets ruffle next to me. My whole body tensed and I didn't move. Not even an inch. Too scared of frightening him away.

We lay like that, both frozen and barely breathing until I heard him exhale, finally relaxing more of his weight onto the bed. I did the same, shuffling into a more comfortable position but staying on my side, too nervous to face him.

With a sound somewhere between a sigh and a growl, he moved in closer, wrapping his arm around my waist and burying his face into my neck so that I could feel his breath warm my skin.

Holy hell, we're spooning!

Before he had a chance to think twice, I grabbed his arm and pulled it all the way around me. Completely wrapped in his embrace, a well of emotions ignited in me as his fingers kneaded gently, but definitely, my arms. I exhaled again and let myself sink into his hold, my soul agreeing with me for once. I felt him shift a little away from me.

Oh.

"I'm sorry, Vi. You're stronger than I am."

I almost fell out of the bed. How could he possibly think *I* was stronger than him?

We lay silently for a time, as I contemplated what he'd said. I looked back over the past few weeks and my gradual but definite unraveling. Then I tried to see it from Lincoln's point of view and realized there had always been something else going on at the time, something that could have excused my behavior in a way that didn't make him think it was him. Even though it was. Always.

The more I thought about it, the more I realized why he was so hard on himself. At the volcano, he'd told me so much more than he'd ever intended. He'd done it to save me but also…There was no hiding from the fact that he'd admitted to wanting to be with me, even though he knew it could destroy me.

I took a deep breath. I'd never told him that I was just as guilty, wanted him just as much. Sure, there was still fear and the deep desire not to hurt him, but he needed to know the truth.

I wriggled a bit, moving his arm a little higher again. I could feel his heart thudding in my back.

"Linc?" I began as my breathing went into overdrive. "You're going to have to tell me not to roll over."

If I thought he was frozen before, I was wrong. Everything about him stopped dead still. I waited, but there was nothing.

This is it.

I started to turn toward him, but his arm clamped back down on me, stopping me in my tracks.

"Violet," he said, his voice low and thick with desire. "Do. Not. Roll. Over."

I smiled. A wave of disappointment from my worse half and then relief from my better half washed through me. I wasn't going to steal his soul.

Not tonight.

"Never think I'm strong, Linc. Not when it's us. I'm always only hanging by a thread." My truth. *And* my warning.

He settled in behind me, softening his hold, and kissed my hair before whispering in my ear, "Well, that makes two threads. We can work with that."

I didn't want to sleep, didn't want to miss a moment of this feeling of…calm.

"Promise me we'll find a way," I mumbled. Because there had to be hope, didn't there? Hope for some day.

My body relaxed, my mind went still, my soul content for now. I fell asleep within moments, but not before I heard him whisper, "I promise."

When I woke in the morning, I was alone. But I knew he'd stayed with me most of the night, could still feel where his arm had held me tight.

I went out to find him asleep on the couch. Spence would be up at some point and Lincoln wouldn't want to risk him thinking something had happened that hadn't. I felt the twinge of guilt that had been guaranteed. I knew it had cost me. Us. That one request to stay. I could already feel the rebloom of pain from being close to him.

Despite my temptation to wake him and thank him for looking after me, I decided not to. He'd only jump into one of his spiels about us never being together, and I knew it already. Plus, he looked so peaceful, so beautiful, that I couldn't.

Instead, I wrote him a note, carefully, knowing Spence might see it too.

Thanks for giving me a place to sleep last night, and for the extra blanket.

Vi.

Because he was a mighty fine extra blanket and I hoped, just this once, my words would make him smile instead of frown.

chapter forty

> *"Destiny grants us our wishes, but in its own way, in order to give us something beyond our wishes."*
>
> Johann Wolfgang von Goethe

I couldn't stay still, so I bought a to-go coffee and blueberry muffin and began walking, relishing the peace of some time alone in the city streets.

I strolled through the park where Lincoln and I had returned that exile and wandered through the trees I'd used for cover. A lot had happened since that night. Lincoln and I had worked so hard to stay away from each other, but still…we were drawn to one another. It went beyond us, beyond angels even, compelling us to want each other and need each other. After just a few hours in his arms, I felt the best I had in months.

Sipping my coffee and nibbling my muffin, I surprised myself by smiling. Not because everything was going to be okay, but because I was finally willing to accept I couldn't control everything. I'm

Grigori. A warrior. I would always fight and do my best to stop exiles from tormenting innocent humans. I would put my life on the line to make sure others didn't have to. And I couldn't control the outcome. My smile widened and I pulled Lincoln's coat around me and breathed in his scent.

He does love me.

Phoenix had won. Resurrecting Lilith had released a nightmare on our world, but also, he'd helped us. He'd sacrificed strong exiles whom he could have used to do his bidding, and I was sure he'd done so because he wanted them gone, stopped. Phoenix had helped us save the people of Santorini. They had no idea what they had escaped.

No matter what else was on his mind today, whatever torment, suffering, and destruction he was planning with Lilith, I knew he'd be thinking of that too. Phoenix had lied.

The human isn't gone at all.

Lost in my thoughts, I hadn't noticed that I'd walked myself all the way to my apartment building.

I didn't have a plan, hadn't made a decision, but I couldn't keep hiding, and anyway, it was midmorning and Dad would be at work.

Chicken!

The security guy waved as I passed, and when I got into the elevator, I couldn't help but realize that the building felt different. I caught sight of my wrists in the mirror, my markings still exposed. For some reason, I hadn't put back on the bracelets I'd taken off in Santorini. Further proof that I wasn't sure if I belonged here anymore, or if I was wanted.

Dad loved me; I didn't doubt that, but he loved only part of me and that part was getting smaller and smaller as the Grigori in me started to take over every facet of my life.

Would it be better if I just left now?

Before he saw who I really was? Before he had to choose whether or not to believe me? Before he had to find out about…her?

I banged my head against the elevator mirror.

Great plan, Vi. Just like he thinks of…Evelyn less and less.

No. I'd promised him an explanation and he was going to get one. I'd tell him everything except the part about her. I couldn't do that to him. Then it would be his choice whether I belonged here or not.

As soon as I opened the door to our apartment, I knew I wasn't alone.

I dumped my bag and headed for the kitchen area. "I know you're here," I said, my voice low.

I made my way to the coffee machine. If she thought I was going to make her one, she was very badly mistaken. On my way, I noticed the open balcony door. We were really going to have to start keeping that locked. Twelve stories meant little for security these days.

My hands fisted when I saw her come from the hall. She'd been in Dad's room. She'd cut her hair—by herself from the look of it—but it was an improvement. The whole hair-to-the-knees thing might look cute on a five-year-old but…Well, it didn't work.

"Thought you'd gone," I said, as flat as I could manage.

She looked no older than Griffin—twenty-five, maybe twenty-six, the age Dad thought she was when she'd died. Or rather, struck her deal. What was really irritating was that, dressed as she was in jeans and a black turtleneck, she looked completely normal, like she could be my sister or something. My better-looking sister. Also annoying.

"Flee instinct." She hitched a shoulder. "It's hard to throw off."

She stayed on the other side of the breakfast bar and moved slowly, keeping her hands in my view, which I tried to pretend wasn't a hundred percent trained on her. She moved to the coffee table, slowly reaching down and picking up the carved wooden box she'd left me.

"He gave it to you, then?"

"What? Did you think he wouldn't?" I asked, aggravated on so many levels, especially now that I'd discovered where my escape instincts came from. "How'd you find us, anyway?"

"Directory services."

Christ, to think exiles can just look me up!

She opened the box and pulled out the envelope, which held her letter. I knew that she'd be looking at its well-worn edges. Marks made by contemplative fingers. I wanted to tell her they weren't from me, but that wasn't altogether true. I'd handled the wretched thing more than my fair share of time since Dad had passed it on.

She held up her other wristband. "Do you mind if I take this back?"

"I don't care what you do. Take it all." I poured milk in my coffee, spilling it with my shaking hands.

Damn.

I watched her from the corner of my eye as she put on the band.

"The rest is yours, but I think I'm going to need this."

I leaned back on the kitchen bench, feigning the best I-couldn't-give-a-damn look. Truth was—I needed the bench to support me.

"Like I said, I don't care what you do with that stuff."

She nodded but put the box back down on the table.

"Is that coffee?"

"Yeah. If you want one, there's a takeout place down the road."

She smiled. "Fair enough."

Then the staring competition began. I cemented my feet to the floor and stared into her wild blue eyes. I couldn't help but wonder just how many secrets they held. A lot, for sure.

"You have his eyes," she said, returning my stare.

"And you have the eyes of a stranger," I said, glad when that made her finally look away from me. "You need to go."

"I thought you might have some questions."

I walked past her, giving her a wide berth, and headed for the door. "You know, I can't think of one thing I want to say to you," I lied.

She nodded and took a step toward me. I backed up instinctively before I was smart enough to stop myself. That one step gave too much away. She paused, putting her hands in front of her again.

"I wouldn't hurt you," she said calmly.

"History says otherwise. And what makes you think you could take me?" I challenged, using the same line Gray had used on me.

She smiled again. "Okay, Violet. I'll leave."

I took the last few steps to the door and reached it at the exact same time it burst open and my father charged into the room, breathless.

"Violet! Violet! Oh, thank God!"

"Dad," I said in complete shock. "What are you doing here?"

"The doorman called the second he saw you come in."

Trust Dad to have everyone spying for him. Before I had a moment to think, he pulled me into his arms, gripping me deathly tight.

"I thought I'd lost you."

"Dad—wait! Dad, I need to tell you something."

Shit.

His arms went limp. It was too late.

I stepped back to see Evelyn. Dad's mouth dropped open and his keys fell to the floor with a metallic clank, deafening in the silence.

"Tell me I'm not seeing things," he said, his voice quivering and tears welling in his eyes.

But when I looked back at Evelyn, I was rendered speechless.

Tears welled in her eyes too. She looked calm except for her hands. Still extended in front of her, they were trembling as she whispered, "Hello, James."

angel hierarchy

The Sole

Violet Eden (G)

1ST CHOIR

Seraphim	*Cherubim*	*Thrones*
Griffin (G)	Rudyard (G)	Phoenix (ED)
Uri (AL)	Nahilius (EL)	Jude (EL)
Nox (AD)	Beth (G)	Becca (G)
Josephine (G)		Evelyn (G)
Lilith (ED)		

2ND CHOIR

Powers	*Dominations*	*Virtues*
Lincoln (G)	Spence (G)	Salvatore (G)
Nyla (G)	Onyx (once ED)	Morgan (G)
Gressil (ED)	Gray (G)	
Nathan (G)	Archer (G)	

Grigori (G) Angel Light (AL) Angel Dark (AD)
Exile Once Light (EL) Exile Once Dark (ED)

3RD CHOIR

Principalities	*Archangels*	*Angels*
Irin – The Keeper (EL)	Zoe (G)	Magda (G)
Kaitlin (G)	Olivier (EL)	Samuel (G)
Max (G)	Whitey (ED)	Hiro (G)
Conductor 1 & 2 (G)	Mia (G)	

acknowledgments

There have been so many people who have played a part in bringing this series together. None more so than my agent and friend Selwa Anthony, whose guidance, know-how, and support have been invaluable.

Thank you to my publishers, Fiona Hazard and the fabulous Vanessa Radnidge, for taking the time to make each book in the series everything it can be. To my editor, Kate Ballard, who continues to treat each manuscript with meticulous expertise, and to the rest of the team, including Chris Raine, Christine Fairbrother, and Theresa Bray.

Having my books published in the United States has been a dream come true and I could not hope for a more amazing publishing house to be associated with than Sourcebooks. Thank you to senior editor Leah Hultenschmidt, who has championed and guided this series since first reading *Embrace*. To publicist Derry Wilkens, who ticks every box in the ideal publicist department and is a total pillar of support. Many thanks must also go to my editorial assistant

Kim Manley, production editor Jillian Bergsma, and to the incredible design team, including Katie Casper, Dawn Adams, and Sarah Cardillo. I'm so grateful to you all!

A huge shout-out to my family and friends for their support and love.

To Matt, who is always the first to read and whose opinion I value so much, and to our girls—I am so lucky to have the world's most supportive family.

Finally, thank you to my readers—those of you I have met; befriended on Goodreads; and talked to via Facebook, Twitter, and my website; and those of you I have yet to meet. You guys make writing books the best job in the world.

Discover more at

embracetheseries.com

Embrace

by Jessica Shirvington

It starts with a whisper.

"It's time for you to know
who you are..."

Strange dreams leave her with very real injuries and there's a dark tattoo weaving its way up her arms. The guy she thought she could fall in love with just told her he's only half-human—oh, and same goes for her. And she keeps hearing a distant fluttering of wings.

Violet Eden is having a very bad seventeenth birthday.

But if angels seek vengeance and humans are the warriors, you could do a lot worse than betting on Violet Eden...

Praise for *Embrace*

"A dark and heart-racing tale."—Book Couture

"Addictive...add to your must-read list."—Entertainment Weekly

"Smart, edgy, and addictive...a must-read."—Kirkus *starred review*

For more Jessica Shirvington books, visit:

teenfire.sourcebooks.com

MORRIS AUTOMATED INFORMATION NETWORK
0 1022 0339040 0

The Kind One